ASTONISHMENT!!!

Works by Francis Lathom

NOVELS

The Castle of Ollada*
The Midnight Bell*
Men and Manners
Mystery
Astonishment!!!*
Very Strange, But Very True!
The Impenetrable Secret, Find it Out!*
The Mysterious Freebooter*
The Fatal Vow†
Human Beings
The Unknown
London
The Romance of the Hebrides
Italian Mysteries*
Live and Learn†
Young John Bull
Mystic Events

STORIES

The One-Pound Note & Other Tales†
The Polish Bandit & Other Tales
Puzzled and Pleased & Other Tales
Fashionable Mysteries & Other Tales

PLAYS

All in a Bustle
The Dash of the Day
Orlando and Seraphina
Holiday Time; or, The School Boy's Frolic
Curiosity
The Wife of a Million

TRANSLATIONS

The Castle of the Tuileries
Erestina

* Available from Valancourt Books
† Forthcoming from Valancourt Books

Gothic Classics

ASTONISHMENT!!!

A ROMANCE OF A CENTURY AGO

Two Volumes in One

BY

FRANCIS LATHOM

AUTHOR OF "THE MIDNIGHT BELL," "THE CASTLE OF OLLADA," "THE IMPENETRABLE SECRET," "ITALIAN MYSTERIES," "THE MYSTERIOUS FREEBOOTER," "THE ONE-POUND NOTE," "THE FATAL VOW," "THE UNKNOWN," "MYSTERY," "MYSTIC EVENTS," &C. &C.

> For my distracted mind,
> What succour can I find?
> On whom for consolation shall I call?
> LYTTLETON.

Kansas City:
VALANCOURT BOOKS
2008

Astonishment!!! by Francis Lathom
First published by Longman and Rees in 1802
First Valancourt Books edition 2008

This edition © 2008 by Valancourt Books

All rights reserved. The use of any part of this publication reproduced, transmitted in any form or by any means, electronic, mechanical, photocopying, recording, or otherwise, or stored in a retrieval system, without prior written consent of the publisher, constitutes an infringement of the copyright law.

Library of Congress Cataloging-in-Publication Data

Lathom, Francis, 1774-1832.
  Astonishment!!! : a romance of a century ago / by Francis Lathom. – 1st Valancourt Books ed.
      p. cm. – (Gothic classics)
  "Two volumes in one."
  ISBN 1-934555-40-1 ((cloth) : alk. paper)
 1. Foundlings–Fiction. 2. Young men–Fiction. 3. Italy–Fiction.
      I. Title.
  PR4878.L175A9 2008
  823'.7–DC22
                              2008003704

Published by Valancourt Books
Kansas City, Missouri

Composition by James D. Jenkins
Set in Dante MT

10 9 8 7 6 5 4 3 2 1

CONTENTS

Note on the Text • vi

Astonishment!!! • 1

Contemporary Reviews • 276

NOTE ON THE TEXT

The text of the Valancourt Books edition of *Astonishment!!!* is that of the first edition, published in two volumes by T. N. Longman and O. Rees, London, 1802. A small handful of printer's errors, such as missing or extraneous quotation marks, have been silently corrected. Other errors, such as the frequent misspelling "lightening" for "lightning," have been retained.

A second edition of the novel appeared in 1821, published by A. K. Newman. The present edition is the first since 1821.

For more information on the author, Francis Lathom, the reader is advised to consult the Valancourt Books edition of his *The Castle of Ollada* (Chicago: Valancourt Books, 2006), which contains an essay detailing all that is presently known of this elusive and fascinating writer.

James D. Jenkins
Kansas City

May 6, 2008

ASTONISHMENT !!!

A ROMANCE OF A CENTURY AGO

In Two Volumes,

By *Francis Lathom,*

AUTHOR OF " MEN AND MANNERS—MYSTERY—MIDNIGHT BELL—CASTLE OF OLLADA—DASH OF THE DAY—ORLANDO AND SERAPHINA, OR THE FUNERAL PILE—HOLIDAY TIME, OR THE SCHOOL-BOY'S FROLIC—CURIOSITY, &c. &c.

For my distracted mind,
What succour can I find?
On whom for consolation shall I call?

LYTTLETON.

VOL. I.

London:
PRINTED FOR T. N. LONGMAN AND O. REES,
Paternoster-Row.
1802.

Title page of the first edition (1802)

Astonishment!!!

Volume I

For the Poetry interspersed in these Volumes the Author is indebted to a Female Friend.

A FEW WORDS TO BEGIN WITH.

To all my brother authors and sister authoresses, I dedicate the following pages, and for this plain reason, that as they must all in their turns, however eminent their abilities, have experienced some of the difficulties and disappointments which attend the labourer after fame, in his endeavours to please the uncertain and capricious taste of the public; from them is to be expected the greatest candour in criticism.

To say nothing of every character in common life having been so twisted, twirled, and strained into every possible shape and variety, that some of the principal personages in every novel are, at least, cousins, if no more nearly related, to some of the most prominent characters in any other you happen to open; such is the present state of the times, that it must require a skilful pen indeed to draw the every-day scenes of life without the introduction of politics. Every body now-a-days, men and women, are politicians: and so let every body be, but an author; for his pen cannot dip into them without shewing which way his own opinion inclines; and by giving this license to his writings, it is a great chance if he makes himself a single friend, and it is an undeniable certainty that he will create himself many enemies. From this motive, and a desire of remaining in amity with all parties, I have stepped back a century for the materials of my story.

Of those who shall say, that an idle hour might have been less pleasurably spent than in the perusal of these volumes: I declare myself their very humble servant, and bound to exert my abilities for endeavouring to please them still better in my next attempt; and to those who may turn up their nose with a fastidious sneer at my wonders, I shall be tempted to make the reply of a certain waiting maid to her mistress, an indolent lady of fashion, who upbraiding her with "Lord, how you have mended my gown! a child of four years old could not have done it worse." The girl replied, "Very likely, ma'am; but could you have done it as well?"

ASTONISHMENT!!!

CHAPTER I.

> Domestic happiness, thou only bliss
> Of paradise that has surviv'd the fall,
> Thou art the nurse of virtue. In thine arms
> She smiles, appearing, as in truth she is,
> Heav'n born, and destin'd to the skies again.
> COWPER.

THE Marchese di Bartelma was descended from a family which had, for many successive generations, been universally esteemed in the dutchy of Tuscany, of which they were natives, not less for their benevolence to the indigent, than for that noble quality of universal good will, which is so ill understood, and so much less practised by the generality of mankind.

The Marchese was one of those few men who have sufficient courage to follow the dictates of an approving conscience, without regarding those petty sneers and censures of a prejudiced world, which too often work the subversion of virtue in hearts naturally inclined to its practice. To a sound understanding, he had added a store of useful and polite learning: he was not unacquainted with the arts: to the muses, he had devoted much of his time, and they had liberally rewarded his assiduities.

His stature was rather below the middle height, but well formed and active; his countenance was handsome and prepossessing, and the quick turn of his eye shewed that it held counsel with a heart of knowledge.

On the fertile banks of the Arno, at the distance of somewhat less than a league from the city of Florence, stood the family mansion of Bartelma, which had devolved upon the Marchese when in his twenty-fifth year. It was a building in which simplicity and elegance united their powers with the happiest effect: in its front, lay an extensive and romantically planned garden, which descended to the margin of the river, where stood a pavilion, which commanded an uninterrupted view of an amphitheatre of fertile hills, crowned with knots of the cyprus, cedar, mulberry, chesnut, and a variety of other trees, which relieved the eye by their different hues, and improved the beauty of the scene. On the side of these hills, were planted, at uncertain distances, villas, vying with each other in taste and magnificence; groves of orange trees, that seemed to glory in the profusion of the sweets they exhaled; ranges of filbert bushes, that courted the frolic squirrel from the more stately pine; and, at intervals, rows of the luxuriant vine. On the plain below, frequent gardens, scenes of active husbandry, and fishermen on the banks of the river, diversified the scene; and behind the mansion, ran a wood of nearly half a league in depth, which descended in a curve, along each side of the garden, down to the brink of the river.

The Marchese di Bartelma had attained his thirty-first year, before he felt the true passion of love: it was then kindled in his breast by the orphan daughter of the Marchese di Padriva, who was a year older than himself. Her stature was small, nor had she personal beauty to supply the deficiency in her height; but the similarity of disposition to his own, which the Marchese believed himself to have discovered in this lady, lighted at the torch of friendship the flame of love.

For some time, however, he could not bring himself to make a declaration of his passion: the woman he loved was devoid of personal charms; to counterbalance the want of these in his own private opinion, she possessed a mind of worth and knowledge: he wished she had possessed nothing more; but she was an only child, and the mistress of an immense fortune; and he feared that the world at large, who glance over intellectual endowment in search of outward perfection, would ascribe to him a mercenary motive in asking her hand.

"That character of virtue, and disregard of wealth, which has for so many successive generations stamped with honour my progenitors, may now be sullied, in the eye of the world, by the very means I had judged most probable to ensure its continuance. Hard, that the opinion of the world should be so falsely drawn!" Thus did he one day say to himself, while debating on the subject dearest to his heart. He paused a moment—then continued: "But is it not the part of those who are conscious of the right intention of their actions, not to omit the performance of an act of merit, because it may be stigmatized with a false censure? It is.—The object of my affection shall be mine: her soul is congenial with my own, and her philanthropy and benevolence shall silence the tongue of sarcasm."

The Marchese never formed a resolution, till he had given the point in question due deliberation, and digested the controversy he had held with his own mind: thus he had seldom indeed been known to swerve from a determination which he had once taken. One month, he had debated on the plan he had formed for marrying her he loved, without incurring that censure he so much feared to have thrown at him from an illiberal world, and finding, at every revisal of his proposed intention, additional reasons to approve it; he made an offer of his hand to Julia di Padriva, which, as he had expected, was received and accepted with a warmth equal to that with which he had made it.

Still, however secure he thought himself from the well-known goodness of his Julia's heart, of not being restrained in the execution of his plan, judging it by no means right to marry her under the determination of distributing a part of her fortune, as he had resolved to do, without informing her of his intention; he candidly laid before her, not only his intention, but the motive by which he had been actuated to adopt this resolution.

Julia declared herself not only pleased, but flattered, by a conduct which would convince the world—how warmly he was attached to her for herself alone.

The Marchese was now more charmed with the choice he had made, than he had ever yet felt himself: Julia's tenderness for her lover encreased; and both anxiously dwelt on the happy prospect of future days of bliss, arising from a love founded on congeniality of sentiment.

Time moved on with heavy steps in the imagination of the Marchese and his Julia, till the marriage morn arrived, and the everlasting bond of happiness was sealed between them.

The Marchese immediately put in execution the plan he had formed: his mansion was for several weeks a house of festivity to the indigent, and of elegant entertainment to the nobility and gentry. Still did he not escape the sneers of all, or his Julia pass uncensured, even in the midst of those scenes of hilarity to which she had given birth; but exalted above that part of mankind who cannot see happiness enjoyed without betraying that they envy its possessors, the Marchese and his Julia determined, after the entertainments, which were considered by them as a due compliment to the city of Florence and its vicinity on their marriage, were ended, to live retired within their own estate, and seek enjoyment where it is alone truly to be found—in scenes of domestic content.

Books, conversation, music, walks in the country, and accidental excursions on the water, rapidly wore away the first year: towards the end of the second, the Marchese began to grow impatient of an heir: he was the only male descendant of his family then living, and he began to be apprehensive of his death terminating a race he seemed to have been born to perpetuate.

The Marchesa observed with anxiety his fears, and his endeavours to conceal them; and she trembled, lest his love for her should diminish, as those apprehensions, of which he must naturally consider her as the cause, encreased.

Nearly three years had elapsed, and no signs of pregnancy still appeared in the Marchesa. Her husband's spirits, and even his health visibly declined, as the successive months, which brought him no hope of his darling wish, rolled on. The Marchesa passed the day in weeping, and prayers to the Virgin: the Marchese spent his hours in endeavouring to subdue a grief which his efforts were ineffectual to render obedient to his reason.

A fourth year rolled on like the former; and not till the commencement of a fifth, did the physician who had the care of the Marchesa's health, pronounce her to be in a state of pregnancy.

Anxiously between the extremes of joy and fear, passed on the period she was doomed to bear about her burden; and on the fifth anniversary of the Marchese's marriage with his beloved Julia, he was declared the father of a son.

Instantly the mansion of the Marchese di Bartelma became a scene of extravagant joy. Scarcely a servant who resided in it had not served under his father, and did not recollect his entrance into the world; and thus, with heart-felt joy, welcomed the birth of his first-born. Five thousand ducats were distributed by the Marchese in presents to the poor on his estate, and an equal number was petitioned of him by the Marchesa for an offering to the Virgin.

In the course of a month, the Marchesa was perfectly recovered, and a state of the most perfect happiness reigned at the villa di Bartelma.

The little stranger throve as well as the most anxious wishes of his parents could desire him to do. The Marchese could hardly bear him out of his presence, and the Marchesa looked upon him not less with affection as her child, than with gratitude as the means of restoring her to the warm affection of her husband.

Thus had passed on two happy years, when the hand of accident, which blesses without security, but does not inflict misery without relief, snatched the darling of his parents to an early grave. Ineffectual must be the pen which endeavors to describe the grief of the Marchese di Bartelma and his Julia; it can only say, that they felt, as tender parents must feel, the privation of a blessing so earnestly desired, so long withheld, and so soon taken away. At length religion administered her soothing aid to their aching hearts; hope also stepped in to cheer their melancholy with the prospect of a future blessing, similar to the one they had lost; but her presages were fallacious, and religion alone remained their firm friend.

Minds of a good disposition are those which recover the soonest from any infliction of providence, convinced, by the worthiness of their own nature, that the Omnipotent tortures not from a wanton disposition of cruelty towards the creatures of his will, but for some wise end which they do not doubt, although they cannot now explain: they raise their thoughts from their disappointments in this state, which a reliance on the rewards of a future has the ability of rendering most light.

Such were the dispositions of the Marchese and Marchesa di Bartelma: serene amidst calamity, they gathered a negative happiness from contributing to the comforts of those who were unable to provide them for themselves, and derived the most soothing composure from the conviction that it was better to suffer than to sin.

CHAPTER II.

>   —Come on, poor babe;
> Some powerful spirits instruct the kites and ravens
> To be thy nurses. Wolves and bears, they say,
> (Casting their savageness aside) have done
> Like offices of pity.
>
> THE WINTER'S TALE.

SIX years had now elapsed, since that unhappy event, which had tinged not only the countenances, but the hearts of the Marchese and his wife, with a melancholy which time only could dispel.

From his early youth, the Marchese had been in the constant habit of attending mass once every morning, in the church of St. Paul in Florence; and, within the last few years, not only the warmth of his religion, but also the zeal of his moral virtues, had been daily augmenting; he hugged both to his breast, as friends whose fervor to him in his affliction was indubitable.

It was one morning about this time, that, as he was kneeling at his accustomed station, with his eyes fixed upon the missal which lay open on the chair before him, and his thoughts raised beyond the scene around him,—he felt himself tapped two or three times successively on the arm by the finger of his neighbour. He looked aside, in compliance with the signal, and saw that an old woman, closely veiled, was kneeling by his side; and as soon as he turned his eyes towards her, she put into his hands a letter, which she accompanied by bowing down her head very low upon the chair before which she knelt, and then clasping her hands together, and raising them in an attitude of supplication.

The Marchese concluded, that the paper he had just received was an appeal to his charity, and putting it between the leaves of his missal, with a slight inclination of his head, by which he meant to convey to her who had put it into his hand, a tacit promise of reading it at his leisure, he closed his eyes, and returned his thoughts to his interrupted devotions.

When mass was ended, and the Marchese rose from his cushion to leave the church, he perceived that his female neighbour was gone. He cast his eyes along the aisles, but he saw her not amongst those who were moving towards the doors.

As soon as the Marchese was seated in his gondola (which had brought him to Florence, and in which he was to return to his villa), he took the letter from his pocket, and having broken the seal, he read as follows:

"The Marchese di Bartelma is blessed with a heart warmed by religion and benevolence. On the knowledge of his possessing these most exalted qualities of the human mind, is the petition which this paper contains addressed to him.

"Marchese, you have yourself been a parent; you have known the pangs of eternal separation from the object of your heart's adoration.—Pardon the writer of these words, that your sorrows appear to be unfeelingly revived on this paper: the heart which dictates these lines sympathises with you from its inmost recesses; but it feels pangs superior to those which you have felt, and it cannot forbear reverting for an instant to your grief, that it may the more feelingly awaken your interest in its own agonies. By that love which you in your prayers beseech the holy Jesus to bestow on your now angel child, the unfortunate wretch who pens this address to your humanity, implores you to become the protector of a babe who, if you cast him from you, will never know the blessing of a guiding hand to lead his faltering steps through those labyrinths of vice and misery, in which his unfriended wanderings through the world cannot fail to entangle him.

"You have an amiable wife; entreat her to become the mother of a child who must never know the blessing of a true parent's protection: he is not the outcast of shame, nor the starving offspring of beggary, for whom I petition; though one bred in the womb of misery, and nursed in the lap of sorrow.

"That child is now in the pavilion of your garden, which stands on the bank of the river:—go to him, clasp the innocent babe to your heart, call him son, and, oh! may the sound be wafted up to heaven, and call down eternal blessings on your head."

The Marchese di Bartelma was not more surprised than affected by the address to his humanity contained in the paper he had just perused: he wiped the starting tear from his eye, read the letter again, and the feelings of the writer crept deeper into his heart. Still the occurrence was of so unparalleled a nature, that with every benevolent intention ripe in his mind, he felt himself without any fixed resolution, when the oars of his gondola were drawn in to land him on the margin of his garden.

Without any hesitation, he proceeded to the pavilion, and before he reached it, he heard the cry of the child; and on opening the door, the little sorrower presented itself to his view, seated on the floor, almost convulsed with shrieking and weeping. The Marchese took it into his arms, and found it to be a beautiful boy, of about two years of age. On finding itself alone in the power of a stranger, its lamentations encreased. The Marchese used many gentle words to sooth its alarm, but for a long time to no purpose; at last, its exhausted breath obliged it to change its screams into sobs, which it mixed with the accents of "Go to papa, go to mama."

It need hardly be said, that the compassionate heart of the Marchese was forcibly excited to tenderness and sympathy in the feelings of the child, and now seeing its grief a little more calm than it had been when he first went to it, he determined immediately to carry it to the Marchesa. As he was leaving the pavilion, his foot kicked against something, over which he stumbled, and looking down, he saw upon the floor, a small oaken box, with a little key, tied by a riband to the handle upon its lid. Directly conceiving it must belong to the child in his arms, he took it up, and proceeded with that and his young charge towards the house.

The Marchesa's surprize, on perceiving how her husband was laden, may easily be imagined, and also her astonishment when he read the letter he had received, and recounted the correspondence of his adventure with its contents. The child was meanwhile seated on the lap of the Marchesa; and, with a female nurse, its affliction seemed in a great measure to have subsided.

"Poor babe," cried the Marchesa, kissing the infant on her knee, "how strange is thy fate!"

"And how much more cruel," said the Marchese, "would be our conduct than even the fates which have hitherto presided over his destiny, were we to cast him from us."

"Your determinations," returned the Marchesa, "ever do

credit to your heart. Fortune frowns upon you, yet you repay her ill temper to yourself in smiles and benevolence to your fellow creatures: surely Heaven will at last appoint some reward for such unexampled goodness."

"Perhaps," answered the Marchese, "this very child is that reward which you expect I shall some time receive; perhaps it may be the intention of providence that he should grow up to recompense us for the loss of——" His voice faltered, and he hesitated a few moments. "At all events," he continued, "it must be conformable to the will of God, that those upon whose bounty a child is thrown in the helpless state of this infant, should supply to it the place of those parents of whose protection it is deprived."

"He shall not want my care," said the Marchesa. "Beautiful boy!" she went on, again caressing the child, "what misery can have been sufficiently great to drive thy parents to cast thee from them? And that he has parents," she continued, after a short pause, and turning her eyes to the Marchese, "is evident, from his having asked to go both to papa and mama."

"I would pledge my soul," cried the Marchese, "that it is the deepest wound which ever stabbed the heart of the father, or mother, which wrote that letter, to have parted from this child: this is not the composition of art; it proceeds from a heart overwhelmed by the misery of contending feelings; and from this assurance, I shall protect their child, with a stronger conviction of the duty reposed in me: yes, thou poor, deserted little one," he added, taking the child in his arms, and folding it to his breast, "would I could tell the suffering minds of thy parents, that I will be thy father!"

"Come then," said the Marchesa, casting an affectionate smile at her husband, as she received the child back from his arms, "come to the bosom of thy mother."

A short silence, during which the glow of conscious and self-approving benevolence breathed its recompencing fire upon the hearts of the Marchese and his Julia, ensued: the latter then said, "you have not yet looked into this box which you found with the child; perhaps it may contain something that relates to him."

The Marchese untied the key from the handle of the box, and found that it fitted the lock; having lifted up the lid, the first thing which presented itself to his observation was a packet, directed to himself, and strongly sealed; he examined the seals, before he broke them; but found them to bear an impression of that common nature, which could not assist him in discovering by whom they had been impressed.—The first sheet of the packet was an envelope, which contained a letter, and a small parcel, also sealed: by the letter, his curiosity was excited; and he found the following lines to be its contents:

"A secret instinct whispers to my heart—that you have adopted my boy: time presses upon me, and I cannot write all the thanks, all the blessings, I would wish to bestow upon you; nor had I the time, have I the power to utter them in a language adequate to the overflowings of a grateful heart.——While the moments are my own, let me proceed to write down some instructions which it is indispensably necessary, to the safety and happiness of the child now under your care, should be most religiously observed:

"First then, let me entreat you—never to make the strange story of his fate a subject of your conversation to any one but your wife: if any questions be asked concerning the means by which he became an inmate of your house, evade them; on no account, answer them with exactness: if you do not comply with this petition, you serve not the unhappy parent who advances it, by giving your protection to the child.—Oh, that the world might believe him yours, and yours only! but this is too much to ask, nothing can pardon the temerity of such a wish, but the agony of the heart which forms it.

"When he shall be arrived at years of reason, if it shall please Heaven thus long to spare his unfortunate life, acquaint him with the little that you know concerning him: tell him that you are his benefactor, and *not* his father; teach him the fortitude of wisdom, that he may endure with patience and resignation—the necessary mystery in which he is doomed to live; and direct him, never, upon any account, or upon any occasion whatsoever, to make the slightest enquiry concerning who he is, or to answer any question which may be asked of him, relative to what he does know of himself; as either of these cases might cause his immediate ruin, nay, even his death.—Be this last injunction that which you shall most forcibly lay upon him, for the sake of his own peace of mind.

"I have only one more request to add—it is, that when he has attained his tenth year, you will fasten round his right wrist, the bracelet contained in the small packet, which you will find enclosed in the same *envelope* with this letter: and command him never again to take it off; as it may one day lead to a secret of the utmost importance. Till the day arrives on which I have appointed you to put it on his wrist, let no eye behold it but your own.—May the angels of God, directed by himself, bless both you and him, according to my prayers for your happiness."

Thus ended the unsigned letter; after some comments on the mystery which it contained, and repeating his determination to protect the unfortunate babe of whom it spoke; the Marchese broke open the small packet: he found it a blank sheet of paper, which served merely as a covering for the bracelet mentioned in the letter: the bracelet itself was not a very remarkable one; it consisted only of a small emerald, set round with pearls, which were displayed about it in rather a peculiar taste; and to this was joined a plain gold chain, with which the stud was intended to be fastened round the wrist: and this, in compliance with the request in the letter, that it should not be seen, the Marchese locked up in his escritoir.

The box now underwent a farther examination from the Marchesa; but it contained only a few changes of linen for the child, and their quality of that undecided nature, that they could not be pronounced, with certainty, to have belonged either to a person of high rank, or one of low circumstances; they were clean and good, but neither remarkably fine nor coarse, and none of them bearing any mark, their examination gave no assistance to conjecture.

CHAPTER III.

> If I depart from thee, I cannot live;
> And in thy sight to die, what were it else,
> But like a pleasant slumber in thy lap?
> Here could I breathe my soul into the air.
> As mild and gentle as the cradle-babe,
> Dying with mother's dug between his lips.
>
> THE SECOND PART OF HENRY THE SIXTH.

> ———————Lay her i' the earth;
> And from her fair and unpolluted flesh
> May violets spring!
>
> HAMLET.

A NURSE was immediately provided for the child, and directions given to the household of the Marchese, that he should be treated as their master's child: and a hint was also given to them by the Marchese, whose wishes his excellent heart had made laws amongst his servants, that the less the addition of his family was talked of by them, the better he should be pleased with them.

As to the Marchese and his Julia, their retired mode of life freed them from many interrogatories concerning their young charge, which, had they been in the habit of living with the world, they would perhaps have found it difficult to answer to their own satisfaction: amongst those of their friends who did visit at the villa di Bartelma, some jokes on the Marchese's gallantry were started on the first introduction of the little stranger to the company; but they soon ceased, in a joint compliment to the parental humanity of the Marchese, and the good-natured conformity of the Marchesa to her husband's inclinations; Julia and the Marchese only smiled in reply, perfectly contented, that the real story of their little charge did not seem to be even suspected.

All the sounds which the child could utter, the Marchesa and its nurse soon discovered to be those of "Go to papa, go to mama;" and as it was consequently unable to inform them what name it had received in baptism, the Marchese resolved to call it by his own name of Claudio.

In a very short time, the little Claudio became perfectly reconciled to his new residence, and those around him; and the words of "Go to papa, go to mama," were now directed to the Marchese and Marchesa. Arrived at his fifth year, uncommon personal beauty graced his face, and extreme good humour ornamented his mind; nothing more was to be expected from his age, and the Marchese, as he saw him grow up in possession of these two attractive qualities of childhood, saw in him all he expected or desired, and blessed his saints for the gift they had bestowed on him.

The Marchese had anticipated, with much delight, the pleasure he should receive from giving the first rudiments of instruction to the mind of his young charge: the period was now arrived, that he judged it expedient to begin the delightful and profitable task; and the ease and promptness with which his pupil attended to the lessons of his instructor, gave the Marchese the warmest encouragement to proceed in his labours, and repaid his toils with the most satisfactory recompence.

Time passed on without any material occurrence, till Claudio had, as nearly as the Marchese could decide, completed his tenth year: one morning about this time, the Marchese having called him into his study, where he was sitting alone; after a few sentences, introductory to the subject, shewed him the bracelet, and asked him, "if he had any recollection of having seen it before?" Claudio, as he expected, replied in the negative.

"Prepare yourself then," said the Marchese, "to hear a secret, which I am selfish enough to hope will not give you pleasure; but, at the same time, I forewarn you not to let the knowledge of it affect you with violence, but to call in the fortitude of reason to your support under its disclosure.——The Marchesa di Bartelma and myself are not your parents."

Claudio fixed his eyes on the Marchese, but did not reply.

"Did you understand me, my dear child," said the Marchese, after a short pause, and taking his hand, "that I am *not* your father?"

Claudio's eye-lids opened to their widest extent, and he burst into tears.

"You repay my care of you with that grateful reward which I have alone desired," exclaimed the Marchese, and clasped the weeping Claudio to his breast; "fear nothing, my dear boy, though I am not your father, you are my adopted son, and shall never know the want of a parent's protection, while I have it in my power to afford it to you, and you continue to deserve my love."

Still Claudio could not speak, he kissed the Marchese's cheek, and their tears mingled as their faces met.

In a few seconds, the Marchese disengaged himself from the embrace of Claudio, and having directed him to sit down by him, he informed him of whatever related to his mysterious introduction into the family of Bartelma, and produced to him as evidences of his story, the letter which had been put into his hand by the old woman in the church of Saint Paul, and also that which had been contained in the oaken box: "you perceive," said the Marchese, as he concluded the narrative, "that although you now know me *not* to be your father, the change in your situation is but ideal; I love you too tenderly to relinquish my name of father to any one but to him to whom it alone truly belongs; and I here promise to you, that you shall, in every respect, both during my life, and after my death, find that I consider you as my son."

Still the tears flowed down Claudio's cheeks, he endeavoured to speak his thanks, but his sobs rendered them inarticulate. There is something in the name of father to the heart of youth which a benefactor may supply in tenderness, but cannot equal in idea.

The Marchese again read to Claudio that letter which contained instructions for some points in the conduct of his future life, and endeavoured, by many explanations, to enforce them upon his mind. Claudio promised to obey; and then addressed a string of questions to the Marchese, which he expected from the tongue of a youth, placed in so unparalleled a situation; but which he had not the ability of answering. Before they parted, the bracelet was placed upon Claudio's wrist, and the cuff of his sleeve drawn over it, to hide it from observation, and screen it from injury.

For some weeks after this discovery was made to Claudio, his spirits were not so good as they had before been; his lessons were not learnt with his accustomed readiness, nor were his sports pursued with his usual alacrity; frequent also were the questions which he started to the Marchese, relative to the mystery which had attended his early years, and he received with a sigh the Marchese's assurances of his inability to answer them. After these few weeks, however, he returned gradually to his naturally lively disposition, and to all his former habits and amusements with his accustomed spirit: the story of himself, which had at first excited his astonishment and curiosity, by being long dwelt upon, began to grow too familiar to his thoughts to divert them any longer from those scenes and objects which were immediately present to him; the encreasing kindness and love of the Marchese and Marchesa made him almost forget that they were not the authors of his being; and he was yet too young a reflector to think, with any degree of pain, upon those parents whom he had never known.

To his twelfth year, the Marchese alone continued the instructor of Claudio; but judging himself inadequate to the completing of an education which it was his earnest desire to see perfect in every science, and embellished with every polite accomplishment, he engaged for hire a private tutor, strongly recommended for the morality of his conduct, and the ample store of various knowledge which he possessed.

Not long after the introduction of this tutor into the family, an event happened, which would, for a time at least, have disqualified the Marchese from attending to the instruction of his pupil, and which rendered it fortunate that a substitute for his assiduities had already been provided; this event was the death of the Marchesa Julia: a malignant fever seized her, and carried her off in less than a week.

The disconsolate husband shut himself within his chamber, and refused to admit into it, either the cheering light of day, or a consoling friend: the unremitting entreaties of Claudio, to be allowed to participate in his grief, gained him admittance, on the third day after the death of the Marchesa, to the apartment of his benefactor. Pale, distracted by sorrow, sickening, and forlorn, did the weeping Claudio find his now only friend: he kissed his hand, and besought him to take comfort.

"I shall soon taste it in the grave with my Julia," replied the Marchese, in a voice of wild despair.

Claudio threw himself upon the floor before him, and clasped his knees—"Oh, my father!" he exclaimed, "for such you have taught me to call you, live, oh, live! for the sake of your son; I have no protector, no friend, no heart wherein to repose my confidence, but your's; if you forsake me, I am the most forlorn wretch that breathes upon this hated earth; if you promise to live, nature again strews flowers along my path, and beams her sunshine on my head."

The Marchese's cheeks became rippled with the smile of misery, and he besought Claudio to leave him.

"Never," returned the affectionate youth, "never, till I have once again led you forth from this depressing gloom to taste the nourishing air; if I shall never do that, I am resolved to die with you."

A long silence ensued; the Marchese at length broke it.—"For thy sake, Claudio, I will endeavour to bear about an aching heart some few years longer; I have promised in every respect to prove myself thy father; it must be the duty of a father to preserve his own life, that he may watch over that of his son."

Claudio wept with transport, and the Marchese permitted himself to be led by him from his dismal chamber. "May the Saints bless Signor Claudio, he has preserved the life of our master!" whispered the domestics, as they passed together through the hall; the Marchese weak and absorbed in his feelings, leaning for support on the shoulder of Claudio; and Claudio breathing through his tears the smile of religious gratitude, and filial triumph.

The funeral of the Marchesa called forth afresh the extacies of her husband's grief, and it was with difficulty that life was retained within him, whilst with slow and uneven steps, he followed her dust to its last abode.—The bitter task being ended, the Marchese returned to his mansion; it was Claudio only whose sight could give him relief; he could not walk, ride, or even attend mass, without Claudio went with him; with Claudio he would sit for hours, and talk to him of his departed Julia, obliging him to join in a conversation which Claudio was aware did but feed his grief, though it falsely appeared to the Marchese a present soother of his afflictions. When Claudio went to attend his tutor in the study, still the Marchese was by his side, glorying in his progress, and labouring to gain him still greater improvement. "Heaven," he would often repeat to Claudio, "sent you to repair to me the loss of my own boy: in gratitude for that reparation, I listened to your supplication when you besought me to live for your sake; the severe trial is past, and I now pray the director of events, that it may be his will to prolong my life till your's shall have attained a wise and happy manhood."

Claudio was now once more blest, his benefactor no longer wished to shake off his earthly life; and Claudio dared to hope, that he should once again see him restored to that happy serenity of temper, under which he had first known him.

Amongst those instructions which it had been one of the Marchese's chief pleasures to convey to the young mind of his pupil, he had earnestly endeavoured to impart to him, some share of that acquaintance with the muses which it has already been said the Marchese himself enjoyed in an eminent degree: Claudio's ready genius had shown a promising taste for the art his preceptor delighted to teach him to court; he had already composed several little pieces of poetry, which though below the summit of excellence, were still not to be passed over without praise; and shortly after the death of the Marchesa, he presented his benefactor with the following elegy to her memory.

Elegy

On the Death of the Marchesa Julia di Bartelma.

'Tis not the parent's all-subduing claim
    That guides my footsteps to yon mouldering heap;
No kindred ties their magnet-pow'r proclaim
    To wake my eyes instinctively to weep.

Beneath my feet are sacred relics laid,
    Deeply embalm'd in the poor foundling's breast;
With mild compassion, she his fate survey'd,
    His early sorrows softly hush'd to rest.

Upon the friendless world, when cast forlorn,
    No passport to ensure him kind relief,
Save but the tear, too oft repuls'd with scorn,
    Save but the lifted hand, to tell his grief.

No badge had he to mark proud grandeur's sway,
    No costly robe bespoke ennobled birth;
Desertion left him helpless on his way,
    And cast him weeping on the friendless earth:

Till JULIA came, and to her bosom prest
    The hapless outcast; ev'n when nature's claim
No motive whisper'd to her pitying breast,
    To shield him safe from infamy and shame.

Alas! 'tis JULIA these sad lines record;
    Julia resign'd, in death, has clos'd her eyes;
Those eyes that beam'd mild transport on her lord,
    Who heaves o'er Julia's grave his fruitless sighs.

But, hark! from yonder breeze the well-known voice
    Of JULIA steals upon my listening ear;
It calls on CLAUDIO—tells him to rejoice—
    Tells him that "virtue soars beyond this sphere."

In JULIA's words, BARTELMA, Claudio pleads
    That he no more may see thee vainly weep,
When by sad instinct he thy footsteps leads—
    To view the grave where JULIA's ashes sleep.

Her spotless soul regains its kindred skies;
    Bids thee dispel thy fast-intruding tears;
Tells thee to hide in CLAUDIO's breast thy sighs;
    In JULIA's bliss forget thy mortal cares.

CHAPTER IV.

There is a kind of character in thy life,
That, to the observer, doth thy history
Fully unfold———

MEASURE FOR MEASURE.

TIME, that most powerful corrector of grief, began now again to deck the countenance of the Marchese di Bartelma with its usual smiles; still however there were moments when recollection was painful, and it was then that the assiduities of Claudio, to pour a lenient balm upon his patron's wounds, evinced equally the delicacy, tenderness and gratitude of his growing mind.

Although it was impossible that Claudio's age could be exactly known by the Marchese, still, his nominal birth-day, which was in fact the anniversary of that day upon which he had first become one of the Marchese di Bartelma's family, had constantly been observed with some little festivity; two of these annual feasts had been omitted since the death of the Marchesa, the third after her decease was now fast approaching, and the Marchese had given notice to his household, and the tenantry upon his estate, that Claudio's fifteenth birth-day should be held with the accustomed rejoicings of former years.—The custom had ever been, for those who were invited to join in the pleasures of the day, to dine in the air, upon the green before the mansion, round a table spread for the occasion; at which the Marchese, with Claudio on his right hand, on that day presided: the Marchesa had hitherto sat on the other hand of her husband: as the Marchese approached the table, he looked upon the vacant seat, and drew a heavy sigh. Claudio asked him a hasty question, to divert his attention, from the object which was engaging it, and before the Marchese again turned round his head, Claudio had beckoned to one of the Marchese's friends to fill the chair whose vacancy had caused him an unpleasant emotion.

Towards evening, when the hilarity of the feast was rising to its meridian, a servant announced to the Marchese, that six pilgrims were at the gate of the mansion, petitioning for rest and refreshment from the well-known hospitality of its owner. The Marchese desired that they might be immediately conducted to the lawn, and on their appearing, he rose to welcome them, and had seats placed for them near himself and Claudio, by the upper end of the table; five of them were of full stature, the sixth was a youth who had not yet attained his full growth.

In answer to the welcome of the Marchese, one of them returned him thanks for himself and his companions, and added, "that they intended to have reached Florence that night, but that extreme fatigue had overtaken them, and reduced them to the necessity of becoming debtors to his hospitality."

Such viands as the Marchese knew would be acceptable to his

guests under their present profession, were by his order immediately set before them. When they had finished their meal, the Marchese pressed them to drink a goblet of wine to the honor of the feast, of which they were accidentally become members, and to the health of him on whose account it was kept: the pilgrims were returning from their penance, and therefore refused not the invitation to a refreshing draught of Tuscan wine.

The pilgrim whom chance had placed by the side of Claudio, was a man of a most prepossessing countenance, his hair, which had once been of the brightest brown, was beginning to be partially bleached with the snow of age; his eyes were dark, and remarkably piercing; his nose was of the Roman mould, and his features admirably suited to each other; his beard was long, and sprinkled with the white hairs, which were stealing the chesnut hue from his still curling locks; and the pensive melancholy which characterized his countenance, rendered it peculiarly interesting; his figure was tall and well made, and his manners were those of refinement and manliness.

After he had, together with his companions, drank to the health of Claudio, he said, "This is, I think, your birth-day, Signor."

"It is," replied Claudio.

"Shall you think me impertinent, if I ask you how many years you have already counted?" rejoined the pilgrim.

"Only fifteen," said Claudio.

"You are a credit to your years," returned the pilgrim; "God preserve your health to enjoy them many times repeated;" as he spoke, he raised his goblet to his lips, and on finishing his sentence, he emptied the wine which still remained in it from his first draught.

Presently the Marchese filled his own goblet, and pushed the flask of wine to the pilgrims on his side of the table. "No, Signor," said one of them, "our devotions do not permit us to do farther honor to your feast, but we have one amongst us who can perhaps add to its amusement. This youth is our minstrel; he has attended us on our pilgrimage, and accompanied our religious songs on his lute; he is also acquainted with many love-tales and romances, any one of which I am sure he will willingly sing, and accompany his voice on his instrument, to entertain the company here assembled."

The Marchese directly turned to the youth of whom the pilgrim had spoken, and desired him to indulge them with a proof of his talents. The youth blushed, returned the request of the Marchese with a silent inclination of his body, and drawing his lute from under his pilgrim's robe, he sang the following tale:

THE LOVES

OF

ROSA & FERRAND.

SWEET Rosa bloom'd a flow'ret fair,
    Health's glowing smiles her joy would speak,
The breeze in kisses woo'd her hair,
    The dimple revell'd on her cheek;

Her laughing eye would clear explain.
    That ne'er a tear had left its trace,
But such as rose at love's mild strain,
    And ask'd the kiss to take their place.

Oft on the Po's inviting side
    Would gentle Rosa love to stray;
Or in the swift gondola glide,
    When eve impurpled fading day.

Rose blushing heard her Ferrand's sigh
    Steal with enchantment on her ear;
She rais'd her mild celestial eye,
    And spy'd, alas! his starting tear.

"Alas, my Ferrand, tell me why
    "That bold intruder dares to come?
"Has grief oppressive made it fly,
    "An exile from thy bosom's home?

"Where now is flown Aurora's glow,
    "That once in health would on thy cheek
"Exulting bloom? Where now the flow
    "Of youthful joy that made thee speak

"That tale, which fancy fond would say
    "The sweetest was that tongue could tell;
"That tale which knew so well the way,
    "To find my heart's sequester'd cell?

"Oh, tell me all; if thou hast seen
    "A form still fairer than thy Rose;
"Ah! let me wear the willow green,
    "And bind with violets the brows

"Of her thou lov'st; and from that bow'r
    "That once was witness of thy love,
"With the meand'ring jasmine's flow'r,
    "I'll dress for thee a bridal grove:

"This task perform'd, my grave I'll make;
    "With my own hands, I'll mark the spot
"On which I'll die for Ferrand's sake,
    "By him—by all the world forgot."

These words, enraptur'd Ferrand heard
    "Am I," he cried, "indeed so blest?
"Ah, Rosa, keep but half thy word,
    "And give my soul its wonted rest!

"Know, my heart's joy, thy sire with rage
    "Has spurn'd thy Ferrand from his door;
"My sighs nor tears his heart engage;
    "My crime is great—alas! I'm poor!

"But if for me my Rose would die,
    "Oh! promise but for me to live;
"No more my soul shall heave a sigh,—
    "Already does my bliss revive!

"O! let us seek in flight to find
    "That peace a father's frowns deny;
"Let us out-rival e'en the wind,
    "And on love's pinions swiftly fly

"To some sweet spot, in some lone dell,
  "Where Peace with artless smiles shall strew
"Wild flow'rets o'er our happy cell,
  "Whilst Heav'n benign our joy shall view:

"For love has wove the rosy wreath
  "That quivering hangs in Hymen's hand;
"Gales, scented by his mollient breath,
  "Shall waft us safe to pleasure's land."

The minstrel sung with extreme sweetness of voice, and received the commendations and thanks of all present. During the song, Claudio's attention had been entirely directed to the minstrel, and when he ceased to touch the chords of his lute, and Claudio turned himself towards the pilgrim who was sitting next to him, he found that the palmer's eyes were stedfastly fixed on his countenance; and when Claudio began to converse with him, he started, as if awakened from a reverie of thought, and Claudio imagined that he saw him wipe a tear from his eye.

"Alas!" thought Claudio, "this poor pilgrim has some heavy sin lying at his heart, for the removal of which from his mind, even his enjoined penance has been insufficient." Claudio drew to him the flask of wine, and passed it to the pilgrim, to pledge him in the health of the Marchese di Bartelma.

"Sincerely," answered the pilgrim, "do I wish the health and happiness of the Marchese, and if the replenishing of my goblet would encrease to him either of those blessings, I would again drink it filled to the brim; but as that ceremony will be of no effect, instead of that, both he and you, young gentleman, shall each have a telling of my beads when I retire to my pallet." He moved on the flask of wine to his neighbour, and Claudio returned him thanks suitable to the compliment with which he had excused himself from tasting a second time of its contents.

Song, joke, and cheerful conversation, in which the pilgrims gaily joined, wore the hours swiftly away, until the cool breezes of evening began to fan the air; and the merry flute, then inviting the younger part of the assembly to join in the sprightly dance, the pilgrims requested to be shown to their respective pallets, which petition was immediately complied with, and they retired from the scene of festivity, excusing themselves from seeming to neglect its pleasures, by saying they had been journeying ever since the rising of the sun.

CHAPTER V.

>   ——————I see men's judgements are
> A parcel of their fortunes, and things outward
> Do draw the inward quality after them,
> To suffer all alike.
>
> ANTONY AND CLEOPATRA.

ON the following morning, when the Marchese di Bartelma and Claudio met at breakfast, the Marchese addressed him by saying, "Good morrow, my dear son; I learn that the pleasures and exercise of yester-evening did not confine you a moment longer than usual to your bed this morning. Paulo tells me, you were up with the lark."

"I am glad to see you so well," returned Claudio. "Yes, I was up an hour after the dawn of day."

"You saw the pilgrims then depart, I suppose," rejoined the Marchese.

"Yes, I did," answered Claudio, "and have ever since their departure been wishing for your coming down stairs; I have something very strange to tell you about one of them: I thought nothing of it at the moment it happened, but a little while after they were gone, the singularity of the circumstance struck me."

"What was it?" asked the Marchese.

"In the first place," replied Claudio, "I must tell you what I remarked in the same pilgrim yesterday: while the minstrel was singing, his eyes were fixed upon me; and when at the end of the song I spoke to him, he started, as if he had before been lost in thought, and my voice had called him back to recollection; and, I may be mistaken, but I thought I saw him wipe a tear from his eye: then, when I asked him to drink your health, he said, he wished it sincerely, and your happiness too; but that instead of drinking your health, he would tell his beads once for you, and once for me. I thought nothing of these things at the time, but this morning, happening to come into the hall at the moment the pilgrims were going to depart, they all wished me good morning, and bade me convey their thanks to you for your hospitality; and the pilgrim who sat by me yesterday at table, asked me to shake hands with him at parting; and though I did not think of it at the time, I am sure he felt of my wrist, in order to learn if the bracelet was upon it; and when he had done so, he said to me, with a look of more than common meaning, "God bless you, and make you happy!" and he then followed his companions.

"Perhaps the whole of what you have told me," returned the Marchese, "might be only the effect of your own imagination, in adapting accidents to yourself and your own situation. I cannot wonder at every little casual circumstance wearing an air of mystery, to one who knows his own life to be an enigma."

"No, no," cried Claudio, "there was, I am convinced, something more than imagination concerned, in adapting to my feelings the circumstances I have been relating to you.—Who could the pilgrim be?"

"Let that enquiry," answered the Marchese, "if even you should be right in your surmises, be confined to your own breast; remember the solemn injunction laid upon you, never to ask any questions relative to yourself, or to answer any that may be asked of you."

"Oh! yes;" exclaimed Claudio, "the more I think upon it, the more I am convinced, he did feel for the bracelet."

"Let me," said the Marchese, "now this opportunity of speaking upon the subject has presented itself, warn you to guard against any moment in which your passions, without a strict rein being held upon them by your own hand, might be irritated to speak on the forbidden topics contained in that letter which I have often read to you: remember, that however unaccountable and unjustifiable it may appear to you for a parent to renounce a child; the obedience due from a child to a parent requires that he should believe, that nothing but the last extremity of some heavy calamity, not otherwise to be avoided, could induce a feeling heart to so apparently unnatural a conduct; and that both for your own sake, and the sake of those whose cruel fate obliges them to live apart from you, it becomes you most solemnly to adhere to those injunctions throughout your life."

Claudio was going to reply, when his tutor entered the apartment, and by his presence, put a stop to the conversation.

A few days after this, the Marchese, going one evening into the wood at the back of his mansion, found Claudio leaning against the trunk of a tree, and buried in reflection. "Come, come, my dear Claudio," said the Marchese, tapping him on the shoulder, "do not let me see you thus immersed in your own thoughts; all reflection which so deeply absorbs the faculties, as I find yours at this moment, is a species of repining, and I must not encourage this disposition in you: I know you will tell me in answer to this, that your strange fate is a sufficient apology for your holding long conferences with your own mind, and that what you related to me, concerning the pilgrim and yourself, affords you an additional excuse for your solitary meditation.—I confess, that there is truth in all this; but I must admonish you, that it is a man's duty to look on the fair side of his fortune as well as on the dark, and by counterbalancing the good against the evil, extract happiness from the equipoise; for the justice of providence has ordained, that there shall be no sufferer without his equivalent of good;—it is true, that your life is a mystery, that you are abandoned by those who confess themselves to be your natural protectors; but be thankful that, in suffering this desertion of parental tenderness, you have never experienced the want of any comforts which it could have bestowed on you; your fate has been kind in placing you under the protection of one by whom you are not less affectionately beloved, than you could be, if even you owed to him your existence."

"I know I appear ungrateful to your exalted goodness," replied Claudio, taking the hand of the Marchese, and pressing it in his, "I know I must, and I could hate myself for it: I entreat your pardon, and promise to correct my conduct. Believe me, Marchese, although my thoughts sometimes wander from you, my heart is yours alone."

"I did not require this acknowledgement," said the Marchese, "to convince me that you are faulty only towards your own happiness; your actions have spoken your interest in mine."

"And how small a part of my daily encreasing debt of gratitude have they been able to cancel!" exclaimed Claudio. "Oh, what have I yet to repay you!"

"The method is easy," replied the Marchese, "let me see your heart free from inquietude, and I am amply rewarded."

The Marchese then gave a turn to the conversation, and the subject was not again resumed.

The months rolled on unmarked by events of consequence, till Claudio had attained what the Marchese called his eighteenth year; and the time being then arrived when his benefactor had resolved to send him to the college of St. Peter at Rome, to receive the finishing touches of a well-grounded education, his private tutor was dismissed.

The youth was at this period ripening into a manhood which promised more than ordinary personal charms: his dark brown hair, hanging in ringlets over his forehead, seemed to recede in curls to his temples, for the happy purpose of leaving unobscured his animated and intelligent eyes, which gathered lustre from the glowing blood that shone transparent through his thin and slightly tanned skin: his nose formed the exact line of Grecian beauty, and his dewy lips seemed to breathe smiles of complacency. His stature was rather above the middle height, and exquisitely turned in a mean between those admired qualities of beauty and strength which separately form the exact proportions of an Apollo, and the nervous vigour of an Hercules. His natural intellects and mental acquirements were adequate to the perfections of his person, and he was besides expertly skilled in every manly and polite exercise.

Such then was the youth on whom rested the pride and happiness of the Marchese di Bartelma, and with whom he was now on his journey to Rome, in order to place him, in person, under the peculiar patronage of an ecclesiastic who held a high station in the college, and who was distantly related to his family.

Arrived at Rome, the Marchese di Bartelma found in the same inn where Claudio and he took up their abode, the Count di Ponta, who was come to place his only son, Lodovico, in the same college in which Claudio was about to become a student.

The Count di Ponta and the Marchese di Bartelma had been fellow-collegians in the very seminary which their sons were now going to enter; for some time after their quitting the college, they had been intimates, but the retired life of the Marchese's latter years, and other of those various accidents which often snap the thread of friendship, had kept them asunder for a considerable length of time: they met however with mutual pleasure, and their satisfaction was encreased by learning each other's errand to Rome.

The name of the Count Montano di Ponta was familiar to Claudio, although this was his first introduction to his person; for he had frequently heard him spoken of, not only by the Marchese, but also by such of his friends as visited the villa di Bartelma.

The Count di Ponta was a man who had experienced a sudden rise to title and fortune, and the histories of such men are always topics of conversation.

The great uncle of the present Count di Ponta had died, leaving only two male relations; the one was his own nephew, Angelo di Ponta, and the other his great nephew, Montano. As his title and estates had, in the natural right of succession, devolved to Angelo, he bequeathed his personal property, and a small estate which was not connected with the family inheritance, to Montano.

The hereditary domains which fell into the possession of Angelo, had their situation in the rich lands of Placenza; Montano had fixed his residence in the city of Parma. In due time, they both married; Angelo selected his wife for her beauty, Montano chose his for her purse. The wife of Montano died in child-birth, that of Angelo received her death from his own hand. Report whispered, that Angelo discovered his cousin Montano in the bed-chamber of his wife; that in the first phrenzy of his rage, he drew his sword to pierce the heart of the invader of his marriage-bed, and that his wife, rushing forward to prevent the blow from falling on her gallant, received her husband's weapon in her own breast, and survived the wound but a few minutes; and that Angelo, still in love, though wronged in his affections, repented with such violence of his rashness, that unable to live in the state of mind to which he was reduced, he put a period to his own existence with the same weapon which had drawn the life-blood of his wife.

Various however were the opinions of the world upon this melancholy event: some averred, that the wife of Count Angelo had fallen a victim to his unjust suspicions; others talked with great freedom of the levity of her manners, and said, that punishment had only overtaken her too late. Some blamed Montano as her seducer; others again said, that if he was in fault, she had been his inveigler into error; and the sum of varying surmises only amounted to prove, that no one knew any more of the real truth, than that Count Angelo's wife had died by his sword, and that he had very shortly after become his own murderer. Montano was the only person acquainted with every particular, and nothing was known from his lips, as nobody was authorized to question him upon the subject, and he never made it a part of his conversation.

In consequence of this domestic tragedy, Montano immediately became the Count di Ponta, and went to reside in the family pallazo, in the neighbourhood of Placenza. The Count was the father of two children only; Lodovico, who was a few months younger than the nominal age of Claudio; and a daughter, named Valeria, who had preceded her brother one year in her entrance into the world.

CHAPTER VI.

>Live you, or are you ought
>That man may question?
>
>MACBETH.

THE Count di Ponta expressed much satisfaction, as did the Marchese, at this renewal of their youthful acquaintance; and when a few general subjects had been discussed, the Count said, "Do I understand you rightly, Marchese, that this young man is your son; for I had learnt that an untimely grave had snatched from you your only child?"

"Such indeed was the case," replied the Marchese, "but Heaven repaired to me my loss."

The Count then complimented his friend on the promising appearance of Claudio, and the Marchese, with truth, declared himself pleased with the prepossessing countenance and manners of Lodovico; and the young men were recommended to cultivate the acquaintance and society of each other.

In consequence of this introduction, a growing intimacy, as might be expected, not only from the recommendation they had received to think well of each other, but also from their being alike strangers in their new abode, and neither of them having any acquaintance, but his newly gained friend, was soon established between them.

Claudio found Lodovico to be rather the pupil of indulgence than of a strict attention to the right; whatever was faulty in him was the effect of habit, not of nature; his gusts of passion were the result of whim, not of disposition; he had scarcely known the name of contradiction, much less its nature; and he thought, with too much perverseness, that whatever he could afford to pay for, he had a just right either to do, or to possess; still his heart was evidently good, and faultily inclined only from having been too much its own director.

In stature, Lodovico was a few inches taller than Claudio, and in person, although decidedly handsome, by no means so striking and interesting as his friend; Lodovico's hair was but a few shades removed from the palest flaxen, his eyes were of a light blue, and his eye-lashes not sufficiently discernable to give them force; his features were of the Roman mould, and well adapted to each other; and in competition with most men, except Claudio, Lodovico di Ponta would have had the palm of beauty decided in his favor.

In a very short time, the society in which Lodovico was now placed, began to rectify those errors in his early education which, while uncorrected, had tended not only to make his intercourse with the world unpleasant to those who mixed in it with him, but also to himself: to the admonitions of Claudio, he was particularly attentive, and in the course of six months' residence in the college of Saint Peter, almost every improper habit which he had possessed on his first entering it, became corrected; except an inordinate desire which he entertained for pleasure, and in the pursuit of which, no advice or persuasion could prevail on him to put the slightest check upon his inclinations.

Claudio himself was by no means one of those young men who pretend, that while they are living on this sublunary earth, they are insensible to those pleasures which the universal opinion of mortals decides to be enjoyment: far otherwise; whenever the goddess of joy presented herself to him, with an invitation to happiness, whether she wore her hair bound with the tendril of the vine, or the cestus of Venus encircled her waist, he did not turn aside from her beckoning finger, unless she pointed with her other hand to the dark labyrinths of vice, and then he refused all intercourse with her; but Lodovico, rash in his grasp at enjoyment, often pursued her over a bed of roses, to trace his way back through the thorns which alone survived the withered flowers.

However, as Lodovico had one prominent fault, he had one prominent virtue, which was his very manifest regard for Claudio, of whose friendship for him he was most decidedly convinced.

At those hours, when the duties of the college did not oblige them to be confined the prisoners of its walls; the employment of their time was left to their own inclinations, and it is hardly requisite to say, that in the city of Rome, two young men, almost novices in pleasure, could not but find entertainment for their leisure moments, without employing much trouble in their search after it.

Thus passed on the happy moments, chequered by study and pleasure, till within a fortnight of the day on which they were to return, and pass a short vacation at their respective homes.—It was one evening about this time, that, as Claudio and Lodovico were sauntering arm in arm, about one of the public-walks, "Claudio," said Lodovico, "when you and I return home, at this approaching vacation, to our fathers' houses, we shall each be at a loss for a companion of our own years; let us agree not to separate, but pass the vacations alternately at the Marchese's villa, and my father's pallazo; what say you to my plan?"

"I shall like it very much, if it meets the approbation of our fathers," returned Claudio.

"Oh!" replied Lodovico, smiling, "mine at least I can answer for, he never thwarts my wishes."

"Then our scheme is settled," answered Claudio. "The Marchese di Bartelma has too much good-nature to refuse me a request of this kind; so let us agree now, that you pass the first vacation with me."

"With all my heart," cried Lodovico, "I won't refuse your invitation, I promise you, for I have never seen Florence; and not alone that, but I am well convinced that it must be a much better field for the amusements that we full-grown students like to pass our holidays amongst, than Placenza can."

"But you must promise me to act with a little more discretion, where I am known, than you are sometimes given to do here," said Claudio.

"Oh! I promise to put myself under your direction," answered Lodovico, his spirits evidently rising with the prospect of future pleasure which he was drawing in his own mind; "I will indeed; and if you don't find me, the best boy, considering it is holiday-time with me, that you ever heard of, I'll forfeit———but look at that old fellow," cried he, interrupting himself, "he has been walking up and down this street all the time we have been here, and every time he meets us, he slackens his pace, stares at us for a few seconds, and then moves on."

Claudio turned his head to the direction in which Lodovico's eyes were pointed, and saw a friar of the Benedictine order, whose looks were fixed upon himself and his friend. In looking for the person described by Lodovico, Claudio made a momentary stop, and immediately on his faltering in his pace, the friar quickened his steps, and taking the turn of the first street, disappeared.

"What can that monk mean by staring so at us?" said Lodovico.

"Is it not in your imagination only that he does so?" asked Claudio.

"I tell you," said Lodovico, "he did so every time he passed us."

"Well, my dear fellow," returned Claudio, "and not much wonder either; you must be conscious, that you are not given to whisper as you walk along the streets, and a friar as well as another person may raise his eyes at the sound of your voice."

"No, no," replied Lodovico, "I am sure this friar looked with something more than accidental curiosity, either at you or me, which I cannot exactly tell."

"Which ever it was," rejoined Claudio, "did not seem much to please his observation, for he is run away from us both."

"I should have thought him the love-ambassador of some pretty nun," replied Lodovico, "if his face had not looked too sour for the office."

"I saw too little of his countenance to recollect it," said Claudio.

The conversation of Lodovico now again returned to the anticipated delights of Florence, on which he expatiated in a style of rapture, till they had almost reached the college gate, in their return from their walk; then suddenly breaking off his subject, he exclaimed, "Claudio, I am convinced, I have seen that very monk before this evening."

"What is there so very extraordinary in that?" asked Claudio.

"Aye, but I mean staring at us, as he has done this evening," returned Lodovico. "Don't you remember our chatting one night with two pretty little make-believe modest girls, at the corner of the street, by the West gate of the College?"

"I think I do recollect something of it," said Claudio. "Well, and what of that?"

"And don't you remember," continued Lodovico, "that as I was on the point of smacking the cherry-lips of the youngest, she cried out—"Oh, Santa Maria! preserve me, there is an old friar looking at us; if he should happen to be my confessor, I shall have double penance for a fortnight:" I turned round, and saw an old fellow standing quite still on the opposite side of the street, observing us; the girls ran away; I swore I would run after them, and have my kiss; you went into the college; I sauntered about a few minutes in the hope of finding them again; the friar who had observed us passed close by me, and I'll swear he was the very same man who stared at us this evening."

"You were doubtful," returned Claudio, "whether this friar was not the messenger of some unfortunate nun: now, if his observation of us had any meaning at all, I should not be surprised to find that he was a spy upon our actions from the college; though most likely we shall never be able to find out the truth of that."

Lodovico turned grave, and answered, "Do you really think so, Claudio? In truth, some of my penances have been very heavy of late, and I have some how been juggled into the confession of some peccadillos that I never meant to have owned, when I first went into the confessional box. I dare say, our confessor has hints from this fellow to worm out our secrets by."

"You form your decisions too hastily," said Claudio, "what I only offer as a surmise, you write down as fact."

"But if this should be the case, it is a cursed hard thing upon us," replied Lodovico; "what is to be done in this case?"

"There are but two ways of taking it," returned Claudio, "either to submit patiently to the penances enjoined on our follies, or to correct our habits of life."

"And upon my soul," answered Lodovico, "I know not which of the two is the heavier punishment."

They were now arrived at the college gate, and no farther opportunity of private conversation was given to them that night.

When Claudio retired to his chamber for the night, his eyes happened to fall on the drawing of a Benedictine monk which hung over his table; it brought to his mind his conversation that evening with Lodovico. What had appeared to him as an accident when related by his friend, assumed a different character now it became the subject of his solitary thoughts: he recollected the impression which had been made on his feelings by the conduct of the pilgrim; how did he know that the friar might not have regarded him with a like expression; nay, that the Friar might not himself have been the pilgrim.

It can be no matter of surprise, that a man whose life is an existing mystery should be moved to reflection and enquiry by every circumstance, even the most trivial, that falls unexplained under his notice; that he should catch at it with avidity, and endeavour to extract from it a key with which he hopes to unlock the ænigma of his life.

He wished to see the friar; but to what purpose, if he did see him? He was forbidden either to answer enquiries, or to advance any question relative to himself, or whatever related to his birth or parentage. Lodovico had said, that on the first evening on which he had seen the friar observing them, when they stood by the West gate of the College, that after Claudio was gone into the College, the friar had passed close by him, but had not spoken to him: this made it appear more probable to Claudio, that if the friar really had any business with either of them, it must be with himself, and this conclusion made him more earnestly desire to see the friar again, notwithstanding the injunctions by which he was bound.

As soon as Claudio saw Lodovico on the following morning, he began to make enquiries of him about the stature and person of the friar; and Lodovico answered, that he had only observed him sufficiently to know that he was tall, and with a face which could not be accused of indicating a heart possessed of much of the milk of human kindness.

The pilgrim was a tall man, but his countenance wore a mild and complacent aspect, clouded only by sorrow; "it might be possible," Claudio thought, "that Lodovico had mistaken melancholy for moroseness in the face of the friar, and that he might still be the man whose conduct had so strangely interested his feelings."

For a few days, this idea held sole possession of Claudio's heart, and then evaporated like all other impressions, which weaken, if they are not "fed with the stuff which created them," and die away, because reflection, unaided by accident, can devise no nourishment to keep them alive.

CHAPTER VII.

———————I see thee still;

Thou marshall'st me the way that I was going.
MACBETH.

IN the morning previous to that on which Claudio and Lodovico were for a short time to leave Rome, Claudio had strolled into a fruit-shop, and Lodovico was waiting for him on the outside, when the latter, running suddenly into the shop, laid hold of the arm of his friend, and pulled him by it to the door, saying, "Yonder comes the Benedictine monk."

Claudio immediately went out into the street; the friar of whom Lodovico spoke was at some distance from the shop, and coming towards it, thus Claudio had an excellent opportunity for observing him: he was tall, as Lodovico had described him, but his form was not that of the pilgrim, he was more slender, and the angles of his body, more pointed; his countenance too was unlike that of the pilgrim; such parts of his hair as had escaped the razor, were entirely black; his face was sallow, sharp, and thin; his eyes sprightly, and yet there was a gloom of mixed despondency and ill-nature which pervaded his countenance. As he passed the friends, he raised his eyes towards them, but without any particular emotion of feature.

Claudio felt disappointed, but he endeavoured to check his feelings, and prevent their rising to his face.

"Well," said Lodovico, when the friar had passed them, "what is your opinion of him? You see, he looked at us."

"Not more particularly than I may happen to turn my eyes upon any one I meet in the street," answered Claudio.

"Do you think so?" cried Lodovico, "Pray heaven you may be right, and he may have nothing to do with our penances; but he did not stare at us now as he did the other evening, when we were walking up and down the street of the Holy Cross:—Well, well, never mind, we shall give him and of all them the slip for a month to-morrow."

In the evening, Claudio and his friend went to bid adieu to some fair ladies, with whom much of their leisure hours had lately been spent; and as they had resolved to pass a few jovial hours with them after sunset, as this was the night of parting, they had pretended in the afternoon to set out on their journey home, and had engaged beds at an inn in the neighbourhood of the residence of their Dulcineas.

Love, mirth, and revelry, crowned the fleeting minutes, till the clock of the nearest monastery sounded the envious hour of midnight, and their fair entertainers warned them, that it was time to be gone.—Lodovico was resolute in passing the night where he was, but Claudio, wishing for the refreshment of sleep previous to his journey, rose to depart. Lodovico asked him to stay one more hour, and he would go with him; but Claudio, aware that the grant of one hour would only be followed by his friend's importunities to stay another, left the house, calling to Lodovico to go with him; but Lodovico heard him not, and the door was closed upon Claudio.

On going out into the street, Claudio found the night to be one of those, when the thin crescent of a growing moon throws a faint and silver light on the objects which come immediately under its influence, and from its partial gleam, leaves an additional blackness on the surrounding shade.—Claudio listened a few moments at the door, to learn if Lodovico was following him, but hearing no footsteps, he went on. He had not proceeded many paces in the direction which led to his inn, when he heard a voice immediately behind him call out, in low accents, "Signor, Signor." He turned round his head, and perceived at the distance of only a few steps behind him, a tall and dark figure, which was moving towards him; it advanced close to him, and he found it to be the Benedictine friar whom he had seen that morning in the street.

"Signor, a word with you, I beseech you," said the friar.

"What would you with me?" asked Claudio, still going forward.

"I beg of you to stop, and give me hearing," returned the friar; "I have long sought to speak to you alone, but it is next to a miracle to find you apart from your friend."

"What have you to say to me which he may not hear?" said Claudio.

"That," returned the friar, "which I dare hardly trust to your own ears, much less to those of your friend. Will you meet me to-morrow night, at midnight?"

"What can you have to impart to me," replied Claudio, "which it is necessary to tell me in the shades of night? Name where I may see you, and at what I hour to-morrow morning, and I will attend you."

"It is impossible," rejoined the friar, "you ask of me what it is not in my power to comply with; at midnight only can I hold conference with you."

"If even I were inclined to accede to the invitation you give me to meet you at that hour, whose dark veil being considered as an apology for the words or actions it may witness, seems to forbid my holding conversation with a stranger who comes to me thus mysteriously; it is not in my power to comply, for I am under the necessity of leaving this city early after the dawn of day."

"You know not what you reject, when you refuse to meet me,"

returned the friar; "listen to me, Signor, I will tell you thus far my business: If you———"

At this moment, the door of the house which Claudio had just left was heard to open, and Lodovico's voice, tremulous with wine, crying out, "Holloa, Claudio, where are you? Here am I! Holloa! stop for me!"

"I must leave you," hastily exclaimed the friar, "but I charge you be secret on what has passed between us, as you value your life, your honour." He spoke these words in a tone that made Claudio's heart thrill, and immediately disappeared in the shade.

In a few seconds, Lodovico staggered up to Claudio, and his intoxication, and the darkness of the night, both being favorable to his not discerning the agitation of Claudio, they went directly to their inn, and separated for the night.

Claudio having entered his chamber, threw himself into a chair, impatient to indulge thought.—Was it probable, that what the monk wanted to impart to him had any connection with the secret of his birth or not? This it was impossible for him to decide; and on this point rested the propriety of his confiding to his benefactor, the Marchese di Bartelma, what had occurred to him. The friar had commanded him, as he valued his life and honor, not to repeat what had passed between them: notwithstanding this injunction, he would, without hesitation, have decided on laying the whole of what had befallen him before the Marchese, had there not been much more than an equal chance, that the friar's business with him might relate to something diametrically opposite to what he had at first suspected it to be, and thus he might only be awakening the anxieties of his benefactor without a cause. After much deliberation, he determined for the present, at least, to be silent to the Marchese upon his adventure with the friar, and he resolved also not to impart what had happened to him to Lodovico; lest it should eventually prove to be connected with what had been a mystery to him from the first moment of knowing what it was to think.

At one instant, he rejoiced that he had not agreed to meet the monk at midnight of the following day, as the injunction laid upon him in that letter which gave him counsel for the conduct of his life, plainly shewed, that he had enemies at large in the world, as well as friends: at another moment, burning with the desire of knowing himself, he started up, and exclaimed, "I will meet him, and brave the worst that can befall me;" but this hasty decision was quickly baffled by his recollecting, that the monk had not said *where* he was to meet him.

After much debate and painful thought, held with his own mind, he resolved to keep the recollection of what had befallen him as much as possible from pressing on his spirits, and to make it his endeavour, so far to command his resolution, as to leave the unravelling of his fate to the hand of chance; lest his attempting to act towards its developement, should only tend to the farther entangling of the already shackled skein, if it did not bring upon him any fatal consequence. He entered his bed about the dawn of day, but the sleep he enjoyed was very unsound.

When the carriage was announced to be ready for their departure, Lodovico was just risen; Claudio went to his chamber, and roused him—"Why did not you take another nap?" said Lodovico.

"I have slept enough," replied Claudio, "the carriage has been some time at the door."

"I think another nap would have done you good notwithstanding," replied Lodovico, "your eyes are as heavy as if you had not closed them."

"If you don't recollect where we passed the last evening," said Claudio, endeavouring to force a smile, "get up, and look in the glass, and your own eyes will tell you what sort of an evening it was."

Lodovico rose, and followed Claudio's advice, and finding his own eyes by no means sparkling with fire, he readily imputed the dimness of Claudio's to the last night's debauch, without considering, or perhaps knowing, that Claudio had returned from it much less affected by the revelry than himself.

After some time spent in yawning, dressing, and drinking coffee, Lodovico was ready to depart, and they set forward on their journey.

CHAPTER VIII.

―――――――Present fears
Are less than horrible imaginings.

I am settled, and bend up
Each corporal agent to this terrible feat.

MACBETH.

ARRIVED at the villa di Bartelma, Claudio flew into the arms of the Marchese, with all the transport of a son to a parent, after a first separation, and the Marchese hugged the adopted son of his heart with equal fervor to his breast. To Lodovico, as the son of his friend, and also the friend of his son, the Marchese was most cordial in his welcome; Lodovico, pleased with his reception, was extremely cheerful, and Claudio, in witnessing the happiness of his friend and his benefactor, forgot a while to reflect on subjects of anxiety: but when he retired to his chamber, and beheld the little oaken box which had been found with him in the pavilion, standing in its usual situation on his dressing table; saw once more ready to receive him, that bed wherein the departed Julia had so often given him her blessing, his emotions could no longer be subdued, and the tears rolled down his cheeks; fatigued however by his journey, sleep soon administered a welcome draught of oblivion to his cares.

Refreshed by the embraces of sleep Claudio arose at the usual hour of his stirring in the mansion of Bartelma, and went down into the gardens; the first being who courted a renewal of friendship with him was the old mastiff, who had been the faithful guardian of the house many years longer than Claudio had been its inmate; he then went in search of the old prattling gardener, who had pointed out to him many a bird's nest, and taught him to climb the hedges, in order to obtain the brittle prize; he next proceeded to the stable, and visited his favorite horse; "you are grown fat with idleness," said Claudio, "but I must give you some exercise, and reduce your bulk:" Claudio clapped him on the side, and pleased himself with thinking, that his neighings were welcomes to his master's return:—lastly, he strolled to the pavilion, where the arms of the Marchese had first raised him from beggary and death to his name and heart; he sat here a few minutes, but finding that the spot gave rise to reflections and sensations which he wished to curb, he left it, and returned to the house.

Lodovico was all impatience to be introduced to the anticipated pleasures of Florence, and Claudio accordingly, as being his entertainer, lost not a day in conducting him to the scenes for which he panted.

Visits to Florence, rides, walks, and the amusements of the gondola, swiftly wore away the month of vacation allowed by the College, and the time being come for their return to Rome, Claudio informed the Marchese of his wish to pass the next vacation with his friend at the pallazo of the Count di Ponta, and having obtained his ready permission, he bade a farewell to his benefactor, suited to the length of time which he was now about to be absent from him; and Lodovico, in his thanks to the Marchese di Bartelma for the pleasure which his visit to the villa had afforded him, made no professions beyond the delight which variety had fed him with.

It is not at this early age, while their intercourse with the great world is yet in its infancy, that the votaries of pleasure begin to discover either the sameness of those enjoyments which she yields, or to feel the sickening lassitude which succeeds them in a mind sated by their repetition; every youthful heart is allowed for a time to think unrestrained pleasure desirable, that its eyes may open gradually to her superior charms when enjoyed in moderation and ensure it a permanency of its wiser opinion.

As Claudio once more drew near to Rome, those sensations of mind under which he had left it began to return; he could think only on the monk and his mysterious conversation, and wonder whether chance would ever throw him again in his way; it was evening when they approached the city; the sun had retired behind clouds, swelled with rain, and the watery gleams of light which he threw at intervals upon the landscape around, gave a cold and melancholy appearance to the scene, which did not tend to raise the spirits of Claudio. Lodovico was answered only in monosyllables, when he spoke of how they should pass their leisure hours, and what new plans of amusement they should strike out:—How strange, that the human mind should be thus acted upon by light and shade, by time and place; the reason must be left to the philosopher to explain, the fact, the novelist may state.

When they entered the city, Claudio's face was placed at the window of the carriage; it was late in the evening, and not a single monastic was to be seen as they passed through several streets in their way to the college. Claudio could not forbear reflecting—"How immense is this city! how long a time may a man traverse it unsuccessfully in the hope of meeting any one particular individual!"

The first meeting of the collegians since their separation, and their recounting to each other how they had passed their time since they had parted, banished reflection for that evening, in some measure, from the breast of Claudio. As soon as his time became his own, on the following morning, he invited Lodovico to walk; but they saw no one in their stroll whom they knew.

Their walks were continued for nearly six weeks after their return to Rome, unmarked by any occurrence which interested the feelings of Claudio; and he began to think, that if the Benedictine friar had knowledge of his being returned, he was kept from crossing him in his way; at all events from noticing him, or speaking to him, by his being always in company with Lodovico: he wished for an excuse to be alone in the streets, but he could not form or devise one which would not inform Lodovico, that he had some concern which he wished to secrete from him.

In a few days, chance favored Claudio in a point where his own imagination had not been able to assist him; Lodovico, coming hastily into his room, said, "Claudio, my dear fellow, you must not think I slight your society, if I go out without you now and then in an evening; but I have introduced myself into a family, into which I have neither the impudence nor the inclination to take a handsome young fellow like yourself with me."

"How so?" asked Claudio.

"Why," cried Lodovico, "tell me, what do you think an old man deserves that marries a young girl?—In my opinion, a very large, young family."

"And what of that?" said Claudio.

"Why," replied Lodovico, "I know an old fellow in this situation, who does not despair of being the father of as many children as king Priam; his wife, poor thing! was quite of a different opinion till she knew me, but now her fears have all subsided.—Adieu! you can't regret my absence, when you know I am employed in making a happy father and mother for handsome children." And away he ran.

The opportunity of being sometimes alone in the streets, which Claudio had wished for, was now given to him, and he never failed to use it when it offered: His walks were always directed to those spots which he had seen most frequented by ecclesiastics, amongst these were the ruins of the amphitheatre, where crumbling grandeur afforded a rich field for meditation; and at a short distance from these, on a still more solitary spot, stood the dilapidated walls and mouldering pillars of a temple, which tradition related to have been built by one of the Tarquins, but whose inferiority, in point of magnificence, to numberless others of the same nature, had caused it to be little visited by the curious, and its origin almost forgotten.

Hither had Claudio, one evening, bent his steps; the day had been gloomy, and the lowering clouds announced a storm; still the unsettled mind of Claudio could not rest at home: he wandered amongst the ruins, observing every face he met which was shaded by a cowl; friars of various orders were kneeling in this sequestered spot, with their crucifixes held to their devout breasts; and the gales of wind which, at intervals, played through the ruins, announcing the rising tempest, with the chanting voices of the monks at prayer, alone broke the awful silence.—Presently Claudio observed a tall figure, in the habit of a Benedictine friar, coming towards him; he stopped to await his coming; the friar passed him, and Claudio, to his disappointment, saw that it was not him with whom he had held converse on the night prior to his departure from Rome.

Claudio seated himself on the fragment of a ruin, by the side of a path, along which most of the holy men were obliged to pass when they left this solitary spot; one by one they had now almost all departed, but Claudio yet remained; because he knew not whither to wander with a greater hope of obtaining the sight of him he so anxiously desired to meet.—In a short time, the blue lightening began to glaze the marble pillars which supported the broken colonade, and the rattling thunder to announce its nearer approach: Claudio felt an undescribable pleasure, which he had never experienced before in witnessing this elemental war, and still kept his seat; at length, the rain began to pour down in torrents, and a loud crash of thunder which burst immediately over his head, drove him to seek shelter from the storm, and he ran for refuge within an archway of the decayed building.

The side of the building on which he stood met the current of rain driven by the North-East wind, and obliged him to retire farther in, in order to find the shelter he sought; the thunder continued to roar with violence through the ruins, and its re-echoed voice along the archway under which Claudio was standing, doubled its clamours, and the lightening, opposed to the darkness of the interior of the building, gleamed with encreased horror through the gaping chasms in the crumbling walls.—Approaching night and gathering clouds united to thicken the darkness which had been for some time coming on, and when the tempest had in some measure subsided, and Claudio had returned to the entrance of the ruin, there was scarcely sufficient of the light of day remaining for him to distinguish objects by; the rain was now thin and slow; the thunder had retired in murmurs to the distant hills, and the lightening gleamed only a pale shadow of its former fierceness; Claudio therefore resolved to return with all expedition to the college.

He had not proceeded more than an hundred paces from the ruin, before he saw a tall figure, in the habit of a monk, advancing towards him with quick steps, and he had not time to comment upon it, before he recognized it to be the Benedictine friar.

"Signor Claudio," said the friar in a voice of surprise, "happily met; I had begun to fear it never would have been my chance to see you again."

"Did you wish it," asked Claudio.

"Can you seriously ask that," returned the monk, "after what I have already told you? I should have thought it only natural, if a desire of seeing me again had been implanted in your breast—Had you entirely forgotten me till this meeting, or have I entered your thoughts since that night?"

"I confess you have, and often," said Claudio.

"If you thought upon me," returned the friar, "you have also thought upon what I said to you; for your wish to learn what I had to impart to you, must have recalled me into your mind. Well, Signor, have you courage to learn the secret I can impart to you."

"I have," replied Claudio, "tell it to me now."

"That is impossible," rejoined the monk; "you must recollect, I told you before, that it only could be divulged at midnight; besides many more agents than my lips must be employed in its developement. Will you meet me to-morrow at midnight?"

Claudio hesitated to reply.

"Why fear me?" the friar continued, "it is uncharitable, signor, to think evil rather than good of any one with whom your acquaintance is scarcely begun; one of my profession too! I should think that alone demanded a more honorable opinion from you:—however, to convince you, I am no enemy; I swear to you by Heaven, that it is to happiness I shall conduct you, if you will meet me to-morrow at midnight."

"If I refuse to meet him," argued Claudio within himself, "I shall only desire to see him again a few hours after I have left him; I will therefore brave this mystery at once."——————"Friar," he answered, "tell me where to meet you, and I will come."

"Swear to me first," returned he, "by your hopes of salvation through the blessed Jesus, that you will not divulge to any living being what you shall see or hear to-morrow night."

Claudio perceived there was no other method of satisfying his burning curiosity, but that of complying with the terms of the friar, and took the oath.

"This bond of silence," said the friar, when Claudio had taken the oath, "is only necessary to restrain you till you shall know what my secret is; when you once do know it, you will want no farther obligation than itself to keep it sacred within your own breast."

"Where am I to meet you?" now asked Claudio.

"Be upon this very spot to-morrow night," returned the friar, "when the clock of the monastery of St. James shall strike twelve; till then, farewell."

"I will be here," answered Claudio.

"Now leave me," said the friar; "Good night."

"Good night," replied Claudio, and walked on, as the friar had directed him; and when he turned round his head, the monk was no longer to be seen.

CHAPTER IX.

'Tis now the very witching time of night,
When church-yards yawn, and hell itself breathes out
Contagion to the world!
HAMLET.

Oh flatter me, for love delights in praise.
THE TWO GENTLEMEN OF VERONA.

THE interval of suspense passed with Claudio in that state of violent agitation which was natural to his present feelings; the monk had said, "that there were other agents to be employed in the developement of the secret which he possessed, besides his lips!"—might it not be possible, that this man was going to conduct him to the first embrace of a father or a mother? nay, might be himself his father!

Overpowered by his ideas, Claudio threw himself on his knees before a crucifix, and prayed to him who suffered in innocence for mankind, to grant him fortitude to encounter any discovery of his fate which might be about to be made to him.

Somewhat composed by this last action, he turned his thoughts solely to getting egress from the college; he had already bribed the porter to let him pass the outer gate, and the man had promised that he should meet no interruption from him; all he feared was being seen by any one of the superiors in descending from his chamber into the garden of the college: it was now one hour before midnight, he accordingly left his apartment, and meeting no one on the stairs which conducted him into the hall, he gently raised a sash, from which he leaped into the garden, and then drew it down again on the outside; the porter was waiting for him at the gate, and in a few minutes he congratulated himself on his safe escape from the college walls.

He proceeded without delay to the ruins of the temple; the

night was cloudy, but a powerful moon gave him sufficient light to direct his steps with ease; he had not yet heard the midnight hour sounded, but he conjectured that it must be on the point of striking; he took his station on a spot where the shade of a broken pillar screened him from the observation of those who might pass near him, and turned his eyes towards the path which led to the center of the dilapidated building; he had not remained many minutes in this situation when the clock of the monastery of St. James began to strike, and before it was again silent, a hand tapped him gently on the shoulder from behind, and the voice of the Benedictine friar said, "Claudio, is it thou?"

"It is Claudio," he immediately answered.

"Then follow me in silence," replied the friar.

The monk moved on towards the ruin, and Claudio followed his steps; at the very arch-way under which Claudio had sought shelter from the tempest, the friar stopped, "Here we must enter," he said; Claudio recollected that even in the light of day no path had been discernible through this arch, and in spite of his curiosity, and the hopes he had formed of some satisfaction to his mind which he could not explain, arising from this interview with the friar, his courage failed him for a moment, and with a faltering voice, he repeated, "Here!"

"Do you distrust me still," asked the friar, "although I have pledged to you my sacred word, that I conduct you to happiness?—but reasoning here is dangerous, I will therefore convince you by my actions of the sincerity of my words;—take this stilletto," continued he, drawing one as he spoke from under his robe, "and if I deceive you, make what use of it you please."

Claudio took the stilletto, and replied, "proceed."

"Give me your hand," said the friar, "I am acquainted with the path, to an unconducted stranger it is dangerous." The monk took Claudio's hand in his, and they moved slowly on.

For a considerable way, the path, which was stony and uneven, underwent no variation, except that it turned sometimes to the right, and sometimes to the left: at length, the friar, slapping the palm of his hand against the wall, said, "Stop! here we must kneel down, and creep through a low arch."

Whatever Claudio's feelings might be, he had ventured too far to recede, and therefore complied with the friar's directions. The friar stooped down upon the ground, and Claudio having done the same, he guided his hand to the chasm through which it was requisite that they should pass in this position, and putting himself first, called to Claudio to come on: a few seconds brought them through it, and the friar then again taking Claudio's hand, led him down a flight of at least fifty steps, some few of which were of stone, but the far greater number appeared to be only the earth hewn out in the form of stairs; a passage of flat pavement succeeded these, and the friar again stopped, "Now, signor," said he, "let me entreat you, for your own sake, and the sake of myself, not to let a single word escape your lips, till I shall tell you, that you are at liberty to speak."—The friar walked a few steps away from Claudio, made a momentary stop, then returned to him, and said, "Stand still while I throw over you this garment."—Claudio assisted him in silence to draw the robe of an ecclesiastic upon himself.—"Pull the cowl over your face," continued the friar, "and as we pass along hold down your head; remember also my entreaty, that whatever you may see or hear which excites your astonishment, you will not speak a single word."

Claudio now heard a key turn in the wards of a lock, and a door immediately opposite to him being thrown open by the friar, admitted them into a small square room of grey stone, on the floor of which burnt a lamp; the friar locked the door on the inside, and taking up the lamp, opened another door, which led into a passage formed of the same stone as the room which they were leaving; the passage was long and narrow, and as they passed along it, Claudio thought that he heard repeated groans and lamentations very near to him; a third door at the termination of the passage was opened by the friar, and through it they entered upon a scene which made Claudio start back with horror; it presented to his astonished sight a lofty space, whose roof was supported by pillars, which, together with the walls, were entirely covered with human skulls; the length of the building was at least one hundred feet, and its breadth not more than thirty; three lamps, which hung from the ceiling, at equal distances from each other, afforded just sufficient light for him to behold, at the opposite end to that across which he was moving, a large figure of Jesus Christ upon the cross, hung round with black drapery, and at the foot of the figure, a few persons kneeling, whose desponding prayers encreased the horror of the scene.

They passed quickly through this place, and it was succeeded by another passage like the first, at the extremity of this was a small unfurnished room, and adjoining to it a chapel, in which a lamp near the altar gave only sufficient light for Claudio to observe that there were two or three persons near it, without being able to decide on their sex, or their habits.

Various turns, rooms and passages, succeeded those through which they had already passed, and they then arrived at a flight of white stone steps; they ascended these, and entered a door on the right which conducted them into a neat apartment, around which many books were ranged on shelves; a fire had lately been burning on the hearth, and in the middle of the apartment stood a table filled with papers and various implements for writing: the friar bade Claudio remain here, and said, "he would quickly return to him."

The friar did not come back to Claudio till the expiration of nearly a quarter of an hour, and while he was gone, Claudio's wonder and anxiety to have the mystery before him explained only continued to encrease; at last the friar appeared, and beckoned to him to leave the apartment. Another long passage conducted them to a second flight of stairs, like the former, which they ascended, and passed into a room which, though small, was furnished with gaiety and elegance. "You are safe, Signor," said the friar, as he closed and locked the door, "throw off your disguise." Claudio obeyed, and the friar then added, "Your liberty of speech is restored to you; compose your dress at that mirror, and we shall then soon reach the end of our journey."

"Will you tell me now where I am?" said Claudio.

"I leave all questions," replied the friar, "to be answered by one whom you will see presently."

The friar took one of the candles which stood on the table in the room, and held it to the glass. Claudio understood by this, that his conductor insisted on his putting his dress in order, and accordingly complied with his wish, though not in a very attentive manner.

"Come, Signor," said the friar, "your hands and face must want the refreshment of water, after what they have been obliged to submit to; in the next room, you will find a vase prepared for you to wash in." He opened the door of the succeeding apartment, and Claudio, on going into it, found a marble cistern filled with water, scented with the perfume of the rose, and a napkin of the finest texture hanging by its side: he washed himself, and the friar perceiving he had done so, opened the third door, which presented a small but elegantly furnished closet; from this the friar then opened another door, and pointed with his hand for Claudio to pass through it; Claudio obeyed the signal, and he had no sooner complied with it, than the monk, with a gentle inclination of his head, closed upon him the door.

The room in which Claudio was now left was a spacious and elegant apartment, brilliantly lighted by wax candles, in massy silver branches, which stood upon slabs of the whitest marble, supported by gilt stands, between the windows; the curtains and sofas were of a pale blue satin; the ceiling and cornices were composed of a light fret-work in white and gold, and the frames of the sofas corresponded with them in taste. At each corner of the room, the golden leg of an eagle formed the stand of a marble jar, in which bloomed every flower that could regale the sense, and please the admiring eye; paintings which described the flight of Daphne, the rape of Europa, Læda and the swans, the ambitious Semele, and many other subjects, drawn from the luxurious pen of Ovid, hung from the ceiling by silken cords; and between these were placed mirrors of a vast length, which multiplied the glare of light, and encreased the beauty of the apartment.

The contrast of the present scene with those through which he had just passed, made the fascination of the one he was now regarding, appear even greater than it really was, in the eyes of Claudio: he looked round with wonder. The dread which had just before hung upon him seemed to have subsided, and he waited the explanation of his present mysterious visit with a degree of pleasure for which he knew not how to account; he even turned to a mirror, to enquire whether his appearance was not disgraceful to the splendor of the apartment. His dress was the black robe of a student; his disordered hair hung round his neck in its natural curls, and the agitation of his mind had imparted a deeper vermilion to his cheeks than they usually bloomed with; thus far only he had observed himself, when a door, opposite to that by which he had entered, opened, and a female figure appeared before him.

The lady whom Claudio now for the first time beheld, appeared to be about thirty years of age; her stature was rather above the common height of women, but from the excellent symmetry of her limbs, it became rather an advantage than a defect; her face formed a most beautiful oval; her eyes were large, blue, and sparkling, yet mild and conciliating; her skin, save where her ruby lips and blushing cheeks opposed a striking contrast to her alabaster bosom, was whiter than the Parian marble: her dress was a plain robe, of thin white silk, which fell to her feet in clinging folds, that displayed the exquisite formation of her limbs beneath; a single amethyst fastened down the top of her robe upon her waist, and while it confined her heaving bosom from bursting its confinement, did not entirely conceal those beauties which it enviously shaded; her silken sleeve scarcely descended below the turn of her shoulder; a small gold chain was bound round her arm above the elbow, and a second of a finer workmanship was fastened round her wrist: her hair was drawn from her neck round her left temple, and fastened with a diamond comb on the top of her head, from whence the playful ringlets hung wantonly on her right shoulder.

With a gentle inclination of her head on entering the apartment, she advanced towards Claudio with a smile, whose eloquence was indescribable; Claudio bowed, but did not move.

"How shall I apologize to you, Signor," she said, "for this intrusion on your time and more agreeable pursuits?—Sit down, I entreat you, and let me enquire in what words I can best thank you for the favor you bestow on me in this visit?"

She placed herself on a sofa, and signaled to Claudio to sit down by her. "If there is any thing in my power to serve you in, Signora———" said Claudio as he took his seat———He hesitated, and the lady relieved his uncertainty how to proceed by speaking herself. "You are serving me now," she replied, "in giving me the pleasure of your society. I am an unhappy woman, cut off from all intercourse with those whose acquaintance can alone make life desirable: the greatest kindness you can bestow on such an object of compassion is, to say you forgive her having used the means she has practised for bringing you into her presence, and that you will, in charity to her prayers, sometimes visit her solitary retreat."

Claudio was uncertain what to think of this address, thus bowed only in silence.

"Are you angry with me, Signor," she asked, "or do you promise that you will sometimes relieve the flat similitude of my hours with your presence; and when you are absent, give me a pleasing subject for reflection, in the anticipation of your return?"

This was spoken with an earnestness that induced Claudio to answer—"If so small a service as my sometimes visiting you, will prove so great a consolation as you describe it to a life which you seem to declare an unhappy one, you may in this command me, signora."

"Kind youth!" exclaimed the lady, "I thought I could not be mistaken in the good-natured smile of those lips, and the eloquent humanity of those eyes."

"Have you then seen me before?" asked Claudio.

"Oh, yes," she replied, "I have more than once seen you before to-night, and you too have seen me."

"I do not recollect your person, signora," said Claudio.

"Most likely you would not even now recognize it, if you were to see me again, in the same place where we have been together before," said she, with an arch smile.

"What place was it?" asked Claudio.

"I will tell you," she answered, "the next time I have the happiness of your company here."

"Why not now?" said Claudio.

"How impatient are you men for the accomplishment of your wishes!" she returned. "How long have I wished in vain to become acquainted with you! I am determined therefore now to enjoy the innocent retaliation of making you wish a little while in vain to know who I am."

"When shall it be then?" said Claudio.

The lady blushed pleasure at this request, and replied, "You must determine when, by saying how soon you will pay me your second visit."

Claudio began to like the face of his adventure, and said, "How soon will it be agreeable to you that I should return?"

"Society," she answered, "cannot return too soon to one who is condemned to enjoy its comforts only by stealth. What would be your feelings if you were snatched from the pleasures of the world, and immured in a solitary prison?"

"This apartment," returned Claudio, "bears little the appearance of a prison."

"How well does that sentence explain your unacquaintance with restraint!" she cried. "You have yet to learn, that a few days confinement from the world renders it alike to the prisoner, whether he contemplates a gaudy apartment like this, or the gloomy walls of a dungeon; it is not food for the eye, but the mind, which the secluded from the world pant for.—Your name, I think, is Claudio, signor?"

"It is," Claudio answered.

"Your father lives on the banks of the Arno, in the vicinity of Florence; I have known the spot, and am well acquainted with the many beautiful females that city boasts, whose daily intercourse with society renders their conversation lively, and adapted to a man of the world like yourself, whose personal accomplishments, unaided by those of your mind, must ensure your way to the heart of any woman. How then have I, whose sequestered life renders me void of conversation which can interest you, dared to request that you will ever return to my solitary abode!—but you have promised that you will, and I am only giving you ideas inimical to myself, by saying that I have no entertainment to offer you when you do come; my conversation must be confined to my thanks for your presence here, unless I tell you how often I shall attempt in your absence to sketch, with my unskilled hands, features which called forth particular labour even from the finger of nature herself when she formed them; and repeat to you, how often I shall condemn and tear the faultless paper to which I shall not be able to communicate the expression engraven on my heart."

Claudio began now more clearly to understand the lady's earnestness for him to repeat his visits. Claudio was a young man whose heart would have revolted from raising the first blush on the cheek of modesty; but he was not stoic enough to turn away from a woman bent on pleasure, and who had sufficient years to judge of her own conduct: accordingly, taking the hand of the lady, he said, "I am sure these fingers, directed by the mind which beams through the eye that is to superintend their labours, cannot fail of completing whatever task they may undertake."

"It is difficult to draw from memory," she replied, smiling.

"But you shall have the original before you, if you will honor it so far," said Claudio.

"I shall not do it justice," she answered.

"I fear," rejoined Claudio, "that if generally viewed, it would appear a flattering likeness, although partially considered, it may be a true one; without you can give me a secret for retaining the same fire in my eyes which you will communicate to them while you gaze upon them in the act of describing them upon canvas."

"Is not there some fear," replied the lady, "that when I once suffer myself to gaze upon the living eyes of my subject, the copy will never be completed at all, if even begun?———But come," continued she, rising, "you must require some refreshment after the trouble you have undergone to arrive at my prison: I would it could be spared you, but that is impossible; and I doubt not but the difficult access to this place will soon sicken you of coming to it."

"I confess I was not much pleased with it to-night," said Claudio, "but in future, I am persuaded, the length and difficulty of the way will only be thought of by me in my return."

The lady moved to what appeared the middle window of the apartment; and having touched a spring, the curtains flew back on each side, and gave to view an alcove, in which stood a table of white marble: on this were placed baskets of various fruits, cakes, wines, and delicacies of different sorts; and over the table, at the back of the alcove, hung a painting which represented Mars reclining upon the lap of Venus, and surrounded by flying Cupids, in whose countenances were described all the fascination and witchery of the passion which they personated.

She invited Claudio to a glass of wine, which he accepted, and then said, "I could here almost fancy myself in a palace of that Arcadia which our poets describe. How strange a contrast is this scene to those dreary and horrid dungeons through which I passed in arriving at it. Will you satisfy my curiosity by explaining what they are?"

"Not to-night," she answered, "at your next visit, you shall find me more communicative; however, Signor, dispel your fears, if you have any, for no evil is intended you, I assure you. I am supreme mistress of every spot which you have passed, and I promise you, that you have nothing to *fear* from me." As she spoke these words, she took his hand, and confirmed her assurance by pressing it with her polished and tapering fingers.

"You are an ænigma, Signora," returned Claudio, "whose mystery encreases; you have declared yourself a prisoner, and at the same time supreme mistress of all which I have seen.—How are these contradictions to be reconciled?"

"Like most riddles," she replied, "when you have discovered it, you will only wonder that you did not find it out before."

"Surely," said Claudio, "the miserable fate of those wretches whom I heard uttering lamentations in that dreadful cavern, whose walls are set with human bones, cannot be in the hands of one so fair, so sensible, as yourself."

"If you pity them," she said, "I could lead you to sights that would———but come," she continued, after a pause, "I invited you to join with me in my hours of pleasure, and you entertain me only with a repetition of what I have thought upon too much already."

There was a fascination in her person and manner which, had she been in the very act of inflicting those agonies, at the idea of which Claudio's heart had just been chilling, must have provoked the coldest breast to passion; Claudio threw his arm round her neck, and imprinted a kiss on her burning lips.

She disengaged herself gently from his embrace; then said, "you must now be gone; it is not in my power to suffer you to remain longer with me to-night. When will you come again?—Will you visit me again on the third night from this?"

"I will," Claudio returned.

"I shall then unfold to you a little of the mystery which so much puzzles you," she replied, smiling. "The friar who conducted you hither, I will send to wait your coming at the same hour, and on the same spot, where you met him to-night; he is a trusty friend, and the only one who is acquainted with your visit."

"You refuse then," said Claudio, "to suffer me to pass one more hour in your society to-night?"

"It is not my inclination," she answered, "but my necessity which sends you away; your next visit I promise you, shall be a longer one; but, signor, take from me one serious admonition before you go: you have already bound yourself by a vow to the friar who brought you hither, not to divulge whatever you may see or hear within these walls."

"I have, and will solemnly observe it," Claudio replied.

"Beware then," she continued, "as you value whatever is dear to you, not to attempt to enter the caverns through which you have passed to-night, unless when the friar is with you. Believe me, upon my honor, that the entrance from them which leads to these apartments, could not be found by any human being, except those entrusted with the secret of it; and that were it possible for you to discover it, your life must immediately and inevitably answer your rashness. Adieu! promise me, that you will be satisfied with seeing me at those hours when I send the friar to conduct you to me, and you will be safe, and I shall be happy."

"It is no merit in me," returned Claudio, "to promise that I will be governed by your instructions, because I wish to act only under their direction."

The lady still held Claudio's hand in hers, and with another gentle pressure of her fingers, she said, "You will find the friar in the last of the three apartments through which you just now passed. Once more, farewell! till three nights hence." Having said this, she suffered Claudio again to kiss her lips, and then retired hastily through the door by which she had entered. Claudio immediately sought the friar, and found him waiting his coming in the apartment which the lady had mentioned.

"Well, signor," said the friar, "do you repent trusting yourself with me? Did I deceive you when I promised to conduct you to happiness?"

"You certainly kept your word," replied Claudio, "but the path through which you conducted me promised me little enjoyment at the end of it."

"Your way to pleasure," returned the friar, "was an epitome of the world, in our passage through the dismal scenes of which, a persevering conduct leads to felicity at the last."

This speech, thought Claudio, might as well have been omitted by a man in the garb of him who spoke it, after having been his conductor to the lady whom he had just left.

The friar requested him again to put on the holy robe, and to observe the same silence he had preserved on his entrance: Claudio promised to obey, and the friar taking up the lamp, they set forward. Claudio observed the same persons still kneeling before the figure of their crucified redeemer, in the cavern whose walls and pillars were covered with human skulls; but he heard no groans in going through that passage where the lamentations of many voices had before struck his ear.

The friar left the lamp where they had first found it on their entrance that night, and took off Claudio's disguise where it had first been put on. After this, they ascended the flight of steps which led to the low arch, and having passed under it, a few minutes brought them into the open air.

"On the third night from this, I am to meet you here again," said Claudio.

"I shall have my instructions," replied the friar.—"Good night."—and disappeared.

Twilight had not yet begun to peep from the heavens, and Claudio was uncertain how long he had been engaged in his adventure, till he heard a distant clock strike two: he proceeded straight to the college, and being admitted by his friend the porter, soon gained his chamber by the same means which had favored his escape from it.

It cannot be supposed that Claudio slept that morning: he had too much subject for reflection to suffer his thoughts to fall into passive oblivion: his strange adventure did not alone dwell on his mind; the disappointment he had experienced in his raised expectations of learning something relative to himself, had no inconsiderable part of his thoughts; but this latter sensation subsided first, and left the whole strength of reflection bent upon what he had just been witnessing.

That the lady with whom he had been conversing should declare herself a prisoner, shut from the world, and debarred society; yet at the same time supreme mistress of the purgatory, in passing through which his blood had chilled, and of the elysium in which he had revelled, was so irreconcileable a contradiction, that it baffled even surmise.

Not less extraordinary did it appear, that a man, whose garb bespoke him the professor of a holy and retired life, should be the instrument of her pleasures; and, if possible to be so, still more unaccountable than these facts, was the lady's declaration, "that she had seen Claudio more than once before, and that if he were now again to behold her in the same situation where he had before seen her, it was more than probable he would not recognize her." He endeavoured to bring to his mind the persons of all the women whom he had ever known: he thought himself successful in recalling them to his memory, but still there was no countenance amongst them which, in the slightest degree, tallied with that of the signora whom he had just left.

He had found the monk's promises to be true, and therefore he resolved to obey with strictness, both his injunctions and those of the lady; but a stroll along the outside of the ruins was not amongst these, and on the following morning, he repaired to the spot where they stood, thinking that he must discover in their neighbourhood some building of unusual largeness which he might pronounce to be that in which he had been entertained. He walked about for a considerable time, and observed houses and monasteries planted thickly round him; but none whose size appeared at all answerable to his ideas of the building through which he had passed the night before. The monastery of St. James was the largest he saw from this spot; but its distance and situation both seemed to contradict that it could have any communication with the ruins of the temple.

The signora had promised him that, at his next visit, she would be more communicative; to that time therefore he was obliged to defer the gratifying of his excited curiosity. Sometimes he believed that the whole of what he had witnessed had been the spell of enchantment, raised by a spirit, in order to win over his heart to some evil purpose; but having very little faith in the division of supernatural agency, and sincerely wishing the signora to prove nothing more than mortal, he soon banished this idea from his brain.

CHAPTER X.

> If music be the food for love, play on;
> Give me excess of it, that surfeiting
> The appetite may sicken, and so die.
> That strain again;—it had a dying fall!
> O! it came o'er my ear, like the sweet South
> That breathes upon a bank of violets,
> Stealing and giving odour.———
>
> THE TWELFTH NIGHT.

ON the third night, with the assistance of the porter, Claudio repaired again, at the time agreed upon, to the ruins of the temple.

A few seconds after, the clock of the monastery of Saint James had struck the hour of twelve, the friar appeared, and with all the same precautions and observations which had been used on the former night Claudio was conducted to the same apartment where he had before met the mysterious lady, and found her ready to receive him.

She advanced towards him with an air of pleasure and unreserve, which invited Claudio to receive his welcome from her lips, as he held her clasped in his arms.——"You are very good," she said, "to keep your appointment with a woman: how much does a man like yourself deserve from the sex, who does not tyrannize over them after they have made a rash confession of their hearts."

She led him to the sofa, then continued speaking thus—"We must now cast aside the formality of Signor and Signora, as we are to become more intimate acquaintance, by promise, before we part. You know I am to let you, in some measure, into the mystery of who I am, and where I dwell: I shall therefore in future address you only by the name of Claudio.—Do you permit me this freedom?"

"Every thing which tends to discard formality, cannot but be an additional pleasure to me, while permitted to enjoy your society;" returned Claudio.

"You are a flatterer," said she, "but I must allow you the merit of being a pleasing one.—Well, then, I will call you Claudio, and you shall call me your Viola.—Will you call me your Viola?"

Claudio's sighs and smiles answered this question in the affirmative; the lady smiled responsive pleasure, and a few moments of eloquent silence succeeded her question:—she broke it by saying, "In order to keep my promise with you in such a manner that you may understand me perfectly, I must give you some of the leading incidents of my eventful life, before I speak of the situation in which you now find me. Shall you have patience to listen to my sorrowful tale?"

Anxious to learn the mystery of her present life, Claudio expressed his desire to be indulged with the recital, at which she had hinted. "When I tire you," she said, "you must bid me break off; but I will endeavour to be as brief as possible in my narrative."

Claudio drew himself nearer to her upon the sofa; her right hand was held between his, and raising her head from the back of the sofa upon which it had been reclined, she thus began:

"The name of my family, I must not disclose, nor is it of any importance to what I am going to impart to you. My father was a man of high rank and great wealth; my brother, who was some years older than myself, was his only son, and myself his only daughter.—Whatever education could bestow on the mind and person, my father was assiduous that we should both be taught. My imagination was active, and I easily acquired those accomplishments whose chief end is to render woman vain, and give her the first ideas of levity of conduct. The reputation of my beauty, sense, and fortune, gained me more admirers than most girls can boast of having held in their chains at the early age of sixteen; and the one amongst them who particularly pleased me, was a youth of about twenty, whose extreme personal beauty, and love-breathing accents, won my heart.—Oh, surely the tale of love was never told with more enchanting sweetness, or by one more feelingly alive to that passion, which is the soul of existence, than by my lover, whom I shall call Rinaldo; but, alas! he had not wealth to equal that which my father was able to bestow on me, and in his want of fortune, my love and his perfections were not attended to by him whose sanction was necessary to form our happiness.

"My father had lost in age the warm and softening fire of

youth, and looked upon rank as the only happiness which a female could derive from marriage. He was constantly representing to me a thousand evils, by which he wished to persuade me, that a woman who threw herself into the arms of a husband merely for love, was exposed to; telling me that the happiness which personal beauty could give, was joy transient as the colours of the rainbow; told me that all passions, especially that of love, were subject to mutability and cessation; and warned me, that Rinaldo's affections might swerve from me after he had been a month my husband;—but he preached to the winds; the heart which is capable of feeling a passion with real fervor, never was known to change its feelings from argument.

"Many were the offers made to me by men of rank and fortune, and unavailing were the persuasions my father used to induce me to give my hand to one of them; I was resolved to become the wife of Rinaldo, or to live unmarried. My mother had been some years dead, therefore I had no parent of my own sex to call upon to intercede with my father in favor of my wishes; my brother was at this time on his travels, and was expected to return home in about six months, and I looked forward to his arrival with the flattering hope, that his entreaties in my behalf might have some weight in moving the heart of my father.—Rinaldo was forbidden to visit me, and when we met, it was by stealth, in the garden behind my father's house; where the midnight hours were passed by us, when opportunity accidentally favoured our meeting.

"While I was expecting the return of my brother with the most impatient anxiety, my father came one day into my dressing-room, and with very little preface to his declaration, told me that he had resolved on giving my hand, in one month at the farthest, to a rich nobleman, who had long solicited me in marriage; and concluded this dreadful intelligence by recommending me to compose my mind to the event, as I must otherwise be dragged to the altar by force.

"In a state of mind which you may easily conceive, I contrived to see my Rinaldo that very night; but, oh, God! how shall I paint our agonies as we hung mourning on each other's necks! The misery of those moments is still as lively in my imagination as if an hour had only passed since their existence. After much debate, and the formation of many plans, which were made only to be rejected, we determined that Rinaldo should set out immediately for Venice, where my brother then was, and endeavour to prevail upon him to return home directly, and use his intercession in our favour with my father. Rinaldo had never seen my brother, but I directed him where in Venice to find him, and gave him a letter of introduction to him, written by my own hand, and containing all the entreaties for his interest in my behalf which the wretchedness of a love-desponding mind could dictate. An agreement was also concluded between Rinaldo and myself, that if my brother refused to become our friend, or my father should reject his mediation, that I would immediately fly from parental tyranny with him I could alone love.

"The first three weeks after the departure of my Rinaldo for Venice, I passed my solitary hours in tears, and prayers to the Virgin to favor my desires: one week now was only wanting to the completion of that moment, at the dreaded expiration of which, my father had declared his resolution of devoting me to eternal misery. Neither Rinaldo nor my brother was yet returned, and my agony of mind arose to an indescribable height.

"At length, as I was one day sitting in the window of my chamber, indulging my melancholy thoughts, I saw a man on horseback stop at the gate of my father's mansion, and, in a few minutes, I recollected him to be the servant who had attended my brother on his travels. Not doubting him to be the harbinger of his master, I flew down to receive his tidings. Little did I expect to meet them such as they were. He brought information that my brother had been dead ten days, that he had fallen into a quarrel with a stranger whom he had met at an inn on the road on his return home, that they had decided their dispute by the sword, and that my brother had received almost immediate death from the weapon of his antagonist.

"I shrieked, and fainted. When my reason returned (which it did not do with any stability till the expiration of two days and nights), I was told that my father had been so much affected by the death of my brother, that he had been instantly, on receiving the intelligence, conveyed to his bed, and that his physicians despaired of his life.

"Still this accumulation of misery was not all I was condemned to bear: a heavier, a maddening grief awaited me; and too soon it reached my agonized senses:—my Rinaldo was the stranger who had quarrelled with my brother, and been his murderer; and my Rinaldo himself had survived his wounds only two days!"

Viola's voice faltered, and she paused from speaking. After a few moments' silence, she said, "Claudio, I cannot immediately proceed in my narrative,—the recollection of past events agitates my spirits more than I can bear. If I go on a moment longer, I shall become a shocking companion: let us change the scene, and endeavour to divert our thoughts from melancholy reflections. Come, I will show you to my garden."

She rose, and opened a door, through which she passed, and Claudio followed her: it conducted into an apartment whose walls were covered with the branching vine, luxuriantly loaded with the most inviting fruit. Orange trees, in jars, placed on stands, at short distances from each other, exhaled from their blossoms a most grateful perfume; and roses, jessamines, and the sweet-scented heliotrope, filled up the remaining vacancies. In the middle of this blooming paradise stood a small table, on which were cakes, ices, and various kinds of wine.

"Well," cried Viola, "how do you like my garden."

"It is excelled," replied Claudio, "only by the goddess of its beauties."

"Do you like music?" asked Viola.

"Harmony attunes the soul to love," answered Claudio, "and must be admired by every one who knows what happiness the passion can bestow."

"Do you mean by that," returned Viola playfully, "that you want some enchantment to inspire you with the passion just now."

"You could only accuse me of a becoming diffidence," rejoined Claudio, "if I confess your conjecture to be right."

"How so?" asked Viola.

"By avowing," returned Claudio, "that I know myself only to be a mortal kneeling at the feet of a divinity."

After a few minutes' dalliance, Viola drew a silken cord which hung from the ceiling, then said, "I will introduce to you, Claudio, a female friend of mine, whose performance on the lute will fill you with rapture; and I promise not to be jealous, if you confess that you are enchanted both with her person and voice."

No sooner had she spoken, than the door opened, and a beautiful girl, whose age appeared to be at most seventeen, entered. Her height rather exceeded the middle stature, her figure was exquisitely enchanting and elegant, and her limbs were turned with a smooth polish that rivalled the glossy firmness of the snow-white ivory. Her face was not sufficiently long to be called an oval, and in approaching nearer to the form of a circle, it gained the advantage of wearing a more bewitching smile of good humour than the oval can command; her hair was black, and hung curling from the top of her head down upon her bosom, to whose pearly whiteness its sable hue gave additional brilliancy; her black eyes sparkled with the lustre of scintillating stars; her blushing cheeks confessed their theft of the rose's vermilion; her ruby lips breathed a dewy fragrance on the bewitching dimple which graced her chin; and her spiral neck, of velvet softness, expanded into a panting bosom, whose charms were concealed beneath the white drapery which composed her simple dress.

"My dear Zelia," said Viola, on the entrance of the other female, "this Signor is a friend who, like yourself, is so kind as to relieve my solitary hours by his society.—Claudio, you two must be acquainted."

Claudio advanced towards Zelia, and without reserve, yet without levity, she suffered him to kiss her hand.

"Come," said Viola, "let us partake of this little repast, and Zelia shall then indulge you with some music." She drew her chair to the table, and sat down; Claudio and Zelia followed her example. While they were enjoying the banquet, Viola was studying to keep up a lively and spirited conversation, in which Zelia joined with a display of sense and good humour mixed, which warmed Claudio's heart to an interest in what she said, and called his attention in some measure from Viola.

Every moment continued to raise Zelia in the *esteem* of Claudio, but without weakening the hold of Viola upon his *passions*. The two females, whose society he was now enjoying, made a very different impression on his heart:—Viola was the woman whom of all others he should have selected as the amusement of an hour devoted to pleasure: Zelia appeared to him a soul of soft vivacity, and a peculiar interest of feeling, with which he could have been satisfied to pass his future days in the rosy fetters of hymeneal love.

"Come, my dear Zelia," said Viola, "string your lute, and attune our hearts to harmony. Claudio," she continued, turning to him she addressed, "I will not allow Zelia all the merit of the song she is going to sing to you; praise her as much as you please for the powers of her voice, but return me thanks for the words, in which your own name is introduced."

"You have honoured me indeed," said Claudio, "by making me the subject of your address to the muses."

"Unskilful mistresses of composition," replied Viola, "like myself, always choose those subjects for their pen with which their thoughts are most familiar."

Zelia now began to strike the chords of her lute, and silence immediately prevailing on the part of Viola and Claudio, she sung the following:

Address

TO THE

GOD OF LOVE.

EXPAND thy wings of Tyrian dye,
    And flutter to this fairy grove;
The azure fillet from thine eye,
    Come and unbind, sweet God of Love.

Thy smiles we court, nor dread thy scorn;
    Sylphs mantling round thy wanton hand
Shall shield us like the clouds of morn
    That tinge Aurora's purple wand.

To Viola's bosom softly creep,
    Entwine thy fingers in her hair;
No elf shall break thy balmy sleep,
    Thy guardian sprite is Viola fair.

Zelia will choose with magic spell,
    Bright visions for thy sportive dream;
And when thou wakest thy tongue shall tell
    The pair who form the lovely theme.

The beauteous nurse who holds thy head,
    And folds thee in her iv'ry arms,
Who makes her breast thy spotless bed,
    Bribes thee to sing her matchless charms.

And Claudio too, with guardian plume,
    Shall chide the gnat that hovers nigh,
Shall o'er thy form shed sweet perfume,
    And veil the sun-beams from thine eye.

This is the pair that court thy smiles,
    That kneeling at thy rosy shrine,
The willing vot'ries of thy wiles,
    Confess thine influence divine.

While Zelia was singing, Claudio's eyes were fixed upon her in mute and rapturous attention. The exquisite sweetness of her voice distilled, with every note, into his heart the tender passion which she sung.

"Well," said Viola, "how do you like my pupil?"

"I think her," Claudio was replying, "so exquisite an———"

Zelia interrupted him, deeply blushing. She said, "Hold, hold, Signor; do not praise me to my face; for I wish to have pleased you, and I shall doubt my having done so, if you are too warm in your commendations while I am present."

"Do you charge the world in general with this false praise, or only my sex?" asked Claudio.

"Oh, no," replied Zelia, laughing, "I lay the fault upon those who expose themselves to hearing fallacies by listening to their own praises."

"You must be so sensible of your powers of pleasing," returned Claudio, "that to hear they have succeeded is an unnecessary conviction of their excellence."

"Signor," said Zelia, still smiling, "you are falling into the very error I have been disclaiming."

"Are you sorry I have been gratified?" asked Claudio.

"Far otherwise," she returned, "I am happy in your good opinion;" and a deep blush stole over her cheeks and neck as she spoke.

"You must reserve your controversy for another opportunity," said Viola, turning her eyes to a dial which was supported on a gilt bracket against the side of the wall, "it is within five minutes of two o'clock, and Claudio must depart."

"Must I retire," cried Claudio, "without any further communication from your lips?"

"We poor women only," returned Viola, "have the laugh against us in the world for not being able to restrain our curiosity; but I have now a fresh instance that the foible is equally chargeable on the nobler sex.—You must wait for a farther explanation of what surprises you till your next visit."

"I can make no appeal from your decision," said Claudio. "When shall I be permitted to return?"

"It cannot be," answered Viola, "till the seventh night from this."

"You increase the time of my absence," replied Claudio, "in order to try my perseverance."

"Only prove it this once more," returned Viola, "and you shall then have much more frequent access to this place, if you shall still think it worth your while to visit it."

Zelia raised her eyes to Claudio, as if anxious to know his answer.

"To that doubt," said Claudio, "I shall let my actions, and not my words reply."

"Farewell, Claudio," said Viola, rising, and held out to him her hand; Claudio kissed it, and then taking the hand of Zelia, he said, "May my lips be permitted to seal a short farewell here?" Zelia smiled compliance, and Claudio remarked that her hand trembled.

"I must have the last farewell," cried Viola, and again extended to him her hand. Claudio imprinted on it a second kiss, and then departed.

He found the friar, as before, in the last of the suite of apartments; and having passed through those scenes which he now began to behold with less horror, he in a short time reached his chamber, in the college of St. Peter.

CHAPTER XI.

> And him beside march'd amorous Desire,
>   Who seem'd of riper years than t'other swaine;
> Yet was that other swaine the elder sire,
>   And gave him being, common to them twaine.
> His garment was disguised very vaine,
>   And his embroidered bonet sete awry;
> Twixt both his hands flew sparkes he close did strain,
>   Which still he blew and kindled busily,
> That soon they life conceiv'd, and forth in flames did fly.
> SPENCER.

CLAUDIO's thoughts rested still on his mysterious adventure, and the more he considered it, the more it seemed to defy his explanation. What best pleased him in it, was his introduction to Zelia; and the more he rested upon the recollection of her person and manner, the more convinced he was that she had made an impression on his heart that would not easily be effaced.

In the evening preceding that on which Claudio was again to visit Viola, Lodovico came up to him in high spirits, saying, he had just received an invitation, for that evening, from the young married lady, his new acquaintance.

"Beware of the old married gentleman, your other new acquaintance," replied Claudio. "Men in his situation are crabbed animals to deal with."

"Aye," rejoined Lodovico, "I can't help thinking but that it is a great defect in the formation of the passions, that if that old gentleman were to know the important service I am rendering him, instead of returning me thanks, he should be inclined to give me a sound drubbing, if he were able. It is a hard thing upon benevolent-minded young men, like myself, to be obliged to perform our benefits to society with so much privacy.—Well, adieu! Claudio; I must leave you either to find amusement for yourself, or to sit at home envying me. I know which I should do in your case."

Lodovico left the college, and Claudio retired to his apartment.

The evening was passed by Claudio in writing to the Marchese di Bartelma; and about midnight he went to bed. As he lay between sleeping and waking, the Benedictine friar, Viola, Zelia, the subterraneous passages through which he had passed, and the fairy scenes wherein his senses had been regaled with pleasure, all floated in his imagination: presently sleep overtook him, and the subjects which had been agitated in his mind whilst awake, did not now fly from his brain.

He dreamt that he was wandering, in the midst of thick darkness, amongst the ruins of a dilapidated temple. For a long time, he was entangled amongst the fallen stones, and could not make his way to a dim light which he saw at some distance from him. With much difficulty, he arrived at a gloomy building, from whence it shone, he applied his hand to an iron knocker, which hung in the center of the gate, and was answered by the loud and repeated reverberations of its echo.—The lock creaked in its sockets, and the gate was opened by a tall figure, habited in the garment of a friar; its face was of the most ghastly appearance, its arms were brown and shrivelled, and its feet had the talons of an eagle. In one of its hands, it held a lamp, the flame of which burnt blue and sepulchral; the other hand held open the gate.

Claudio started back—the figure spoke, "Welcome;" its voice was hollow, and corresponded with its visionary appearance. Claudio continued motionless—the figure spoke again, "Enter." The sound of its voice proceeded not from substance, it was the vent of air. Claudio trembled—the figure addressed him a third time, "Welcome, enter."—Claudio became still more alarmed, but guided by the inconsistency of action and ideas natural to dreams, he went in.

No sooner had he passed the threshold than the heavy gate shut with a crash that shook the echoing walls; the figure grinned upon him with a murderous smile, which discovered its horribly fanged teeth; then dashed the lamp from its hand, and vanishing with a loud yell, left the astonished Claudio in utter darkness.

Silence and obscurity reigned uninterrupted for some moments. Claudio's blood congealed in his veins, and his flesh shrivelled on his bones. A noise like the hissing of serpents drew his eye to the spot from whence it issued, and he perceived, playing on the surface of a lofty ceiling, snakes of flame, from whose distended jaws dropped particles of luminous fire that stung him in every part: almost immediately the roof gaped, and admitted through the aperture, two animals of hideous form, enveloped in flakes of fire, which, extending their wings, flew to the ground, and brought with them a black car, around which fluttered innumerable visionary beings, of unpleasant forms, apparently composed of a blue and liquid flame.

Claudio was placed by them in the car, and the two animals instantly began to wing their way through the air, with a swiftness that stagnated Claudio's breath, and obliged him to shut his eyes. The most dismal shrieks aroused him from his unwilling lethargy: on again opening his eyes, a light so painfully strong met his sight as obliged him swiftly again to close them, and as he drew his suspended respiration, he swallowed a fiery air that scorched his vitals.

Immediately he felt his clothes stripped off, and a wet sponge applied to his eyes, which caused him to open them without pain. He looked around—torture stared him in the face on every side— horrid demons, standing in the midst of flames, were lacerating human bodies, which appeared to be alive, but deprived of the power of speech, while vultures, seated round the dome, gorged sulphur into the flames to keep them alive. The iron car was every moment becoming more heated by the fire with which it was surrounded, and Claudio shrieked aloud from the pain it occasioned him;—instantly the demons sent forth a horrid grin of malicious satisfaction, which rang through the place; the ground before him opened, and a figure, resembling a mutilated corpse, rose slowly from the aperture, and with its mortified hand, beckoned to Claudio to follow it;—he found himself released from the car, and proceeded forward. His conductor passed through a black gate, which opened heavily on its hinges, into a dark passage, and closed again with a violent crash; in the midst of thick darkness, the figure was still visible, and waving to him to come on: by degrees, a faint glimmering of light began to shine on the path they were treading; the ground, which had before been rough and flinty, became more pleasant to the feet, the air grew purer, and Claudio's skin began to recover from the smart of the fire.

After some time, they arrived in an apartment of modest appearance, lighted by four wax tapers at the corners: the figure groaned and vanished.—Invisible hands began alertly to wash Claudio; they combed his hair, poured a pleasing liquor down his throat, rubbed perfumes upon his skin, drew upon him a muslin tunic and vest, and threw a silk robe across his shoulders. This done, a door in the apartment opened, and a beautiful girl, dressed in all the fantastic gaiety of unrestrained pleasure, waved to him with her silver wand to follow her.

He obeyed, and passed into a gallery, on either side of which stood lofty pillars of marble; and around these were entwined garlands of roses, interspersed with lamps of various colours. Transported by the scene, he moved quickly forward; he ascended some steps of granite decorated like the gallery; the softest music began to steal upon his ear, and his guide, turning round her head, smiled upon him as an encouragement for him to proceed. They entered a lofty hall, ornamented with all the emblems of love, wine, and revelry; the strains of music grew louder and sweeter as they advanced; a gate of mother of pearl now presented itself, his guide touched it with her silver wand, and it flew open, and presented to the sight of Claudio, an apartment which seemed to be composed of columns of clouds, interspersed with the rays of a golden sun; and at the extremity of the room lay, on a bed of roses, a female, the most beautiful imagination could conceive; cupids flying round her, fanned her with sprigs of myrtle, and shook perfume on her bed from their wings; her eyes were turned towards Claudio, and she smiled graciously upon him; his guide pointed to him to advance; and he darted forward to the scene of bliss: immediately a crash like thunder rent the air, the lights vanished, the bewitching scene disappeared, and Claudio sunk into a deep vault; the current of air which met him in his descent awoke him, and he started up in his bed.

When perfectly awakened, and convinced that the past was but a dream, Claudio began to compare its events with those of his past adventures, and found that they tallied, with more than the usual similarity of dreams to fact, with his adventures of the few last weeks: the figure which had bid him welcome to the gloomy building, was no other than the friar, conducting him through the subterraneous passages of the ruinous temple; the terrific features of which had been furnished by his recollection of the dungeon, whose walls were covered with human skulls; the palace of enchantment, represented to his sleeping fancy, was the apartment of Viola, and the beautiful female resting on the couch, herself. What alone did not correspond with his adventure, was his being disappointed in clasping in his arms the lady, when he was on the point of approaching her; but this he considered rather as an inconsistency natural to dreams, than as an omen of his future fortune. After a few minutes passed in thought, he turned himself on his pillow, and again sunk into the arms of sleep.

At the accustomed time, Claudio again left the college, and was met, at his usual station, by the Benedictine monk, as the clock of the monastery of Saint James struck twelve. In the same manner as before, Claudio was conducted to the apartment where Viola was waiting for his coming. After a few tender greetings, she led him to the sofa, and Claudio urging his impatience to learn more of the mystery which encompassed her, she spoke thus, "Do you remember, Claudio, where I left off in my narrative? it was at the death of my ever-to-be-regretted, ever-to-be-loved Rinaldo."

Claudio having declared, that her words were still vivid in his imagination, she proceeded by saying, "Need I explain to you the agony which a love-devoted heart feels on the privation of that object on whom its desires are placed?—So excessive was the misery which I experienced, that a few hours brought upon me an entire stupor of faculty; from which I believe nothing but the intelligence of my father's being at the point of death could have roused me. I flew to his chamber, I hung over his dying bed, I endeavoured, by every means in my power, to repair to him the injury which he might, and which I am persuaded he *did* think, my passion for Rinaldo had been productive of to him. In six days he died, and I was left alone in the world, a friendless, unprotected orphan: I had wealth, it is true, but what are riches to a mind which has lost the object on which its soul is fixed?"

"You think that I have now related to you the worst that befel me from these tragical events, alas! I had yet suffered nothing! You are amazed; remember, that every degree of pleasure and pain is rated by comparison, and when I found myself alone in the world, my feelings were happy, compared to those sensations which followed my discovery—that I should speedily become the mother of a partaker in my sorrows."

As Viola spoke these words, she hung down her head upon Claudio's shoulder; then added, "I am sure, you have a heart sufficiently tender to look with compassion upon the weakness of a woman, whose deviation from what the coldness of the world calls virtue, brought upon her a calamity more than adequate to her love for Rinaldo."

Claudio sighed, and answered her by an embrace, which the near contact of their persons authorized: Viola threw her snowy arms round Claudio's neck for support, as she hid her face on his breast; and Claudio's arm was stealing to entwine itself round Viola's waist, when suddenly starting from her position, Viola caught the right hand of Claudio with both hers; fixed her eyes for an instant, in the wildest transport of passion, on the bracelet which encircled his wrist; and uttering a loud shriek, she fell upon the floor, and fainted.

Before Claudio's astonishment was sufficiently abated to suffer him to act towards her restoration, the Benedictine friar and Zelia entered the apartment from opposite doors, eagerly enquiring, what had happened to Viola? Claudio answered their questions, by entreating them to afford her assistance: The friar knelt down upon the floor, and supported her head on his arm; Zelia ran into the adjoining room, and brought from thence a vase of water, with which she sprinkled her face. Presently Viola opened her eyes, but no sooner did she turn them towards Claudio, than she uttered a second shriek, and relapsed into a state of insensibility.

A much longer time was now required to restore her to recollection; and when she again recovered the use of her faculties, she exclaimed in a low, but frantic voice, "Take him away; I command you to take him from my sight."

"How have I offended you? How have I agitated you?" asked Claudio, kneeling by her side. "I conjure you to inform me, if the———" He recollected the injunction under which he lay, and stopped speaking.

"Leave me! I entreat you, leave me," cried Viola, without raising her head from the bosom of Zelia. "I command, that he be taken away immediately."

"Come, Signor," said the friar, rising from the ground, "you must leave this place."

Claudio stood fixed, in mute surprise, over the body of Viola, as it lay reclined on the bosom of Zelia, and did not reply.

The friar grasped him by the arm, and drawing him by it towards the door, said, in a louder tone than he had before spoken, "Signor, you *must* depart."

"I entreat you to let me remain a few moments longer," cried Claudio.

"You know not what you ask," returned the friar, "when you request to stay in opposition to the command of her who bids you go." "What have I to fear?" asked Claudio.

The friar rolled his eye-balls upon Claudio with a terrific sternness, and replied, "The vengeance of the Inquisition, for having disobeyed one who is under its protection."

Claudio's blood turned cold within his veins, and the friar dragged him hastily, without resistance on his part, from the apartments of Viola.

Claudio felt himself constrained to pass without speaking through those dungeons where silence had been before so solemnly enjoined him; but no sooner did he regain the subterraneous passages, than he addressed his guide, by saying, "I beseech you, father, let me hear to-morrow of the health of Viola."

"I cannot make you any promise," returned the monk sullenly.

"Where may I see you?" continued the anxious Claudio. "Will you be near the ruins about noon, or in the evening?"

"I cannot agree to make any appointment," answered the friar, in the same tone in which he had last spoken.

"But you will speak to me, if we should meet by chance?" said Claudio.

"That time will prove;" replied the friar.

Several more questions were advanced by Claudio, but he could gain only the like unsatisfactory and ambiguous answers from the friar. When they were arrived within a few paces of the last archway, the friar said, "I think you have already been warned never to attempt entering these walls?"

"I have made a solemn promise to Viola, that I will not attempt it;" returned Claudio.

"Listen to one admonition which I shall give you," rejoined the friar; "let no temptation urge you to break that promise; your life depends upon your keeping it sacred. I have already told you, that Viola is under the care of that earthly power from which there is no appeal; remember, that these walls share the same protection."

"You mean the Inquisition?" said Claudio.

"I do," answered the friar—"You have as yet nothing to fear from it; but if you were to attempt to enter these walls, or divulge even a hint of what you have seen within them, your life is not of an hour's value."

Claudio was already without the arch, and the friar returned with a quick step into the ruin.

The first idea which had struck Claudio on the emotion of Viola at seeing the bracelet was, that she had discovered in him the fruit of her passion for Rinaldo; and the first action after his return to the college, was to offer thanks to the power which had preserved him from the commission of incest. His mind continued forcibly impressed with this idea, and to know his conjecture either certified, or explained away, was the anxious desire of his heart.

CHAPTER XII.

> Close to the gates, a spacious garden lies,
> From storms defended, and inclement skies;—
> Here the blue fig, with luscious juice o'erflows,
> With deeper red the full pomegranate glows:
> The branch here bends beneath the weighty pear;
> The verdant olives flourish round the year;
> Here order'd vines in equal ranks appear;
> With all th' united labours of the year:
> Some to unload the fertile branches run,
> Some dry the black'ning clusters in the sun.
> The balmy spirit of the Western gale
> Eternal breathes on fruits, untaught to fail.
> POPE'S ODYSSEY.

THE Benedictine friar had not positively said that Claudio should not see him, either at noon or in the evening, near the ruins, and accordingly, with the hope of meeting him, Claudio strolled towards the spot at both these seasons of the day; he wandered about each time for a considerable while, but met not the friar, and returned home disappointed. On his arrival at the college from his evening walk, a note was delivered to him by the porter, which the man informed him was given to him by a little boy: Claudio tore it impatiently open, and read the following words:

"*You will no more be admitted to the society of Viola, nor must you, on any account, address the Benedictine friar who has before introduced you to her, should you meet him by accident in the street, or in any place whatsoever. Observe these injunctions, and maintain a strict silence on all that is past, and you have nothing to apprehend.*"

This was all contained in the note. Claudio's disappointment and curiosity both returned on reading it, but he had no alternative, except submission to its contents, or subjecting himself to live under the dread of a worse evil.

In a short time, Claudio found that suffering his thoughts continually to dwell on that ænigma which he was forbidden to seek the means of solving, injured both his spirits and his health; and in order to shun those questions which arose from a change in his habits and constitution, he resolved to make the attempt of driving away thought, by returning again to the pleasures which had once possessed a charm for his senses.

A firm resolution is the ablest physician of the mind; and against the vocation, which was to be passed by Claudio with his friend at the seat of the Count di Ponta, his mind had regained its wonted tone: once only had he met the Benedictine friar in the streets of Rome, and the monk had then passed him with a quick step, and without turning upon him his eyes.

A pleasant journey brought them to the borders of the estate of the Count di Ponta, and here nature began to open to the view of Claudio, a splendor that outrivalled even the beauty of the famed banks of the Arno:—they entered a valley which seemed formed for a retreat from the heat of the sun by the hand of nature herself, in one of her happiest dispositions; the easy hills, which formed its sloping sides, were clothed with a turf, whose softness emulated the downy velvet, and whose bright hue vied with the rich emerald; their circling tops were crowned with thick ranges of the chesnut, the wild strawberry tree, and the pine, whose interwoven branches admitted only a twilight gloom upon the mossy path beneath them. From this valley, a winding road, shadowed by knots of the broad leaved myrtle, the almond tree, the acacia, and the fig, around the stems of which entwined themselves the sweet-scented jessamine and ever-blowing rose, brought them to an eminence from whence the passage wound into the bosom of a scene, fertile in every tree and plant which could delight the eye with its blossoms and verdure, or promise a rich harvest of its grateful produce. On the left, was seen a natural cascade, tumbling in murmurs down the rocky cliff into a lake below; across a branch of the lake, hung a rude bridge, whose foot, at the distance where Claudio was standing, was lost in the foaming surges of the agitated water; the cliffs above the cascade were thickly crowned with the majestic cypress; and the luxuriant thickets which ran along its sides, sparkled under the spray with which the water sprinkled them in its current. On the right, lay lofty masses of cliff, formed of the most beautiful marbles, whose rich veins vied in the brightness of their colours with the flowers and mosses which sprung up in tufts amongst their variegated masses; on their tops, grew the erect and lofty cedar, and the rudeness of its long trunks was hid by the flowering almond and the strawberry, beautiful in blossom and fruit. Beyond the pallazo, the long-extended prospect was checquered with verdure, and the distant spires of Placenza, glowing beneath the warm tints of the departing sun, whose retiring rays cast a semicircle of purple light upon the misty clouds, which closed the view.

As they approached nearer to the pallazo, Claudio was struck, not less by its size than grandeur: the building itself was sexangular, placed in the center of a circular colonade, which reached to the second story; the piazza beneath formed a cool retreat, both from the sultriness of the apartments, and the heat of the open air; and its pillars and floor of white marble, delicately veined with streaks of the topaz, conveyed the same coolness to the eye which its structure gave to the sense. The center of the building rose into a well proportioned dome, which finished in a bold statue of a defensive gladiator.

As they continued to advance towards the mansion, statues of warriors, heathen gods, saints, crosses, and emblematical devices, distributed amongst the knots of shrubs that fertilized the gay *parterre*, attracted Claudio's attention; grottos also, and temples inscribed to various protectors and deities, peeped from amongst the branching verdure; at last, a winding and broad sweep of grass, encircled on either side by festoons of chains, which seemed intended only to connect a group of dancing fawns and satyrs, in whose hands they were held, led to the principal entrance of the pallazo.

On entering the house, they were informed that the Count was out on a ride, but that he was shortly expected to return; and Claudio admiring the beauty of the hall in which they now stood, Lodovico said, "he would take the opportunity of his father's absence to make him acquainted with the different turnings and windings of the pallazo, that when he once knew them, he might find himself the more at home amongst them."

Claudio readily accepted his friend's offer, and they passed through a variety of apartments on the ground floor, of which every one appeared the most elegant, till the next in succession was seen: the windows of them all descended from the ceiling down to the floor, and the center one opened into the colonade on the outside, which was only an easy step below them; the banquet hall, as it was called, was beneath the dome, which Claudio had observed on his approach to the palazo; the dome itself was divided alternately into spiral windows and painted niches, in each of which was represented the figure of a heathen god in bas relief; a broad and striking cornice of fretwork, in purple and gold, succeeded these, and the perpendicular walls below the dome, which were divided into the eight compartments of an octagon, were supported by as many pillars of Parian marble, capped with purple and gold trophies, in various devices, to correspond in effect with the dome itself, and surmounted by statues cut from the same snow white marble: between the pillars, were painted by the ablest artists, in figures of the size of nature, eight of the most striking scenes drawn from the poems of the inimitable Tasso. The sofas were gold and purple, to accord with the decorations of the ceiling, and the tables were of the most richly-veined marble, supported in frames of silver gilt.

Opposite to the door by which they had entered the banquet hall, was a corresponding entrance, which Lodovico threw open, and preceded Claudio into an apartment whose form was a semicircle, four large windows were placed at equal distances in the curve; they opened into the colonade, and on the outside of each was an arbour level with the floor of the apartment, and entwined with all the sweets which the flower garden of art and nature can produce. Claudio's eyes fixed first upon these perfume-exhaling bowers, but they quickly wandered to the decorations within the apartment, which exceeded all the ideas of elegance, imagination could devise: the hangings, the curtains, and the sofas, were of white silk, richly and fancifully embroidered with the rarest of flowers, shrubs, and insects; the ceiling and the pannels between the windows were composed of a silver ground, on which was described the rose of maiden blush, expressed by a pencil which defied the rivalship of nature, and decorated with its leaves and buds, formed of a glossy substance, which had stolen the glow and transparency of the emerald. The curtains hung flowing from the ceiling, and were drawn back on each side by female figures of the whitest marble, which were placed in the interstices between the windows. On each side of the door, a silver Cupid, holding out a flaming torch, supported, in the center of its rays, a glass lustre for several lights, and immediately opposite to the entrance was a mirror, of a sufficient size to repeat in its reflection all the splendor and extent of the banquet-hall.

"You have doubtless," said Lodovico, "heard report mention the unhappy fate of Count Angelo di Ponta and his wife, who were my father's predecessors in the possession of this pallazo, and the surrounding estates?"

"The story which is current in the world of the Countess having died by the hand of her husband, and his having afterwards put an end to his own existence, has undoubtedly reached my ear," replied Claudio—"Does report speak with truth of their fate?"

"In this instance," returned Lodovico, "common fame contradicts her usual system, and speaks no more than fact. What I was going to tell you, when I asked you whether you had ever heard of them, was, that the embroidery which so much pleases you in this room, is the work of that countess' own hand; so admire it as much as you please now, or at any time when you are here alone, but don't mention it when my father is by; because it gives him pain to hear any thing said which revives in his memory the late Count."

Claudio recollected, that the Marchese di Bartelma had told him, that suspicion had whispered the Count Montano to have been the gallant whose attention to his wife had raised the jealousy of Count Angelo to the desperation to which it had arisen; he accordingly considered, that Lodovico was the last person to whom the subject ought to be continued, and immediately suffered it to drop.

They now proceeded to the second range of apartments: the bed-chambers equalled in elegance the rooms of entertainment; and after some slight observations on the statues which ornamented the grand staircase, and surrounded the hall of entrance; they entered an apartment where refreshments were prepared for them, and where the Count di Ponta soon joined them.

The reception which the Count gave to Claudio was both flattering and cordial; the report of the college had informed him, that Claudio possessed a mind of principle, firmness, and erudition; and he conceived such a friend as a most valuable acquisition to the happiness of his son; well aware, that the effervescence of his passions required the restraint of advice, and convinced that it would be much more readily attended to by him from one of his own years and pursuits, than from the tongue of age and gravity.

On the following morning while at breakfast, the Count addressed his son, by saying, "Lodovico, you must this week contrive to amuse your friend, as well as you are able, with walks about the grounds, which are new to him: rides to Placenza, and occasional recourses to the library. Next week, I invite you both to accompany me on a journey to Mantua; I am going to fetch home my daughter, Valeria, from the convent of the Holy Virgin, where she has for some years past been receiving her education: she was to have returned to me before this time, but the Abbess required permission of me to suffer her to remain in the convent till after the festival of the Virgin, which takes place next week, that she might have the honor of assisting at its solemnities; and this devout and noble sight, we shall now have the pleasure of witnessing."

The young men both expressed their satisfaction at this projected expedition, and the Count went on speaking, "After our return from Mantua, we shall have more additions to our family than Valeria."

"Who will those be?" asked Lodovico.

"What think you," said the Count, "of a visit from Signor Roderigo di Viratti, and his daughter, Clementina?"

"Oh, I shall delight in their company," cried Lodovico—"Claudio, prepare your muscles to laugh all day long, for you'll have food for merriment, I promise you."

"Signor Roderigo," continued the Count, addressing Claudio, "is a distant relation of my late wife's, who continues, about once a year, to pay me a visit for a few days; a good-natured old gentleman, but there are certainly some whimsical points about his character and manners, which make his good nature very often appear the result of folly."

"But this is not the season of the year at which they usually visit you;" said Lodovico.

"No," replied the Count, "but they have sent me word that they are to be at Mantua next week, and will return home with me on the day following the festival of the Virgin: those young women who are designed by their parents for a monastic life, and have passed their probationary years in the convent of the holy virgin, are to take the veil; and Signora Clementina's eldest daughter, being one of the number who are on that day to pronounce their vows of retirement from the world, she and her father, Signor Roderigo, are to be present at the ceremony."

"I always thought," said Lodovico, "that her own vanity would make her shut up her pretty daughter in a convent. Claudio, I must give you a sketch of the history of these oddities, that you may be prepared for your introduction to them. Signor Roderigo is at least sixty-five, and has his full share of the infirmities which belong to that venerable age: early in life, he married a woman of nearly twice his own age, who brought him only one child, the Clementina of whom we have just been speaking: like all only children, she heard of nothing but her own perfections, and experienced no other treatment but the most foolish indulgence; her father was known to be rich, so she easily procured a husband, but, alas! poor man, his only consolation in the marriage state was, that his father-in-law was equally miserable with himself; but this difference attended their misery—Clementina's dissatisfied temper and ill usage soon killed her husband, and Signor Roderigo's less tender feelings gave him the happiness of following his passionate old dame to her last abode. Once relieved from his termagant wife, Signor Roderigo thought himself happy, and attributing all the infelicity which had attended his marriage state to his first wife having been many years older than himself, he resolved to marry a second who should be as much younger. After an infinite number of fruitless attempts to obtain for himself the handmate he wished for; a mercenary old woman, who had the care of an orphan niece, promised him the girl's hand in marriage; but on the morning of the intended wedding-day, when Roderigo went to claim his destined bride, he found that she had fled the night before from her aunt's house. This is now almost three years ago; the girl has not been heard of, and the old fellow has ever since been travelling into every city, town, and village in Italy, in the hope of recovering his runaway."

Claudio smiled, and the Count said, "Strange as this account of the old gentleman's motive for travelling appears, it is not exaggerated, I assure you; you will not have known him many hours, before he will himself give you the history of his unfortunate case."

"Beyond a doubt, he will," added Lodovico, "he asks every body he meets, if they have not seen his dear, bewitching little Livia."

"And if," said Claudio, "he should unfortunately meet at last with a man who replies, 'I am her husband, Signor.'"

"I can't promise you," returned Lodovico, "that he would have the complaisance to wish his rival joy; but at the same time, nothing more terrible need be apprehended from such a meeting, if it ever should take place."

A laugh followed, and Claudio then said, "Pray proceed to describe Signora Clementina,"——"Her age," returned Lodovico, "is forty-five; her person what most women's are at those years; she has three daughters, the eldest of whom is about nineteen, and being prettier than her mother, is destined to be a nun, and the other two, who are some years younger than their sister, make up the travelling party with their mother and grandfather."

"Oh! then, Signora Clementina accompanies her father in his wanderings;" said Claudio.

"Yes, yes," replied Lodovico, "he travels to find a wife, and she travels to look for a husband; for ever since the death of her *caro sposo*, she has taken as much pains to replace him, as her father has done to get him a new wife, and with less success; for I am positive, she has never had an offer of changing her situation, though her vanity is so great, that she actually believes every man she sees is in love with her, and that she is guilty of hourly cruelties in frowning upon those young men who sigh and smile at her, and though she is affectation itself personified and caricatured, she is constantly exclaiming, 'I hope I am not thought affected; I would not appear affected for the world; I wish to harmonize with all my fellow creatures, but I am unfortunate in seldom meeting with a soul congenial to my own: I know you think me affected.' And then she grins like a monkey, to shew her teeth, which were once white and a complete set; and languishes to describe the wire-drawn feelings that inspire her heart of sensibility."

Lodovico paused, and Claudio cried, "Go on, go on, for Heaven's sake, let me hear all her delicate sensibilities."

"No, positively, not another word," replied Lodovico, "I have said just enough to set your expectation on tiptoe, and now I am determined not to curtail the pleasure of your introduction by making you too familiar with the portrait of your new acquaintance—Yes, I will tell you one thing more, and then I am dumb; you shall hear her daughters' names, and if they don't describe the mother to you more fully than any likeness I could paint, why I pity your want of imagination."

"Nothing less than the names of Goddesses, I guess;" said Claudio.

"Oh, no, no!" exclaimed the Count, "any body may have such common names as those; Signora Clementina invented these herself; repeat them, Lodovico, for I am sure it puzzles me to recollect them."

"Beginning with the eldest," cried Lodovico, "these incomparable young ladies are named, Delicatilla, Sensibilla, and Langualilla."

Another laugh followed the recital of these expressive names, and Lodovico adhering to his resolution of not enlarging upon the sketches he had given, the subject was dropped.

CHAPTER XIII.

———————————'Tis dreadful!
How reverend is the face of this tall pile,
Whose ancient pillars rear their marble heads,
To bear aloft its arch'd, and pond'rous roof!
By its own weight made stedfast and immoveable.
Looking tranquillity, it strikes an awe
And terror to my aching sight! the tombs
And monumental caves of death look cold,
And shoot a chillness to my trembling heart.

CONGREVE.

THE time passed on pleasantly, though unmarked by any particular occurrence, till the party set out from the pallazo on their journey to Mantua; at which city, they arrived in the afternoon, previous to the festival, from witnessing the solemnity of which they expected much satisfaction.

The Count di Ponta and his son were impatient to see Valeria, and accordingly, after having taken refreshment, they proceeded to the convent of the holy Virgin. The grandeur, solemnity, and awful majesty of the structure, were remarked even by Claudio and Lodovico, who had been living in the midst of religious buildings at Rome. A loud knock at the outer gate of the convent, brought to them the porter, by whom they were admitted through a dark portal into the chief court of the convent, whose leading feature was gloom. They walked on, for a considerable time, between a double row of the sorrowing cypress, whose nodding tops seemed to mourn for those who were destined by fate to sigh out a life of melancholy within the walls they enclosed: at intervals, the tall spires of the church, and the roofs of the cloisters, all ending in a crucifix, or an image of the Virgin, peeped through the gloomy branches; and amidst the boles of the trees, were scattered the figures of saints, and small chapels, whose altars were scarcely rendered visible by the gleam of twilight which shone upon them through a single window of dimly stained glass. Presently the path widened, and the trees falling off gradually to the right and to the left, opened to a full view of the cloisters, above the center of which, rose the grand East window over the great altar of the church, and towering over these, appeared the lengthening spire.

The porter having consigned them to the care of a friar at the center door of the left wing of the cloisters, retired; and the friar having learnt that they wished to see the Lady Abbess, conducted them through a variety of passages, each terminating in a large figure of the Virgin, to which they were desired to make obeisance, and at last brought them to a handsome apartment, where he left them.

"This is a novel sight to you, young men," said the Count, "who have never before been within the walls of a convent; how do you like the appearance?"

"I trust," replied Claudio, "I am not deficient in respect to the opinions of our religion, but I fear mine would never be sufficiently warm to shut me up in a cloister for life. Here is nothing to invite the soul to love retirement; an universal gloom meets the eye, and communicates through it a chill to the heart."

"Poor dear little creatures," cried Lodovico, "only think of three or four hundred of them being shut up here, one in a cell, like a solitary turtle in a cage, without a single mate within hearing of their plaintive cooings."

"And yet, I doubt not," returned the Count, "but that many more amongst them are happy than you give credit to for being so. I would never force a daughter of mine to accept a monastic life, but I should think if such a choice were her own, that it was a happy one. How many temptations are there to evil in the world which are here avoided." He sighed, and paused.

"That is but a negative goodness," replied Claudio, "which is immaculate because it has never had the opportunity of sinning."

"But it is a positive happiness never to have done wrong," returned the Count, "whatever the means which have restrained us from evil."

The words and habits of the Count di Ponta had appeared to Claudio a contradiction, ever since he had had the opportunity of observing them. He was a man who lived in splendor, and to whom the expences of a large and sumptuous establishment, seemed a cause of pride and pleasure rather than dislike; yet he was often extolling the comforts of a contented sufficiency, and repining over the cares of grandeur: he talked constantly without reserve of the faults of his younger days, and even the errors of his manhood, without apparent remorse; and yet, the next hour, he would launch out into the blessings of possessing a mind which had never known the reproach of a single error.

Claudio had yet seen too little of him to form any determinate judgement of his heart; but he concluded him to be a man who had been the slave of his evil passions, and who was still unhappy under their temptations; restrained from their present free indulgence only by the fear of a future punishment, and at times tortured by reflections on the past: one hour he would be lively, and the first to promote the laugh and joke; at another, he would sink into silence, yet without appearing to be buried in reflection. His passions were quick, but his temper was naturally good: his devotion appeared the effect of superstition rather than a conviction of the right. Without being a man of learning, he was a pleasant companion; and without apparently studying to please, his society generally gave pleasure. His age was about fifty, but he looked a younger man than he really was; his person was good, and his manners were those of one who had lived with the best society.

The Lady Abbess now coming into the room, put a stop to the conversation. The Count di Ponta was already well known to her, and his son and Claudio having received their introduction, she informed them that Valeria was well, and would attend them in a few minutes. "I am glad," said she, addressing the Count, "that you have made choice of this season to visit Mantua; the festival of our holy mother," and she crossed herself as she spoke, "should be attended by every true Christian, as an act of devotion most acceptable to the highest God: the pomp and splendor which attend it will besides afford you one of the noblest exhibitions of grandeur which man can pay to those blessed beings to whom he owes his Redeemer from sin and death."

The Count requested, that his son and Claudio might be shown the church of the convent. "You shall see it now, my sons," said the Lady Abbess, "but you must attend it also to-morrow morning, at the performance of mass, previously to the commencement of the holy procession: all its riches and beauty are not now exposed to view; on the morrow, the blessed Virgin permits them to the gaze of the public eye."

She rang her bell, and a veiled nun attending, she was commanded by the Lady Abbess to conduct Lodovico and Claudio to a friar, who should show to them the church. They followed the nun, and passing through the refectory, a large marble hall led to the door of the church, where the friar, of whom the Lady Abbess had spoken, met them.

The massy grandeur of the nave, built of grey stone, and supported by pillars of immense bulk, at the foot of each of which was a small altar; the figures of the Apostles, and various Saints of marble, in niches along the side of the wall, and the windows of painted glass, describing in succession the events of the New Testament, first struck their attention. They proceeded to the choir, and having admired the silver rail which surrounded the altar, they passed some minutes in viewing the painting which ornamented the back of the altar, and which represented the salutation of the angel Gabriel to the Virgin: and in the compartments on each side of the altar, were two very large paintings, the one of the birth, the other of the crucifixion of Jesus Christ: the altar itself was of white marble, golden censors hung on each side of it, and upon the base, a silver eagle supported the sacred volume from which the priest of the convent read the divine word.

"You think nothing of our church today," said the friar who attended them, "for you see it only as it is kept in common, for the use of the nuns; to-morrow, if you visit it, your opinion will be much changed; it will scarcely appear to you the same place."

"I think then," replied Lodovico, "we had better defer our farther investigation till we attend mass here in the morning. Come, Claudio, I dare say my sister is by this time in the Abbess' apartment."

The friar seemed very well pleased at their readiness to depart; for, he said, "the nuns were only waiting their absence to begin the decorations for the next day;" and they returned to the room where they had left the Count and the Lady Abbess, with whom they now found Valeria. Lodovico met her with the pleasure and affection of a brother who had been four years absent from an only sister; and when the tear of joy which Valeria dropped at again clasping him in her arms was wiped away, he introduced her to his friend Claudio. Valeria still wore the white flowing and simple drapery of the boarders, which she was in a couple of days to throw off for ever; and Claudio thought it so admirably adapted to the interesting softness of her person, that he doubted whether some part of her charms would not suffer from discarding her present dress. She was about the middle stature, and her every limb appeared so well proportioned to the whole, that it was difficult to decide which feature of her entire person gave the greatest grace to her face and frame: she was delicately fair, and her soft blue eyes, and the mantling blush which painted her cheeks, accorded in unison with her pale auburne hair; her teeth were exquisitely white, and her melodious voice, breathing softness, declared there was no single perfection of which she was destitute.

After a short conversation, Valeria said, "You must excuse me, my dear father, if I shorten your visit to-day; my sisters are all employed in preparations for the splendor of to-morrow, and I must not be idle while they are at work; in a very short time, I shall be wholly yours and my brother's." The Count readily accepted his daughter's excuse for hastening their visit, and they very shortly after having received her good-humoured hint, left the convent.

On the following morning, they returned to the convent of the Holy Virgin, at the hour the Lady Abbess had acquainted them the grand mass would be performed, and were conducted, by her order, into a private gallery in the choir which commanded a full view, both of the altar and of the nave of the church: and Claudio and Lodovico found it indeed an altered place, as the friar had informed them would be the case. The statues of the saints and apostles, in the niches on each side of the nave, now wore rich robes of satin and scarlet cloth, studded with various gems, and edged with broad laces of silver and gold; and in one of the hands of each was placed a thick taper of wax lighted; above each of the small altars, at the foot of the pillars, was now fixed a figure of the Virgin of silver gilt; the altars were each lighted by four wax tapers, in silver candlesticks, and their sides and bases were hung with garlands of artificial flowers.—The floor, from the great gates of the church to the steps which led into the choir, was thickly strewed with the leaves of the cedar, acacia, fig, and mulberry; and from the entrance into the choir to the rail of the great altar, the marble pavement was scarcely visible through the sprigs of myrtle, roses, jessamine, heliotrope, convolvulus, and a variety of other natural flowers, which gave animation to the scene, and exhaled a perfume most grateful to the senses.

On each side of the great altar, ranged upon the steps which led to the ascent on which it stood, were placed massy silver branches, filled with wax tapers; above the base of the altar, erected on a silver bracket, supported by angels, was a silver figure of the Virgin Mary, of the size of life—a coronet of the most valuable stones was placed upon her head, a robe of cloth of gold was thrown across her shoulders, and swaddled in folds of white satin, studded with diamonds and rubies, lay on her knee a small golden image of the child Jesus. Silver candlesticks, in which burnt wax tapers, were continued on brackets against the wall to a considerable height above the head of the figure of the Virgin, and rich festoons of artificial flowers, made by the nuns of the convent, and representing nature with the most skilful art, were twined around the candlesticks, and carried from one to the other in a variety of fantastic turns and shapes.

But what most rivetted the attention of the spectators, were those compartments in the wall between the great altar and the angle of the choir, where had been seen on the prior evening, the paintings representing the birth and crucifixion of the Son of God: the paintings were now gone, and in their places appeared spaces of several feet in depth; at the back of one of which was represented, by figures as large as life, in coloured sculpture, the pangs of purgatory, and at the back of the other, the joys of Heaven. The former were expressed by figures whose countenances were depicted full of horror and agony, and whose hands were upraised in prayer, kneeling in the midst of flames, and surrounded by demons, who were extending towards the unhappy sufferers their tridents, in an attitude of triumph, and with a malicious grin painted on their countenances. In the other, was seen mount Calvary, with Christ upon the cross, the thieves crucified on either side, and the three Marys kneeling at the foot of the cross; and above these were the same figures represented sitting in the clouds, surrounded by rays of glory, and with the Holy Ghost resting above them.

Little time was given to Claudio and Lodovico for observing those things in the church which excited their attention, before the melody of the full-toned organ, accompanied by the voices of the concealed nuns, bursting on their ears, informed them that the bishop was approaching; they turned their eyes towards the great gate of the church, and saw a procession of priests advancing in the following order: first, twelve youths bearing censers, and distributing around the most grateful perfume, by throwing thyme in the air as they passed along; next six priests, in their rich vestments of white muslin, embroidered with figures of the cross on their breasts and shoulders, in green and gold; then followed a band of instruments, dressed in robes corresponding with those of the priests; next, under a canopy, supported by twelve other priests, in dresses like the former, the bishop, habited in his festal robes of white satin, richly worked in tissue of green and gold; on his head, he wore his golden mitre, studded with precious stones, and in his hand he carried his golden crosier, enriched with a diamond head; and then followed the like number of priests and censer-bearers as had preceded him.

Arrived at the altar, the bishop gave his benediction to the priests, and they distributed it to the assembled congregation; the bishop next dipped his hands in a vase of holy water, and having kissed a small crucifix which stood upon the altar, and knelt in silent homage to the image of the Virgin, the ceremony of mass began. At the conclusion of it, the Count di Ponta and his companions repaired to the house of a friend, from a balcony of whose mansion they were to observe the procession pass. In about half an hour after their arrival, the procession appeared in the following order.

First, an extremely fine band of music, in rich dresses of green and gold; next, several of the different orders of friars in Mantua, walking two and two, each order headed by its superior, and its banner borne before it on a silver staff;—then followed the different companies of artizans, with the emblems of their trade, consisting of various devices, and their arms cut in silver, carried in the midst of them, and followed by a troop of men and boys, bearing lighted tapers;—next came the kings of the different companies of archers, musketeers, and gladiators, who had that year gained the prizes of skill given by their companies, habited in grand Roman dresses of various coloured silks, and wearing a wreath of laurel on their heads, and a golden collar round their necks;—then followed the priests of the different parish churches, each carrying in his hand his venerabilis, and lighted, some by two, others by four little boys, in white surplices, with wax tapers, in silver candlesticks;—after them, on a platform carried by eight priests, and under a canopy of green silk, fringed with gold, and headed by a golden crucifix, borne by an equal number of priests, came the figure of the Virgin Mary, which, during the performance of mass, had been placed upon the grand altar;—on each side of the canopy walked eight ecclesiastics, carrying flambeaux, and a double number of youths, some with wax tapers, others flinging perfume into the air from their golden censers;—immediately after these, walked a number of young girls, representing angels, wings of pale blue silk issued from their shoulders, their heads and waists were bound with garlands of flowers, and they had each a silver wand in their right hand;—then came the magnificos of the city, richly dressed, and each carrying a lighted thick wax candle;—and after these, a troop of boys, equal in number to the girls who had preceded them, also carrying white wands, on the top of which were fixed small effigies of the Virgin Mary;—next after these, under a smaller canopy than that borne over the Virgin, came the Host, likewise attended by priests and censer bearers, and followed by the archbishop; these were succeeded by many more friars, headed by their banners; and the procession closed with a band of music, similar to that which had preceded it.

The streets were crowded with spectators, who fell on their knees to the image of the Virgin as it passed by them; and Claudio and Lodovico had just risen from their homage, when Lodovico catching hold of Claudio's arm with one hand, and pointing into the street with the other, cried, "By heavens! there's the very Benedictine friar that I used to think a spy upon our actions at Rome, staring at us as hard as ever."—Claudio directly turned his eyes the way which his friend had guided them, and no sooner had he caught a glimpse of the friar, sufficient to convince him it was the same he had known at Rome, than he disappeared in the croud.

"What can have brought that old fellow to Mantua?" said Lodovico, "Perhaps the same business, or rather pleasure, which brings us here;" answered Claudio.

"Hardly, I should think," replied Lodovico, "he must have sights enough of this kind at Rome, without traveling for them:—however, we are not at College now; the old boy can have no authority over our actions here."

And with this satisfactory conclusion, Lodovico dismissed the subject from his thoughts: from the mind of Claudio, it did not so immediately retire.

CHAPTER XIV.

> Where that old woman day and night did pray,
>   Upon her beads devoutly penitent,
> Nine hundred pater-nosters every day,
>   And thrice nine hundred aves, she was wont to say;
> And to augment her painful penance more,
>   Thrice every week in ashes did she sit,
> And next her wrinkled skin rough sackcloth wore,
>   And thrice three times did fast from any bit.
>
> SPENCER.

AFTER the procession was ended, the image of the Virgin was restored to its place upon the altar, to be visited in the afternoon by the penitents who had vowed to it a pilgrimage, and who had arrived in Mantua in a large body the preceding day.—There was something inviting to Claudio in the name of pilgrim, although it was folly to imagine, that he should see the one who had so particularly noticed him, on his fifteenth birth-day, at the villa of the Marchese di Bartelma, as it was to be supposed he had long since quitted the habit of penitence, having been on his return from a pilgrimage when he stopped at the villa di Bartelma; however, whatever might be the feeling which actuated him to the wish, Claudio felt a desire to see the pilgrims enter the church on their homage to the Virgin, and prevailed on Lodovico to accompany him to witness it.

They now entered the church by the great gates from one of the principal streets of the city, and not through the garden, as on the preceding evening: they found the gates open, and a banner in white and gold fixed before each of them: upon that on the right hand was written, "Whoever remains at prayers in this church throughout the whole of the following night, shall receive absolution for whatever crimes he may commit in the course of the next forty days."—And upon that on the left, "Whoever says five Ave Marias and five Pater-nosters at every altar in this church, delivers a soul from purgatory."

Lodovico was beginning a remark upon the latitude of the first of these holy declarations, when the soft music of several lutes, joining in the same hymn, and voices chanting to the strain, cut short his observation by announcing the approach of the pilgrims. A vast concourse of people preceded them into the church, and they entered to the number of about three hundred, following their minstrels. Claudio and Lodovico had taken their situation near the steps which led to the choir, and as the troop of pilgrims approached, Claudio beheld amongst them the very minstrel who had accompanied the pilgrims that had shared the hospitality of the Marchese di Bartelma: after recognizing him, Claudio looked with anxiety, and something like expectation, for the pilgrim whose countenance and manner were so strongly impressed on his recollection. The pilgrims passed slowly by, but he whom Claudio wished to see was not amongst them.

Claudio now wished for an opportunity of speaking to the minstrel, though he hardly knew what he wanted to say to him; but that opportunity was not then to be obtained, for no one was allowed to follow the pilgrims into the choir of the church.

"There is a minstrel with these pilgrims," said Claudio to his friend, "who was once entertained at the villa di Bartelma with a band of pilgrims whom he was attending: I should like to speak to him, and learn if he recollects me."

"Let us stroll towards the square then," said Lodovico, "where the pilgrims met to come in procession to their devotion to the Virgin, and where they will probably separate when they go to their respective inns: come, it makes no difference where we walk."

Claudio and Lodovico accordingly proceeded to the square; and in little more than half an hour, the pilgrims entered it, and separated into detached parties, as Lodovico had predicted they would.

The minstrel, and those whom he attended, passed very near to where Claudio and his friend were standing; and Claudio, having motioned to him with his hand to stop, went up to him, and said, "You recollect me, do you not?"

"I have some remembrance of your face," replied the minstrel, "but I don't know where I have seen it before, or what your name is."

"You saw me," returned Claudio, "on my birth-day, at the villa di Bartelma: you stopped there with five pilgrims, to ask refreshment of my father, the Marchese."

"I rejoice to see you well, Signor," replied the minstrel, "I recollect you now; but you have added to your growth within these four years."

"Are any of the pilgrims with you now whom you were then attending?" asked Claudio.

"Oh, holy Saint Peter be praised! not so soon again after their last penance," returned the minstrel.

"Have you seen any of them since?" rejoined Claudio.

"No," answered the minstrel, "they all came from beyond Belluno, and I seldom travel that way."

"Don't you remember one amongst them," said Claudio, "a tall man, with dark and impressive eyes, who sat next me at the table?"

"I remember him well, Signor," answered the minstrel.

"What was his name?" asked Claudio.

"We called him brother Iachimo," returned the minstrel.

"Whence came he?" asked Claudio.

"He joined the other pilgrims at Belluno," was the reply.

"And did he return thither with them?" was the subsequent question.

"No, he parted from us about nine leagues on this side of Florence."

"Is that all you know of him?" said Claudio.

"All," replied the minstrel, "but that he was a good-tempered and a good-hearted man."

Claudio put a ducat into the minstrel's hand, and wishing him a good journey when he should leave Mantua, walked away.

"You seem to be strangely curious about this pilgrim," said Lodovico.

"My vanity was flattered by his notice when I was a boy," returned Claudio, smiling.

"And so you are enquiring where you may get a little more of the palatable dish now you are a man," cried Lodovico.

Claudio made an equivocal reply, and suffered his friend to enjoy his mirth, as the easiest method of dismissing the subject.

On the following morning, the Count said, "Come, we must go and resume our old places in the gallery of the choir, that we may see to advantage the ceremony of taking the veil."

"No," cried Lodovico, "I go to church on no such errand; prudence forbids me to excuse myself from being of the party, for I should certainly commit a sacrilegious outrage, and snatch the dear little angels from devoting themselves to eternal seclusion."

"You have nothing to fear from their eyes," said the Count, "for they are veiled."

"Oh," returned Lodovico, "but I should see the impression of their fluttering little bosoms, panting under their sable robes, and I could not stand quietly by, I assure you."

Lodovico continued firm in not going to witness what he called, "the living death of the pretty girls;" but said, he would reserve himself for the Lady Abbess' concert in the evening; Claudio and he accordingly set out upon a walk about the city, and the Count went alone to the church of the Holy Virgin, out of compliment to the Abbess, who had ordered a seat to be reserved for him.

When they met at dinner, the Count informed them, that he had that morning seen the Signor Roderigo di Viratti, and his daughter, the Signora Clementina, in the church.

"Oh," cried Lodovico, "what a hard-hearted old monster, to go and see her pretty little chicken cooped up for life in a nunnery, so well convinced as she is herself of the pleasures of liberty. Oh, that I had but the power of turning into nuns a few of those old widows that have grown-up daughters, and yet want the fluttering moths to singe their wings at their candles."

"I saw them scarcely for a minute," the Count went on, "as I was leaving the church. They told me they were at the house of a friend in this city, and should leave it to-morrow for my pallazo; so, I suppose, they will arrive there much about the same time we shall reach home."

"Let them come," exclaimed Lodovico, in exultation, "I'll read her a lecture about shutting up her daughter, because she is prettier than herself.—But we shall see them at the concert this evening;" added he, after a pause.

"No, they will not be there," replied the Count, "I enquired of Signora Clementina, if we should meet her at the Lady Abbess' fête, and she answered me with one of her pathetic looks, "that it would be too much for her tender feelings to enter the convent of the Holy Virgin again in some time."

Claudio and Lodovico joined the Count in a laugh against the tender feelings of Signora Clementina; and the entrance of a friend of the Count's, who was to dine with them, put a period to the subject they were discussing.

At the appointed hour in the evening, they went to the concert, and were conducted into the marble hall through which Lodovico and Claudio had passed to the church on the evening of their arrival in Mantua.—In a lofty gallery at one end of the hall, before which was drawn a deep curtain of grey silk, were stationed the nuns who were to be the performers in the concert. Below this gallery, but extended much farther into the hall, was a screen of silver net-work, behind which the Lady Abbess, the noviciates, and the boarders of the convent, had their seats.—The other parts of the hall were elegantly decorated with festoons of flowers, and lighted with thick wax-candles in magnificent branches.—Next to the screen, were seats for the nobility of Mantua, and those strangers who had received invitations from the Lady Abbess, and behind these were benches occupied by some of the pilgrims, and the superiors of the monasteries of the city:—The screen of silver net-work had a door into the hall, by which the Abbess only entered it, and through which the archbishop and the confessor of the convent alone were allowed to pass, and hold with her a short conversation of ceremony.

The united voices of the nuns, formed a harmony that enchanted the senses of the listeners, and made them regret the signal given by the Lady Abbess, to express that the concert was concluded.

Light refreshments, of which the company stood to partake, were then brought into the hall; Claudio and Lodovico were meanwhile walking about amongst the benches, and Claudio's eyes fell upon the face of the Benedictine friar, almost hid beneath the hood of a pilgrim, with which his dress now corresponded. The friar's eye met his, and he immediately turned his head towards another pilgrim who stood close to him, and to whom Claudio conjectured that he whispered. The other pilgrim directly raised his head in the direction where Claudio was standing, but his hood entirely concealed his face,—Claudio's curiosity was raised, he wished to see the countenance of the pilgrim to whom it had appeared to him that the friar had pointed him out. The croud of company rendered it difficult to approach nearer to them, without evidently pointing out to Lodovico that something, or somebody, in that part of the hall, had attracted Claudio's attention;—this he wished to avoid, and while deliberating what steps to take, the friar and pilgrim both had left the spot where he had just before seen them.

He cast his eyes around, as far as the intervening heads would allow him to throw them, but he saw not those whom he sought, and imagined that they had left the hall. Claudio sunk into thought and Lodovico began to rally him on having fallen in love with a nun: Claudio endeavoured to regain his spirits, and talked as much as his friend required, although his tongue and reflection were not directed to the same subject.

In a short time, they left the convent: it was late in the evening, and the cloisters were lighted with tapers. As they proceeded amongst many others who were issuing out by the same way, Claudio happening to turn his head on one side, saw a face beneath the hood of a pilgrim, on which the light of an opposite taper falling, brought to his recollection a countenance with which his sight was familiar, but he could not immediately remember where he had seen it before. Another pilgrim stood close by the one he had just remarked, and though the light did not fall favorably for Claudio to behold his face, yet he was convinced, from only observing his figure, that it was the Benedictine friar.

He had scarcely proceeded an hundred paces, before a sudden start of recollection explained to him, that the countenance on which the light of the taper had fallen was that of the lovely Zelia, whom he had seen in the apartment of the mysterious Viola; and that the change of her dress had for a few moments perplexed him in his endeavours to recollect who she was.

He immediately turned back his head to look for her, but she and the friar were both gone; and a number of the magnificos, who were leaving the concert-room, were moving along under the very taper where he had seen them standing. The Count at this moment called to his son to keep up to him, and Claudio having no ready excuse for drawing his arm away from that of Lodovico, was in a few minutes hurried by him into the street.

The conversation at supper prevented Claudio from indulging

in reflection. When he retired to his chamber, the strange accident of his having seen Zelia in the habit of a male pilgrim, became the subject of his thoughts; he had felt a prepossession in her favor from the first moment of his beholding her. If it were possible, that the same interest towards him had taken possession of her feelings, why come to Mantua to catch only a transient glimpse of his person, when it was in her power to see him every day at Rome? And why make that very friar her companion who had been the ambassador of her friend Viola's passion? Again, he thought that it could only have been the result of accident that they had met; but then how strange, that Zelia should appear in the disguise in which he had seen her! There was something in this circumstance, when connected in his thoughts with the mystery of his first introduction both to her and Viola, which he was unable to dismiss from his mind: one reflection brought on another, and drove off the attacks of sleep, till Claudio, wishing to compose his mind for her embraces, took up his pen, and endeavoured to sooth his agitated senses, by writing the following lines to the power whose influence he wished to feel.

Address to Sleep.

What were our state, O power benign!
    Shouldst thou deny thine opiate balm?
Thy aid has influence divine,
    Thou bidst the tortur'd wretch be calm!

Oh! hear me then, sweet sleep, and shed,
    Luxurious shed o'er me thy charms;
Weave thy blest chaplet round my head,
    And bind me in oblivion's arms.

Thy poppy canopy unroll,
    Shade my tear-swoll'n and brimful eyes,
Enchantment's web spin o'er my soul,
    Nor let peace fly me when I rise.

CHAPTER XV.

> The day thus spent, my Lord for music calls;
> He thrums the base, to which my lady squalls;
> The children join, which so delights these ninnies,
> The brats seem all Guadiccie's, Lovatini's.
>
> GARRICK.

ON the following morning, at an early hour, the Count di Ponta went to the convent of the Holy Virgin, to receive his daughter Valeria, at the hands of the lady Abbess. As soon as they arrived at the inn, Lodovico, flying up to his sister, exclaimed, "Come, jump, Valeria, cut a caper as high as the moon for joy, and then fall on your knees, and thank all the Saints in the calendar, that you have escaped from the walls of that dungeon."

"I shall ever remember it with pleasure," answered Valeria, "for I was always treated under its roof with kindness."

"Ay, ay, very likely," half-whispered Lodovico, in return, "but the kindness of an old Lady Abbess, and the kindness of a young lover, are very different things, my dear sister; and now you have got foot loose into the world, you will have the opportunity of making the discovery for yourself."

The Count's carriage was now announced to be ready, and they proceeded on their journey without delay.

During their first day's ride, it was Claudio's fortune to be seated opposite to Valeria, and he found that the simple, yet elegant dress, which she had substituted for her boarder's robe, had robbed her of none of that delicate beauty which she possessed in so eminent a degree; her conversation was lively, and bore the marks of a well-informed mind, and her manners were gentle, without bashfulness, and refined, without affectation.

On the third day of their journey, Lodovico and Claudio found horses waiting for them on the road, and proceeded forward on horseback, and arriving at the last stage where they were to stop between Mantua and the pallazo of the Count di Ponta; they found already in the inn, Signor Roderigo, with his daughter and granddaughters, who had proceeded thus far on their journey.

"Here they are, by all my hopes of fun!" cried Lodovico: "Come, Claudio, let us take a saunter round the inn, and give you a peep at them before I introduce you."

Lodovico's plan was followed, and Claudio's transient sight of the party through the window, gave him the following ideas of the individuals that composed it:—Signor Roderigo was extremely short, and very corpulent; appeared at least sixty-five, and yet was dressed with all the splendor and show of a Neapolitan youth of fashion. Signora Clementina was as much above the common standard of female height, as her father was below that of men generally rated, and her taper shape was in direct opposition to his corpulency: her eyes were grey and small, her lips shining, and her mouth wide; the color of her cheeks was 'what it pleased the painter,' and her hair was of a sandy brown. In all these points, except the color of her cheeks, she resembled her father; in that particular, he wore a natural purple where she glowed in artificial vermillion. In age, she appeared to be about twenty years younger than he, and in the rainbow colors of her dress, she outrivalled even his gay suit. The two daughters appeared as the true children of their mother.

After having twice passed the window, they returned into the house; and Lodovico walking without ceremony into the apartment where they had seen the party assembled, introduced to it his friend. Signor Roderigo rose, the very caricature of politeness, to receive them, and brushed about the room as fast as he could wield about his little fat body, to place them chairs. Signora Clementina was reclined on a sofa, and, extending her hand to Lodovico without attempting to rise, she said, in a languishing tone, "Signor, you must excuse my getting up to receive you, my nerves are shattered with the journey.—I hope your friend won't think me affected for not rising."

Claudio bowed in silence.

"He is too well bred, you see," answered Lodovico, "to speak the truth; but you know I always think you horribly affected."

One of the daughters shrieked, snatched a bottle of perfume from the table, and ran and held it under her mother's nostrils. "Exquisite child!" cried Signora Clementina, "how well did I divine your sensitive nature, when I gave you the name of Sensibilla. This dear girl feared my spirits would experience a shock from your abrupt accusation of affectation, because she knows it to be what my nature most dislikes to be suspected of, and flew to me with this essence of roses to arrest my senses in their fall." She kissed her daughter's neck, then added, "Don't be alarmed, dear child; I don't mind Signor Lodovico's raillery."

Lodovico threw himself carelessly upon the other end of the sofa on which the Signora Clementina was reclining, and replied, "Come, I will deal fairly too by you, Signora; I'll tell you when I dare say you were not affected at all, not half so much as even I could have wished to have seen you."

"Pray let me hear when that was?" returned she, with a simper which indicated that she had some expectation of receiving a compliment.

"When you saw your pretty daughter take the veil," replied Lodovico: "if you had been half as much affected at that sight as I should have been, you would have rescued her from the gloom of a convent's walls before it was too late."

"Oh, Signor," rejoined the lady, evidently piqued at the compliment having been turned from herself to her daughter, "Delicatilla was too tender a composition to move in the world at large with comfort to herself; for that reason, I placed her in the happy seclusion to which she has just retired. You may conceive what a convulsion rent my nerves, when I heard her pronounce the vows of eternal separation from her affectionate mother:—but I suppose you call both that, and the tears which now rush into my eyes, affectation." She put her handkerchief to her eyes, but there was little doubt that it returned from them without moisture.

"What think you, Signor," continued Lodovico, turning to Roderigo, and winking at Claudio, "is it not a shame to deprive the world of so many sparkling eyes as are shut up within the walls of convents?"

"*Mon cher papa,*" returned Signora Clementina, proud of her knowledge of another language, besides her mother-tongue, and eager upon all occasions to display it in the use of those three words. "*Mon cher papa* is perfectly assured of my happy and accurate judgement in the education and disposition of my daughters. I hope you don't think me affected in this declaration, Signor Claudio, but *mon cher papa* knows with what propriety I have acted."

"Well," resumed Lodovico, "and are these young ladies to pass their lives in the same happy seclusion from their fellow creatures?"

"Oh, no!" replied Signora Clementina, "I study the dispositions of my children, and am convinced the gloom of a convent would affect the senses of Sensibilla: delicately alive to the tenderest touch of feeling, she would expire when she was deprived of animated objects to give her the bliss of calling forth her sensibility; her soul of exquisite sensation expands over a romance, and her heart feels all the warmth of friendship and affection for that little dog Lupetto. It is not long ago, that she neither slept nor eat for six-and-thirty hours, because she thought the dear little creature had got the tooth-ache."

"Then as to Languililla," Signora Clementina went on, "you see in what a waking slumber, what a trance of languishment, the sweet girl now reclines upon that chair; nothing but music can rouse her soft powers;—strike the lute, my dear Sensibilla, and invite your sister to cast her soft blue eyes upon us for a moment."

Sensibilla complied with her mother's request, and Languililla raised her head, half opened her eyes with a faint smile, breathed a smothered sigh, and as soon as Sensibilla laid down the lute, she again closed her eyes, and sunk into her former position.

It was evident to Claudio, that these young ladies had not been christened according to their natural dispositions, but tutored to assume characters corresponding with the names given to them by their ridiculous mother. He despised the folly of the one, pitied the blind compliance of the other, and felt it very difficult to suppress his inclination to laugh at both. As he was on the point of motioning to Lodovico to depart, their horses were brought out, and no excuse was now requisite for quitting the party.

"We shall see you again in a couple of hours at the pallazo, I suppose," said Lodovico.

"If I am not dead with fatigue before that time," answered Signora Clementina, "don't think me affected for saying so; but I am always killed with weariness when I travel in a close carriage."

Lodovico and Claudio now made their escape. "Well," cried the former, as soon as they were mounted, "now tell me honestly, did I exaggerate my account."

"No," returned Claudio, "for once in your life, I will allow that you fell short in your description of the ridiculous; but we heard nothing from the old gentleman of the cause of his travels, as I expected we should have done."

"You are not quite intimate enough yet," replied Lodovico, "you will hear the whole account of Livia's falsehood, take my word for it, before you have been together at my father's pallazo twelve hours."

"I must live on expectation," said Claudio, and they then clapped spurs to their horses, and rode on.

It was late in the evening before all the travellers arrived at the pallazo, and on account of the fatigue they had experienced on their journey, the ladies retired to bed at an early hour. They had not many minutes left the apartment, before Signor Roderigo began to open his budget of sorrows to Claudio, whom he believed to be the only person present to whom his story was new. The old gentleman was then questioned on the success which had attended his travels, since the Count and he had last met, and he was obliged to answer, that he had shared the common fate of lame old men who pretend to run after nimble girls; though these were not exactly the words in which the old gentleman expressed his own case.

When Claudio left his chamber the next morning, he met a servant, who put a letter into his hand—"Whence comes this?" asked Claudio. "A pilgrim left it with the porter, Signor, very early in the morning; he enquired whether you were at the pallazo, and being answered in the affirmative, desired that letter to be given to you."——Claudio tore open the paper, and found that the contents were written in a hand with which he was unacquainted. The words were these—"The intelligence of your eyes was fallacious, or you loved Zelia the first moment you beheld her in the apartment of Viola. If you have felt that love, cherish it; if you have not, endeavour to acquire it, for Zelia is prepared, at some future time, to make you the best of wives." The strange means by which this information was conveyed to Claudio, caused him for some time to be undecided, whether he was pleased or vexed by what he had read—How strange! that a woman should thus mysteriously, either by herself, or through her friends, offer her affections, her hand, to a man with whom she had only once in her life conversed;

and that with this offer she should neither acquaint him who she was, or where she might be seen; only say, that the time fixed for the happiness she designed him must be distant.

He had lately dwelt so much on the mystery of Viola, and the friar who attended her, that the letter he had just received, which was only a part of the same ænigma, did not so much raise his anxiety, or curiosity, for the explanation of its contents, as it would have done, had he received these lines without having gone through the series of adventures which had preceded them.

It now appeared evident to him, that Zelia had come to Mantua on purpose to see him; but he could not account why both she and the Benedictine friar, who it was clear was her colleague, should have avoided any intercourse (as had been the case at Mantua) with the very man whom they were soliciting to become her husband.

He went to the porter, and enquired a description of the pilgrim who had left for him the letter, and the porter's account of him tallied exactly with the person of the friar.—Claudio asked, "If he was alone?" and to this particular, he received an affirmative answer.

He was convinced, that it was folly to dwell upon a subject which all his conjectures could not explain, and therefore endeavoured to drive it from his thoughts; but it continued resolutely to haunt his mind, and reflection did not make him the less enamoured of Zelia's person; he only wished to see her throw off the garb of mystery, for he was well assured that he had never seen a woman whose embraces he should prefer to those of Zelia, without this disguise.—However pleasing a face any mystery may carry with it, it is still coupled with distrust; this truth Claudio felt, and he felt also that it is equally hard to love truly where there is any cause for distrust, as it is to drive from the heart any object, however enveloped in shades, which has once warmed the passions.

A few days after the Count di Ponta's return from Mantua, a large party of his friends were invited to pass the day at the pallazo, and welcome the return of Valeria to her father's house: music was the pastime of the evening, and Valeria evinced a taste and execution of the first excellence. Signora Clementina hoped so often, "that she should not be requested to sing or play, as it looked so affected to refuse, and she really was not either in voice or finger;" that the company present were *obliged* to invite her to an exhibition of her skill, though there was not a single person amongst them who would have thought of making the request, if she had not artfully put them in mind that it would be agreeable to her. "Well, if I must play," she said, "you shall see my little girls exhibit with me; indeed, I should not have been prevailed on tonight at all, if I did not think they could afford you a few minutes entertainment.—Go, my sweet children," she continued "and prepare yourselves for music."—The girls left the room, and returned in a short time with garlands of flowers on their heads, festoons descending from their shoulders to their feet, and with each a shepherdess' crook in her hand. "Here come my little nymphs," said the mother, and placed herself at the piano. "I hope you don't think them affected," she continued, "they do it to please me." She then began a symphony, and her daughters, dancing up to her in a fantastic figure, placed on her head a garland of roses, and began a duet, which they performed in the style of opera singers; and at its conclusion, Languililla fell into the arms of her sister, Sensibilla.

The company was *obliged* to express itself highly gratified, and Signora Clementina, rising from the instrument, said, "I am afraid you think them affected, but indeed all they do has only the merit of being the impulse of unadulterated nature, and to the same mistress must be attributed their defects."

"Positively," said Lodovico, "you do not get up, you must sing us a solo."

"I shall faint, I shall expire! and if I don't comply, you will call me affected;" returned she.

"I certainly shall, if you don't consent to entrance us," returned he, leading her back to her seat.

"Oh, you annihilate me by this cruel alternative;" cried she, and then began to sweep the keys with an inward exultation that betrayed itself in her eyes.—In a few minutes, she burst out into strains more loud than harmonious, and quavered through a song, of which the concluding lines were—

> He gave a hint—a hint's enough,
> Her faith in man is gone for ever!

The praise of the party was now again conveyed to the delighted ears of the Signora, who retired to a window, to which Lodovico followed her: "I have a favor to beg of you, Signora," said he, "I want to solicit a copy of the beautiful lines which compose the song you have just given us with such wonderful effect."

"Oh, mercy!" exclaimed she, "then Sensibilla has betrayed me; I should scold her violently, if I was not persuaded, that it is her love and partiality for her mother's little talents that have drawn her into a confession of these words having been written by me."

"Even so," replied Lodovico, "and I must have them."

"Upon one condition only," she returned, "if you will confess to me, whether she told you who is the subject of them."

"A hint's enough," replied Lodovico, as if endeavouring to recollect the concluding lines of the song—"her faith in man is gone."

"Ay, *for ever!*" sighed out Clementina, making an attempt at looking interestingly.

"A hint *is* enough," returned Lodovico; "you are yourself the betrayed and innocent sufferer of the poem; yet I can hardly believe, that he who has tasted the sanctuary of those lips could ever profane the bliss he had enjoyed by a hint."

The Signora rose with affected bashfulness, and said, "I shall certainly quarrel with Sensibilla; go, go away from me, Signor; I will not be questioned any more on this subject; I can't think why I did not choose some other song?" She moved to a card-table by which Claudio was standing, and he addressed her with, "Don't you play, Signora?" "I dare say, you will think me affected," she replied, "when I tell you I do not, and that my reason is, that I always feel myself so full of spirits in company, that I despair of fixing my mind sufficiently on one object to do justice to my game."

"Signora Clementina would certainly do injustice to the animate objects around her, by giving up her whole attention to the card-table;" replied Claudio.

"Do you ever play, Signor?" she asked, with a low curtsey.

"Very often;" Claudio answered.

"I give you much credit then," she returned, "for the neatness with which you have transferred to me a compliment which must so often have been addressed as a truth to yourself."

The Signora attempted to look so amiable as she spoke these words, that Claudio began to be apprehensive, she was going to make love to him. Lodovico came up to his relief: "Signora," said he, "much as I extol the beauty of your lines, I must quarrel with you about the sense of the last; you say, "Her faith in man is gone *for ever!*" What! because she has found one wretch who was sufficiently presumptuous to confess that he had been happy? You can find no defence for the injustice of this assertion."

"Oh! yes," she replied, "the best defence of a wronged female in so trying, so wounding a situation, is to arm herself with a shield against all future temptations which might involve her in the like dilemma."

"I must first know what was the exact quantity of happiness which the offender tasted," answered Lodovico.

"Merciful Virgin!" exclaimed Clementina, "did not Sensibilla, when she blabbed me for the author of the song, say he only kissed my hand?"

"*Only!*" exclaimed Lodovico, "*only* kissed your hand! there are men who would walk a pilgrimage to Loretto, only to kiss the nail of your little finger."

The Signora raised her fan before her face, and walked back to the window.

"There is one man," continued Lodovico, following her, "but he does not venture even to look his passion——There is a man, who wanders every morning between five and six, near the orange grove—who sighs—who——I am not convinced, Signora, that his life is not in danger from his fear of confessing his adoration of a nameless object; he has to-night heard the last line of your song, and I have seen a visible change from pleasure to melancholy in his countenance ever since."

Lodovico was now walking away in his turn, but the Signora's curiosity was raised to a pitch that required gratification, and following him, she exclaimed, "Signor Lodovico, one question, if you please."

"Not a word more on the subject for the world;" answered he, in a low voice, and enjoining her to silence by holding his finger to his lips, he went to the other end of the room. The agitation of inward triumph, pleasure and vanity joined, were now marked on the countenance of the Signora Clementina, and placing herself on a window, she sat exercising her fan.

When the party broke up, Lodovico called Claudio into the garden, and told him his conversation with the Signora Clementina. "Now," said he, "just by way of a harmless frolic, let us try whether the old woman has the vanity she appears to have: you can write verses, compose a few lines, referring to the two last of her song, and I'll send them to her, with a *hint* that shall tell her, that they came from the gentleman who wanders every morning between five and six o'clock in the orange grove. We will contrive to be going that way with our nets at the time appointed, and we shall discover, whether her credulity in love affairs is as great as it appears to be."

Claudio saw no mischief that could arise from this trick, which would only afford him and his friend a laugh in private; for they resolved not to mention it to any one, and considered that the time in the morning Lodovico had mentioned that the ideal gentleman walked at, was an hour when none of the family were hardly ever stirring.

"But you told her," said Claudio, "that the gentleman who feared to confess his passion had heard her song; she must imagine it to be your father."

"Oh! no," replied Lodovico, "she has been long acquainted with all the young and old fellows too who dined here to-day, and they, you know, were all present when she sung."

"But how should any of them get into your father's garden at five o'clock in the morning, or indeed at any time of the day?" said Claudio. "You can't deceive her in that; a few moments recollection will point out to her, her error in believing you."

"Oh! you are mistaken," rejoined Lodovico, "all the principal families in the neighbourhood have keys of my father's grounds, and this she is as well acquainted with as I am."

"Then my objection is removed," said Claudio.

They then repaired to Lodovico's apartment, and together composed the following lines:

VERSES addressed with the humblest adoration to the lovely Signora Clementina, by him who, ever since her arrival at the pallazo di Ponta, has wandered every morning between five and six o'clock in the orange-grove, opposite to her chamber-window, in the presumptuous hope of inducing her to grant him a private interview.

  AND dared he give the cruel hint?
    And could he bear to hear her sigh?
  And could he see the damask tint
    Fade on her cheek, and let her die?

  Ah! how unlike the faithful youth
    Who loves—but loves, alas! in vain;
  Who, emblem apt of silent truth,
    Scarce ventures even to complain.

  If then a niggard in my woe,
    I veil my grief from every eye;
  If while my tears in secret flow,
    I hide the pangs of which I die:

  How much more niggard should I prove,
    How much more secret, more on guard;
  If in return for boundless love,
    My sweet passion met some soft reward?

  Oh! grant me then, with silent sip,
    Soft prelude to more fervent bliss,
  To steal from off that rosy lip,
    The dewy fragrance of a kiss!

  And then, by yonder God of day,
    It never from this mouth shall part,
  Until for others to make way,
    I store it safe within my heart.

  Thus when some maid to love devoted,
    Shall wish to justify her plan,
  I, as an instance, shall be quoted,
    To prove the secresy of man.

The letter was sealed up without delay, and given by Lodovico to a confidential servant of his, with orders to deliver it to Signora Clementina's woman, and if she made any enquiries whence it came, to say it had been put into his hands by a person with whom he was unacquainted.

During supper, the letter was presented to the Signora by one of the Count's footmen; Claudio and Lodovico continued eating, and were careful not to catch each other's eye. The Signora read the note, smiled, read it again, and put it into her pocket, whilst her eyes snapped with agitation, and her neck coloured with triumph.

At a little before five in the morning, Lodovico, as had been agreed upon between them, rapped at Claudio's door, who, in a very few minutes, drew on his clothes, and came out into the gallery; Lodovico motioned to his friend to follow him in silence, and they went down together into the great hall. Behind the hall was a passage, with a door at each end, and close by each of these doors was a flight of stairs, leading to the chambers on the different sides of the mansion. "If Signora Clementina ventures down," said Lodovico, "she will come by these stairs on the left, because this door at the foot of them leads straight to the orange-grove."

"Surely she has got the start of us," returned Claudio, "the bolts of this door are undrawn."

"No, no," cried Lodovico, "I dare say, it has not been bolted at all to-night; the servants are careless."

With their nets in their hands, they proceeded to the orange-grove, and took their station behind a knot of trees, on the margin of the lake, from whence they could command a full view of the place of appointment. Immediately opposite to the spot where they stood, an arched grotto terminated the walk, and through it a narrow recess led to a small apartment, which was a convenient dressing-room for those who bathed in the lake which wound round it, and this apartment had an entrance from a walk behind it, as well as through the grotto; behind it, the water was shallow, and suited to timid bathers; those who preferred a deeper stream for swimming, came through the grotto, and flung themselves from the bank on which it stood, into the body of the lake.

They had waited nearly half an hour in expectation, when Claudio affirmed that he heard footsteps. They peeped from their hiding place, but seeing nobody, concluded that Claudio had been deceived; in less than five minutes more however, the sound of footsteps became audible to them both, and Signora Clementina appeared, stealing into the grove. She wore a light morning dress, loosely put on, and a long veil of white gauze. They now sunk down behind the shrubs which grew around them, content to watch her conduct through the foliage: she wandered about some time without looking on either side; presently she began to turn about her head, as if searching for the expected swain amongst the surrounding trees; she next hummed a few notes of an opera song; and lastly, stopping in front of the grotto, she seemed undecided whether or not to enter it. She threw up her veil, and took another turn of the walk; again she stopped for some moments at the mouth of the grotto; at length, she appeared to have summoned resolution to enter its recesses, and had moved one step forward, when out darted from the inner apartment, the Count di Ponta, habited only in dame nature's plain buff regimental.

For about a couple of seconds, both parties staring each other full in the face, made a dead stop. Signora Clementina then screamed loud enough to have split the tail of a comet, if one had at that moment been passing over her head, and the Count, as if surprise had rendered him unconscious of his situation, cried out, "What can bring you here at this time of the morning, Signora?" To *see* a naked man was enough to unstring every nerve in the Signora's composition, but to hear a naked man deliver a sentence of near a dozen words in length, and addressed to her, was almost sufficient to annihilate her on the spot, and throwing herself upon her face on the ground, she lay motionless, and apparently dead. The Count now first recollected his immodest appearance, and going back to the dressing-room, he drew on his bathing trowsers and robe de chambre, and returned to the lady's assistance. Kneeling down by her side, he raised her head upon his arm: much pains were requisite to make her again open her eyes, and when she did so, the Count said, "I hope, Signora, you are convinced, that the unlucky accident which has taken place was unintentional on my part; I did not expect to meet you abroad at this hour."

"For mercy's sake," she replied, "conduct me back to the house; the air during the night has been so very warm, that I came abroad for a little refreshment. I see you think me affected for saying so, and don't believe me."

"Not at all," answered the Count; "the warmth of the air induced me to come down thus early to take a dip in the lake."

"Let me conjure you," cried the Signora, as she rose from the ground, "never to let this accident, so distressing to my feelings, transpire from your lips; I could not live under the idea of its being known."

"You may depend on my not mentioning it," replied the Count.

"How could I expect to meet you here," she rejoined, as she took his arm to move towards the house; *Could* I expect to meet you here?" she said, throwing at him a side-long glance.

"By no means, certainly not, Signora," returned he; "at least, I can faithfully I assure you, that the meeting you here was the farthest thing from my thoughts."

The Signora sighed, and the Count and she moved slowly on. When out of sight, Claudio and Lodovico escaped directly to some distance from the spot where they had been stationed, and gave a free loose to their mirth: "Thank Heaven," cried Claudio, "that we kept ourselves concealed; she would certainly have suspected us, if we had shown ourselves."

"I think," replied Lodovico, "she won't come back in a hurry to meet the wanderer in the orange-grove. How unexpectedly she must have been surprised with the sight of a full grown Cupid, bursting upon her from the bower of pleasure! ha! ha! ha! It was my father, I dare say, who opened the door we found unbolted."

"No doubt," said Claudio, "and his footsteps coming to the bath that I heard when we could not see any body near us."

"How fortunate," exclaimed Lodovico, "that I made the appointment just at this place! I can never be sufficiently thankful to chance for the favor she has done me in giving a lift to my scheme."

"As we are up," replied Claudio, "let us rather throw our nets than return to bed."

The proposal was agreed to by Lodovico, and they did not return to the pallazo, till all the family, except the Signora Clementina, were assembled at breakfast: a bad head-ache was alledged as her apology for her breakfasting in her own room.

CHAPTER XVI.

> O, my offence is rank, it smells to Heaven.
> ───────────O! what form of prayer
> Can serve my turn?───────────
> ───────────O bosom, black as death!
> O limed soul! that struggling to be free
> Art more engaged!—Help, angels, make essay!
> Bow, stubborn knees!
> HAMLET.

AT dinner, Signora Clementina made her appearance; but complained that her head-ache had not yet left her, and not a word was dropped, either by the Count di Ponta or herself, relative to the cause of her indisposition. Sensibilla paid her mama's head-ache the same compliment of refraining to satisfy her appetite, which she had conferred on her lap-dog's tooth-ache; and Languililla even exerted herself almost to open her eyes, and enquire after her mama's health.

Claudio and Lodovico managed to get through the day with perfect composure, notwithstanding it was a very difficult task to the latter; and on the following day, Signora Clementina declaring herself perfectly restored to health, Claudio advised his friend to be satisfied with the joke he had enjoyed, and not to run the hazard of becoming her tormentor in any new shape; which advice he promised for the present at least to follow.

Towards the conclusion of the vacation, the Count di Ponta one day thus addressed Claudio: "Are you acquainted, whether it is the Marchese di Bartelma's intention that you should travel on leaving the college of St. Peter?"

"I believe it is," replied Claudio, "I have heard him say, that he thought no education complete without it."

"Exactly the same is my opinion," returned the Count; "it is my plan, that immediately on his final return from Rome, my son should visit France and Germany. If you should like still to continue his companion, you will give him infinite satisfaction, and I will write to the Marchese to inform him what arrangements I have made in my own mind for Lodovico, and enquire if they meet his approbation for you: one tutor will then be sufficient for you both, and on receiving your father's answer, I will employ my endeavours to engage a man suitable to attend you on your tour."

This proposition met Claudio's warmest acquiescence, and the Count accordingly dispatched a long letter, without delay, to the Marchese di Bartelma. Claudio sent one, at the same time, to express his satisfaction of what the Count had written; but referring the decision, with all respect, to the Marchese.

As soon as it was possible for the answers to these letters to arrive, the Count and Claudio each received one from the Marchese di Bartelma; the former containing the most flattering opinion of the Count's arrangements; and the latter expressing to Claudio all those sentiments of benevolence and affection which the conduct of the writer had ever convinced him were the growth of his heart; and the result of the application being what was not less anxiously desired by the Count and his son than by Claudio, the Count immediately put abroad enquiries for a travelling tutor of the first abilities.

From the first moment of the acquaintance of Claudio and Lodovico to the present hour, not a day had passed which had not augmented their friendship. Claudio saw, with true satisfaction, that Lodovico's errors became corrected through his advice, and Lodovico found in Claudio the safe pilot to steer him through many a storm which his folly raised, and his repentance, unaided by friendship, could not quell. Lodovico expressed extreme joy at the idea of their anticipated travels, and declared that the friendship of Claudio, and the pleasures of Paris, would give him happiness too great for the enjoyment of a mortal; yet, however, notwithstanding this declaration, he did not seem to be at all apprehensive of sinking under the excess of extacy, although he never thought of claiming rank above a sublunary being. Claudio was well convinced, that Lodovico's heart was fundamentally well disposed, and that all his improprieties of conduct originated in the wildness of his temper, and the warmth of his passions; and he regarded the correcting of these effervescences of nature, knowing them to spring from a good soil, not only as a pleasure, but a duty he owed to the intimacy in which they were placed; and Lodovico, notwithstanding his many faults, had the good sense to perceive the right intentions of Claudio, and to feel grateful for his admonitions, though he had not always resolution enough to follow them.

As Claudio's knowledge of Valeria increased by living in her society, he found more to admire in her than even the first favorable impression she had made on his senses had led him to believe her possessed of: she enjoyed, in a most eminent degree, an acquaintance with all the fine arts, and she exercised them with the unaffectedness that gave them additional force; her form, which had always appeared to him delicately beautiful, encreased in interest as it became more familiar to the observer; and her heart, above all her other qualifications, was eminently the seat, not only of the most perfectly acquired talents, but also of the purest and brightest virtues.

On retiring from her presence, Claudio often felt more than an uninterested recollection of her perfections, and he would sometimes even entertain something like a wish that he had never seen Zelia; but in the heart of man, passion is a stronger advocate in favor of women than virtue, and his debates with his own mind generally ended in a self-conviction, that Zelia had all the power over his senses which she wished to possess: again, he would reflect on the folly of suffering his affections to place themselves on a woman with whose person only he was acquainted, and whose dark and mysterious offer of herself to him for wife, seemed to carry with it a tacit confession of there being some point in her conduct, or fate, which she feared openly and honorably to explain; when perfection of body and mind was continually before his sight in the person of Valeria:—but, alas! all his arguments with his own heart concluded only in his discovering that Zelia was at that time its sovereign.

Valeria entertained an esteem for Claudio, because she saw him individually as a young man of worth and knowledge, and particularly as the friend of her brother; her days of seclusion from the world had been so chaste in precept and thought, that no ideas of a more tender nature had yet found their way into her mind.

Signora Clementina, with her daughters, and the Signor Roderigo, their grandfather, had now left the pallazo, the last week of their residence at it having been suffered by Lodovico to pass without any greater interruption of their habits and happiness, than the occasional raillery which their affectation and particularities called from him; and which, like most foolish and affected people, they excused, as it brought their darling foibles into notice; and the evening was arrived which preceded the day on which Claudio and Lodovico were to return to Rome.

Claudio had delayed packing up his portmanteau, till he went to his chamber at the hour of retiring to rest; and he then recollected that he had left his missal in the private chapel of the pallazo. The book in question was a large volume, bound in embroidered velvet, printed on vellum, and enriched with paintings, in colors and gold, of the different saints; it had been the last present of the Marchese Julia di Bartelma to Claudio on her death-bed; and since that day, he had never attended mass without using it: it was much too large to travel in his pocket, and he accordingly took up his candle, and proceeded towards the chapel in search of it.

The Count di Ponta had retired to his chamber at an early hour, as was his usual custom when the pallazo was without company. Claudio had been employed above an hour in his chamber: thus all the family were retired for the night, and he passed on to the chapel without hearing a single breathing or footstep, or catching the glimmer of an expiring light. As soon as he entered the chapel, the groans and confused murmurs of a person in agony and prayer met his ear, and he saw a dim lamp burning on the rail of the altar. On the left side of the altar, an iron rail parted off from the chapel a space of about six feet square, which was paved with sharp flint stones, and called the cell of penance: here it was customary for the penitent of any heinous crime to kneel, subject to the inconvenience of the points of the sharp stones; and hence proceeded the voice which Claudio now heard.

He deemed it a complaisance due to the penitent, whoever he might be, to disturb his devotion as little as his errand to the chapel would permit; and therefore setting down his candle by the outward door, he proceeded to the chair on which his missal lay; and having taken it up, immediately retired.

Claudio's heart was warmly susceptible of the sorrows of his fellow creatures, and he felt himself moved to pity by the very great agony of mind which the deep groans of the penitent had expressed him to be suffering under.—Having once more gained his chamber, he deposited his missal in his portmanteau; and having said three pater-nosters for the peace of the unknown penitent, he entered his bed.

The Count di Ponta had bade farewell to his son and Claudio on the preceding evening, as had the fair Valeria; and, at an early hour, they began their journey.

"I had an adventure last night," said Claudio, as they rode along; "having left my missal in the chapel, I went, after we had parted in the gallery, into the chapel to fetch it——"

"And there found my father at penance," replied Lodovico, with a gravity of countenance very unusual with him; "but, for God's sake, do not let it escape your lips that you saw him there: I hope he did not know you saw him."

"No, he did not," returned Claudio; "I went in, treading softly and in the dark, in order not to disturb the unhappy sufferer I heard in the cell of penance; but, I assure you, that I was entirely unconscious of its being the Count, or I should not have mentioned the circumstance as I have done."

"Every surmise is worse than the truth," said Lodovico; "I will therefore commit the truth of his penance to your friendship.—Yesterday was the anniversary of that fatal event, the death of Count Angelo's wife, the Countess Horatia di Ponta, by the hand of her husband!"—He paused, then added, "You have, I dare say, heard that my father was the man with whom the Countess Horatia had broken her vows of fidelity to her husband, and driven him to the desperate act he committed: my father feels himself an accomplice in the guilt of the Countess, and endeavours to expiate his crime by penance."

"I give you my honor," said Claudio, "that I will never revive the subject." Lodovico regained his wonted cheerfulness, and a fresh topic of discourse was started.

When they drew near to Rome, Viola, the Benedictine friar, and particularly Zelia, with all the concomitant circumstances and mysteries which had attended them, began to float with renewed strength of imagination in the brain of Claudio; and when he once more entered the city, an agitation, composed of doubt, passion, distrust, and expectation, only natural to the peculiar situation in which he stood, seized upon his heart.

CHAPTER XVII.

> ————Praising what is lost,
> Makes the remembrance dear.
> ALL'S WELL THAT ENDS WELL.

MONTH rolled on after month, till the time allotted for the residence of Claudio and Lodovico at the college of Saint Peter was nearly elapsed.—Lodovico was looking forward with elated spirits to their approaching travels: Claudio felt disappointed when he looked back upon the length of time which had passed without his having seen the Benedictine friar, or heard any intelligence of Zelia, or of the mysterious Viola; and the idea of being on the point of leaving that city which appeared to him the most likely place to gratify his curiosity, encreased the gloom which hung over his mind.

Still, however, whatever Claudio felt, he contrived to conceal from his friend Lodovico's observation those depressed feelings of which he did not intend to explain the cause, and indulged himself in reflection at his moments of solitude; but reflection tended not to remove the knotty points which gave it birth: and when thought had exhausted itself upon the mystery of Viola's invitation, and her subsequent horror at the sight of his bracelet; his ideas would turn to the more pleasing side of the ænigma, and indulge themselves with contemplating, in imagination, the beauties of Zelia, and the promised happiness contained in the note which had been left for him by the pilgrim at the pallazo di Ponta. When fancy, fed by passion, drew Zelia to the imagination of Claudio in the exercise of every polite art and elegant accomplishment, he would forget that he had only seen her in circumscribed solitude, and under the pilgrim's garb of restraint, and his ideas would follow her through the ball-room, the gaily decorated *parterre*; then place her at the lute, charming the senses of an admiring circle, and when the vision began to fade from his senses, eager to preserve the picture which had enchanted them, he would transmit to paper the vivid colours which had warmed the painting of his brain.

TO ZELIA.

HOW much too swift those moments flew,
Oh, Zelia! which I pass'd with you!
How sadly slow each tedious day
Has crept along, from you away!

No joys for me, the festive board
Which once had charms, can now afford;
No former pleasure I pursue,
But wish to sigh, and think of you.

Wrapt in the folds of smother'd love,
Along the midnight beach I rove;
Bid fancy take her airy flight,
And bring my absent fair to sight.

The little rosy dimpled smile,
That decks the loves in Cyprian isle,
Perch'd on her blooming cheek, I see;
Then fondly hope—'twas meant for me.

In raptures of ideal bliss,
I dare to think I steal a kiss,
And folded in a high-wrought dream,
Happiest of happy men, I seem.

I hear her touch the trembling string,
Attun'd to love:—I hear her sing:
And as she trips the trembling dance,
At me she casts the side-long glance.

But soon these fancied joys retreat,
When reason reassumes her seat;
And all these fond illusions prove,
Is, that there's witchcraft sure in love.

Thus would he give his passion for Zelia vent, and as his mind cooled from the warmth of any freshly conceived idea, his thoughts would turn to the folly of having fixed his affections with such violence on a woman of whose personal charms only he had been able to form any estimate: he would consider that Zelia, being ostensibly the companion of Viola, was by no means a trait of character in her favor, and that the offer she had made to him by letter, did not at all bespeak that delicacy of mind which he should wish to find in the woman he made his wife: he would then turn his ideas to Valeria, and see in her every perfection of person and mind unshaded by mystery, and pure from the shadow even of an indelicacy. Violently would he then upbraid his heart for still inclining with the fervor of contradiction to Zelia: he resolved to make it his study to forget Zelia, and to dwell on the amiability of Valeria.

The travels of the two young friends were to commence from the pallazo of the Count di Ponta; from whence they were immediately to cross the Alps, and proceed in a direct route to Paris.—In their way from Rome, a few days were passed by them at the villa di Bartelma, in bidding farewell to its worthy possessor; and an equal time having been spent by them at the residence of Lodovico's father, they set out, accompanied by the tutor who had been provided to attend them.

As it is not our intention to relate any of the travellers' observations or adventures upon their journey, but such as intimately refer to the history which we are engaged in recounting, we shall immediately transport them to the foot of the Alps, where they arrived at the close of an autumnal evening. On their entering the inn where they were to pass the night, they enquired of the host for a guide to conduct them across the mountains; and he informed them, that there was a large party of travellers in his house awaiting the morning to perform the same journey, and that it was usual for parties who met at his inn, to cross the mountains in company, which he pointed out to them as a very discreet plan for the pocket, the expence of the guide's attendance being lessened by his receiving his pay from several masters.

To this plan, Claudio and Lodovico saw no objection, but were rather pleased, by the anticipation of not travelling the dreary route before them without company, and accordingly retired early to rest, that they might be prepared to rise with the dawn and set forward; this early hour being the time at which, their host said, he always advised his guests to begin their journey at that time of the year, as the day was else scarcely long enough to bring them to the *auberge*, at the opposite foot of the mountain, while it was light.

With the first glimpse of approaching day, Claudio sprang from his bed, and roused his friend, who having quickly joined him, they went out together, and found the mules on which they were designed to travel, already brought out before the door of the inn, and preparing for them to ride. One of the guides, and five of the party, who were like them going to cross the Alps, had already ascended about half a furlong up the side of the craggy steep, and it was still only just light enough to show that there were persons preceding them, without discovering their sex or age.

In a few minutes, the second guide mounted his mule, as a signal for the second division of travellers to begin their journey, and in a few seconds more, the whole party was in motion.

The morning was cold and uncomfortable; and when the sun rose, it appeared only to tantalize the travellers, who saw its beams reflected on the surface far below them, and were only cheered by the sight of its enlivening rays, while they coveted the warmth in which the shepherd lay basking on the plains beneath.—At length, however, as the day continued to advance, the influence of its invigorating beams began to play upon the travellers, and with the refreshment of the warmth thus afforded them, their spirits became enlivened, and a pleasant conversation wore away the hours.

The first guide and his party, from the uniform pace in which they had all continued to travel, had kept, throughout the morning, at very nearly the same distance from them at which Claudio had observed them from the inn when he had first risen; towards noon, however, on a commodious spot, where it was usual for the travellers across the mountains to stop and refresh themselves, the first guide and his party halted, and the second division soon came up with them.

The travellers all alighted, and having turned off their mules to graze, seated themselves on the grass, each bringing out from his budget, such provision as he had stocked it with before his departure from the inn.

Claudio, when seated on the grass, continued in conversation with a French ecclesiastic, whose spirited and sensible discourse had entertained him during the journey; and he did not, for some time, turn round to his neighbour on his other side, till the sound of his voice struck his ear as being familiar to it; he then immediately turned round, and found that the person next to whom he was sitting wore the dress of a monk of the Franciscan order, and that his face was entirely covered by his cowl.

Again the monk spoke, and Claudio was again convinced that the voice was familiar to him, but the monk did not raise his head, and without the assistance of beholding his features, Claudio could not determine to whom the voice belonged:—presently Claudio invited him to drink a horn of wine from his flask, which the monk accepting, and raising his head to drink—'Claudio's prosperous journey;' the latter beheld the features of the pilgrim who had so strongly interested his feelings at the villa di Bartelma.

At the sight of the pilgrim, Claudio felt a chill of surprise run through his veins, which was immediately succeeded by a fervid glow of satisfaction: he fixed his eyes steadfastly on those of the pilgrim, in the hope that he would address him; the pilgrim's eyes fell upon Claudio's countenance as he returned him the horn, and thanked him for the draught it had contained, but there was no expression in his countenance that indicated his recollection of Claudio.

Claudio was disappointed, that his old friend did not recognize him; he hesitated whether or not to make himself known to him.— From the mystery which had marked the pilgrim's conduct on the morning of his departure from the villa di Bartelma, not less than the injunctions by which he was bound never to lead to the subject of himself, he was at a loss to determine whether the pilgrim might not now know him, but be restrained from confessing that he did know him, by some cause with which he was unacquainted. This possibility was still supposing the pilgrim acquainted with his fate; and interested in his happiness, and this made him still more eager to learn, whether he really was recognized by the pilgrim or not.

Whilst debating with his own mind, and experiencing an anxiety which he could ill conceal; the guide who had led the way in the morning, called to his party to mount their mules, and the pilgrim was among the first who rose to go in quest of his beast.—Claudio immediately sprang up from the grass, determining to mount his mule likewise, and join the first division of travellers, in the hope of some opportunity being given him of offering his person to the recollection of the pilgrim.—He looked about hastily for his mule, but he saw it not; that of the French Abbé had also strayed, and it was some time before the whistle of their guide brought them, with a sluggish pace, up to the spot where their companions were feeding. The delay occasioned to Claudio's proceeding on his journey by the wandering of his mule, proved fatal to his wish of riding in the company of the pilgrim; for by the time he was mounted, the party which had preceded in the morning were nearly twice as far as before in the van of their companions. The path was calculated only for one certain pace, and Claudio had no means of getting up to him by whose side he wished to travel.

Uneasily passed the remainder of the journey to Claudio, he wished for its conclusion without having any fixed idea how to proceed when it should be terminated; at length the village at the foot of the mountain appeared in sight, and the travellers began their congratulations to each other on their safe journey across the Alps.

The hamlet to which they were now advancing, appeared to consist only of a few scattered dwellings, seated in the bosom of a fertile grove of the chesnut and acacia.—Lodovico had been for some time riding by the side of two peasant girls and their father, who had been informing him of a journey they had been making into Italy, to visit a rich relation; and he now addressed them by saying, "I think, damsels, from what I observe of the village where you tell me you dwell, you'll find it but dull living after the gay scenes of Turin, which you say you have been visiting."

"Oh! no, Signor," replied one of the girls, "we shall have so much to tell our neighbours who have never been from home, that the relation of our adventures will afford us amusement for a long while to come."

"And," added the other, "our neighbors will make so many rejoicings at our return, that we must feel happy at going back to a place where we see ourselves respected."

"And most likely, I think," rejoined Lodovico, "there are a couple of young men, who will be foremost in the throng of those who express their joy at your return."

"Ay, ay, Sir," returned the father, "you guess rightly enough; they have both sweethearts, or they would not be so well satisfied to return home to our village, I warrant me; but they are both good young fellows, and I am thankful for any cause that may attach them to the place where they were born:—not, sir, but what they have been telling you about the rejoicings of our neighbours at seeing us safe home again, is true enough; we live in our village in the harmony of one family. If you think it worth your while, sir, to step down to our cottage after the moon is up to-night, you'll see young and old assembled on the green before it, dancing, and welcoming us home with the pipe and tabor."

The girls joined in their father's invitation, and Lodovico having accepted it, with much gaiety, and joked with the girls upon his bad chance of getting a partner, as they had both sweethearts, they found themselves arrived within a few paces of the village.

The old man and his daughters struck into a different path from that which led the other travellers to the *auberge*, and Lodovico, at parting from his new friends, promised to find them out by the time the moon was up, and the girls replied, that they should be quite affronted, if he broke his word.

On arriving at the inn, Claudio, eager again to see the pilgrim, enquired for the travellers who had preceded him; and his mortification was far from small, when he learnt that there were two inns in the village, and that the first party had gone to the other, as one auberge was not large enough to contain them all.

CHAPTER XVIII.

Mar. It is offended.
Ber. See, it stalks away,
Hor. Stay, speak: I charge thee, speak,
Mar. 'Tis gone, and will not answer.

HAMLET.

WHILST partaking of the refreshments which had been prepared for the travellers at the inn, Lodovico informed his friend of the promise he had made to join the dance by moonlight, and pressed Claudio to go with him. To this invitation, Claudio first replied in the negative, having formed the resolution of making some excuse for visiting the other inn in the course of the evening, and at least once more seeing the pilgrim, if chance denied that he should have any intercourse him; however, as the entreaties of Lodovico would admit of no denial, Claudio promised to accompany him, purposing, in his own mind, to steal away on the first opportunity given him, and go to the inn where the pilgrim had taken up his abode for the night.

When the moon was risen in full splendor, and Lodovico thought it time to keep his appointment, a little boy of the inn was engaged by him to conduct them to the cottage of old Jacques and his fair daughters. A few minutes' walk brought them within the sound of the pipe and tabor, and it produced an agitation of mirth throughout the frame of Lodovico; for he began to caper forward in elastic bounds, that soon left Claudio behind him.

By the time that Claudio came up to the party, Lodovico was acquainted with almost every individual of which it consisted, and prepared to introduce his friend to the rustic circle.

The scene before him was irresistibly cheering even to the senses of Claudio, though occupied principally by matters of nearer importance to his heart; and he could not immediately summon resolution to quit the spot of enchantment. The *paysannes*, dressed in their white petticoats, little jackets of coloured stuff, and their flowing hair bound round their heads with a wreath of flowers, culled from the uncultivated bed of nature, looked like the fairies of the scene, as they tripped along in light bounds, and exact measure to the melody of the pipe. The shepherds of the mountains, for such were their partners, moved by their sides with steps not inferior in grace to those of their shepherdesses: they were neatly dressed, and their spirits were the result of light and happy hearts; and under a tree, near the cottage door, sat the advanced in years of both sexes, drinking their lemonade to the happiness of their children.

Notwithstanding the fears that Lodovico had expressed of not getting a partner, where sweethearts were so plentiful, one was soon brought to him by old Jacques' daughters; and another being at the same time introduced by them to Claudio, he thought it impossible to refrain from going down one dance, however his inclination might lead to quitting the party; and accordingly taking her hand, with a compliment for the pleasure she conferred on him, he led her to the dance.

The name by which Jacques' daughter had introduced to Claudio the young girl who was just become his partner, was Nina de Saint Pierre: her face and figure were amongst the most attractive he had ever beheld; her stature was about the middle size, her limbs exquisitely turned, and every part so formed as to add to the regular beauty of the whole; her countenance was of the most interesting kind; her hair was nearly black, and hung curling, in natural ringlets, of the most playful glossiness, below her waist; her eyes were dark, and expressive of a heart where mildness of temper and good sense were united; her skin was fairer than that of most women whose eyes and hair are dark; the blush of the rose painted her cheeks, and the vermillion of the cherry stained her lips, upon which the smile of good humour constantly played. In her manner, there was a *naïveté* which betrayed innocence without displaying a want of that portion of sense without which the quality becomes a folly. Her dress added to the interest excited by her figure and person; she wore a white petticoat, round the border of which she had fastened the leaves and fruit of the wild strawberry; her jacket was of a pale blue, and her little straw hat was adorned with a wreath of the same shrub which ornamented her petticoat;—a single rose was stuck carelessly in her bosom, and her blooming cheeks appeared its twin flowers.

Lodovico's partner was a young woman of not so delicate proportions as Nina de Saint Pierre; her chief beauty was the florid health that marked her countenance; and Claudio observed, that from the beginning of the dance, Lodovico cast upon Nina an eye of admiration, which almost entirely abstracted his attention from his own partner. The moment the dance was concluded, he came running up to Claudio, and having whispered in his ear, "Did you ever see so lovely, so bewitching a creature as her with whom you have been dancing?"—moved up to her, without waiting Claudio's answer to his rapturous exclamation, and engaged her hand for the succeeding dances.

Claudio declined dancing any more for the present, and retiring by degrees from the throng, who were too much occupied to observe his actions minutely, he stole into the shade, and continued to move slowly towards that part of the village where he had been informed stood the little inn at which the pilgrim was a lodger. Being arrived at it, he had no excuse for going in, but that single apology for entering a house of public entertainment, of calling for his pint of wine. To his satisfaction, he was ushered into a public room, where he found all the members of the first division of travellers across the mountains, except him whom he wished to see.

To leave the room again immediately was almost to betray the cause of his having entered it: he accordingly constrained himself to sit down, and pretend to drink his wine. Out of the number which the room contained, the greater part were dozing over the fire, and of those who were perfectly awake, two only were conversing. Their topic was a point of religion; and after they had talked some time, not happening to agree, one of them said, "I wish the monk who journeyed with us across the mountains was here now: he would soon resolve us."

"I wish he were," replied the other, "I wonder where he is."

To this, a man in the chimney corner, who had hitherto been silent, answered, "I saw him just now, going towards that lump of rock at the foot of the mountain where the cross stands; likely he may be gone to tell his beads there."

Upon this, the disputants agreed, that they must wait his return for the decision of their debate; and Claudio knowing the pilgrim to be meant by those who had called him the monk, on account of the dress he now wore, made haste to finish his wine, and left the inn with a determination of walking towards the cross which the man in the chimney-corner had mentioned.

He left the inn, and meeting, by accident, near the door, with the same boy who had conducted him and Lodovico to the cottage of old Jacques, he enquired of him, if there was not a cross near to the spot where he was standing.

The boy replied in the affirmative, and asked if he should conduct him to it.

Claudio answered, that he wished only to have the path to it pointed out to him, which the boy having done, Claudio rewarded him for his trouble, and ordered him to leave him.

Gathering clouds had, in a great measure, obscured the light of the moon, since Claudio had entered the inn; and the uncertain light which it now cast on the objects around, rendered Claudio, for some time, at a loss what he discerned, where the entire scene was strange to him.—He proceeded about a furlong in the direction pointed out to him by the boy; and beginning to ascend a small eminence, which he concluded to be the lump of rock of which the man in the chimney-corner had spoken, he imagined, that on a spot where the light of the moon fell with a silvery and uncertain light, he beheld the figure of a man standing with his hands stretched out towards Heaven.—He concluded this must be the pilgrim; and feeling averse to interrupting his solitary devotions, he resolved to wind round the little eminence which he was ascending, and to watch his departure from the place where he now stood.

He accordingly changed his path from the straight direction in which he had been proceeding, and bent his steps to the right, which led him away from the figure he had just observed, though it still kept him within view of it. He had not proceeded many steps, when a lengthened groan, accompanied by the violent clapping of hands, as one in agony of mind, arrested his wandering senses: he saw no one, and continued to proceed for a few moments, imagining his ideas had deceived him; but a second groan, close to the spot on which he was moving, convinced him that the first had not been the result of imagination, and a voice, which then became audible to him, exclaimed, in smothered accents of grief, "Oh! protect, protect them."

Whether the sound of his steps aroused the devotee from his prayer, or whether his devotions were ended, Claudio was uncertain; but these words were no sooner pronounced, than a figure, which had hitherto escaped Claudio's observation by kneeling in the shade, advanced a few paces into the light, and Claudio immediately recognized it to be the pilgrim in his monk's habit.

"Who art thou?" the pilgrim said, in a voice of no very complacent tone, "that under the shadow of night's concealing veil, stealest thus upon me, to listen to the secrets of my soul, sent forth in prayer? Answer me: what was thy intention?"

"Neither to interrupt you, or to learn your secrets," replied Claudio: "had I known how you were engaged, I had bent my steps another way."

"Who are you?" asked the pilgrim.

"One whom you have seen before, but do not recognize," answered Claudio. "Do you not recollect being once entertained at the villa di Bartelma, in the vicinity of Florence, on your return from a pilgrimage?"

"I remember it well," was the reply; "proceed."

"You honoured the son of your entertainer with your particular notice," returned Claudio; "It is he who now addresses you."

The pilgrim started, and a few moments of silence ensued; he broke it by saying, "Tell me, I command you to tell me, *what* you heard me utter."

"When?" asked Claudio, in an agitation which he could not easily command.

"*Now*, in my prayer," returned the pilgrim, in a voice of horror, that made Claudio tremble.

"I only heard you sigh, and then say, 'Oh! protect, protect them.'"

"Do not deceive me!" exclaimed the pilgrim, seizing Claudio by the throat, "or by Heaven———"

"Indeed, I heard no more!" exclaimed Claudio, interrupting him in alarm.

"God be praised!" returned the pilgrim, and he crossed his hands upon his breast, as he bowed down his body towards the earth.—"Leave me, leave me immediately," he added, after a short pause.

"I hope I have not offended you," said Claudio.

"Leave me, boy," repeated the pilgrim with emphasis, and turned his back towards him as he spoke.

Claudio walked slowly away, distracted by his doubts, and agonized still more by the improbability of having them explained.—He walked on, without being conscious which way he moved, and with his eyes bent towards the ground;—presently he ran with violence against something which obstructed his progress; he raised his eyes, and found it to be the cross, which he had before, at a short distance, supposed to be a man in prayer. The force of the blow had almost stunned him, and with his hand pressed upon his head, he turned his face accidentally round towards the spot from whence he was proceeding, and saw the pilgrim, at some distance, following his steps. He doubted whether to stop, or to go on; but the injunctions under which he had lain from his birth, rushing forcibly on his thoughts, and being uncertain whether obtruding himself into the society of this very man might not be acting in opposition to them, he moved quickly away. The Marchese di Bartelma, he recollected, had told him that it was evident, from the nature of the injunctions laid upon him, that he had enemies as well as friends in the world.—Might not this man be an enemy whose society he had been thus eagerly seeking?—This idea, backed by the strange conduct of the pilgrim within the last few minutes, alarmed him, and he quickened his pace, without knowing or regarding which way he turned his steps.

He had proceeded some way without stopping, when a rivulet, which ran across his path, intercepted his course; he looked behind him, and seeing the pilgrim advancing close upon his steps, he was on the point of trusting to the shallowness of the water, and wading across to the other side; when the pilgrim, in the same voice of complacent mildness which had so much won his heart on his visit to the villa di Bartelma, called out, "Stop, my dear Claudio, hear me; I beseech you to hear me; by heaven! you have nothing to fear from me."

The prepossessions of the human heart are unaccountable; such were Claudio's in favor of the pilgrim; his softened voice pleaded to Claudio's heart, and although he was not free from alarm, a preponderancy of idea in favor of this stranger arrested his steps, and induced him to suffer his hand to be taken by that of the pilgrim.

The hand which the pilgrim had taken was not that on the wrist of which the mysterious bracelet was fastened. The pilgrim pressed the hand he held with the strict grasp of friendship, and said, "Are you happy with the Marchese di Bartelma?—Fear not to tell me."

"I have not an ungratified wish under his protection," replied Claudio.

"Do you feel grateful to him for his care of you?" asked the pilgrim.

"I were a monster of ingratitude not to adore him for the interest he has ever taken in my welfare," replied Claudio.

"Heaven be praised that you are happy," rejoined the pilgrim; "But is it really true, that you have no wish ungratified?"

Claudio knew not how to reply, and hesitated in silence.

"I see your fears," rejoined the pilgrim, "and I will relieve you—first swear to me, that however you may be interrogated, or by whomsoever, you will not divulge that you have——" At this moment, the voice of a shepherd, close behind them, calling home his goats from the mountain, roused the pilgrim from the trance of reflection into which he had fallen; he started, and exclaiming, "We are interrupted; I cannot hazard remaining with you.—Thanks be to the Almighty powers that you are happy. Do not expect ever to see me again; if we *should* ever meet *again* by chance, I charge you, as you value your hopes of heaven, not to let it appear that we have ever met *before*; farewell."——And having thus said, he again pressed the hand of Claudio, and ran swiftly up the side of the mountain, where the thick underwood, and the partial shadows of the overhanging crags, swiftly shut him from the sight of the astonished Claudio.

END OF THE FIRST VOLUME.

Astonishment!!!

Volume II

ASTONISHMENT!!!

CHAPTER I.

> ————————This is a creature,
> Would she begin a sect, might quench the zeal
> Of all professors else, make proselytes
> Of who she but bid follow.
>
> THE WINTER'S TALE.

BEFORE Claudio had time to reflect on the past, the shepherd came up to him, and addressed him with, "Good even, Signor. Whither stray you at this late hour?"

"I am a stranger in this part of the country," replied Claudio, "and have been wandering about I know not where; if you are going to the village, I shall be glad to accompany you."

"Yes, I am," replied the shepherd. "I seldom go home thus early in an evening; but I expect to find my father and sisters returned from a long journey, which they have been making into Italy, and that hurries me home to-night."

"Is your father's name Jacques?" asked Claudio.

"Pray, if I may be so free, Signor, how could you, that are a stranger here, guess that?" rejoined the youth in surprise.

Claudio then explained to him how his acquaintance with his father and sisters had commenced; and Robert hearing of the frolics which were going forward at home, whistled lustily to his flock to accelerate their pace. In a short time, they arrived at the field where Robert enclosed his sheep for the night; and this task being performed, it took but a few minutes more to conduct Claudio back to the dancers on the green.

On the arrival of Robert, the dance was immediately broken off, and his sisters led him between them to their father. Nina de

Saint Pierre was still dancing with Lodovico; but on the interruption of the dance, she came running up to Claudio, and with that simple frankness which marks the innocence and good humour of the heart, she said, "I fear I have offended you, Signor."

"Why do you express this apprehension?" asked Claudio.

"Because," replied she, "it is customary for our young men to dance alternate dances with the woman whom they first lead out, and you have been absent now four dances."

"Upon my word," returned Claudio, "you are much mistaken, in thinking that I could have received any other than the greatest pleasure in having your hand for the dance; and had I known, that the rules of your society had decreed me the happiness a second time, you should not have found me absent at the moment the satisfaction was to be enjoyed."

"Oh, Signor!" returned she, "I did not speak with the intention of receiving this fine compliment from you, I only mentioned my fears, that if I had displeased you, I might have an opportunity of expressing to you, how unwillingly I had offended."

"We will banish all doubts then," said Claudio, "in dancing together immediately."—He was then leading her to the dance, when Lodovico running up to them, exclaimed, "No, upon my honour, I won't give up my partner; if you had wished to have had her again, you should have kept in the way at the time she was yours by right; now you have forfeited your pretensions, I swear she is mine for the rest of the evening."

Lodovico attempted to speak this sentence in the voice of good humour and raillery; but Claudio observed, that the quick turn of his eye, cast in raptures on the countenance of Nina, denoted a warmer interest than that of common gallantry to be concealed for her in his heart. "We must follow the rules of the ball," replied Claudio, smiling. "Nina claims me for another dance, and you cannot object to our taking it, as it is to be the reconciler of a little quarrel we have had; but after that, if she will accept solely of your hand for the rest of the evening, I will petition her to excuse my dancing any more, as I am fatigued with my journey, and shall be glad to retire to rest."

Lodovico complied with this arrangement with but an indifferent grace, and Claudio joined the dance with Nina for his partner.—"It is very kind of you, Signor," she said, in the same playful innocence of voice and manner with which every sentence she had spoken had been uttered, "to give up dancing yourself, that your friend may enjoy the more of the amusement; and indeed it is but fair of you so to do, for he seems much fonder of it than you do."

This was a reproach upon his thoughtfulness, which Claudio perceived that the speaker did not intend to convey, yet evidently felt.—"My friend," said Claudio, "is a merry young fellow, in full health and spirits: I am not quite well, or you should find me a better partner."—"If that is the case," said she, "and you only go down this dance on purpose to make it up with me; believe me, I'll forgive you, without your putting yourself to the pain."

The dance was now beginning, and Claudio had no further opportunity for conversation with his partner, till they reached the bottom: he then said, "I am sure my friend ought to hold a higher rank in your estimation than myself; for whilst you have been dancing with me, he has remained disengaged."—"Notwithstanding his being so fond of dancing," said she.—Lodovico advanced towards them, and Nina, turning round her head, said to him, "I am sorry that your complaisance to me, should have prevented all the other damsels from so engaging a partner as yourself."—"If you really flatter me by thinking so," replied Lodovico, with a satisfaction sparkling in his eyes which he could not conceal, "it is but a justice due to your compliment, that I should reserve myself wholly for you."—The dance was just then concluded, and Nina, addressing Claudio, said, "Are you *sure* you sha'n't dance any more, signor?" To which Claudio having answered in the affirmative, she turned to Lodovico, and said, "Then, signor, I won't dance with any body but you the rest of the evening, that it may not be my fault if you are without a partner."

It did not require much penetration in Claudio to observe, that Lodovico was struck with the little *paysanne*, and that she was evidently pleased by the attention which he showed her; and Claudio was also convinced, that however unable Lodovico was to deny himself any pleasure which his heart pointed out as desirable, and his ability rendered attainable, still he feared no evil from his friend's attacks upon the vanity of Nina; for he was well convinced, that a heart of innocent simplicity is a safeguard to its possessor against the *open* attempts of evil; and that Lodovico's departure in the morning, would render it not worth his while to begin a *covert* siege upon her affections. From these reasonings with his own mind, he felt satisfied, that no ill would accrue to Nina from the flattery of Lodovico, but perhaps the shedding of a few tears at his departure from the village where she dwelt; and from this assurance of his own mind, he felt satisfied to let them enjoy the innocent pleasures to which the evening gave opportunity without interruption.

When Claudio left the dance, in order not to appear proud or reserved, ill adapted as was his mind to conversation, especially such as he could have no interest in, he joined the party of elders, who were chatting under the shadowing boughs of two lofty chesnuts.

Their chat was upon the qualities, tempers, and accomplishments of the gay group before them; and their commendations fell principally on Nina.

Claudio enquired who she was; and his neighbours informed him, that she was the daughter of Louis de Saint Pierre, who sat on his other side.

Claudio turned to observe him, and found him a hale, healthy man, who appeared about sixty years of age: the snow of old age had whitened his head, but the damask of the rose had not fled from his cheeks; his stature was rather tall, and not bent by the infirmities of age. He was somewhat corpulent, and strongly made; but what particularly pleased Claudio in his appearance, was the smile of content and cheerfulness which constantly sat on his countenance, and bespoke the gratitude of his heart to a superior power.

Claudio entered into conversation with him, and Louis' favorite topic soon became the subject of their discourse; this was his daughter Nina. The old man led instinctively to the description of her beauty and attractions; and then dwelt, parent-like, with rapture on their repetition from the lips of Claudio.

The envious clock of the village now striking eleven, and the moon beginning to withdraw her light, Jacques announced to the group of dancers, that it was time to put an end to their diversion;—which information was received with a faint murmur, and the pipe immediately flowed through a soft cadence, which announced its dying breath for that night.

After a cheerful good-night, pronounced again and again from every mouth, they all took the different paths which led to their humble dwellings. Lodovico resolutely drawing the arm of Nina through his, and declaring that he would see her safe home: Louis de Saint Pierre, who had witnessed his attention to his daughter during the evening, well knew that to raise no objections to his walking with her, was the best method to make his marked conduct of the least consequence, proceeded along on her other side, in chat with Claudio. Arrived at the cottage of Saint Pierre, he went in with his daughter; and wishing Claudio and Lodovico a good night, closed his door with resoluteness, though not with impertinence.

Lodovico was chagrined at not having been invited to enter the cottage; but he was obliged to content himself with calling out aloud to Nina, that he would pay her a visit before his departure in the morning, and hoped to find her not fatigued by her dance.

As soon as they were out of the hearing of those in the cottage, Lodovico burst, with all the vehemence of a man whose passions are violently raised, rather than the warmth of one whose heart is sensibly touched, into all those raptures with which Claudio expected to hear him declare the lovely Nina had inspired him.

Well acquainted with the effervescence, as well as changeableness of his temper, Claudio suffered him to proceed in the relation of his extacies with little interruption, not doubting, but a few days, if not a single night's, absence from the goddess of his present adorations, would considerably weaken, perhaps entirely extinguish, the flame which was now burning with such fierceness in his heart.

CHAPTER II.

> *Fal.* Go to; you are a woman, go.
> *Host.* Who I? I defy thee; I was never
> Called so in mine own house before.
>
> FIRST PART OF HENRY THE FOURTH.

ON reaching the inn, those who had been their fellow travellers through the day had already retired to bed; their tutor alone was waiting their coming, and having ordered in an *omelet* and a boiled chicken, which he had provided against their return, they sat down to supper. The tutor, however, was the only one of the party capable of enjoying the meal of which himself had been the caterer. Claudio had no appetite, and complained of a head-ache as an apology for not eating; and Lodovico endeavoured to persuade himself, that his love for the cottager's daughter was so violent, as to preclude the passage of his supper into his stomach.

"Oh, lovely Nina!" exclaimed Lodovico, walking about the room in all the agitation of a delirium, "impossible that thy form, thy eyes, and thy lips, can be those of a cottager's daughter! impossible that thou canst be the daughter of Louis de Saint Pierre, the shepherd!"

The hostess had just brought upon the table her smoking *omelet* and ragged pullet, as Lodovico uttered this rhapsody to the fair maid of his devotions; and turning about her head at the conclusion of his sentence, she said, "Aye, Signor, very true, that is what many people hereabouts say."

"Say, what?—What do you mean?" exclaimed Lodovico, awakened from his trance of reflection by the interchiming of his hostess' voice.

"Why, what you said just now, Signor," replied she, "that Nina de Saint Pierre has too much beauty and delicacy to be a shepherd's daughter."

"Do they say so?" asked Lodovico, impatiently.

"Oh, yes," answered the hostess: "I for my own part often say so."

"And what is your reason?" enquired Claudio.

"Nay, I can't say that I have much reason," returned the landlady, "only I have heard other people say so.——You would like a little pepper with your *omelet*, I dare say, Signor," she added, addressing the tutor; and, without waiting for a reply, left the room.

Lodovico immediately began to call her back with all the lustiness of voice he was capable of exerting; and finding that she did not directly return, he stamped about the room, to wear away the moments till she came. When she appeared, "Leave the room again at your peril, till you have answered me all the questions I want to have resolved," said Lodovico, leaning his back against the door.

"I only went for the pepper, Signor," returned the hostess; "and if it had not been to grind, I should have been back in half a second; but my husband uses the pepper-mill to grind his snuff, and so————"

"What the devil does all this signify to me?" cried Lodovico. "Cannot you hold your tongue one moment, and listen to what I have to say to you?"

"Certainly, Signor," she answered, "I am at your service now, to listen to any thing you have to say; I shall not attempt to leave the room, without the Signor at supper calls for any thing that is not upon the table; and then————"

"Let him fetch it himself, or go without it," cried Lodovico.

Lodovico had no sooner uttered this sentence, than finding he had been too hasty in his expression, he turned to his tutor, and said, "I beg your pardon for the words which escaped my tongue; but the impertinence of this talkative woman, threw me off my guard." And the tutor, like many who have followed, if not resembling any who had then gone before him, loved eating much better than letting a delicate supper get cool, either while he took offence or acknowledged apologies, and consequently, continued eating in silence.

"Why do you think, I ask you," said Lodovico, again turning to the hostess, and still maintaining his situation against the door, "that Nina is not a shepherd's child?—Do you think that Louis de Saint Pierre is not her father, or that he is not what he seems to be?"

"Why as to that, we can't exactly tell," returned she: "Louis is not a native of this part of the country, and his wife that is dead came from Paris, I know, because my great aunt knew her grandfather.—Louis' wife has been dead now sixteen years, and I reckon Nina is about seventeen years old."

"But you can tell whether she was born here, or brought to Louis' cottage when she was an infant."

"No, I can't, Signor," replied the hostess, "because the winter she was said to be born, there was a very great fall of snow from the mountains, so violent that we could not stir out of our own doors for almost six weeks, and when we began to get out again a little, my husband brought news home, that Louis de Saint Pierre's wife was brought to bed of a little girl."

"And why should not this have been the case?" asked Lodovico.

"Because," answered the hostess, "she had never appeared to any of us to be with child, and if she really had been brought to bed in the fall of snow, the goodness of God must have been all the help she had in her trouble; for I am sure, no mortal could get near the cottage to help her."

"Then," said Claudio, smiling, "it must have been equally impossible for any one to have conveyed a child to Saint Pierre's cottage during the fall of snow."

"Aye, how can you explain that difficulty?" asked Lodovico, impatiently.

"Oh! as to that," replied the hostess, "great folks can find roads that poor men can't discover; money will make bridges over snow and water; neither fire nor sandy deserts can stop them that have gold to pave the way with."

"You imagine then that some person of consequence had her conveyed to Saint Pierre's cottage?" said Lodovico.

"Oh, I don't pretend to say any thing for truth," answered the landlady; "I have only been telling you my guessings. And as to her being a great body's child, all I knew of the matter is, that an old man that used to live in our neighbourhood, and pick up a little money by telling fortunes, once said, in the kitchen of this very house, that he firmly believed her who was called Nina de Saint Pierre to be the bastard of a duchess."

At this information, and particularly the means by which it had been obtained, Claudio, and even Lodovico himself, burst into a fit of laughter.

"Well, Signors," cried the landlady, rather nettled at the contempt put upon what she regarded in a serious light, "you need not believe me without you please; but the old man I mention was the son of a seventh son, and if such as he don't know, I can't pretend to say who should."

"Pshaw, an old fool!" exclaimed Lodovico.

"I shall keep my opinion of him for all that," returned the landlady; "and I thank my stars, I have not the profaneness to speak thus of one whose wisdom, when he was alive, must easily convince us, that he has the power of punishing an insult to his memory now he is in the happy abode of the blessed;" and having so said, she crossed herself, pulled open the door, in spite of the weight Lodovico was still impressing upon it, and bounced out of the room.

After the departure of the hostess, who did not again make her appearance in the supper room, Claudio and Lodovico began to review the hints which she had thrown out relative to the noble birth of Nina; and having coolly weighed them, they concluded, that from the little certainty with which the hostess had been able to speak of what she called her most successful guesses, there was little reason to believe, that there was any foundation for such a report, but the talkative credulity and superstition of the ignorant neighbourhood.

At all events, Lodovico's passion was fixed on Nina as a woman, and not on her pedigree. Thus the subject which he had encouraged the hostess in speaking upon, only because Nina was its topic, he now quickly dropped; and Claudio felt no interest in attempting to dive into the private history of a girl whom, in all probability, he should never see again after the following morning.

After some time, Lodovico, who declared he could not sleep, was induced to go to bed, and Claudio, on retiring to his chamber, found indeed that reflection banished sleep. The whole of his mysterious life passed in review before his thoughts; but most forcibly, as is always the case with last impressions, did his interview of that night with the pilgrim engage his reflection. Why did the pilgrim first upbraid him for approaching him, and then follow him with terms of kindness?—For whom could he have been imploring the protection of Heaven? And above all, what could it be that he was on the point of imparting to him?—Then, how strange that he should have said, they should never meet again; and his having charged him, if they ever *did* meet again, not to let it appear that they had been known to each other *before*. Was it possible, that the man with whom he had that evening been in conversation was the author of his being?—He shuddered upon the possibility, and thought became suspended in a chaos of contending feelings.

Claudio had informed the Marchese di Bartelma of what had occurred between him and the pilgrim, on the morning of the latter's departure from the villa of his benefactor, after he had been entertained there on his way to Florence; and his mind was now engaged in considering, whether it did not become him, in conformity with his former conduct, to inform the Marchese, by letter, of what had now passed between him and the same mysterious personage.

After much debate with himself, he concluded, that in the precarious situation in which the papers in the possession of his benefactor declared him to be living, it was dangerous to trust a communication of the importance of his discourse that evening with the pilgrim to writing; and, accordingly, he resolved to reserve it for the delivery of his tongue to the private ear of the Marchese, on his return from his present travels.

Unable to rest, he undrew the curtain which shaded from his view the towering mountains over which he had that day been journeying: the moon was sinking behind them, and its faint beauties just tinged their snowy tops with its fading influence. Beneath the foot of the Alps, the hamlet, of which the auberge he was now in formed a part, was faintly visible; and the solitary lamps which were seen in some few of the cottage windows, appeared a spark of fire compared to the pale face of the declining moon.—The scene was in unison with his feelings; and tearing a leaf from his pocket-book, wrote with his pencil the following

SONNET.

Behold! the moon beams on yon mountain's brow,
    Silv'ring the cedars on its rugged side;
Its barren top congeal'd with whit'ning snow,
    Inur'd to cold, the northern blast derides.

The glim'ring taper from yon lowly cot
    Beams the glad witness of domestic bliss;
Views the fond wife exulting in her lot,
    Whilst on her babes the father prints his kiss.

Sure sights like these might sooth the ruffled mind,
    Obliterate the pangs of sorrow past;
Anticipation gild with joys refined,
    And smooth the brow by memory's cloud o'er-cast:

But whelm'd in doubt, each stranger form I view,
May be *that father* whom I never knew!

At an hour by no means so early as that at which they had risen on the preceding morning, Claudio and Lodovico met in the passage from which their respective doors opened.—"Well," said, Claudio, "how have you slept?"

"Oh, vastly well!" replied Lodovico, "after I once fell asleep; that little gipsey I danced with though, kept me awake full *half an hour.*"

"Well, well," said Claudio, "if you experienced no greater inconvenience from the scintillation of her eyes; you won't die this bout, I promise you."

"Oh! I don't expect it," rejoined Lodovico; "but upon my honor, Claudio, and setting all joking apart, I am most desperately in love with her for all that.—Do you think there would be any impropriety in going to the old man's cottage, and inviting ourselves to breakfast with him?"

"Upon my word, I think it is an unwarrantable liberty for any man, but one who is prepared to offer a girl his hand, to take in the house of a father of a family to whom he is almost a stranger," replied Claudio.

"Then we will certainly wait to pay our visit till after breakfast," answered Lodovico; "for as to making an offer of my hand to any woman, is at present the farthest thing from my thoughts, I assure you; especially to a shepherd's daughter, though my hostess vouches for her being the bastard of a duchess, upon the authority of a seventh son's son, who is now in the happy abode of the blessed."

Breakfast was accordingly ordered to be got ready directly; and when it was concluded, Lodovico having told his tutor he should be ready to depart in little more than an hour's time, took Claudio's arm to proceed to the cottage of Louis de Saint Pierre. On their way thither, they met Mathurine, Jacques' eldest daughter, and having informed her whither they were going, Lodovico would admit of no denial to her accompanying them.

Arrived at the cottage of Louis, they found the door shut, and the shutter of the lower window closed.

Lodovico knocked, but received no answer: he repeated his summons, but still in vain: and as he was on the point of again announcing with his fist, that there were visitors waiting on the outside of the door, an old woman put out her head from an opposite cottage, and said, "Do you want Louis de Saint Pierre?"

"The same," replied Lodovico.—

"You will not find him at home," she returned; "he and his daughter set off early this morning into the country, and will not return in some days: they left this message with me before they set off, that I might inform any one who might enquire for them in their absence."

"In what direction are they travelling?" asked Lodovico.—"I am not acquainted;" answered the old woman, and drawing in her head, closed the door.

"Is it usual with Louis thus to leave his home, and take his daughter with him?" said Lodovico, addressing Mathurine.—"Yes," she returned, "he generally goes out for about a week at a time once every year."

"Is this the time of the year he usually goes?" asked Lodovico.

"The time of the year is uncertain," she answered, "but this is the month he went in last year."

"Where does he go to?" was the subsequent question.

"To see some relatives he has about twenty leagues from hence; but I do not know exactly the situation of their dwelling, or the name of the place," replied Mathurine; "it is somewhere amongst the mountains."

This discourse brought them to the cottage of Jacques, to whom and his other daughter, Jeannette, Claudio and Lodovico had promised to bid farewell, previous to their departure from the village.

They were invited to sit down; and grapes and new bread were brought out to them, of which they partook, in compliment to their entertainers. During their stay at the cottage, Lodovico mentioned what had the evening before passed between him and the hostess, relative to Nina de Saint Pierre, and enquired of the family where he now was, whether any credit was to be given to her assertions?

Jeannette replied, "That the hostess was a censorious woman, and an unpleasant neighbour; that her giving credit to the fortune-teller was accounted for in his being her own cousin, and that no reports of Nina being the child of any one but Louis de Saint Pierre and his wife Maria, who had long been dead, had ever been circulated in the village."

After some further conversation at the cottage, and promising to call in upon its inhabitants, if chance should ever lead them again to that spot, Claudio and Lodovico rose to depart; Lodovico not forgetting to entrust a soft message for Nina to the care of her friends, Mathurine and Jeannette. Claudio desired them to inform her, that he had remembered her at quitting the village, though he did not convey his remembrance in so rapturous language as his friend; and the girls having promised to deliver the messages with which they were entrusted, and intreated the Signors to accept some grapes, the growth of their vineyard, to regale themselves with on their journey; Claudio and Lodovico pronounced the last farewell to their fair entertainers, and then proceeded to the inn, where finding every thing prepared for their departure, they in a few minutes sat forward on their journey.

CHAPTER III.

> ————Pry'thee, see there!
> Behold! look! lo!————
> ————Hence, horrible shadow!
> Unreal mockery, hence!————
>
> MACBETH.

CONTRARY to Claudio's expectation, the impression which Nina de Saint Pierre had made on Lodovico proved a durable one: not a day passed in which he did not extol some one of her perfections, or draw a comparison much in her favor between her and some other woman in whose way accident threw him.

With equal obstinacy, did Claudio's mysterious meeting with the pilgrim continue to rest on his spirits, as the perfections of Nina dwelt on the mind of Lodovico; with this difference only between their feelings, that the subject of Lodovico's thoughts afforded him a constant topic of conversation; Claudio's were confined to his moments of solitary reflection.

The introductory letters which the Count di Ponta's interest had enabled him to put into the hands of his son and Claudio, procured them numerous attentions and civilities in every city which they visited: at Vienna, they were particularly fortunate in the formation of acquaintance, and received an introduction to the court of the emperor. But what particularly contributed to the pleasure of their residence in the capital of the German empire, was their knowledge of a family who, having formerly been indebted for civilities of a similar nature to the Count di Ponta, were strenuous to return the politeness they had experienced.

That branch of the family which was the particular entertainers of the Italian friends, consisted of a young man, a few years older than themselves; his wife, a most beautiful and accomplished woman; and their five children. The happiness of this couple appeared uninterrupted, nor did they seem to form an idea of any enjoyment beyond the circle of their domestic bliss. Their felicity was such as could not escape even the observation of an inconsiderate brain like Lodovico's; and one evening, when Claudio and himself returned to their hotel, after having passed the day in this enviable family, Lodovico exclaimed, "Upon my soul, Claudio, I have thought to-day, for the first time, that it is possible for a man to be both married and happy. What think you of the matter?"

"It has long been a decided opinion with me," returned Claudio.

"Indeed!" ejaculated Lodovico; "if this is the case, you must have seen the woman with whom you imagine you could enjoy this happy state. I must quarrel with you for not giving me as full a share of your confidence as I place in you."

"My observation," returned Claudio, "referred to no particular object, I assure you."

"Well," cried Lodovico, "it appears strange indeed to my weak brain, how you can imagine a happiness, of which you can't call to your fancy all the component parts of the pleasing fascination Now were it possible for me to think of matrimony, I should place myself in the situation of our German friend, put Nina by my side, instead of his *cara sposa*, and as to the children—why, I think, the picture will be highly enough finished to my taste without the addition of them."

Claudio smiled, but did not reply.

"And so you positively don't prefer any one woman in the creation to another?" exclaimed Lodovico, after a pause.

"I did not say that either," replied Claudio.

"Aye, aye; but I mean in the way of a wife," rejoined Lodovico.

"So do I," answered Claudio.

"Oh! you do confess then that one of Cupid's sly arrows has touched your heart," cried Lodovico. "I'll guess her name in three times for any wager you please."

Claudio smiled again in silence; for being unable himself to decide whether the woman he best loved was Zelia or Valeria, he feared not that his friend should make a discovery in a random guess, which he had himself not been able to decide in many months' reflection.

"I know your secret, I'll swear I do," exclaimed Lodovico, rubbing his hands, in exultation. "The shaft that wounded your tender heart was shot from the eyes of my wicked sister, or I am a nun."

"Why do you think so?" asked Claudio, endeavouring to keep a composed countenance, and wishing to hear Lodovico's sentiments upon the subject in question.

"Oh! I am sure of it," replied Lodovico. "Her name is never mentioned but you heave a sigh, which you endeavour to smother in a pretended cough; and then, when you are at the pallazo, you pluck a rose, and carry it to Valeria, because you heard her praise the colour of that particular sort: she receives it with a blush and a smile; and you are fit to drop a tear upon it, in the extacy of your heart, at seeing that she is pleased with it."

"Oh! you become quite ridiculous," said Claudio.

"Not half so ridiculous (begging your pardon, my dear friend) as that confusion of yours makes you appear. Come, come, don't be angry, because I have found out your secret. I don't ask you to confess: perhaps there is some agreement of secrecy between you, and I won't tempt you to break it by urging you any further upon the subject; so give me your hand, and I have done."

Claudio extended his hand to meet that of Lodovico, who pressing that of his friend in a strict grasp, said, "If it is as I suspect, I wish you happy with all my heart. I know no man whom I should be so well pleased to call brother as yourself; and there let the subject rest, till you think proper to begin it again to me."

Claudio nipped the hand of his friend with a warmth equal to that with which he had pressed his, and turned away in silence.

"Oh, that I had never seen Zelia!" again burst from the lips of Claudio on entering his private apartment. "Of the actual possession of how much real happiness does her idea deprive me? Why cannot I summon resolution to ensure my permanent felicity, by closing my eyes upon the mysterious phantom of pleasure which is continually flitting before my senses in the shape of the incomprehensible Zelia? How unaccountable, how strange, that the feelings of man should be thus at variance with his felicity! It must be the part of man, to pluck out from his mind the vividly coloured weeds of giddy fascination, which would choke up the modest flower of true pleasure. Zelia shall be banished from my thoughts, and Valeria become the reward of my conquest over the error of my heart. With this resolution firm in his mind, he closed his eyes, and enjoyed a night of calmer repose than he had ever yet experienced, when sleep had overtaken him with his fancy burningly alive to the charms of Zelia.

Claudio and Lodovico had been rather more than eleven months absent from Italy when they entered the busy scenes of Paris. Here they found letters from the Count di Ponta and the Marchese di Bartelma, which gave them the satisfaction of learning, that those they left behind them were well, and anticipating the pleasure of their return.

Lodovico indulged himself freely in the society of the Parisian ladies, but still there was scarcely a day that he did not break out into raptures in the praise of Nina de Saint Pierre.

Claudio acted neither the part of the libertine, nor the Stoic; and feeling, with extreme satisfaction, that a firm adherence to the resolution he had taken at Vienna, of not suffering Zelia to occupy his thoughts, had already effected a considerable change in his heart in favor of Valeria; he now formed the pleasing idea of making a declaration of his passion to her at his return into Italy.

One evening, after retiring to his chamber, he held a longer than usual conversation with his own mind, and finding himself capable of devoting his thoughts solely to the happiness of one object, which he conceived it the duty of every man to have determined to do, before he should make any woman an offer of his hand; he resolved on the next morning to impart to Lodovico his intentions of addressing Valeria in the character of her admirer.

Having extinguished his lamp, as was his usual custom before retiring to rest, Claudio entered his bed a little before midnight, and in a few moments, a soft doze, which announced the approach of sounder sleep, took possession of his frame.—How long he had been in bed, or whether a profound sleep had overtaken his senses, he was uncertain, when the sudden undrawing of the curtains at the foot of his bed made him start up in that wild alarm which attends the abrupt interruption of sleep.

He cast his eyes forward to that part of the chamber from whence the noise had proceeded, and to his astonishment beheld a number of thin and sparkling flames dancing before his sight on the wall opposite to the foot of his bed.—In a few seconds, his senses became capable of abstracting ideas; he recollected where he was, and knew that the rapid undrawing of the curtains at the foot of his bed had awakened him, and he now perceived that the flames upon the wall formed these words,

> Valeria must not be the wife of Claudio!
> She whom he is destined to wed,
> shall be shown to him in
> A VISION.

No sooner had he decyphered the burning letters, than the whole faded from his sight in a momentary eclipse, and the curtains of the bed were rapidly drawn back into their former situation.

For some minutes, Claudio continued sitting up in his bed, uncertain how to act; he had hitherto possessed no faith in supernatural appearances, and would have immediately been convinced, that what he had just seen was the effect of mortal hands, had it not been a mystery beyond his solution, how any one could have become acquainted with his love for Valeria, which he had kept the close prisoner of his own breast.

Determined however to ascertain whether any juggling trick had been played him from the adjoining apartment, he sprang from his bed, and hastily drawing on a few of his clothes, he issued out into the passage upon which his chamber opened, and where a light constantly burnt throughout the night, resolved to explore the adjoining room, and if possible discover the means by which the strange appearance had been introduced to his sight.

Having left his chamber, he took down the lamp from the wall of the passage, and without considering who might occupy the adjoining chamber, he went in: he looked eagerly round, but nothing was to be seen, except the disorder of clothes, which denoted some one to have undressed in the room: he stood still, and listened; the suspiration of a person asleep met his ear from the bed; he approached it gently, and drawing the curtain aside, beheld Lodovico buried in sleep.

He again looked round the room, narrowly searching whether there was not some closet in the wall which separated his apartment from that of his friend, but no such was to be found; he knelt down, and examined whether any one had secreted themselves under the bed, still nothing was to be seen:—he again walked round the chamber, dissatisfied with his search; again he listened; all was motionless, and not a sound met his ear, save the breathings of Lodovico, and the ticking of his watch upon a table by his bed-side.

After some time, Claudio returned to his own chamber: he lighted his lamp, and closing his door, threw himself into a chair, almost afraid to acknowledge to his own mind, that he believed the appearance which he had that night witnessed, to be supernatural.

The present mystery, like every one which had hitherto attended the life of Claudio, became more complex by reflection.—"Why must not Valeria be the wife of Claudio?"

"And who could be the destined wife that was to be shown to him in a vision!"

These last words seemed to imply, that he had never yet seen her: had not such seemed to be their import, he would immediately have concluded, from the contents of the letter which had been left for him at the pallazo of the Count di Ponta, that this predestined wife, thus strangely announced to him, could be no other than Zelia. But then, how could Zelia, or indeed any one connected with her, have gained the slightest hint that his heart had ever been inclined to the sister of his friend? Or had that fact, which he considered as an impossibility, have reached the ears of Zelia, or any of her agents, how could they have found the means of entering a private hotel at that hour of the night, and of escaping, unheard or unseen by him, with all the apparatus which must have been necessary for the artificial performance of the mysterious writing on the wall?

He rose from his chair, and taking the lamp in his hand, examined attentively every part of the wall on which the luminous letters had appeared; but to no purpose: there was not the slightest incision in the tapestry by which the lights that composed the letters could have been admitted into the chamber, or indeed any mark whatever which denoted any such transaction as that which Claudio had just witnessed to have transpired.

After pacing his chamber for some time, he threw himself upon his bed, but without the hope of that night enjoying the refreshment of sleep. He thought not so much on the past as the future.

The promised vision rested most forcibly on his mind. Was he to expect its appearance in a similar manner to that he had just witnessed? or was it to be represented to him in his sleep? These were questions naturally arising in the mind of a man, situated as Claudio then was; but they were obliged to be dismissed from his brain unanswered. After much irresolute debate with his own mind, he determined to postpone the intention he had a few hours before entertained, of confessing on the following morning to Lodovico, his love for Valeria, although he could not decide, whether or not he had any just cause for so doing; and he also resolved not to impart to any one the occurrence of the night, as he considered, that if it was the trick of mortals, his publicly speaking of it might be the means of his never discovering the truth; and that were it otherwise, it were better, for his own sake, to conceal what he could not explain.

In the course of the following morning, Claudio took occasion to enquire of several of the family, whether they had not heard a noise in the house about midnight; and being replied to in the negative, he turned off their enquiries into what cause had led him to ask this question, by saying, he believed he had been disturbed by a dream; and as he treated the subject thus lightly, no one enlarged upon it to him, and the conversation was dropped.

Claudio was possessed of a resolute mind; and his efforts to conceal from Lodovico, that an unpleasant subject was rankling in his breast, were as successful as he desired them to be.

The two following nights passed on uninterruptedly in the chamber of Claudio. The ideas which had floated constantly in his brain during the day, danced throughout the night before his sleeping fancy; but he had no dream of sufficient consistency for him to decide it the promised vision.

CHAPTER IV.

―――――Fancy's hand delights in youth to spread
Delusive colours on the future hour.

Moist from her pencil tempting scenes arise:
On common life, Romance's tints she lays;
Till cold reality her hand applies,
And at the touch each flatter'd form decays.
MRS. OPIE.

ON the third day after the mysterious letters had appeared on the wall of Claudio's chamber, Claudio and his friend were engaged to sup at the house of a Marquis, who held a high situation at court, and to whom they had received letters of introduction from a distinguished character at Placenza.

At the usual hour of visiting, they kept their appointment, and on entering the house of the Marquis, found a large company of both sexes already assembled.

Some were engaged at the card-tables, and the majority were formed into conversation parties.

Their introduction to the mistress of the house was succeeded by her inviting them to play, which Lodovico declined, and Claudio accepted.

In a few minutes, La Marquise summoned him to join a party who were moving to a vacant card-table. Having introduced him to the two ladies with whom he was to play, she next turned to the gentleman who was to be his adversary, and announced him to Claudio as the Chevalier de Gramont; Claudio stepped directly forward to acknowledge the introduction, and to his extreme astonishment beheld in the Chevalier de Gramont—the person of the pilgrim!

A visible emotion was instantly pourtrayed on the countenance of Claudio and the Chevalier; but it passed unnoticed by those around, who had no interest in their changes of countenance, and the party took their seats.

The solemn injunction which Claudio had received from the pilgrim at their last meeting, carefully to avoid letting it appear they had ever met before, if chance happened again to throw them in each other's way, allowed him now only to receive him as an entire stranger.

The Chevalier acted strictly up to the conduct which himself had marked out for their observation, and the game passed without either much correct play or conversation on the part of the gentlemen.

When the party rose from the table at the conclusion of the game, the Chevalier and Claudio moved to different parts of the saloon; and Claudio felt happy in being immediately called to another table, that his thoughts might be amused from winking into the gloom of reflection.

When he again rose from the card-table at the end of his second game, one of the ladies with whom he had been engaged at the first table, addressed him by enquiring the success of his second attempt. Claudio took a seat by her, and after a few immaterial questions and responses had passed between them, he said, "The Chevalier de Gramont, with whom we played, appears an agreeable man; is he an inhabitant of Paris?"—"No," replied the lady: "I think I have heard my brother mention that his residence is in Normandy; he is introduced to the Marquis where we are visiting by a banker at Toulon."

Claudio was on the point of making a rejoinder, when supper was announced, and the company called upon to quit the saloon.

At table, chance placed Claudio the sixth person from the lady of the house; Lodovico was on the other side of the table somewhat lower down, and almost immediately opposite to Claudio sat the Chevalier de Gramont.

They had not been long at table before La Marquise, addressing Claudio, said, "Signor, will you have the goodness to repeat to me the name of your friend, for I want to invite him to partake of this dish, and I am so careless as to have forgotten by what title he was introduced to me."—"Signor Lodovico di Ponta," returned Claudio, in answer to her question.

Claudio had observed that the Chevalier listened attentively for his reply to the Marquise's enquiry, and no sooner had Claudio pronounced the name of his friend, than he observed the color to fade from the cheeks of the Chevalier, and his hand to shake so violently, as to oblige him to lay down the fork with which he was eating.

A strange sensation, inexplicable even to himself, filled the breast of Claudio, and he continued accurately to observe him who had caused it.

The Chevalier de Gramont immediately called for a glass of water, and put it to his lips, in the manner of a person who sips for relief from any painful feeling, rather than of one who drinks to slake his thirst.

Claudio pretended to eat, but still kept his eye indirectly fixed on the Chevalier, who presently resumed his fork, but his use of it was only pretended, and he shortly after sent away his plate unemptied.

Claudio felt not less averse to food than appeared to be the Chevalier; but he constrained himself to do some little honour to the entertainment.

In about ten minutes' time, the violent emotion which had at first seized the Chevalier on the mention of Lodovico's name, began to subside; but a visible agitation still ran through his frame.

La Marquise had remarked, that the Chevalier's plate had been empty almost from the first of his sitting down to table, and pressed him to suffer it to be replenished.—Having replied to her request in the negative, she rejoined, "I fear you are not in health. Is there any thing not upon the table which you would like to take?"

"Nothing, I assure you," he replied in a trembling voice; "I am subject to affections of the head which seize me suddenly, and render me unfit for society during their attacks; I have suffered such a one since we have been seated at table."

La Marquise eagerly enquired what could be done to give the Chevalier relief; he answered, "if you will pardon my abrupt retiring, I will immediately return home; quiet is the only medicine I am able to reap any benefit from in these cases." So saying, he rose from the table, and bowing to La Marquise, who, in wishing him good-night, lamented the privation of his company to the party, and wished him better; he left the room.

A few remarks were made by some of the company, upon the complaint under which, no doubt seemed to be entertained that the Chevalier was suffering; and his name was then mentioned no more.

Claudio, though anxious and distressed, still felt a negative relief in the absence of the Chevalier, and endeavoured to restore his thoughts to the company, from which they had been some time abstracted.

At a late hour, Claudio and Lodovico returned to their hotel.— Lodovico had passed an evening much to his satisfaction, and was in great spirits; Claudio did not say that it had been otherwise to him, and they parted for the night.

When Claudio was left to his solitary reflections, a greater chaos of ænigmas than had ever yet filled his mind, danced in his brain. Already, before this evening, had his surprise been forcibly excited by the different garbs in which he had seen the pilgrim, and the sudden changes which he had witnessed in his passions; but it was now, if possible, encreased to a still higher pitch, by the situation, in which he had seen him within the last few hours.—Most of all, he was impressed with the emotion which had so evidently shaken his entire frame on hearing pronounced the name of di Ponta.

"Was it possible," he then asked of himself, "that the pilgrim could by any means have been accessary to, or acquainted with the extraordinary occurrence of the luminous letters which had appeared in his chamber?" The subject of his reflections was one where thought was lost in an infinite maze of conjecture; and he was obliged to confess, however reluctantly to his own mind, that his powers of reasoning could not assist him in the explanation he so much desired to obtain.

On the following day, Claudio arose in a far from enviable state of mind: anxiety was not the only disagreeable feeling which filled his mind; a dissatisfaction at the complexity of his fate was mingled with the other unpleasant sensations which he was doomed to experience. Obedience to the will of a first cause, had ever been registered in the heart of Claudio as the most eminent of duties; but the strange complication of distressing events which appeared every day to be multiplying upon him, almost irritated his mind into a murmur against the decrees of that omnipotence, from which his cooler moments of reflection would, by convincing him that they had arisen, teach him to bear with resignation.

In spite of his efforts to conceal the gloom which he felt to have cast a veil over his mind and features, he found that the real feelings of his heart would break out into observation: Lodovico remarked at breakfast, that he was unwell; and Claudio urged the trite excuse of a cold and head-ache.

The rays of the rising Sun tended not to dispel the mists of Claudio's mind; and feeling himself fitted only for solitude, he stole from the side of his friend, and sought a shady recess in the garden of a sequestered monastery, to indulge thoughts which he could not keep down, although fully aware of their evil tendency to the mind that nourished them. When the shades of melancholy cast their dark clouds over the mind, every object contemplated by the eye which holds conversation with a heart thus oppressed, wears the raven-tint of sadness.

As Claudio reclined upon a bank of grass under the thickly spreading foliage of an ash, the walls of a neighbouring convent caught his eye; and with the true spirit of human weakness in misfortune, which experiences a negative, and indeed inexplicable pleasure, nearly bordering on the confines of pain, in concluding that he is not the only unhappy mortal upon whom the sun rises and sets; his thoughts wandered from his own situation to that of the virgin shut for ever from the access of a friendly heart to sooth her on the bed of sickness, or the luxury of a responsive sigh, echoed to her love-torn heart by a breast feeling with equal sensibility the pangs her own experiences.

The subject took hold upon his heart, it diverted for a short time his mind from the more painful subject of himself; and with the idea to which his imagination had given birth, warm in his fancy, he drew a consolitary amusement in penning the following

SONNET

TO THE

SORROWING NUN.

Yon glimm'ring taper guides my eager eyes
  To that fair form who courts the cloister's gloom,
To witness why with tenor sad she sighs?
  Why tears of sorrow wet the mould'ring tomb?

Why, when chaste virtue glows upon her face,
  She strikes her bosom with so harsh a blow?
When guilt's dark characters she cannot trace,
  Why clasp'd with fervor are her hands of snow?

Ah, me! pale superstition bows her head,
  On the hard pavement bends her trembling knees,
Drags her at midnight from her spotless bed,
  No beam of hope beyond the grave she sees.

But Heaven indulgent marks her silent tear,
And angels waft it to a happier sphere.

"The curse of life," exclaimed Claudio, "is memory.—Could that poor nun forget the world, she might be happy. Could I forget the past, I might taste comfort in existence; but while that baneful picture of the mind, called memory, paints in her vivid colors what we wish oblivion's water to wash out from our brain, no mortal can be happy; for he who has tasted only of such banquets in the world as have left no regret upon his mind after the feast was concluded, is composed of a stuff which allies his soul to a purer world, although his corporeal frame may wander on this sublunary earth; no mortal can be happy."

"Oh, memory! thou curse of life;" he repeated, after a pause of phrenzied thought; and the cause of misery driving from his mind the unhappy, and leaving the source of sorrow stampt upon his brain, with an agitated hand, he poured forth his soul, in the fever of its workings, against the power whom he experienced to be his enemy, in the following words:

SONNET TO MEMORY.

Fly from my bosom on the breeze's wing,
    Thou bold tormentor of the human mind!
The cup of happiness thou canst not bring,
    Thou giv'st its contents to the passing wind.

Thy unsteady hand, no cooling drop will bear,
    To quell the fever of my thirsty lip;
For thou bestow'st alone the dregs of care;
    Compell'd by thee, the bitter draught I sip.

In joy's mild garb, thou canst not deck thy form,
    For tears in natal sadness slowly steal
Down thy deep furrow'd-cheek, and life's rude storm
    Buffets the rainbow-smile thou fain would'st feel.

Thy sullen frown pourtrays my state forlorn,
Thy rose is blighted by the circling thorn.

CHAPTER V.

  Ber. 'Tis here!
  Hor. 'Tis here!
  Mar. 'Tis gone!
  Bar. Is not this something more than phantasy?
What think you of it?
  Hor. Before my God, I might not this believe,
Without the sensible and true avouch
Of mine own eyes———
                    HAMLET.

THE chill of the evening distilled from the clouds, which were quickly gathering to expel the rays of day, first awakened Claudio from his trance of meditation to the recollection of where he had passed the day: he arose from his seat of grass, a dewy coldness shivered his limbs, and a burning fever agonized his head; no nourishment had that day passed his lips, and a sick faintness, which immediately came upon him when he began to move, reminded him of the neglect of himself to which thought had induced him.

He was acquainted with a bye-path through the gardens, which led by a much nearer way to his hotel than did the broad walk by which he had entered them; he accordingly turned into the narrow path; it lay through an assemblage of shrubs and branching beech-trees, whose arms being artfully entwined as a screen from the warmth of the mid-day sun, now almost totally excluded from the path along which Claudio was moving the little remaining light of day which beamed from the Heavens.

The lateness of the hour had caused the gardens to be totally deserted, and as Claudio passed along, not a sound, but the wafting of the leaves, fanned by the gentle breeze of evening, was heard by him; he continued to proceed hastily along, eager to gain his hotel, and procure some refreshment for the relief of his unhinged frame, when in passing through an angle of the labyrinth where the thick foliage opposed an impenetrable screen to the twilight of the hour, he suddenly heard a voice call upon him by name.

His mind was in a state to be affected by trifles; he started, and even trembled: for some moments, surprise and uncertainty suspended his every faculty, but reason quickly lending her aid to dispel the stupor, momentary fear had given birth to, he replied to the call, by demanding who had uttered it.—No answer was returned to this question; he continued, silent for a few seconds, and then repeated his demand in a louder tone.—Still no reply was given. "If thou bee'st ought that dares to face man, I charge thee to appear, or speak to me again," he cried; still all continued silent; not a breath was heard to move, or a footstep to fall.

Claudio proceeded slowly on his way, not knowing what to fear, what to expect, or what to desire.

For several minutes, he continued his path uninterrupted, and began to believe that his imagination had deceived him, in thinking that he had heard his own name pronounced aloud by the voice of some invisible being; and a distant light from the gate to which he was approaching, had just cheered him by a momentary glimpse which he had caught of it, when the same voice was again by his side, pronouncing, "Claudio!" "What wouldst thou with me?" he exclaimed aloud.—"Bid thee *Beware of Di Ponta!*" returned the voice.

Again Claudio started; the warning was as strange as unexpected; but the moment called for action, and not for thought, and he exclaimed aloud, "Who art thou?"—"Seek not to know me!" returned the voice.—"If thy purpose is evil," replied Claudio, "justice calls upon me to become thy punisher; if good, thou canst not fear to show thyself to me: who art thou? Speak, I charge thee, or dread my fury."

No reply was returned, and Claudio immediately rushed into the thicket from whence the voice had proceeded; a figure entirely white, and rendered just discernable by the opposition of its colour to the shades amongst which it was moving, swam hastily across his path; Claudio followed the direction it had taken, and at the turn of an angle of the grove, he caught a nearer view of it, and again called upon it to answer him.—No answer was returned, and Claudio still continued to follow; at length, pursuing the only path which presented itself, and turning round a clump of trees on its margin, a white figure, of immense tallness, stood motionless within a few paces of his reach.—Claudio made a momentary stop, while he convinced himself that his imagination was not deceived in what he saw, and then darting upon it with all the strength he could command, it sunk at his feet from its erect posture, and he fell with it to the ground.

Notwithstanding his unexpected fall from the want of resistance which had attended his assault upon the object of his surprise and curiosity, still however Claudio had not omitted to grasp that which he so anxiously wished to investigate, and almost instantly again rising with it clenched in his hands, he, to his astonishment, found that he held only in his grasp the white habit of a Carmelite friar.

Rage, disappointment, and the anxiety of desiring to explain what he could not comprehend, jointly tortured his breast, and throwing down the garment, he ran wildly from one spot to another, in fruitless search after him whom he supposed to have worn it.—Overcome by the contending feelings of his mind, he threw himself upon the ground in a stupor of melancholy and despair; the climax of his misery seemed now complete; the friend to whose attachment he owed the greatest happiness of his life, next to the love of the Marchese di Bartelma, was now mysteriously, if not supernaturally pointed out to him as an intimate with whom his connection was dangerous! And what most distressed him was, that from the Chevalier de Gramont's sudden emotion at table, on the preceding evening, at the mention of Lodovico's name, he could not doubt but that the present warning came either immediately or indirectly from him.—Was he then to believe the pilgrim, in whose favor his mind had always inclined to take so dear an interest, or Lodovico, from whom he had never experienced any other conduct than the very heart of friendship, to be an enemy.—The necessity of believing one so, and the impossibility of deciding with certainty which, almost maddened him; the tears rolled in scorching drops down his quivering cheeks, and raising himself upon his knees, in an agony of mind which no reflection could calm, he prayed to his Saviour, with the rhapsody of a maniac, for relief from the strange circle of miseries which surrounded him.

Having ended his prayer, he again fell with his face on the wet earth, and almost dared to breathe a wish of never again rising from its cold bed.

At the voice of the bugle, which sounded from the entrance into the gardens, to announce to the wanderers in their groves, that their gates were about to be closed for the night, Claudio started up, and rather from habit than any present intention, he passed the drawbridge which conducted him into the street. Here the busy hum of men recalled his scattered senses, and with them, in some measure, his fortitude of mind, and a slight portion of composure was also restored to his feelings, by his resolving not to follow the admonition of an adviser in the dark, to distrust one whom years of friendship never abused, had made it a justice for him to confide in.

On entering his hotel, the landlord met him, and exclaimed, "Oh, Signor, where have you been all day? your friend has been searching for you every where."

"Where is he?" asked Claudio.

"Far enough from hence," replied the landlord. "You know not, Signor, what you have lost by being out of the way: there is a *grande fête* given to-day by *sa Majesté* at the palace of Versailles, consisting of a play and a ball, and I have procured the Signor Lodovico a ticket, and would have done the same for you, if you had been at home at the proper time to take it out; but I did not know of it till after breakfast this morning, and you were then no where to be found; I am extremely sorry for your loss."

"I am obliged to you, for your consideration," returned Claudio, "but pray don't make the matter any cause of uneasiness to yourself; I assure you, it is none of regret to me. Pray let me have some supper got ready immediately;" and having said this, he was proceeding to his apartment.

"Pray, Signor, allow me just to speak to you," said the landlord, contriving to interrupt Claudio's progress; "I have ten thousand pardons to beg of you for a liberty of which I have been guilty; I thought by your absence from home during this day, and its being so late before you returned this evening, that you would not perhaps come home at all to-night, at least only to sleep, and I have introduced a gentleman into your apartment who is now going to supper there; he is a constant customer at my house, and having no other room vacant, I felt unwilling to turn him away."

"If your guest is a gentleman, and known to you, I can have no objection to supping with him," returned Claudio.

"Oh, Signor," cried the host, gaining spirits from Claudio's easy manner of receiving the intelligence, which he had been doubtful how he might take, "do you think that I would introduce any one but a gentleman into your apartment? The Sieur Fronval, for such is his name, is one of the most respectable gentlemen in the province of Brittany, and has been known to me these thirty years."

In his present state of mind, Claudio felt something like the anticipation of pleasure from the conversation of a stranger, which might amuse his senses without leading them back to any topic of distress; he accordingly ordered his host to lead the way, and introduce him to his other guest: at these forms, the landlord shew himself very expert, and having mentioned to the Sieur Fronval, that his supper was to be served up with that of the Signor Claudio di

Bartelma, made up the fire, and wished the gentlemen a pleasant conversation: he retired.

Claudio's companion soon showed himself to be, if not a man of learning, at least one well acquainted with the ways of the world; various were the scenes of life through which, according to his own account, he had passed, and his observations upon them proved that they had not glided through his mind unreflected upon.

Fatigued almost to an imbecillity both of body and mind, Claudio had called for wine immediately on seating himself in the hotel; he felt his strength refreshed by it, and when supper was brought in, contrary to his expectation, he found a willingness to partake of the repast.

The Sieur Fronval, who said he had been travelling many leagues that day, did ample justice to the cookery of the hotel; and when the cloth was removed, he addressed Claudio by saying, "You complain, Signor, that you are fatigued with the exercise in which you have passed the day, what say you to joining me in a refreshing draught which I always take in an evening upon the road?"

"What is it?" Claudio enquired.

"It is a mixture of brandy, white wine and water heated, which is commonly known here in France by the name of mulled brandy; you will find it a pleasant and composing liquor, I assure you."

Any thing which appeared to have the capacity of restoring his debilitated mind, was inviting to Claudio, and he readily assented to the proposal of his companion.

The Sieur Fronval then rang the bell, and the host coming in, he directed him to make some mulled brandy without delay.

"Your usual quantity, I suppose?" said the landlord.

"No, no, a double portion," replied Fronval: "the Signor here has agreed to drink some with me."

The host retired again, and in a short time made his third appearance with a small bowl of the liquor which Claudio's companion had ordered.

"Come, Signor," said Fronval, "let me help you to the first glass, and give me your opinion of my choice."—Claudio drank, and his companion appeared not a little pleased at his assurance of the mixture being both pleasant and refreshing.

"I am a moderate man," continued Fronval, "and never exceed the half of what this bason contains; so we must regulate our draughts according to the time we mean to sit."

"To confess the truth," answered Claudio, "I feel myself almost ready to retire at present, for this warm dose has composed my feelings most agreeably to sleep."

"Let us have one half hour's more chat, with your leave, Signor, and then it will about my usual time of going to bed," rejoined Fronval.

To this proposition, Claudio readily agreed, and felt not a little satisfied as the minutes passed on, at the approaching attacks of sleep, which promised an oblivion of his cares for the few hours his head should be reclined on his pillow.

At length, the clock struck eleven, and Claudio and his companion then parted for the night.—Claudio immediately retired to his chamber, and had rested his harrassed frame but a few minutes on his bed, when "the balm of hurt minds," cast its veil of peace over his senses.

CHAPTER VI.

Where should this musick be? i'the air, or the earth
——————————————Sure it waits upon
Some God———————————————————
This is no mortal business, nor no sound
That the earth owes———————————————

My spirits as in a dream, are all bound up.
TEMPEST.

STRAINS of the softest music floating through the air, aroused Claudio from the embraces of sleep; he cast his eyes around, and a brilliant light met them at every turn; he raised himself from his recumbent posture, and found that he was not in bed, but reclining on a low couch, whose furniture was of satin, expanded over the softest materials; a loose robe of silk was thrown over his shoulders, and descended in thick folds below his feet, and his flowing hair was slightly confined under a light net; the apartment in which he was, bore the appearance of an artificial garden; long branches of the sweet scented acacia rose in curves from the floor, and entwined their spiral tops to form an harbour over his head; amongst these, were scattered knots of roses, heliotrope, hyacinths, jonquils, and almost every flower which could delight the eye with its vivid colours, or regale the sense with its perfume, and the light which illuminated the apartment proceeded from variegated lamps, thickly intermixed amongst the verdant foliage.

The shape of this fairy palace was an oblong; at one end of it was placed the couch upon which Claudio found himself reclining, and at the other appeared a flowing curtain of white silk, surmounted by various devices in silver, and colours, emblematical of the passion of love. There was no visible entrance to the bower, and Claudio concluded it to be concealed behind the silk curtain; but he felt a heaviness and reluctance to move from his situation in order to investigate the wonders around him; for which he found it not less difficult to account, than for his being there at all.

The music, which was invisible, continued still to sound with equal sweetness as it had first played upon the ears of Claudio, and in a few minutes, two voices of extreme melody joined it in these words.

> Claudio! from this goblet sip
>   The draught that gives thee happiness,
> That gives thee power to view the fair,
>   The fair, thy future days shall bliss!
>   Sip, Claudio! sip
>   The happy draught,
>   That from thine eyes
>   Shall tear the veil,
>   To view thy prize;
>   Sip, Claudio, sip!

Whilst Claudio's attention was occupied by the singing of these words, an infant Cupid suddenly appeared by the side of the couch on which he was reclining, and presented to him a silver goblet, which contained a perfumed liquor. "Sip, Claudio! sip," was again repeated in the most persuasive accents by the invisible songsters. The smiling Cupid approached the goblet to Claudio's lips, with a silent invitation to taste its contents, sparkling in his laughing eyes. Once again the concealed voices sang "Sip, Claudio! sip:" the laughing Cupid insinuated the brim of the goblet between his lips, and Claudio swallowed a draught of the most delicious beverage.

Immediately the voices ceased from their song, the infant Ganymede disappeared, and the music was changed from the jocund tone in which it had accompanied the exhortation for Claudio to taste the offered cup, to a full strain of the softest harmony: this lasted for some minutes, and then dying away in a gentle cadence, the sound of the instruments became scarcely audible; the faintest murmur of the former strain was only to be heard, and the silken curtain, at the extremity of the bower, opposite to the couch, began to rise gently from the ground.

With a scarcely perceptible motion, the curtain continued to mount in gathering folds, till it became lost behind the branching verdure which composed the bower. The receding of the curtain gave to view a small arbour, whose foliage was solely that of the ever-blowing rose, in the midst of which, on a couch of moss, whose transparent verdure rivalled in brightness the sparkling emerald, lay reclined the beautiful Zelia! a thin white drapery alone composed her dress, and her dark hair playing in airy folds on her rising bosom, displayed the whiteness of her skin to the most enchanting advantage. On one of her hands, she supported her head, and her other arm hung carelessly across her waist. Her eyes smiled pleasure, and were fixed on Claudio.—A light net-work separated the arbour from the other part of the bower, and above the net-work appeared, in letters of gold,—

"THE DESTINED WIFE OF CLAUDIO."

Zelia did not speak; and Claudio felt a languor stealing over his whole frame, which deprived him of all ability either to address her, or to approach nearer to the spot where she reposed, earnestly as he endeavoured to exert strength for both these purposes; still he continued to gaze upon her, and her eyes remained fixed upon him.

The music continued to die away, till it was heard no more; and the whole scene vanished gradually from the senses of Claudio.

The exclamation of "Holloa, Claudio! do you intend to sleep till midnight? or are you dead in good earnest?" uttered by the voice of Lodovico, and attended by the speaker giving him a pull by the arm, was the next occurrence to which the senses of Claudio awoke.

At this address, he started hastily up, and found himself in his own bed, in the chamber of the hotel, and Lodovico standing by his side.

"Are you returned already?" asked Claudio.

"Already!" repeated Lodovico, "why it is upon the stroke of four o'clock in the afternoon, and I am almost famished for want of my dinner. Come, make haste and get up, I dare say you have been raking out all night. I thought you were upon some scent of that kind, by your not coming home any part of yesterday. Make haste, there's a good fellow, and I'll see after dinner, while you are getting up;" and with these words, he left the room.

No sooner did Claudio awake, than the recollection of what he had witnessed in the night, burst full upon his mind: that he had seen the vision promised by the luminous letters, he had no doubt; but whether the vision had appeared to him in a dream, or in a trance of waking stupor, he was unable to determine.

What most surprized him was, that he had slept so long beyond his usual time; but he attributed it to the fatigue which his mind had undergone on the preceding day; and he judged also, that the liquor which he had on the former evening drank with the stranger, being of a stronger nature than he was accustomed to take, might have had some influence in protracting his sleep.

With his thoughts busily employed in reflection on the occurrences of the night, but without being able to form any decision upon the nature of the appearance which he had witnessed; he dressed himself, and went down into the apartment where Lodovico was impatiently waiting his coming, to summon dinner upon the table, which meal Claudio declined joining in, and ordered some coffee for himself at another table.

"You have slept late, Signor," said the host, addressing Claudio, as he placed his breakfast before him. Claudio replied carelessly, "that he had over-slept himself."

"The gentleman who supped with you last night did not keep

his bed so late," rejoined the landlord; "he was on his journey by seven this morning." Claudio did not reply, and the host turned to the table at which Lodovico was dining, to perform some little service which should bring him into notice there.

Lodovico's appetite was whetted by his ride from Versailles, and he did not attempt to converse till he had done ample justice to the *bouillié* before him; he then drew his chair up to Claudio's table, and recounted to him the amusement he had received from being present at the *fête,* given the preceding evening at the court; and having concluded his account, he cried, "Now let me hear what kept you in bed so long?" To this question, Claudio returned an evasive answer, which Lodovico immediately construed into a confession of his hours having been spent in the service of the ladies, and having passed a few jokes upon his friend's drowsiness, he suffered the subject to drop.

That the vision of the preceding night, which was only another mystery added to those that had already occurred to him, proved no relief to the mind of Claudio, need hardly to be said, for can it require to be explained, that the reflections of succeeding days only confused, instead of elucidating the subject which alone occupied his mind.

The final event of his debates with himself, proved a determination to recount to the Marchese di Bartelma, without the slightest reserve, every circumstance which had occurred to him during his life; and to ask his advice how to act under the strange fate which seemed to be hanging over him.

For a moment he hesitated, whether it was consistent with the principles of honour, and his own safety, to divulge to the Marchese his adventures with the Benedictine friar and Viola; first, on account of the promise he had made not to relate the particulars of Viola's private abode; and next, on account of the threat which had been held out to him of the anger of the Inquisition falling upon him, should he make any such revelation.

But then, without divulging this part of his story to the Marchese, he could not ask his advice, with propriety, relative to making an offer of his hand to Valeria; because, unless he mentioned Zelia, he should hold back from the knowledge of the Marchese the very circumstance which must bias his determination; and then, if he spoke of Zelia, it was equally necessary that he should say where and how he had become acquainted with her, in order to assist the Marchese, as much as possible, in forming his judgment upon the good or evil intentions, not only of Zelia herself, but more particularly of those connected with her, of whom she might very probably be the tool for accomplishing some unexpected end.

After debating many days with his own mind how to act, he resolved, that as he was well aware that his secret would be as sacred in the breast of the Marchese as in his own, and as the exigency of his fate seemed to require the advice of some one more experienced than himself, to ensure his safety amongst such a chain of unparalleled and inexplicable events, to relate to his benefactor all that had befallen him in Rome; his subsequent adventure with the pilgrim; the mysterious warning which had been given to him of Di Ponta; and the visions which had pointed out Zelia to him as his destined wife.

When a resolution is once formed, the mind gains a sort of composure from the anticipation of putting it into effect, and from the expectation of its event proving favorable to its wishes. Such a negative calm now possessed the heart of Claudio; and during the remainder of his stay in Paris, which was scarcely a week, he met with no occurrence to revive unpleasant feelings in his mind.

CHAPTER VII.

> With what a grace and tenderness he loves!
> Complacency and truth, and manly sweetness,
> Dwell ever on his tongue, and smooth his thoughts.
> ADDISON.

ON leaving Paris, the route of the young friends was immediately directed towards Placenza, and pursued without interruption, till they arrived at the pallazo di Ponta; Lodovico having many times, in the course of their journey, expressed his vexation, that their destined route did not again lead them through the hamlet where dwelt the beautiful Nina de Saint Pierre.

With every mark of pleasure at their return, they were received by the Count and Valeria; the former of whom acquainted Claudio, that he had received an invitation from the Marchese di Bartelma to himself and his daughter, pressing them to visit him at his villa in the neighbourhood of Florence; and that he intended accompanying Claudio and Lodovico thither, when they had rested a few days from their journey at his pallazo.

Claudio beheld Valeria with all that warmth, that a mind which has built love upon esteem, beholds the object of its adoration: in her he beheld a blaze of unshadowed modesty and mental worth, which entirely eclipsed the glittering fascination of Zelia's charms: he studied to inspire her with those feelings which were to crown his happiness, and he studied also to deserve that her affections should be placed on him.

It is easily perceived by the man who loves, whether those attentions which are the first hints of his passion to the object who inspires it, are auspiciously received; and Claudio's discerning eyes soon communicated satisfaction to his heart, in observing the delicate, yet encouraging smiles with which Valeria received from his hands those little offices which the heart of love is ever studying to perform.

Still, however, Claudio considered it an obligation imposed on him by the peculiarity of his situation, not to make an open declaration of his passion to Valeria, till he had communicated its existence to the Marchese di Bartelma. A few days would now transport him to the embraces of that revered friend; and anxiously did he pant for the moment, when he should once again receive the blessing of him who had called the deserted foundling his son.

On the morning prior to their departure for Florence, as Claudio and Lodovico were strolling about the extensive gardens of the Count di Ponta, they entered a path which led to a romantic pavilion, which was often the favorite retreat of Valeria from the mid-day sun; and several papers, scattered on the grass, immediately caught their eyes. Lodovico stepped forward, and picking up one of them, exclaimed, "By Jupiter! my sister has been poetising in the pavilion, and has dropped some of the flights of her fancy from her port-folio, in her return to the house. Now, Claudio, what would you give me for a peep at them?

"Nothing," replied Claudio; "for I think it would be taking an unfair advantage of an accident."

"Phoo, nonsense," rejoined Lodovico, "girls, you know, are always modest about showing their compositions, and I really think it will be doing my sister quite a service, if we take this opportunity of finding out whether her pen has any merit, without putting her to the blush about it."

Claudio had not time to reply, before Lodovico began reading aloud the following

Sonnet to Memory.

> Benign enchantress! give my longing eyes
>   Again those scenes my artless childhood knew;
> Bid once again those fairy visions rise
>   Which youth with brilliant touches painted true.
>
> Oh! once again thy matchless pencil dip
>   In the clear sparkling vase of happiness,
> With fervid glow tinge youth's carnation lip,
>   Revive the smile that rapture would express.
>
> Let me once more th' extatic transport know,
>   When fairy smiles, with mild instinctive power,
> Would stamp their image on the clouded brow,
>   Moist with the dew, fallen in affliction's hour.
>
> Make me again behold the morn of youth,
> Sparkling with beauty from the beams of truth!

Claudio was going to speak, but Lodovico stopped him from proceeding by exclaiming, "Don't interrupt me; I won't hear a syllable, till I have read one on the other side of the paper, for I see it is addressed to a Nun, and I want to see what consolation she attempts to give to the poor prisoner's panting little heart."—he then continued reading,

SONNET TO A NUN.

WITH placid step, behold that airy form,
    Lifting to Heaven her mild celestial eye;
Her soften'd brow, unruffled by a storm,
    Ne'er into being called the heaving sigh.

But from the guileful world, no voice she hears
    To lure her footsteps from the path of truth;
Friendship no more with treacherous smile appears,
    And steals the secret from the lips of youth.

Love vainly flutters round those sacred walls,
    Flaps his light pinions at the casement rude,
With Syren voice each fair enthusiast calls:
    In vain each fair enthusiast is woo'd.

Oh, sacred haunts! unclose your gates to me,
And screen me safe from friendship's perjury.

"Good Heaven!" exclaimed Claudio, "how differently may the human mind be impressed by the same subject! Perhaps at the very moment that my fevered brain was giving birth to lines on the same subjects on which these are written, Valeria penned those sonnets in all the happiness of a mind at peace with itself. How strangely does the world, in all its parts and mutations, take color from the despondency or cheerfulness of the mind which contemplates it!"

Lodovico heard not the exclamation of Claudio, for he had stepped aside to gather up some more of the papers which the wind had dispersed; and the Count at that moment appearing in the walk, with some friends who were come to pass the day with him at the pallazo, previously to his journey to Florence, Lodovico directly joined them, and Claudio stole apart to indulge his reflections, and more particularly to examine the papers which Lodovico had put into his hands at parting. He found that they contained many successful efforts of Valeria's poetical genius, on all of which he dwelt with the rapture of a lover; but one, in particular, met his feelings, and raised his ideas of the worth of her who had composed it: it was entitled

THE

BALL-ROOM.

Sweet music strikes my listening ear,
And lures me to the ball-room's sphere,
Where lights in glittering myriads shine
To mark the dancers' mystic line.
Nature by art is sweetly won
To bless the work by her begun,
And round the winding columns weaves
In emerald foliage her leaves.
Here Cupid lifts his purple wing;
Here heedless twangs his silver string;
Tears from his eyes the fillet blue,
And smiles his destined prey to view.

Oh, fairy scene! what bliss were yours,
Did TRUTH but consecrate your bowers;
Did she instinctively reveal
What each fair bosom *feigns* to feel:
Did she but prompt the Syren tongue
To soft insinuation strung.
Who is that lovely form that leads
Attraction to the spot she treads?
Whose sandall'd feet with bounding spring
But mock the viewless Zephyr's wing,
And emulously seem to vie
With her light heart that bounds as high:
Whose jewels glittering from afar
Fix rapture on their fairer star?
"A victim, sacrificed in youth,"
Exclaims the thrilling voice of truth;
"That beauteous fair, to wealth a prey,

Hails with a sigh the dawn of day.
Splendor, from mild Contentment's cot,
Woo'd her to taste a happier lot;
But e'er the moon had thrice revolv'd,
The flame of Cupid's torch dissolv'd,
Repentance, clothed in Fashion's dress,
Exiles the Syren, Happiness:
The suppliant at the fortress stands,
And entrance begs with open hands.
In vain the hapless outcast calls:
Unheard her prayers,—she fainting falls.

"And yonder youth, whose dauntless air
Unmov'd beholds each lovely fair,
Each morn the pebbly beach explores,
To catch the sigh from India's shores;
For there, amidst her plantain groves,
Juellen mourns their widow'd loves:
Ambition broke pure Hymen's band,
And tore from his her Æthiop hand.
To distant climes condemn'd to roam,
Fancy still paints his happier home;
And whilst he views Italia's fair,
Juellen robs him of a tear.

"That form, where honour should repose,
Plucks in its bud yon opening rose;
In secret meditates her shame,
And blasts her once unsullied fame,

"And that smooth face that scarce can smile
Gives the full goblet, to beguile
The senses of yon wealthy heir
Who whirls the dice-box high in air,
Till, reft of all, despair prevails,
And Suicide her victim hails.

"And yonder form——" Ah! Truth, forbear!
No more I'll seek this dangerous sphere;
No more this fairy scene I'll tread,
Where the heart's volume is not read;

Where smiles are heralds of deceit;
In the grasp'd hand no friend we greet;
Where each soft voice to ruin calls;
Where vanquish'd virtue sinking falls.

Rous'd by thy call, oh, Truth! I fly
To yield myself thy votary.

"Valeria, thou art the blessed genius of my fate!" exclaimed Claudio. "With a woman possessing a mind like thine, what man can fail of being happy? Soothed by the reason and philosophy of thy mind, cheered by the smiles of thy pleasure-breathing lips, my soul shall taste repose from the tortures which have hitherto racked it."

With his heart more at ease than he had felt it since his first acquaintance with the Benedictine friar at Rome, Claudio rose on the morning he was to begin his journey towards Florence. His companions appeared not less in spirits than himself; and a week of pleasant travelling brought them to the villa di Bartelma.

It was towards noon, on the eighth day of their journey, that the carriage of the Count di Ponta stopped at the mansion of the Marchese di Bartelma; and Claudio, forgetful at that moment of all ceremony to his companions, was the first to spring out of it, and run into the hall. An old servant of the Marchese met him, and Claudio addressed him with, "Where is my dear father?"

The old servant shook his head sorrowfully, but did not speak.

"Almighty powers!" exclaimed Claudio, "what means your dejection? Explain it this instant, I entreat you."

"My poor master," returned the man, his voice scarcely audible through the tears which were choking his utterance, "was taken so violently ill in the middle of last night, that———"

"That, what?" exclaimed Claudio, in a voice of frantic terror. "He cannot be dead!"

"No, he is not dead," returned the servant. "Praised be Heaven, that has spared his life to behold you once again: but the physician who attends him had no hope that you could have seen him alive."

The Count and his son were by this time in the hall: they had heard enough to explain to them the truth. Claudio was flying hastily to the chamber of the Marchese: the Count detained him. "Your suddenly breaking in upon him," he said, "in his present state of health, may accelerate the very event you fear."

Claudio saw the danger, and suffered himself to be led to a seat.

"I will acquaint the physician who attends my master, that you are arrived," said the old servant, and left the hall.

An uninterrupted silence reigned till his return.

"Well, Paulo, can I see him?" exclaimed Claudio, starting up, when the old man came back.

Paulo did not reply, but introduced a gentleman, whom Claudio recollected to be the physician who had attended the Marchesa Julia in her last illness. There was something, if not ominous, at least heart-rending to Claudio in his appearance; and he turned aside, no longer able to suppress his tears.

The physician informed them, that he had administered a sleeping draught to the Marchese, and that it had a few minutes before their arrival, thrown him into a gentle slumber.

The Count enquired the nature of the attack under which he was labouring, and learnt, that in consequence of a cold which he had caught a few evenings before upon the water, the cramp had seized him in the stomach.

"Why was I not sent for? Why was not my return home hastened?" said Claudio.

"Your return could not be accelerated," replied the physician; "for I was not summoned myself to attend the Marchese, till five o'clock this morning."

A silence ensued: Claudio broke it. "Do you think it is impossible for him to recover?" asked Claudio.

"I shall be better able to judge of the event when he awakes from his present slumber," returned the physician.

"You confess then that you have little hope," said Claudio.

"I have ordered mass to be said for him in the cathedral at Florence," replied the physician; "and you may rely, that no efforts of which I am capable shall be omitted for restoring him:" and with these words, he left the apartment to return to his patient.

Claudio threw himself upon a sofa, and buried his face in his hands: his recollections may be easily divined.

In a short time, the physician again entered the room: Claudio sprang up to meet him in silence, but with the most eloquent enquiry of despairing sorrow painted on his countenance.

"I fear the die is cast," said the physician.

"Oh, God of mercy! spare my father!" exclaimed Claudio, clasping his hands in the agony of his feelings.

"Have you fortitude to see him once again?" asked the physician. "He knows that you are arrived, and wishes the Count di Ponta and yourself to go up to his chamber: he has something of importance, he says, to communicate to you both, if his agony will permit him to utter what he is desirous to say."

"Of importance!" echoed the heart of Claudio. "Can he be going to divulge to the Count the mystery of my introduction into his family?"

"Come, let us lose no time in seeing him," said the Count, addressing Claudio.

Claudio heard him not.

Claudio, at that moment, thought only of the mysterious warning against di Ponta, which had been given to him in the gardens of the monastary at Paris. "Should he be about to divulge to the Count that I am not his child," thought Claudio, "and should the voice of that awfully invisible being who bad me beware of di Ponta have spoken the truth to me, in asserting him my enemy; what becomes of Claudio when his protector dies?"

"Come, Claudio," repeated the Count; "we must not lose time."

Claudio threw himself upon a sofa, and breathed a groan of agony: his brain almost maddened by what he feared to be the business of the Marchese with the Count and himself at this awful moment. He might indeed have avoided it by going first alone to the Marchese, and communicating to him the warning of the mysterious voice; but then to lay a weight of agony for his future welfare on the heart of that man who had been the father of his orphan state——Impossible! Equally impossible did he feel it to refrain from seeing him once again; and with a heart assuming fortitude rather from despair than hope, he sprang from his seat, and extending his hands towards heaven, he mentally exclaimed, "To the God who has hitherto protected my orphan state, I resign my future fate;" and then beckoning to the Count to follow him, he left the room.

At some distance from the chamber of the dying Marchese, Claudio caught the sound of his groans, and running forward, he burst into the chamber: a servant by the side of the bed pronounced the name of Claudio.

"My dear boy," faintly articulated the Marchese.

Claudio rushed to the bed, and snatched the Marchese to his own arms from those of the attending domestics.

In the gripe of mingled agony and pleasure, the Marchese held Claudio entwined, till a flood of tears relieved his overpowered spirits. Claudio snatched a napkin from the hand of a servant, and wiped the dew of agony from the forehead of his father. The head of the Marchese fell upon the shoulder of Claudio. Claudio imprinted the kiss of gratitude on his cheek, and their tears were mingled.

A sudden pang tore the Marchese from the arms of Claudio; and when the strength to combat with his agony failed him, he sunk on the bed, breathing out his miseries in smothered groans. Claudio fell on his knees by the side of the bed, and clasped the holy cross which lay on the Marchese's pillow. The physician feared the present struggle to be the last. The confessor of the Marchese was immediately summoned to the chamber, and the extreme unction administered by him to the dying man. The exertion used in its performance recalled the Marchese into life. He cast his eyes on the Count di Ponta, who was standing at the foot of the bed, and beckoned him to his side. The Count obeyed. The Marchese made several ineffectual efforts to speak: at length, he with difficulty pronounced the name of the Count. After a few minutes pause, a sudden spark of strength seemed to be restored to him, and he proceeded to say, "My friend, Montano, friend of my youth, it is of my boy, my dear Claudio, that I would speak to you."

Claudio turned faint and sick, and his head fell upon the bed.

"He is the friend of your son," continued the Marchese. "He is amiable: you know him to be so. He has no friend on earth but your family. He is my sole heir: I reserve nothing from him at my death; but it is in your power alone to suffer me to die happy. Oh, my friend! Oh, my Claudio! bless me by agreeing to the wish of my heart."

The Count requested the Marchese to proceed.

"Let your daughter," continued the Marchese, "become the wife of Claudio, and I die content."

Claudio was relieved, though astonished by the request of the Marchese: more surprised perhaps by its unison with his own private wishes, than at the inclination expressed. He spoke not.

The Count said, "My friend, Bartelma, I am much mistaken if the hearts of my Valeria and your son have not long since united in the very wish you now express. I have been a silent observer of the first growth of a mutual passion. How say you, Claudio, have my observations been falsely drawn?"

Claudio spoke the truth with diffident firmness.

"Then be happy, my friend," said the Count, addressing the Marchese: "I approve the choice of my daughter, not less as the son of my esteemed friend, than for himself. Henceforward, Claudio is my son as well as yours."

For a few minutes the Marchese sunk on his pillow, overpowered by the joy he received at the ready compliance which met his dying wish from all the parties concerned in the request dearest to his heart. His desire of connecting Claudio previously to his death with a family, his alliance to whom would support him through every emergency, was now accomplished. When he was again able to speak, he begged the Count to go and acquaint his daughter with what had passed; and to request of her, that she would come to his chamber, and receive the blessing of his dying breath.

The Count left the chamber to comply with the request of the Marchese.

When alone with Claudio, the Marchese again raised himself in his bed, and endeavored to address the child of his protection; but the power of speech had fled from him for ever, and an inarticulate sound only remained to him.

The Count's conversation with his daughter was not long. An explanation, for which the hearts of either party are prepared, is quickly discussed; and in a few moments he led her into the chamber of the Marchese. Claudio met her, and taking her hand in his, he said, "Does my Valeria consent to bless the man who has never yet, but by his actions, declared to her the affections of his heart?"

"Let your affections hence forward," replied Valeria, "speak in your actions as they have hitherto done, rather than in your words, and I fear not to be happy with you."

Claudio led her to the side of the bed, and they knelt by it. All strength and presence of mind was now quickly fading away from the frame of the Marchese. Paulo and the physician supported him, as he leaned over Claudio and Valeria to bestow on them his blessing. He clasped his hands, and raised his eyes to heaven—a scarcely audible sound passed his quivering lips—the effort was his last—he sunk back upon his pillow, and expired.

The sigh of old Paulo announced the death of his master. Claudio caught Valeria in his arms, and hurried her into the gallery. The Count and Lodovico received her at his hands; and Claudio ran to his own chamber, to give vent to the first overflowings of his grief in private.

CHAPTER VIII.

———————Ere the bat hath flown
His cloister'd flight, ere to black Hecate's summons
The shard born beetle, with his drowsy hums,
Hath rung night's yawning peal, there shall be done
A deed of dreadful note.
MACBETH.

A PLACID resignation to the will of providence, drawn from a reliance on its ultimate benevolence to its creatures, though its purposes may for a while be enveloped in a shade impenetrable to mortals, is the most soothing balm under the pressure of affliction. Claudio sipped deeply from its cup of restoration, and it expelled the cloud of sorrow from his brow.

What most agonized his feelings was, that the only friend to whom he dared to have entrusted the many mysterious adventures which had occurred to him in the course of his life, had been snatched from him, at the very moment he had resolved to apply to his advice, for the direction of his future conduct under them.

The principal point however in which he had desired to ask the assistance of the Marchese, that of obtaining the hand of Valeria, was already effected, by the very means he should have desired it to be accomplished, and with this first wish of his heart gratified, he resolved to seek happiness in dwelling on such events of his life, as had been succeeded by pleasant consequences, and in endeavouring to banish from his memory, such as had only given him pain: amongst the latter, the mysterious warning he had received against the name of di Ponta, was the most difficult to be driven from his mind; for every action of the entire family who bore that name, towards him, was so contrary to what the invisible admonisher had signified them to be, that he hesitated not to pronounce the admonition to have been a calumny, or the attempt of malice to separate friends whose happiness consisted in each other's society.

When the funeral of the Marchese was past, it was agreed, that the Count di Ponta and Valeria should return to Placenza, till the time which decency required to be dedicated to the memory of the Marchese di Bartelma, should be elapsed, at which period, Claudio was to visit Placenza, and receive the hand of his Valeria in marriage.

On the ninth day after the death of the Marchese, the Count and his daughter left the villa di Bartelma; Lodovico remained with his friend. Claudio, although he constrained himself to appear cheerful in society, still wore the garb of sorrow in his heart; and being unfitted for the gay society in which Lodovico loved to mix, his time was passed chiefly alone, and he amused himself either by reading, or more frequently by the never-failing book of reflection. Again and again would he revise his past life, and re-act, in imagination, all the scenes which had composed it; but his reflections always were doomed to end where they had begun—in a chaos of mystery.

Thus had two months passed away unmarked by any event worthy of notice, when, towards the close of a sultry evening, which Lodovico was gone to spend in Florence, the rays of the departing sun, gilding the waters of the Arno with their glowing beams, invited Claudio to throw himself upon a bed of grass which ran along the margin of the river, at the foot of the garden, and enjoy the cooling zephyrs which succeeded a burning day.

The prospect around him, though familiar to his eye, still pleased his observation; and some time was passed by him, in contemplating the amphitheatre of nature's fertility, enriched by the labours of the most successful art, which bounded the view on every side; till the distance becoming obscured by the shades of night, made him search for an object of attention nearer to the spot on which he was seated. The sound of oars regularly cutting the smooth water, caught his ear, and to the sound he directed his eye, and perceived a gondola gliding along the glassy surface of the river: it approached towards him, and he raised himself on his elbow to view it as it passed by him.

As it advanced nearer, he perceived the prow turned towards the spot on which he was sitting; he next saw the oars drawn on board, and in a few moments, it stopped directly opposite to him.

Two men in masks immediately sprang on shore, and having each seized a hand of Claudio with both theirs, he was hurried on board by them, the oars thrown out, and the gondola again on its way, before he could sufficiently recover himself from his surprize, to enquire why he was thus treated.

"Who are ye, why is this?" was his first demand.

A man who was also masked, and in the habit of a priest, answered him, "Fear nothing, my son, no harm is intended to you: the purpose for which you are now detained, will not only be the means of benefit to you through life, but, perhaps, of preserving your existence till the period Heaven has ordained you should enjoy it."

"What is that purpose?" asked Claudio.

"You will presently know it,"' returned the priest. "I am forbidden to explain: the motive must unravel itself. Be satisfied that no evil is intended against you."

"Every restraint inflicted on one who is not criminal must be evil!" exclaimed Claudio.

"Answer me, I command you," he continued, with encreasing warmth, "why I am detained here?"

"I have already told you, I cannot," replied the priest.

"You mean, you will not," said Claudio.

"So, if you please: I will not," returned the priest.

Claudio sprang from the bench on which he had been seated,

and seizing the collar of the priest, threw him from him; at the same instant, leaping on the side of the gondola, and bending forward to throw himself into the river (knowing that he was an expert swimmer, and hoping thus to escape the toil into which he had so strangely fallen), the gondoliers caught his waist, and in an instant he was again placed on the bench, and his arms tied to his sides.

"If, as you say," exclaimed Claudio, "it is to good that you would conduct me, why refuse to explain that good, and thus render me willing to obey you?"

"I am not convinced that you would think as I do," returned the priest.

"Then you are not convinced," replied Claudio, "that the hope of future benefit, which you hold out to me, is founded in truth, or you would not hesitate an explanation which would ensure my compliance."

"None of us can be certain that a probability will be," answered the priest.

"Nor can the law of God or man," cried Claudio, "authorize you to act evil upon any individual, in the expectation of good arising from it."

"I have authority for what I do," returned the priest, harshly. "Bring the bandage," he continued, addressing himself to a man who stood by his side.

The bandage was produced, and Claudio, in the struggle which he made to avoid its being tied over his eyes, caught a momentary glimpse of a building he was well acquainted with; and which convinced him, the gondola was entering that part of the river which bisects the city of Florence.

The bandage being tied over his eyes, a mask was placed before his face, his hat was again put upon his head, and a loose robe was thrown over his shoulders; he was then again made to sit, and the priest, having placed himself by his side, said, "Be advised, my son, to conduct yourself with gentleness and obedience in what is required of you, until you shall again be landed on the spot from whence you have just been brought, and you may depend on no insult or injury whatever being offered to you; should you refuse to comply by gentle means——" The priest seemed to hesitate how to proceed.

"What then?" interrupted Claudio.

"The end for which you are now here must be accomplished by force," replied the priest.

"Release me instantly," exclaimed Claudio, "or, I swear by Heaven, the law shall give me vengeance for the insolence you are practising towards me."

"We fear not the law," replied the priest, "nor your prattle, after the end for which we detain you is accomplished, and we have means to free us from the fear of it at present; therefore be silent, or you will repent this hardiness."

Notwithstanding this threat, Claudio continued to give vent to the feelings of his mind.

The priest interrupted him by saying, "You provoke us to treat you as it is not our desire to do, would you behave with gentleness."

Claudio's mask was instantly lifted up, and his utterance stopped by a gag.

The gondola moved swiftly along, and in a short time stopped; but although Claudio was well acquainted with the course of the river, he was unable to determine to what place it had brought him, from the number of angles and circuits which had been made by the rowers, in the space of the few last minutes; and which, from the regularity of that part of the river, he did not hesitate to conclude having been performed in order to baffle the efforts of his memory or imagination.

He was immediately led by two men up about a dozen steps; and after being hurried along a few paces, he was made to ascend a single step, and he then heard a door shut close behind him, which led him to conjecture, that the last step he had ascended, had brought him into the hall of some building.

Again he was led forward, and after turning many angles, and alternately ascending and descending an uncertain number of steps, a second door was shut; and the voice of the priest called to Claudio's conductors to stop, which command they instantly obeyed.

The flat pavement along which Claudio had last proceeded, had sent forth a hollow echo to the footsteps that had trodden it; and their motion now ceasing, he caught the sound of distant voices in prayer.

A footstep approached towards the spot where Claudio's conductors held him; and he heard the buz of whispering voices very near to him, but he could not distinguish a word they uttered.

Two persons, one of whom he conjectured to be the priest, now seemed to recede from the spot where he stood, and presently a door at a little distance from him was opened; quickly it was again closed, and again he heard the sound of discoursing voices, apparently stationed very near to the place where he had heard the creaking and flap of the door.

Presently he was directed to be led forward; his guides caused him to advance a few paces, and the mask and bandage were then ordered to be taken from his face.

The first object which his eyes fixed upon was a small altar, at the foot of which he was standing; and a little elevated from the ground, on a platform on which the altar was raised, stood the priest still masked.

Eagerly he cast his eyes around him in pursuit of other objects, that might either gratify his excited curiosity, or explain his mysterious situation.

On his right, stood the two men who had forced him into the gondola, and next conducted him to the place where he now was: they were masked, and defied the enquiry of his eyes.

A little to his left, stood another man in the habit of a friar, whose cowl entirely shaded his countenance; and in his hand, he held that of a woman, in a white garment, whose face was hid beneath a thick black veil, the sides of which were fastened upon her shoulders.

"You are called upon, Claudio di Bartelma," said the priest, "here, in the sight of Heaven and us present, to receive that maiden as your lawful and only wife, and to acknowledge her as such whenever you may be called upon so to do."

"That female then is, doubtless, Zelia," exclaimed Claudio's heart; "and I am now brought hither to fulfil the prediction so mysteriously announced to me." Maddened by the authority so unlawfully and unjustly exercising over him, Claudio struggled with the utmost vehemence to split the gag, and extricate his arms from the cord which confined them: in vain were his efforts. The men again seized his hands. He threw himself upon his knees in tacit supplication to the priest. The priest only commanded him to rise, and then waved his hand to the female to approach the altar.

She obeyed the signal, and the friar moved by her side.

Claudio, still kneeling, raised his eyes to Heaven in silent supplication for its interposition: it was denied him. The marriage ceremony was performed throughout with apparent devotion by the priest. The hand of Claudio was forcibly guided by the men who held him, to place a ring on the finger of the female who stood by his side; and the priest, having closed his book, knelt, and blessed them.

No sooner was the ceremony concluded, than the female raised her veil; and the friar who stood by her, at the same moment removing his cowl from before his face, the countenances of Zelia and the Benedictine friar were presented to the sight of Claudio. His surprise was not great, for they were the persons he expected them to be. His misery and vexation at the event just past exceeded all the bounds of human patience to endure. They did not address him; and in a few instants, the bandage was again placed before the eyes of Claudio, and the mask stuck under his hat. Immediately he was made (by what he could conjecture of the way) to retrace the path by which he had been led to the devoted altar; and being placed in the gondola, the oars began to cut the yielding waves, and the vessel to gain a swift movement.

Claudio sat lost in a stupor of rage, uncertainty and despair.

At length, the gondola stopped; and Claudio being lifted on shore, and the bandage taken from before his eyes, he found himself precisely on the same spot from whence he had been taken. Having unbound his arms, and taken the gag from his mouth, the men jumped into the gondola, carrying with them the mask and the robe which had been put upon Claudio; and having turned the prow of the gondola towards Florence, they threw out their oars, and ran swiftly down before the tide.

Claudio stood motionless, with his eyes fixed on them, till they vanished from his sight; and he was then, for some moments, at a loss to determine, whether the past was a reality or a vision; but cruel conviction soon explained to his heart, that the mysterious Zelia was now indeed the wife of Claudio di Bartelma.

CHAPTER IX.

> ————————There is a power
> Unseen that rules th' illimitable world,
> That guides its motions, from the brightest star
> To the least dust of this sin-tainted mould;
> While man, who madly deems himself the Lord
> Of all, is nought but weakness and dependence.
>
> THOMSON.

THE night was far advanced, and a sickly moon alone opposed its faint beams to the darkness of midnight. Claudio, almost ignorant what he did, walked slowly towards his house, and rang at the gate. Old Paulo received him with astonishment at his long absence, and joy at his return. With a slight, but unsatisfactory answer, Claudio passed him, entered the house, and proceeded to the supper-room.

The first object he beheld on entering that apartment, was Lodovico pacing the room in the wildest agitation, and with a frown of anxiety (the most unusual garb for his countenance to wear) painted on his face. The moment Claudio opened the door, Lodovico ran towards him, and seized his hand. "Thank God, I see you!" exclaimed he. "Where have you been?"

"I am well, and safe," returned Claudio: "let that answer satisfy you for the present."

"What do you mean? Has any thing happened to you?" exclaimed Lodovico.

"I thought your anxiety had arisen from my absence from home at this late hour," said Claudio.

"Oh, no," replied Lodovico; "some thing has occurred to me which—thank Heaven, that I am here alive!"

Claudio's curiosity was excited, and his mind, for the time, diverted from himself; and he eagerly enquired of Lodovico an explanation of his mysterious hints.

"Listen to me," returned Lodovico, "and I'll give you as clear and exact account of my adventure as I am able. The moon shone so very bright about ten o'clock this evening, that it tempted me to walk home from Florence through the pine-grove, about half a league from your villa. I proceeded two-thirds of my way without interruption, or indeed meeting a single individual, till I arrived at the double row of wild chesnuts which divide your estate from the neighbouring plantations. I was scarcely amongst the trees, before a voice, entirely unknown to me, called to me by name to stop. The voice was behind me; and turning my head suddenly round, I beheld a tall figure, muffled in a dark-coloured drapery, following me close upon my heels. I immediately conjectured the person to be no other than a hired assassin, sent out to murder me in revenge for some favors I had received from the lady of some jealous gallant; and I felt for my sword to defend myself with. To my disappointment, I found I had it not upon me, and I instantly ran forward in the hope of escaping my pursuer. For a few paces only I outstripped his velocity: he then came up with me, and seizing me by the arm with both his hands, again commanded me to stop. His superior strength rendered me unable to disobey his order, and he spoke thus: "Are you not Lodovico di Ponta?" I did not reply: I feared my affirming the question might cause my instant destruction; and I hoped from his reposing the question, that there was a possibility of his being uncertain whether he indeed held him he sought for.

"Fear not to answer me," he continued, after a short pause. "I know you, and intend you no harm. Tell me, do you not call Claudio di Bartelma your friend?"

"I do," I replied.

"Is yours the friendship of the tongue or of the heart?" he rejoined.

"Upon what authority do you enquire?" I asked.

"Give me an answer," he replied: "I want no questions."

"Who are you," said I, "that dare accost me with this insolent familiarity?"

"One," he answered, "whom you will never know more of than you do at this moment. Answer my question, and I shall soon leave you for ever: is your friendship of the tongue or heart?"

"Why should you doubt that it is of the heart?" I asked.

"Once more, I conjure you to be explicit," he exclaimed. "Are you ashamed to answer me the truth?" he added, after a short pause.

"No," I replied, "I shall never blush to assert, in the face of the world, that Claudio di Bartelma is my dearest friend."

"Are you sure of that?" he asked, with emphasis.—"As sure as that I hope for Heaven," was my reply.

"You will not then," he returned, "object to take the vow which I shall require of you?"

He loosened one of his hands from my arm as he spoke, and moved it up to my neck, which he seized in a firm grasp; having done this, he continued speaking: "Swear to me, by the Saviour of the world, and the hopes of your own salvation through his sufferings, that no event on earth shall cause you to think otherwise of Claudio di Bartelma, than you do at this moment.—Swear to continue his friend through every emergency, though ruin stare you in the face for your reward. Swear! or this poniard stabs you to the heart!"

As he spoke these words, he took his right hand from my arm, and sliding it under his cloak, drew out with it the weapon he had named, and held it over my breast, prepared to strike the blow of death.

"Believe me, Claudio, the friendship which I bear you would have authorized me, without scruple, to have taken the oath dictated to me; but the strange midnight arrest which accompanied it, rendered me, I hardly knew why, averse to complying with the demand of him who had proposed it, and without answering, I struggled to free myself from his gripe.

"Villain!" he exclaimed, "thy professed friendship is a lie, and thou shalt perish in thy falsehood:" and while uttering these words, he contrived to throw me upon one knee, which alone supported me from falling upon the ground; his hand was now again raised with the poniard over my breast, and my exclaiming, "Hold, hold, and hear me!" alone prevented his driving it to my heart. I remonstrated with him, but in vain, on the unlawful authority with which he was treating me: he would hear no apologies for my not obeying him, and to preserve my life, I took the oath he had required.

"May heaven so bless or curse thee, as thou abidest by thy vow!" he exclaimed, and instantly throwing me from him upon the ground, he disappeared amongst the trees.

"You may imagine that I was not long in returning home, and that my anxiety has not been slightly tortured for your return, in order to participate my strange adventure to you, and to learn your conjecture upon its cause and actor."

Contrary to the expectation of Lodovico, who had in his own mind predicted that the most excessive surprise would seize his friend on the recital of this adventure, Claudio sat wrapt in thought, he neither spoke, nor did his countenance betray any strong symptoms of astonishment.

The occurrence which had that night befallen Lodovico, appeared to Claudio a part of the mystery contained in the warning he had received in the gardens at Paris; and he knew not how to answer Lodovico, without betraying, that he was acquainted with something which lessened his astonishment at his friend's adventure.

"Why do you not speak?—Is not this strange?" asked Lodovico.

"Strange things have also happened to me," replied Claudio, "much stranger than you have encountered."

"Good heavens! what mean you?" exclaimed Lodovico. "Are they of the nature of that which has befallen me?—I entreat you to tell me?"

"The time may come," said Claudio, "nay it *must* come, when you and all the world shall be made acquainted with what has this night befallen me."

"Almighty God!" cried Lodovico, "you alarm me beyond all bearing. What can have befallen you this night, to hang so heavy on your mind?—I *am* your friend, I *shall* be your brother. Do you doubt my capacity or my will for fulfilling both these characters as becomes an honest man, that you hesitate to trust me with your afflictions?"

Lodovico spoke these words in a tone of honest fervor which penetrated to the heart of Claudio. He threw himself upon Lodovico's neck, and said, "No, my friend, heaven forbid that I should be base enough to entertain a doubt of the honour of a tried friend; but much more than what has this night occurred to me, must be known by you, before I can expect that any credit will be given by you to my present adventure. I can only say that it is true; explain it I cannot.

"The mysteries which have for a long time attended my life, I had resolved to keep locked up in my own breast; till their quick succession on each other, rendered me unable any longer to support the burden in my single breast. When I two months since left your father's pallazo for this villa, I came prepared to open my heart to the Marchese, as him to whom my confidential duty most belonged. I need not tell you how that plan was frustrated, by one of the cruel and unforeseen accidents of existence. He who had the first right upon my confidence being now torn from me, I hold my friend most worthy to supply his place. Will that friend consent to receive a confidence, which is only entrusted to him in default of a dear father's existence?"

"You make me the substitute of so excellent a man," replied Lodovico, "that I feel honor in being ranked his successor."

"You promise me your secrecy," said Claudio.

"On the faith of a friend," returned Lodovico.

With the exception of his not being really the son of the late Marchese di Bartelma, Claudio then recounted to his friend, every occurrence which had befallen him since the commencement of their acquaintance at the college of St. Peter in Rome.

Lodovico heard his friend's account with wonder, and when it was concluded, he knew not how to reply; the whole appeared to him wrapt in shades of impenetrable darkness, and he could only recommend fortitude to his friend, without being able to give him any consolation, drawn from a rational conjecture of the truth.

"With you, my friend," said Claudio, "who know my heart, the tale of my strange fate gains credit; but were it to be publicly told, what would the multitude of uninterested hearers believe it? Either the fiction of a villain, or the wanderings of a madman's brain: yet, from them it may be concealed, but from your father, your sister, it cannot; and what will it appear to them, but a plea for breaking off the intended marriage, aggravated by the glaring dress of apparent falsehood.

"When I have said that I am already married, does not the question naturally follow, to whom?—To Zelia.—Where is your wife?—I know not.—Who is she?—I am not acquainted.—Where did you gain a knowledge of her?—In a place where I never but once saw her, and which I am bound, not only by an oath, but by the ordinance of the inquisition, not to point out or name, if even it were in my ability to do it, which I solemnly believe it is not.

"Oh, Lodovico! the misery of my fate is more than the weak heart of a mortal can bear up under without breaking. I will fly to the deserts, herd with the savage beasts, and by avoiding man, free myself equally from repeating my incomprehensible fate, and from again falling into the toil of such invidious wretches, in the form of humanity, as this detested earth swarms with."

Lodovico besought Claudio to be calm: he assured him, that the hearts of his father and Valeria were too much biassed in his favor to believe him dishonourable, because unfortunate. He said, he would write to the Count on the following day, and request his presence alone at the villa di Bartelma, when Claudio might be guided by his advice, what plan to pursue for his restoration to happiness.

To this scheme, Claudio at first assented, won to it by the eagerness with which Lodovico advanced it, and with the fervor with which he declared himself persuaded that his father would embark in his cause; but on a more deliberate reflection, he judged it better to defer giving information of his unfortunate connection to the Count, as there was a possibility that his forced marriage might prove to be the stratagem of some artful persons, who intended to release him from his engagement on the payment of a sum of money, which they might demand of him for his absolution from the bond by which he was now connected. Lodovico entered into his idea, and they resolved to secrete for a month, at least, the transactions of that night from every individual, which the distant time appointed for Claudio's nuptials with Valeria very much favoured.

Lodovico slept little that night: Claudio tasted not at all of repose. At an early hour they met in the garden: "Come, come," said Lodovico, "you must not brood over your sorrows, that is fighting your enemy's battle instead of your own: take my advice, I beseech you; appear at Florence as you used to do in former days. The Marchese your father has now been interred a sufficient time to authorize your again mixing with the world, and by going into it as you were wont to do, show your enemies that you are not debarred from the enjoyments of society by their contrivances."

"Not only from the cause you mention," replied Claudio, "but also from the possibility of my encountering some of those persons from whom alone I can hope for the solution of the mystery in which I am enveloped, I will certainly accompany you on your rambles to Florence: after breakfast, if you please, we will go thither for the first time."

"Agreed," returned Lodovico, "and I must insist on your going by the pine-grove, that I may show you where I last night encountered my midnight assailant."

At the time agreed upon they sat out. On reaching the double row of chesnut-trees, Lodovico stopped, and was beginning again to recount his preceding night's adventure, marking, as he spoke, the spot of action. Claudio listened to him, till something which he perceived glittering amongst the grass attracted his attention; he stooped down to pick it up, and to his surprize found it to be a bracelet, exactly resembling the one which he had worn on his wrist ever since he was ten years old.—For a few moments, he could scarcely believe that he had not dropped his own without having been conscious of its fall: he drew up the sleeve of his coat, and found it firm on his wrist. An exclamation of astonishment insensibly escaped his lips: it drew the attention of Lodovico, who interrupting himself in his narrative, came up to his friend at the moment he was comparing the bracelets with each other.

"What have you found?—What thus violently agitates you?" asked Lodovico. "You picked up this bracelet, did you not?" continued he, finding Claudio did not speak.

"Yes, I did," replied Claudio gravely.

"And it corresponds with one on your wrist?" rejoined Lodovico.

Claudio's head swam in agony: he struck it with the palm of his hand, and staggered to a tree, against the trunk of which he supported himself.

"Claudio, for heaven's sake, what affects you?" said Lodovico, following him.

Claudio hid his eyes with the hand which had been placed upon his forehead.

"You cannot still distrust me," continued Lodovico: "recollect the vow by which I bound myself on this very spot."

"I wrong your friendship, I fear," said Claudio, taking Lodovico's hand; "and yet, believe me, my friend, I know not how to be just to you and to myself."

"Tell me nothing that will injure your own happiness," replied Lodovico.

"I must suffer by concealing any thing from such a friend," rejoined Claudio. "Inclination prompts me to tell you all I feel: duty to a parent whom I have never known, forbids the disclosure of all my miseries."

"How!" exclaimed Lodovico, "a parent whom you have never known!"

"Oh, God!" cried Claudio, "the agony of my soul has betrayed me into the very confession I feared to make—you know my secret, and I throw myself upon your mercy."

"May the God of mercy abandon me, if I desert my friend in his extremity!" exclaimed Lodovico.

Claudio burst into tears, and clasped him to his breast. Some minutes were given by the friends to the composure of their agitated feelings.—Claudio broke the expressive silence: "I can proceed no farther now," he said. "This bracelet is to me a sacred gift of chance, and must be carefully bestowed: let us return home for the present."

Arrived at the villa di Bartelma, a full confession to his friend flowed from the tongue of Claudio; and Lodovico, with the heartfelt warmth of a brother, renewed to his friend his solemn promises of secresy upon all the points with which he had, within the two last days, become acquainted.

CHAPTER X.

>————————To be worst,
>The lowest, and most dejected thing of fortune,
>Stands still in esperance, lives not in fear;
>The lamentable change is for the best:
>The worst returns to laughter. Welcome then,
>Thou unsubstantial air that I embrace!
>The wretch, that thou hast blown unto the worst,
>Owes nothing to thy blasts.
> KING LEAR.

"Have I done wrong in disclosing the secret of my birth?" was the reflection which principally occupied the mind of Claudio throughout the night; but reason replied to his enquiry, "That the heart of friendship is indivisible, and that they are no friends who have secrets apart from each other." This gentle whisper to his heart, silenced his doubts, and the bracelet next occupied his ideas; from the sum of which, he could only collect what Lodovico had immediately concluded, on having heard the full of his adventures, that the man who had on the preceding night way-laid him in the pine-grove, could be no other than the mysterious pilgrim, whom Claudio had already seen under so many different shapes.

According to his recent determination, Claudio once more entered into the great world, and mixed in the societies he had before been accustomed to frequent; but no event occurred to elucidate any part of the mysteries by which he was encompassed.

The time rolled heavily along, though immersed in dissipation, till a month only was wanting to the completion of the period, at which it had been predetermined that Claudio should pass over to Placenza, and receive the hand of Valeria in marriage.

Claudio's distraction of mind increased as the moment advanced which would extract from him the confession he so much dreaded to make.—Lodovico, with the true sympathy of friendship in his feelings, beheld the anxiety under which he laboured, and again urged Claudio to permit him to request the presence of the Count di Ponta alone at the villa di Bartelma.

To this plan, Claudio at length consented; and Lodovico wrote to his father a letter, from the contents of which, the motive of his son desiring him to visit the villa di Bartelma immediately, and alone, could not be conjectured by him; and wherein he at the same time hinted to him, that there was not a cause for his request of sufficient evil nature to alarm his feelings.

This letter had been dispatched about a fortnight to the Count, when Lodovico came running one day into Claudio's room almost out of breath, and his eyes sparkling with pleasure. As soon as he could speak, he exclaimed, "What think you, Claudio, Nina de Saint Pierre is at this moment in Florence. "How do you know that?" asked Claudio, "you have not been to the city to-day." "I have just learned the information," returned he, "from my servant, who travelled with us, and who knew how much I was struck with her in her native hamlet. He tells me, that he saw her not a couple of hours ago, walking about Florence, and leaning on the arm of her old father, Louis. Oh, Claudio! I am out of my wits with rapture: I must see, I must speak to her before this day closes, or I lose my senses. I have sent Julius to find out where in Florence they lodge, and if possible what can have brought them to it at all."

"And have you, Lodovico," said Claudio, attempting to raise a smile, "after all your gaieties and libertinism, resolved to become the tenant of some humble cottage, hung with woodbine, and capped with straw: to rise with the lark, go to bed with the sun, dine because it is mid-day, and sup when the chickens are at roost; and all for the sake of calling this enchanting little rustic your wife?"

"Hey day!" exclaimed Lodovico, in a loud laugh, "have the thoughts of matrimony so far beguiled away from you the recollection of past pleasures, that you think no dish can now have any relish for another which has not been said grace over by a friar?"

"Is this your plan?" said Claudio, gravely. "For shame! for shame!"

Lodovico felt the justice of the reproof; but the present application of it was one in which he did not choose to acknowledge that he felt it, and, endeavouring to continue the laugh he had raised at the commencement of the last sentence he had spoken, he said, "I cannot help being diverted at the solemnity of a rake like yourself, going to turn married man."

"I have been a rake, I confess it," replied Claudio; "at least, I do not pretend to have been the phlegmatic stoic who would turn away from an engaging woman bent on love, and with sufficient years of discretion to judge for herself; but I never was the first to raise the blush on the unsullied cheek of modesty. The very inequality of the combat between the man who is skilled in the deceits of a life of libertinism, and an innocent rustic, should deter a man of principle from tampering with an untutored heart.

"Be a rake, if you will, Lodovico: Florence affords opportunities enough for diversion. Look round, you will find numerous sunflowers that will make you their orb of light, and face you, turn which way you will: with them, you may repent the folly of your ill-spent moments; with an innocent girl like this, the time would arrive, that your heart would ache without expiating your crime."

Lodovico continued silent for a few moments, then said, "Well, I do confess, that you have always been more principled in your pleasures than myself, and I solemnly swear, that hereafter I will take pattern by you; but, in this one instance, I feel my happiness depend so strongly on possessing her, that———"

"That you would sacrifice the eternal peace of mind of an innocent girl, for the momentary gratification of a wanton gust of passion," said Claudio, and then returned his eyes to a book he held in his hand.

Lodovico paced the room, apparently not well pleased with his friend's admonitions, and yet convinced of their truth, although unable to subdue the spirit which tempted him to act in defiance of them.

An uninterrupted silence prevailed, till Lodovico's servant, Julius, was announced to be returned from Florence, and immediately ordered by his master to come into the room. Julius entered almost breathless with the speed he had used in his return; and Lodovico instantly addressed him with, "Well, Julius, have you discovered any thing? Where do they live?"

"At the hotel of Saint Luke," replied Julius.

"What brings them to Florence? have you learnt that?" continued Lodovico.

"Pretty nearly, I fancy, I have, sir," returned Julius. "I am well acquainted with the landlord, and he says———"

"What, what?" interrupted Lodovico.

"Why," returned the useful messenger, "he says they seem strange kind of people, and he can't make them out at all."

"Blockhead," cried Lodovico, "is this all that you———"

"Your patience, sir," interrupted Julius: "he says his wife has a shrewd guess about their business."

"Indeed!" said Lodovico. "Well, what does she think?"

"She does not pretend to go nearer than a guess," returned Julius; "but she thinks, she says, that they are no better than they should be."

"Why, why does she conjecture this?" asked Lodovico, triumph and joy lighting up his countenance.

"Why," went on Julius, "she says, they know nobody in Florence; and she has overheard them often wondering, that some gentleman does not come and fetch away the young girl."

"Indeed!" exclaimed Lodovico.

"Yes, sir," continued Julius; "and she says, they are always asking if no enquiries have been made at the hotel about them, by any gentleman; and that the old man is always taking Nina out to walk about the city, as if he wanted her to show herself, and gain attention."

"Very well, very well," cried Lodovico: "I have heard enough to make me happy."

Julius was dismissed, and Lodovico went on speaking thus: "How strange, that the old fellow should fight so shy of me in his own village, and now have brought Nina to Florence with these evident proofs of sacrificing her to his own benefit: proofs so plain, that they strike even the hostess of an inn. It must have been done to answer some end in the way of gain: however that is immaterial, as long as chance points me out a spark of hope for obtaining her. Don't you wish me joy, Claudio?"

"If she is what this account seems to bespeak her," replied Claudio, "I can have no farther objections to offer to your being the man whom her charms are to make happy in preference to another."

"And I," returned Lodovico, "can have no reason for delaying any longer to pay her a visit."

"Beware," said Claudio, "both for your own sake and hers, how you act on your visit: remember, your opinion of her motive for being in Florence is but conjecture."

"It will soon be reduced to a certainty," rejoined Lodovico, laughing. "Farewell!" and left the room.

His heart beating high with anticipated joys, Lodovico immediately proceeded to Florence, and bent his steps to the hotel of Saint Luke. He enquired for the host, and requested him to make known to his lodger, that a gentleman desired a few moments' conversation with him.

With a significant grin, the host received his message, and left him to impart it. In about five minutes, he returned, and requested Lodovico to follow him.

A few steps brought Lodovico to an apartment, the door of which the host opened for him, and then left him. On entering, he found Louis de Saint Pierre alone in the room. The old man advanced to meet him with the salutation of, "You're welcome, sir." His eyes then meeting Lodovico's countenance, he started back, and added, "Do I behold the Signor Lodovico?"

"The same," replied Lodovico, extending his hand, which the old peasant directly met with his, and greeted with a fondly pressure. "How fares the beautiful Nina?" asked Lodovico.

"Very well, very well, Signor," answered Louis.

"Heaven be praised," returned Lodovico. "It is of her," he continued—then suddenly reflecting that he might be mistaken in his conjecture concerning the motive of her visit to Florence, he said, "I came to speak to you, good old man, on a subject in which my heart is deeply interested."

"I doubt it not, I doubt it not," rejoined Louis. A tear started in his eye; he endeavoured to hide it from the observation of Lodovico, and added, "Pray, Signor, speak on."

"I shall be brief," continued Lodovico, "in coming to the purport of my visit: the exquisite girl who accompanies you to Florence is————"

"I knew it well, I knew it well," replied the old peasant. "You are come to take her from me."

Lodovico was now confident in the opinion of the hostess, and assured in his own desires, he answered, with a rapture he could ill conceal, "You understand my meaning then?"

"I do, I do," answered Louis de Saint Pierre.

"You shall find your account therein, be assured," said Lodovico.

"Alas, sir!" replied the old peasant, "I ask no return for what I have done for her: I love her too tenderly to lessen the regard I have shown her, by the acceptance of the requital you are pleased to offer me."

This was a strange language to Lodovico at the present moment: he knew not how to understand it, otherwise than thinking the requital for the prize he was going to receive from the old man laid entirely upon him, and accordingly saying, "Your state cannot be affluent: I entreat you to accept this trifling sum." He put into the hand of old Louis a purse of gold.

"Kind, sir," replied Louis, "I thank you. Your bounty may serve to cheer my latter solitary days; for solitary they will be indeed bereft of my dear Nina. Excuse an old man's tears; but I cannot choose but weep, though I well know it is to her interest to leave me."

"Let that certainty, and the knowledge of my ardent love for her, console you," rejoined Lodovico.

"May Heaven will it so!" exclaimed Louis; and, after a momentary pause, he added, "I will bring her to you, Signor, and tell her the happiness that awaits her." He made some steps towards the door; then stopped, and looking Lodovico full in the face, he said, "I little thought this, Signor, when I saw you in my humble village."

"My heart was then the same," answered Lodovico.

"And fate is incomprehensible," replied the old man, and left the room.

Libertine as Lodovico was, and unaccustomed as he had ever been to suffer the feelings of an indifferent person to interrupt his plans of private happiness, he felt something like remorse, for which he found it difficult to account, at the tears which flowed from the eyes of the silver-headed Louis. For a few moments, the ardour of anticipated pleasure became damped in his breast: he paced the room, stopped, reflected, and at length smiled again. "What cause have I to feel remorse," he exclaimed, "when the old man's easy accession to my proposal, before I had scarcely hinted it, authorizes my conduct, had I never before designed it?" This reflection re-assured him; and the voice of Nina at that moment, heard without the apartment, strung his every nerve to rapture.

What Nina's words were, he did not correctly understand; but he immediately heard Louis say, "Come, come, bear up, thou wilt shortly forget old Louis."

"Forget thee!" exclaimed Nina, "never, never forget to love and honour thee."

They now entered the apartment, and Louis de Saint Pierre pointing to Lodovico, said, "Behold, my love, the Signor who demands you."

The voice of Nina had wound the feelings of Lodovico to the highest pitch of extacy: the sight of her left him scarcely master of himself; and darting towards her, he grasped her hand in his, and, as if yet fearful of the completion of his wishes, he asked, "Lovely girl," do you consent to the happiness I propose for you?"

Nina trembled: it appeared to be with difficulty that she commanded her utterance. After some minutes of hesitation, she replied, "My duty, Signor, bids me yield compliance to your will. Pardon me: my heart is now too full of various emotions to grant me utterance for all that passes in it; but I entreat you to conceive me all I ought to be to you, and you will then conceive me all I will endeavor to be."

"Thou exquisite perfection!" exclaimed Lodovico, clasping her to his breast, and imprinting on her lips the first kiss of love, "the sweet confession tingles on my heart, and fires me with the ardor of returning all the fond delight your smiles can give."

Again Louis de Saint Pierre wiped a tear from his eye, and raised his hands to Heaven in silent supplication for the welfare of his beloved Nina.

"Come, lovely girl," said Lodovico, "are you ready to put yourself under my protection?"

"Oh, Signor!" cried Louis, "before you tear her for ever from me, grant me the only boon I shall ask of you—once more to see her, ere I quit this city?"

"You shall, old man," answered Lodovico, "most willingly you shall."

"Where, Signor, shall I find her," asked Louis.

"Enquire," returned Lodovico, "for Lodovico di Ponta, at the villa di Bartelma, about half a league from this city."

"Once more embrace me, my dear, beloved child," said Louis, extending his open arms towards Nina.

Nina threw her arms round his neck, kissed his cheek, and exclaimed, "Farewell, thou kindest, best of men!"

"May Heaven grant thee to be as happy as old Louis wishes thee!" exclaimed the old peasant. Nina retired from his embrace with a tottering step: Lodovico caught her trembling frame in his arms, and conveyed her to the gondola which: had brought him to Florence.

CHAPTER XI.

My hour is almost come———

HAMLET.

THAT the beautiful Nina de Saint Pierre was his own, every rapture-beating pulse in the frame of Lodovico di Ponta told him: by what extraordinary means the innocence of her character was converted into the most refined art, he was at a loss to comprehend. It occupied his thoughts for a few moments; but the heat of his passion soon dismissed the subject for one of nearer interest to his own pleasure, which was—where he should, for the present, lodge his lovely prize.

He determined to ask the advice of Claudio; and accordingly ordered the gondoliers to convey him back to the villa di Bartelma. Nina was placed by his side in the gondola: one of his arms encircled her waist, the other hand held hers. She did not withdraw herself from his caresses; but a frown of distrust and anxiety, which she appeared in vain to be endeavouring to dispel, sat on her countenance. Lodovico exerted himself to reassure her by every protestation of his love and friendship: she heard his vows without interruption, and seemed to gain confidence and ease from their repetition.

When they arrived at the margin of the garden, Lodovico caught Nina in his arms, and carried her on shore.

"Do you reside here?" she asked, pointing to the house.

"No," replied Lodovico: "this is the villa of a friend of mine."

"Of a friend," repeated Nina, in a voice of distrust.

"Yes," answered Lodovico: "of that Claudio whom you must recollect having seen with me in your village."

"Oh!" returned Nina, a faint smile adorning her coral lips, "I remember: he who danced so little, and———" she hesitated—

"By his laziness," added Lodovico, "gave me the opportunity of tasting some of the happiest moments of my life. Were you angry with him?"

"I cannot say I was displeased at dancing with you," answered Nina, with the air of *naïveté* she had before been accustomed to speak in.

Lodovico again pressed her hand in ecstasy between his: they were surrounded by too many observers for him to return her a warmer acknowledgement for her confession.

Paulo was at that moment advancing from the house; and Lodovico, having beckoned to him, led Nina to the hermitage which stood a few paces from the margin of the river, saying, "I must entreat you to remain here a few moments, my dearest Nina. Fear no interruption during my absence: you will meet with none, I assure you; and I will return as quickly as possible."

"Pray do," replied Nina: "I am almost afraid———" she hesitated——

"Dear girl," exclaimed Lodovico, "would I, for the sake of my own happiness, ask you to remain where you were unsafe?"

"Oh! no, no;" she returned, "I am a foolish, timid girl: it is my duty to confide in you. Go."

Lodovico imprinted a second kiss on her love-inviting lips, and leaving the hermitage, he ran to meet Paulo.

"Paulo," he said, "will you perform me a service?"

"Most willingly, Signor," replied Paulo.

"Then," said Lodovico, "remain during my absence, which will not be long, near the hermitage, and prevent any one from entering it."

Paulo bowed in the affirmative to Lodovico's request.

Lodovico put a piece of gold into his hand, and asked where he should find Claudio.

"In the library," Paulo replied; and Lodovico immediately bent his hasty steps towards the house.

Claudio was just awoke from his *siesto*, when Lodovico burst into the room. "Wish me joy, my dear fellow," he cried: "I am the happiest man in existence. Nina is mine."

"How so?" asked Claudio.

"Upon the only terms I would take the trouble of calling any woman my own," rejoined Lodovico.

Wine was standing on the table before Claudio. Lodovico filled a goblet, and drank to the health of his fair prize. Claudio followed his example, and then enquired the particulars of his friend's interview with Louis de Saint Pierre, which was speedily recounted by Lodovico; and while Claudio was expressing the same surprise which had already been occupying the mind of Lodovico, at the easy compliance which had attended his wishes, Lodovico drank another goblet of wine, and continued, "Come, Claudio, now advise me: where am I to give Nina a habitation? I can't for a moment encourage the idea of bringing her into a house, of which I hope soon to see my sister the mistress. I am unacquainted with any person or situation in Florence where I can place her to my liking. What am I to do with her?"

Claudio was for a few moments silent: he then said, "How should you like a cottage close by the margin of the river, which she might have entirely to herself?"

"Are you acquainted with such a one?" asked Lodovico, eagerly.

"I know one which was vacant a few days ago," replied Claudio; "and if you should like to have it, I will directly make enquiries about it for you myself."

"Oh! by all means," exclaimed Lodovico: "you cannot more highly oblige me;" and again the wildness of pleasure lifted the replenished goblet to his lips.

"First," said Claudio, "I must exact one condition from you, and I go immediately: do you assure me, upon your honour, that you have used no art to inveigle this girl into your power? that she is now with you from inclination, not treachery; and fully aware of her own situation?"

"My dear fellow," cried Lodovico, smothering a laugh, "I only wish you could have seen the readiness with which my proposals were accepted, nay anticipated, I may say, both by her father and herself. However, to ease your scruples, upon my honour, no deceit has been used towards her on my part: my conduct has been open and honourable."

Satisfied with this assurance, Claudio instantly sat out to make enquiries relative to the cottage of which he had spoken, saying, he should bring what information he could collect about it to Lodovico at the hermitage.

Lodovico now, for the first time, recollected, that a little of the beverage which the heat of the day had rendered so very acceptable to him, might be as welcome to Nina. Quarreling with himself for his forgetfulness, he snatched the bottle from the table, intending to run with it immediately to the hermitage: he raised it to the light, and found it empty. It was full when he first came into the room. He could now scarcely forbear cursing his own selfishness: he had emptied a bottle, she had not been offered a drop. Violently he called for a fresh supply of wine: it was brought to him. He ordered some lemonade and biscuits to be added. His agitation had again raised the fever of drought in his mouth and throat, and again the wine was called in to dispel it. At length, the different refreshments which he had ordered were all placed before him on a salver, and he took it up in order to proceed with it to the hermitage.

He was surprised that he could not support it steadily: his hands trembled under the weight of the salver. He did not stay to investigate the cause, but called to Paulo, from a window, to leave his station for a moment, and carry what he found to be unsafe in his own hands. Paulo obeyed; and it required little penetration in Paulo to discover, that the combined effects of extravagant joy and anxiety, operated upon by a few goblets of wine, had left Lodovico little in possession of his calm reason.

Claudio soon found the owner of the cottage; and a bargain being easily struck, which made Lodovico its tenant at option, Claudio returned homewards. Instead of entering the house, he proceeded towards the hermitage, as had been agreed upon between Lodovico and himself that he should do, when he had seen the landlord of the cottage. As Claudio advanced towards the hermitage, he heard the voice of Lodovico in no very gentle sounds; and he fancied, though he believed that his senses deceived him, that he heard a faint shriek. He continued to move on, and was arrived within fifty paces of the hermitage, when Nina de Saint Pierre, her hair dishevelled, her dress torn, her lips breathing incoherent accents of distress, and the wildest agony painted in her frantic eyes, rushed from it.

Claudio started: he feared what he felt averse to confide even to his own heart. A moment convinced him of the truth of his suspicion: it presented to his sight, Lodovico pursuing the fugitive with unsteady steps, but a determined countenance, lighted by the sparkling rays of libertinism and intoxication.

Claudio advanced towards them: Nina flew to meet him; and throwing herself upon the ground before him, she clung to his knees, exclaiming, "Oh, Signor! save me: I am betrayed, insulted. Oh! for the love of God, save a defenceless, unprotected girl from ruin."

Lodovico followed, and attempted to seize the arm of Nina: Claudio stepped forward before her, and said, "Lodovico, is it thus you pledge your honour?"

Lodovico was beyond the reach of argument: *the noblest passion prophaned, and the most degrading vice indulged*, held his senses in subjection. With a stubborn laugh, he exclaimed, "Come, come, you know my determination;" and endeavoured to pass Claudio, who still stood between him and the kneeling Nina; Claudio again moved his station to counteract his intention of passing him, and said, "You know, Lodovico, that I never profess a principle to which I dare not act up: you well know the principle to which I at this moment allude. Beware you do not provoke me to treat you harshly:" then turning to Nina, he added, "Sweet girl, confide in my protection."

"Claudio," cried Lodovico, endeavouring to command a clear utterance, "we have hitherto lived friends; but unless you forego that hand, the name by which we know each other must change."

With calm firmness, Claudio replied, "Will you abjure me for your friend, when I am proving myself most worthy of the sacred title?"

"My passions are at this instant in no state for argument,"

exclaimed Lodovico, with fierceness. "Do you persist to thwart my will?"

"Shall I become a party concerned against the honour of a defenceless woman?" said Claudio.

Again Lodovico attempted to pass Claudio, and again Claudio frustrated his design. Wound up almost to madness by his uncontroulable feelings, the accents of Lodovico's rage were scarcely any longer to be understood. "My servants shall force her from you," was alone spoken in distinguishable sounds; and a subsequent effort produced,—"Julius, Cassio; Julius, Cassio."

Claudio attempted to catch hold of Lodovico's arm: "My dear friend, my dear Lodovico," he rejoined, "I entreat you to be composed, to suffer yourself to be convinced."

At that moment, a spark of strength, together with a momentary power of speech, returned to Lodovico: hastily drawing his sword, he called out, "By heaven, I will not brook your usage of me! Suffer me to pass you, or, by the Almighty Powers, my sword shall force me a passage through your heart to her arms."

Nina clung to Claudio, and shrieked aloud for help.

All remonstrance was in vain: Lodovico continued to press forward upon Claudio with his naked sword, and Claudio, in defence of his own safety and that of Nina, was compelled to draw his sword; with pointing which, at arm's length, against his adversary; he hoped he might prevent his coming too close upon him and his trembling charge.

Still Lodovico continued to push his way; and Claudio disengaged himself from the grasp of Nina, not doubting but that, with both his arms at liberty, he could keep his adversary at bay, by foiling his thrusts, till the servants, whom Nina's shrieks must have alarmed, should come up, and assist him in disarming the insanity of Lodovico.

For some minutes, his stratagem succeeded, till Lodovico bending suddenly forward, rather from the uncertain swing of intoxication than from any design of pressing forward, fell upon the sword of Claudio, before he was aware of the danger of his friend; and when Claudio hastily withdrew it, the blood rushed from the wound, and Lodovico sunk upon the ground, exclaiming, "I am killed, basely murdered, murdered by Claudio—by my friend!"

The servants at that moment came up, and the last words of their master were immediately echoed by Julius and Cassio, Lodovico's two servants. In vain did Claudio, with coolness, but not without heart-rending agony, recount the truth: in vain did the innocent lips of Nina support his assertions: the servants of Lodovico heard their declarations, with countenances which were far from appearing to receive their words as the truth.

Claudio knelt down on one side of Lodovico, and endeavoured to ascertain if the life had really fled. Paulo dispatched a servant for a surgeon. Nina, the injured Nina, forgot her wrongs; and tearing her muslin robe, bound it round his wounds to stop the flowing blood.

In a few moments, Lodovico's servants proposed carrying their master to his bed. Claudio had no reason to disapprove of this wish, or if he had, they did not appear likely to have attended to it; and, accordingly, the body of Lodovico was taken up between them, and they moved with it towards the house.

Claudio stood with his face buried in his hands, in a stupor of misery. A shriek of joy from the lips of Nina roused him from his reflections. "Oh, Louis! my father, my dear father!" she exclaimed, "blessed be the Virgin that I behold you once more!"

Claudio was standing within a hundred paces of the river. He looked around, saw Nina running towards its margin, and immediately beheld a gondola drawing in its oars opposite to the garden. Without any fixed design, he followed Nina towards the brink of the river; and as he approached it, he saw Louis de Saint Pierre spring from on board, and having taken Nina in his arms, directly return with her into the vessel. No sooner had he entered it, than he presented her to a man who was muffled in a long cloak; and who, throwing it aside to embrace her, presented to the astonished sight of Claudio—the features of the *mysterious pilgrim*.

What were their words at meeting, Claudio could not hear; but scarcely had the pilgrim released Nina from his embrace, and the oars of the gondola were again thrown out, than a second gondola appeared in view, on board of which, Claudio discovered the Count di Ponta, whose attendants and baggage bespoke him to be then concluding a journey, which he had doubtless made to Florence, in compliance with Lodovico's letter.

Before Claudio had time to feel that his misery was encreased by the arrival of Lodovico's father at this unseasonable moment, the gondola which had on board the Count, and that which contained the pilgrim and Nina, passed each other. The Pilgrim and the Count were so situated in their respective vessels, that their countenances fell on each other at the moment of their passing. Their eyes met. A sudden start betrayed the inward emotion of each. "The Count di Ponta!" burst from the lips of the pilgrim. "Thou here!" thundered forth the voice of the Count. The pilgrim drew his cloak over his face, and the Count sat fixed in mute surprise. A few movements of the oars carried the vessels to a considerable distance from each other, and that of the Count was drawn up to the margin of the garden.

Paulo had not left the side of Claudio, since the fatal event which had a few minutes before taken place; and now taking hold of his arm, and leading him away from the spot where he had been standing, he said, "My dear master, for Heaven's sake, do not be the first to meet the Count di Ponta at this dreadful moment. His eye has not as yet fallen upon you. Come to the hermitage: let him gain the intelligence of his son's fate from any tongue rather than from yours."

Claudio replied only by a smothered groan, and suffered himself to be led by Paulo to the hermitage.

"Rash, rash Lodovico!" exclaimed Claudio, as Paulo placed him on the bench; "Couldst thou revive, and know the misery of thy friend, what would be thy feelings?"

"Be composed, my dear master," said Paulo, "indeed, I don't believe him dead: the wound cannot be a mortal one: I am sure it is not near his heart."

"Would the surgeon were come," rejoined Claudio. "To know the worst would not be so terrible to me as this wretched suspense."

"Promise me you will not leave this spot; pray promise me that," said the faithful Paulo, "and I will go to the house, and endeavour to learn what you have to hope or fear."

"I shall not leave it, be assured," replied Claudio: "I have here all I now desire—solitude for my reflections."

Paulo then moved towards the house with all the celerity threescore and ten years would allow him to exert, and Claudio sunk down upon the bench almost devoid of sensation.

CHAPTER XII.

> ————Our compell'd sins
> Stand more for number than account.
>
> Virtue is bold, and goodness never fearful.
>
> MEASURE FOR MEASURE.

WHEN Paulo returned to the hermitage, which he did not do till nearly the expiration of two hours, Claudio raising his eyes to him on his entrance, said, "I read in your countenance the intelligence you bring—Lodovico is no more."

Paulo shook his head in silence, then replied, "You must take sanctuary."

"No, no," cried Claudio, clasping his hands in despair, "let me expiate by death, the crime of death which I have committed."

"My dear master," replied Paulo, "you have not a heart capable of committing an intentional crime: it would be therefore unjust, that you should suffer for an accident as a deliberate criminal."

With all the eloquence of tenderness and fidelity did Paulo continue to implore Claudio to seek his own safety. Unmoved he heard his entreaties, till Paulo added to his arguments, "You must not suffer the death of a common malefactor: you must not suffer this disgrace to rest on the son of he Marchese di Bartelma."

Claudio instantly started up: "Lead me where you will for safety," he exclaimed. "There is not that sacrifice I would not make to the memory of Bartelma."

"It is already growing dusk: the gondola lies by the side of the garden," returned Paulo. "My brother, in whom I can confide, is within call: we will convey you to Florence, and there you will find no difficulty in gaining the altar of Saint Paul."

Paulo gave the signal to his brother, who almost immediately appeared: "Come," said Paulo, "enter the gondola, we shall be ready in a few moments."

Claudio followed him. In his way to the gondola, he passed the pavilion: "Perhaps," he said within himself, "I now behold thee for the last time; farewell! I owe thee something, for thou wert my first protector when I was cast friendless on the mercy of strangers." A tear stole down his cheek: he felt his fortitude weakening at every moment he remained on the beloved spot where he stood; and exclaiming hastily, as he threw his eyes towards the house, "Farewell for ever!" he sprang into the gondola.

Without difficulty, Claudio reached the church of Saint Paul: his faithful servant, Paulo, no entreaties could prevail upon to pass the night apart from his master.

Reflection occupied the mind of Claudio: whether to dread the resentment of the Count di Ponta, or to believe that he would accept the truth as an apology for the unfortunate event of the day, was a point on which Claudio could not resolve; nor was the strange circumstance of the meeting between the pilgrim and the Count di Ponta, entirely absent from his mind, although his own immediate concern occupied by far the greater part of his thoughts.

With the morning, Paulo went out to endeavour to learn whether the Count had taken any measures for the apprehension of Claudio. About noon, he returned: with impatience Claudio urged him to speak.

"I bring strange information," replied Paulo, "and I know not whether to deem it good, or bad."

"Whatever it be, speak," returned Claudio.

"About an hour ago," answered Paulo, "as I was standing in the street of Saint John, I saw the officers of justice leading a man to prison: he appeared about forty or forty-fire years of age; his hair grey from premature old age, and his dress plain almost to shabbiness. I enquired for what offence he was arrested, and one of the by-standers told me, that he was accused of murder by the Count di Ponta."

"This is strange indeed!" exclaimed Claudio: "how can this mistake have originated? The error must lie with the officers of justice; for I cannot think that Lodovico's servants, who saw me with the blood-stained sword in my hand, would do otherwise than bluntly accuse me to their master's father."

"I think it must be so," returned Paulo, "but my dear master, this mistake at all events favours your departure from Florence, as it will not in all probability be discovered, till you are beyond the reach of your enemies."

"And from my absence," rejoined Claudio, "an innocent man may suffer an unjust punishment.—Oh, no! though I did not hold myself bound to deliver up my life for the forfeit of an accident, it is surely my duty now to surrender up my person, and spare the horrors of a prison, the apprehension of an ignominious death, to an innocent man."

"Oh! for Heaven's sake, be not so rash," exclaimed Paulo: "consider what you just now said of the Marchese di Bartelma, my poor dead master———"

"It is my regard for him," interrupted Claudio, "which urges me on to this step; the principles of honour were the first instructions he gave to my youthful heart, and though the world may call it a reproach upon his memory, that his son should suffer an ignominious death; yet the heart of that son teaches him that, were his father alive, he would think him less culpable in suffering this ignominious death in expiation of an unforeseen accident, than in permitting a fellow creature to pay the forfeit of his fault by the loss of an innocent life.—I am resolved: which is the prison?"

"That of the Holy Cross," answered Paulo; "but on my knees I entreat you, my dear master, not to quit the protection of God, which the altar here affords you."

"God is every where alike the protector of the upright heart," exclaimed Claudio; and bursting from Paulo's hands which were entwined round his knees, he rushed into the street.

Arrived at the prison of the Holy Cross, he entered the outer court, and rang the bell at the great gate: the jailor opened it, and Claudio rushed in.—"What would you, Signor?" demanded the jailor. "Is there not a man in this prison, accused of murder by the Count di Ponta?" asked Claudio. "There is," the jailor replied. "He is innocent," exclaimed Claudio; "release him instantly, and put your chains on me." "Signor!" ejaculated the jailor. "I am the guilty man," continued Claudio: "I surrender myself up to justice." "Excuse me, Signor," returned the jailor, "but indeed I believe you are a little out of your senses: pray go away." "On my faith and honor, I am your just prisoner," said Claudio, with calmness but emphasis. The jailor laughed, then replied, "Ah! Signor, I see very well what kind of confinement it is you want: I'd lay my life you have broke out of some bedlam, and think you are come back to it now; but I assure you you are wrong: pray go away." "Well, think me mad, if you please," returned Claudio: "I am only sorry it is so rare to hear a man acknowledge himself in fault, that when he does so, he is accounted mad. If I am mad, I have my lucid intervals: I am sure you will perceive my fit is off when you handle this;" and with these words, he put a couple of pieces of gold into the hand of jailor. "Why you are not so bad as I thought you, Signor," replied the jailor, with a grin of satisfaction. "Now lead me to this man's prison," said Claudio. "Why, Signor," returned the jailor, "I would with all my heart, only I believe he wishes to be alone." "And I," answered Claudio, putting two more pieces of gold into the prepared hand of the jailor, "believe he wishes to see company." "It would be unhandsome of me, Signor, to dispute what you say," returned the jailor; "so please to follow me."

Through a chain of dark passages, the jailor preceded Claudio to a door fastened by many bolts, which he undrew; and then thrusting in his head, addressed his prisoner with, "Here is a Signor who—"

"Will speak for himself," said Claudio, interrupting him, and at the same moment entering the cell, which was faintly illuminated by the gleam of a single lamp, suspended against the dusky wall.

"Well, speak for yourself, if you will," cried the jailor, "and I'll leave you together to settle it;" so saying, he closed the door, and disappeared.

Claudio advanced, and a dark figure stepped forward from a recess in the cell to meet him: Claudio moved on, the rays of the lamp fell on the countenance of the figure which was approaching towards him, and discovered to him, the features of the mysterious pilgrim.—Claudio started back.—A chaos of undigested ideas floated in his brain: he remembered the exclamation of the pilgrim, and the surprise of the Count di Ponta on the preceding day, when the gondolas passed each other in the river.—His eyes continued fixed on the form before him.—The pilgrim came up to him, and took his hand, "Is Lodovico di Ponta then dead?"

he said.—Claudio was still more surprised at this question. "Oh! yes," he replied, "and"—"Well, well," exclaimed the pilgrim, with a mixed emotion of pleasure and agony, "We shall then at least *die* together."

This was to Claudio a strange, an incomprehensible exclamation; he answered it by saying, "You will not *die*; I come to save you; I come to deliver myself up as the unfortunate destroyer of Lodovico di Ponta."

The pilgrim's eyes in his turn gleamed with the wild enquiry of surprise; then turning aside from Claudio, and striking his hands upon his forehead, he exclaimed, in a scarcely audible voice, "Oh God, what a moment is this!"

In as few words as the subject would admit, Claudio went on, endeavouring to administer consolation to the pilgrim, by recounting that his imprisonment must be an error, as he was himself the actor of the unfortunate crime for which the pilgrim was suffering a false confinement.

"Oh, almighty powers!" cried the pilgrim, the violence of his emotion encreasing. "Are you then not arraigned by justice, but here only at your *own* will?"

Claudio answered in the affirmative.

"Then fly, instantly fly!" returned the pilgrim, "while there is yet a possibility of your life being saved."

"What!" exclaimed Claudio, "think you I could fly, and leave you here to suffer for my crime?"

"It is not your crime for which I stand accused," returned the pilgrim; "there is now no time for explanation, but it is not your crime."

"Oh, I see your motive," replied Claudio, "but I cannot yield to it.—I have ever through life perceived that you have taken an interest in my fate, and you would now deliver up your life upon the scaffold to save mine."

The whole frame of the pilgrim became convulsed, his eyes rolled with frantic wildness, and he exclaimed, "Forbear to torture me, and fly as I command you."

"Never!" replied Claudio, with emphasis, "never! you shall not suffer for my crime."

"I repeat that it is *not* yours:—I call on heaven to witness, that it is *not* your crime," shrieked out the pilgrim in a paroxysm of phrenzy.

"To what am I to attribute this interest in my fate?" cried Claudio, wound up to a pitch of feeling which rendered him unmindful of the charge under which he lived.—"Who are you?—Why have I met you at every important moment of my life?—Why have you shown yourself unable to quit me, and yet studious to shun my observation?—Why————?"

"Away, away," interrupted the pilgrim, "thoul't madden me."

"Why," continued Claudio, unmindful of his command, "why now offer your own life to expiate a murder for which mine is the just forfeit?—Oh! on my knees———"

"Kneel not to me," exclaimed the pilgrim; "It's I whom thou should'st curse—'tis I who have driven thee an outcast upon the world—torn thee from a parent's arms, to give thee to the bosom of a stranger—fated thee to plunge thy sword in the heart of thy friend for my error; and thou, the innocent sufferer, art now condemned either to atone thy honourable fault by an ignominious death, or to live the despised offspring of an executed malefactor."

"Oh! of whom shall I be the despised offspring? let me know my father; if it be but to share disgrace with him, let me know my father," cried Claudio.

The pilgrim uttered a groan of agony.

"Oh! who, what is my father?" repeated Claudio.

"A murderer!" replied the pilgrim, in a voice of thrilling horror.

"Murderer!" echoed Claudio, faintly.

"Aye;" continued the pilgrim, "the murderer of thy mother."

Claudio rose slowly from his knees, and clasped his hands in silence.

"Now, wouldst thou still know thy father?" asked the pilgrim, with a frantic solemnity of countenance.

"If I could serve him;" returned Claudio, after a pause.

"Thou mayest serve him," replied the pilgrim, "and die with his blessing on thy head."

"Oh!" exclaimed Claudio, "point out to me the means."

The pilgrim fell hastily on one knee, and presenting a poniard to Claudio, he cried, "Plunge this into my breast, and preserve thy father from death upon a scaffold."

Claudio sunk, from the wildness of expectation, into an attitude of astonishment and horror.

The agony of mind, and frantic exertion of the pilgrim during the few last moments, had entirely wasted his mental and bodily powers; and he fell back upon the floor in a state of insensibility.

The fall of the old man roused Claudio from his lethargy of thought: he ran to him, and supported his head on his arm, and after some minutes, recalled him into existence:—The fever of his mental agony had evaporated in the burst of passion which had wasted his strength, and he now opened his eyes with a serene calmness, which recalled to Claudio the recollection of his person on that day when he first beheld him at the villa di Bartelma. "Art thou still with me?" he said, in accents of faint pleasure. "Hast thou not fled from a father first known to thee as a parent in a loathsome dungeon, with the thunder of justice denounced against a murderer, pressing on his head? Oh my boy, my boy! for nineteen years I have not clasped my child to my bosom; do not now withdraw thyself from his embrace. Oh! my son, my son!" he added, in a voice choked by contending feelings, and fell upon the neck of Claudio. Rising from the earth, he continued, "I told thee I was a murderer—I have not been so, my child, without wrongs to provoke me to the bloody deed which has since cursed my fame, and blunted my happiness in this world. It was the baseness of others, rather than my own error, which drove me to commit the action I am now doomed to expiate by my death; but fly, I charge you, fly, and leave me!" he exclaimed, interrupting himself, "You may yet preserve your life; every moment you remain here, endangers it: I had forgotten your safety was at stake. Oh! forgive me, I have a full heart of misery for my excuse—one more, one last embrace, and then—farewell for ever!"

"By Heaven, no!" cried Claudio, "no power shall tear me from a father, whose situation so peculiarly requires the support of a son's affection."

Again the pilgrim burst into tears, and threw his arms round Claudio's neck; he spoke not, but the strictness of his embrace conveyed the gratitude of his overflowing soul.

"You said true, my father," rejoined Claudio, "we shall at least *die* together."

"My expression," replied the old man, "was the first exclamation of a heart weakened by affliction, and overpowered by the sudden appearance of one so tenderly beloved, where so little expected to be seen.—But surely, surely the Count di Ponta will spare you, when he learns the cause of your misfortune, although I do not expect that he will ever show mercy to me."

"To you!" exclaimed Claudio, "Is then the Count di Ponta the enemy who imprisons you here, and seeks your life?"

"He," returned the pilgrim, "even he, who once called himself my friend."

Claudio's soul was on the rack to learn an explanation of the mystery before him, and he besought his father to develope it to him,—"Yes, my son," he returned "since I am known by my enemy to be in existence, there is no longer any reason for my son to be debarred the confidence of his father; my motive for secrecy has now subsided.—Grant me a few moments to collect my wasted powers, and thou shalt hear, in full detail, the wayward destiny that has attended thy father, and doubly wounded him in its descent on his innocent and unhappy children."

Claudio drew a bench, and having placed his father upon it, he sat down by his side. After a few moments' pause, the old man spoke thus: "You must have heard, in your intercourse with the world, that Count Montano di Ponta gained his right to the pallazo and estates, which he now holds in the neighbourhood of Placenza, by the death of his cousin Angelo, who having put to death his wife in a moment of jealousy, could not outlive the racks of his conscience, and died by his own hand."

Claudio replied, that he was acquainted with the circumstance.

His father then went on: "That Angelo," he continued, "supposed to be no more, is *thy father.*—'Tis Angelo who now addresses thee.—Montano and myself are cousins.—I, the immediate nephew of the then existing Count di Ponta; he, one descent removed below me.—At the death of the old Count, the hereditary pallazo and estates near Placenza devolved on me: to his great nephew, Montano, the old Count bequeathed his personal property, and a mansion in the city of Parma; still however his possessions were very inferior to mine, and Montano (of which I was then entirely ignorant and unsuspicious), looked upon my superior fortune with the most invidious malignancy.

"Shortly after the death of the old Count, Montano married a lady, whom he selected for her fortune, rather than any preference he felt for her mind or person: at the expiration of a twelvemonth after their nuptials, she brought him his daughter Valeria.—Shortly after the birth of Montano's child, I first saw your mother: Oh! my son, how exquisitely beautiful a woman was then my Horatia, scarcely eighteen years had rolled over her head; every grace adorned her person, every fascinating accomplishment lived in her mind, every inviting beauty ornamented her face; I loved and married her.—Ere another year had elapsed, you were born, and a few months after your entrance into the world, the wife of Montano gave birth to Lodovico, and expired in the pangs of becoming the mother of a son.

"From this period, Montano was constant in his visits at my pallazo, nay he frequently made it his abode for many weeks together. I suspected then neither his friendship, nor my wife's honor; but the time was rapidly advancing, when the fatal discovery to my peace was to be made.

"I shall pass over many intervening circumstances, which you could take no interest in having recounted, which, at the time, appeared to me innocent; but which I now look back upon, and perceive to have been the dawnings of my wife's infidelity and my misery, to the hour when she presented me with a daughter. About three months after this event, going one day unexpectedly by her into her closet, I found—(Oh, my son! judge whether I had not sufficient provocation for the rash act which I committed)—I found my wife locked in the arms of Montano di Ponta!

"In the phrenzy of my passion, I drew my sword, intending to pierce the heart of my false friend: your mother rushed between us to prevent the blow, and sheathed my sword in her own breast."

Angelo gave a short pause to reflection; then proceeded thus: "The villainy of Montano now displayed itself in glaring colours. For three days, he detained me a prisoner in my own house, on his accusation of my having murdered my wife. At length, to save my guilty life from terminating on a scaffold; I bound myself to fly my country, to leave behind me my offspring, under the care of strangers, pledging myself farther, never to let them know their true parent. The base Montano allowed me a month to dispose of yourself and your sister. I immediately took you with me to Florence, intending, if possible, to find out the nurse who had received me into the world, and who was warmly attached to my father's family, to make her the *confidante* of my sad story, and to ask her advice concerning the disposal of my children.

"With little difficulty I found her. She was grown old and infirm: she was without the means of supporting you, and I had them not to give her. By her advice, I wrote those letters, which you must long ere this have seen, to the Marchese di Bartelma. I had heard the story of his anxiety to become a father, and of his sudden loss of his only child; and I considered, that such a man could not be deaf to the entreaties of a heart-broken parent. The old nurse was my messenger to the church of St. Paul with my first letter to the Marchese; and she it was who conveyed you, and the little oaken box which contained the bracelet you now wear and my second letter, to the pavilion on the margin of the river.

"A few days taught me, by the means of my faithful old nurse, that my most sanguine wishes relative to yourself had succeeded; and all my anxiety was now for my infant daughter."

"Does my sister still live?" asked Claudio.

"Her unsullied honour," returned Angelo, "is your recompence for having been the unfortunate instrument of your friend's death. She whom you yesterday rescued from the violence of Lodovico di Ponta, is your sister, Fulvia."

"Oh, God! I thank thee," exclaimed Claudio, "that an unintended crime has been the produce of a real good."

Angelo took a cross from his bosom, kissed it, held it for a moment to his breast, and then passed it into the hand of Claudio. With his eyes fixed upon the sacred remembrance of his salvation, Claudio fell upon his knees: "Saviour, of eternal mercy," he cried, "who knowest the motive of my crime, and the innocence of my heart; if it shall seem good to thee that I atone my error with my life, grant me thy fortitude in suffering, that I may meet death without a murmur against thy will."

Angelo knelt by the side of his son, and in interval of expressive silence followed Claudio's prayer.

CHAPTER XIII.

>   ———Spirits are not finely touch'd,
> But to fine issues: nor nature never lends
> The smallest scruple of her excellence;
> But, like a thrifty goddess, she determines
> Herself the glory of a creditor—
> Both thanks and use.
>
> MEASURE FOR MEASURE.

ANGELO continued his narrative in the following words: "About a week after your introduction into the family of di Bartelma, my old nurse thus addressed me: 'If you can consent to let your daughter be happy without affluence, I have found a situation for her, where she will enjoy comfort and kindness.' This was an offer of the most consolitary nature to a parent situated as I was; and I eagerly declared myself satisfied with the words of my nurse: she then explained herself by saying, 'My only daughter, who came on a visit to me yesterday, and is going to remain a few weeks with me here in Florence, is married to a worthy peasant, one Louis de Saint Pierre, on the other side of the mountains. They both earnestly wish for children, but the Virgin is deaf to their prayers; and my daughter says, that if you will permit her the care of your little girl, to bring up as her own, it will be the greatest happiness you can bestow both on her husband and herself.'

"To this proposal, I readily and thankfully agreed; only conditioning with my old nurse, that she should secrete, even from her daughter, who was the parent of the unfortunate child thus cut off from the protection of its natural fosterers: which she faithfully promised, and honourably performed.

"The month allowed me by Montano being elapsed, I immediately quitted Italy. My death, as a suicide, was noised about; a fictious funeral, at which Montano appeared inconsolable, was performed; and my pallazo and estates were directly usurped by the destroyer of my peace and honour.

"The many hardships I have undergone, I shall pass over in silence; for they are light compared to the agony of mind I was constantly enduring for the welfare of my children. A hundred ducats were yearly paid to me by a banker at Toulon, from Montano; and on this slender pittance, I was compelled to subsist. I remained in France, wandering about in the true disposition of an uneasy mind, until within a few weeks of the time at which you saw me at the villa di Bartelma. Desirous, if possible, to learn some intelligence of my children, I disguised myself in the manner you saw me, and joined a party of pilgrims above Belluno: they were journeying to Loretto: I accompanied them, and by my contrivance, they stopped for refreshment at the villa di Bartelma. Ah, my son! what did I not experience on once again beholding you! I could scarcely believe you were indeed my boy. Thirteen years had elapsed since I had seen you: you told me you were happy—ah! how earnestly did I then pray you might be mine. On the morning of my departure, I felt upon your wrist that bracelet which I had commanded you to wear, and I was satisfied.

"In journeying through Florence, I visited my old nurse. A few moments only did I venture to stay in her house: they however served to inform me, that my daughter was also well and happy.

"For nearly four years after my pilgrimage, I enjoyed a tolerable calm of mind from the knowledge of your welfare. I then began to reflect, that the uncertain wheel of fortune might one day turn in my favour, either by the death-bed repentance of Montano, or some other one of those causes which almost invariably lead to the detection of villainy, and the restitution of happiness to the oppressed. This reflection brought on a subsequent one, which was, that at the time such an event might take place, if ever it should arrive, my old nurse might be dead, and no means left me of regaining my daughter. I accordingly once more passed over to Florence, for the purpose of concerting some plan with my nurse, by which my daughter might be restored to me at any moment I should again be able to take her under my protection.

"On this second journey into Italy, I altered my disguise, from that of a pilgrim's garb to a monk's habit. It afforded me the screen from public notice and suspicion which I wished to derive from it, and my business with my nurse being concluded, I was journeying into Switzerland; where it was my intention to spend some time in wandering amongst its romantic scenery, when we met in crossing the Alps.

"That I felt satisfaction in again beholding you, I need not repeat: that I concealed my feelings from you, need not also be told you. Your conduct soon explained to me, that you recognized me for the pilgrim that had been entertained at the villa di Bartelma; and I perceived as clearly, that the manner in which I had noticed you on that day, had excited your interest and expectation, and that our second meeting called forth your feelings with redoubled emotion.

"My surprise was, as you must have remarked, great, when I found you close by my side as I knelt to pray at the foot of the rock, in the evening after our journey. I feared that you, nay perhaps also some companions who might be attending you, had heard my prayers uttered aloud for my children; but you heard me only exclaim, "Oh, protect, protect them!" and little did you then imagine for whom I had preferred the petition to heaven.

"I could not forbear questioning you, whether you were happy. Scarcely could I refrain from discovering myself to you; and I drove you from me, that I might not be tempted to make the confession, of which I dreaded the consequence. You left me—I know what misery must be passing in your breast: I hesitated a few moments—I resolved to ease your doubts, by telling you the strange fate that was impending over yourself and your wretched parent.—I followed you for that purpose—I overtook you on the brink of a rivulet—How our conversation was broken off by the approach of a shepherd, you cannot have forgotten.

"I knew not then that your sister and her protector were inhabitants of the village through which I was passing: chance had led me to it.—Many months were then passed by me, as I had predetermined, in wandering amongst the wilds of the Swiss cantons: at length, weary of continual solitude, I repaired to Paris, where, under the name of the Chevalier de Gramont, and by means of letters from my banker at Toulon, I was received as a stranger into many families of the first respectability."

"Well do I recollect our meeting at the house of the Marquis," exclaimed Claudio; "and the violent emotion which your features betrayed when you learned that my companion was Lodovico di Ponta, is now fully explained to me."

"Oh, what a moment of misery was that!" returned Angelo; "and with what various plans for securing your safety was my brain racked, after I left the house of the Marquis, and returned to my own hotel. On the following evening, I wandered about the hour of twilight into the garden of the Thuilleries; and seeing you reclined on the grass, absorbed in reflection, I judged this would be a happy moment for warning you to beware of di Ponta, though I scarcely knew in what words to convey my admonition: to disguise myself however from your recognizance, was my first business: I accordingly hastened to a place where I could procure the habit of a Carmelite friar; and having dressed myself in it, I returned to the gardens at the moment that you were rising from the grass. What followed need not be repeated to you: I need only remark, that in your desire of ascertaining from whom the voice had proceeded, which had addressed you, you pressed so close upon my heels, that I saw little probability of escaping you. I feared the elucidation which would then follow: a sudden thought darted across my brain to strip off my white garment, and hang it upon a tree I was passing, trusting that in the uncertain light of evening, your sight would continue fixed on the white robe, and I should escape unseen. My plan produced the effect I had desired from it.

"I felt now somewhat relieved in mind again, although the method I had used for putting you upon your guard against the family of your enemy, was a vague and uncertain one. In a few days, you left Paris. Now I knew you thus intimately connected with di Ponta, I felt it an impossibility to keep myself at a distance from you, and followed you to the neighbourhood of Placenza, where I took my abode in a vacated hermit's cell, in the guise of his successor. When you accompanied the Count on his visit to the villa di Bartelma, I pursued your road as a travelling mendicant; and as severe a stroke as yourself did I experience in the death of the worthy Marchese."

"It was then doubtless you," said Claudio, interrupting his father, "who met Lodovico by night in the pine-grove, between Florence and the villa di Bartelma, and exacted from him an oath of eternal friendship to me."

"Do you not see my motive for this conduct?" rejoined Angelo. "I had learned that Montano's daughter was to become your wife: I thus secured to you the eternal friendship of her brother, and my sanguine hopes flattered me with the expectation, that we might all one day be friends again; but fate has ordained it otherwise, and we must bow to the will of providence. On that night, I dropped from my wrist a bracelet similar to the one you wear: by their correspondence, it was ever my intention to prove to you that you were my son, should any doubts have attended the explanation to you.—They were the first gift of my love to your mother."

Angelo wiped a tear in silence from his eye: Claudio put into his hand the bracelet which he had found in the pine-grove; and after a short silence, during which Angelo fixed his eyes on the bracelet with a sort of mournful pleasure, he spoke thus: "I shall now proceed to inform you of what relates to your sister. The last time I saw my old nurse before her death, was at my second journey into Italy, after my banishment from my estates and titles by my unnatural cousin. I have already told you my reason for coming to Florence a second time, and thus I executed the purpose of my visit. Having learnt that my nurse's daughter was dead, but that her husband, Louis de Saint Pierre, continued to protect my child with a father's care, and to delight in her as if she had been his own; I addressed to him a letter, wherein, after expressing the thanks of a father for his love of my child, I said, "When she is arrived at her nineteenth year, if in the interval I do not come and demand her of you, bring her in the first week of October to the hotel of St. Luke in Florence; where she will either be met and claimed a near male relative, or a sufficient sum of money be given to you to support her through life; but as you value your existence, make no endeavors to learn who she is, as such enquiries might endanger her life."

"When the time specified in my letter arrived (the first week in the month of October, the very week in which we are now living), with a heavy heart, I counted the advancing of the hours which would bring my child hither. The rotation of fortune's wheel had not given me the power of acknowledging her in the face of the world; and I had resolved to return with her, and her protector, to their humble dwelling, to share with them their simple happiness, and to enjoy the felicity of living in the society of at least one of my children. With this determination, I proceeded to the hotel of Saint Luke: Louis de Saint Pierre received me, and my visit was soon explained to him. Guess, Claudio, if you are able, the surprise, the horror, the agony which rent my heart, when I learned from the lips of the old peasant, that *my child* was just gone away from the hotel, with a man who had called himself *di Ponta!*

"All fear for myself was lost in my apprehensions for the safety of my child's life and honour: I instantly confessed myself her father to the astonished peasant, and not a moment was lost in procuring a gondola to carry us in pursuit of her. She was found, she was recovered—recovered immaculate. I clasped her to my breast: I fell on my knees to pour out my thanksgivings, in the fullness of my heart, to Heaven for her safety. As I rose from my short prayer, she, for the first time, blessed my ear with the delightful sound of "father." At that moment, the gondola which contained Montano di Ponta passed ours. He heard the exclamation of your sister,—from that instant, his vengeful heart decreed her an orphan.

"No more remains to be said, but that I am now a prisoner here, on the accusation of Montano di Ponta, for the murder of my wife."

"Where are now my sister and her venerable protector?" asked Claudio.

"They are not permitted to lodge in the prison," replied Angelo, "and I have not seen them yet this morning."

In the strain of heart-broken sorrow, Angelo continued to expatiate on the strange fate which had attended his house. Claudio interrupted him by saying, "Still more strange has been the mysterious fate which has attended your son." Angelo eagerly enquired to what he alluded; and Claudio, in as few words as the subject would admit, recounted his first acquaintance with the Benedictine friar, and Viola, at Rome; Zelia's subsequent ænigmatical offer of herself to him in marriage; the luminous writing on the wall of his chamber in Paris; the vision; and, lastly, his still more unaccountable marriage.

Angelo heard the tale of his son's eventful life with surprise; but the incidents which had composed it were all unknown to him, and he could not offer him the solace of even a surmise from what cause they might have arisen.

Scarcely was Claudio's account of himself concluded, when the door of the cell was opened, and Louis de Saint Pierre and Nina entered. The thanks which Nina was about to bestow on Claudio as her preserver from dishonour, she was quickly taught by Angelo were due to a brother; and the emotions of her elated and innocent heart were poured forth to him, in the joint words of gratitude and astonishment.

When the first transports of brotherly affection were in some measure subsided, Angelo called upon Nina to join him in entreaties to Claudio to fly from Florence, while yet a prospect of his escape from justice presented itself to him.

A scene of the most affecting nature followed. Angelo beseeching his son to fly with Nina, and ensure her safety and his own. Claudio, in the honest fortitude of an affectionate heart, asserting his resolution to live or die with his father. Nina, in the fullness of her heart, and the weakness of a woman's feelings, leaning alternately to the arguments of Claudio and her father. Louis de Saint Pierre catching sometimes the weakness of Nina, sometimes the spirit of Claudio, and endeavouring to stifle both these emotions in order to render himself the consoler of all. It was a scene which can be acted only by the feelings, and defies the description of words.

CHAPTER XIV.

> My heart laments, that virtue cannot live
> Out of the teeth of emulation.
>
> JULIUS CÆSAR.

AGAIN the heavy door of the cell rolled back upon its hinges, and the jailor entered: "Is there a Signor here who calls himself Claudio di Bartelma?" he asked.

Claudio was stepping forward to answer to his demand, when Paulo burst in: "Oh, my dear Signor!" he cried, "I trust, I hope, all will yet be well. Here is a letter: Julius has been seeking you all the morning, to deliver it into your own hand."

Claudio tore open the paper, and found its contents to be as follows:

"My dear friend,

    Julius writes this, by my command, to inform you, that the wound I received is not mortal; that the bed of sickness has opened my eyes to reflection; that I entreat your forgiveness for the provocation you received from me; and beg to see you immediately on a concern of the utmost importance to my future happiness. I shall constrain myself to sign this letter with my own hand, that you may not doubt its authenticity.

Your ever sincere friend,
LODOVICO DI PONTA."

"Thank Heaven! he lives," exclaimed Claudio. The sound of joy was caught and echoed by all present. On a sign from Claudio, Paulo and the jailor left the cell. Claudio then spoke: "I am safe, but my father is not; and I shall not comply with Lodovico's request to visit him."

"He is your friend, and entreats to see you on a bed of sickness," replied Angelo.

"But as the son of the Count Montano di Ponta," rejoined Claudio, "he must be my father's enemy."

"Is it not possible," said Nina, "that the concern of importance he mentions, may be something in our father's favour?"

"Remember his vow," added Angelo, as if agreeing in the suspicion of his daughter.

"Invited by that shadow of hope, I will go to him," answered Claudio. "Lodovico's frailties have, at times, mastered his reason, yet I have always believed him fundamentally well principled. Farewell."

"My fate, my son," said Angelo, "cannot be made worse than it is: remember, therefore, that you have a sister to protect, and be careful of your own safety."

"While I remember Nina as my sister," replied Claudio, "I shall not forget, that you are the father of us both." An affectionate embrace from his father and Nina followed these words, and he then hastily left the prison.

With a mind hurried almost beyond a consciousness of its own actions, Claudio repaired to the villa di Bartelma. He enquired for Lodovico, and was shewn to his chamber, Lodovico was reclining on a sofa, wrapped in his night-gown. Julius entered first to announce Claudio. "Admit him instantly," was the reply from Lodovico.

Claudio heard it, and stepped forward to the chamber: on his entrance, Lodovico attempted to rise, extending towards him at the same time his hand.—Claudio moved hastily forward to prevent his leaving the sofa, and received his offered hand in his.—"Oh, Claudio!" exclaimed Lodovico, "do you, can you forgive me?"

"I have done that long ago, Lodovico," replied Claudio, "when a man repents, it is a base heart that will deny him forgiveness."

"How could I ever disregard the salutary counsels of a friend like you?" Lodovico rejoined. "Sit down—closer to me—I am weak through loss of blood, and unable to exert myself, though I have much to say to you."

"Defer it till your strength is better renovated," returned Claudio: "conversation will now overpower you. Try and repose: I'll come to you again when you are refreshed by sleep."

"Stay, stay, I entreat you to stay," replied Lodovico.—"I cannot rest unless I open my heart to you.—Where is Nina?—Is she in safety?"

"Be assured she is," answered Claudio.

"Heaven, I thank thee!" exclaimed Lodovico. "Yes, Claudio, I speak from my soul: now my foul passion has abated, a worthier love has filled my heart, and to know her immaculate is the chief blessing of my restored existence.—You are doubtless acquainted where she now is?"

"I am," Claudio answered, in a faint voice.

"Be then, my friend, the messenger of my heart to her," Lodovico went on: "kneel for me at Nina's feet—implore her forgiveness for me. Yet one thing more, my friend: use all your eloquence in my behalf, entreat her to accept the hand and heart of a penitent who adores her."

Claudio trembled, a dewy coldness stood upon his forehead, and after a pause, he replied, "You, Lodovico, become the husband of Nina!"

"As the first of gifts this world can crown me with!" exclaimed Lodovico, in ecstasy. "Oh, Claudio! I never knew the raptures of a virtuous passion till now."

Claudio's agitation encreased, as combating sensations met in his heart, and he said, "Do you know who Nina is?" "A peasant's daughter," rejoined Lodovico, "but she is perfection's heiress, and her beauty and virtue shall reward me for the humble sphere from which I take her to my heart.—Oh, Claudio! you will not, you cannot, refuse to be the ambassador of my love to her."

"I must indeed, except on one condition," answered Claudio: "you must first obtain your father's consent to your marriage? when you have done that, send for me again, and I will visit Nina with your petition; till then, farewell!"

"Promise me," said Lodovico, "that you will not leave the house. I expect my father every moment in my chamber: I will lay my case before him, and I trust to the honesty of my principle for procuring me my wish."

Claudio promised that he would not leave the villa, till he had seen Lodovico again; of which promise, his friend had no reason to be suspicious, as he was totally unacquainted with the ties which were inviting his heart back to Florence.

Immediately on the departure of Claudio from his apartment, Lodovico dispatched his servant to request the Count to visit him; with which petition the Count in a few minutes complied. On his entering the chamber, he said, "My dear Lodovico, you must wonder that I have not more frequently visited you to-day; and that when I have been with you, my mind has seemed to wander from you,—I should have passed much more of my time with you; but I have been disturbed:—unfit to see you in your present weak state."

Lodovico immediately enquired what had occasioned his father trouble. To which demand, the Count thus replied—"Angelo di Ponta, he whom you have so often heard me pronounce my bitterest enemy; he whom all the world but myself have, for nearly twenty years past, supposed to be dead; he who has lived only by my mercy, has broken through the conditions on which he held life, and shown himself publicly this day in Florence; but I have accused the murderer of his wife to the laws of his country. Angelo shall now pay the atonement of this crime, which I have thus long spared him."—Towards the conclusion of this speech, the Count's anger rose to great warmth; and when he ceased speaking, he continued to traverse the chamber with hasty steps.

That Angelo di Ponta, the reputed murderer of himself, still lived, for a few moments created the surprise of Lodovico; but a subject of nearer interest to his heart claimed his first attention; and after a short pause, he spoke thus: "Let me intreat you to dismiss for a while from your mind a subject which I see distresses you, and to give your ear to one which I wish to introduce to your attention."

The Count's brow began to unruffle its frown, and he enquired what that subject was.

"I have formed a wish," Lodovico replied, "to the completion of which, my hopes almost flatter me, nothing is wanting but your sanction."

"What is this wish?" the Count asked.

"To call a lovely woman by the tender name of wife," Lodovico answered.

"Who is she? What is her rank and name?" the Count enquired.

These were questions ill-suited, at the present moment, to Lodovico's circumstances and feelings. After a few moments' hesitation, he said, "You may conceive me visionary in the prospect of happiness I have formed to myself; but it is indeed the result of much reflection with my own mind.—I shall ensure myself happiness by the action which will reward an insulted girl."

"Whom say you?" asked the Count, in an elevated tone of voice.

"The wronged Nina," Lodovico replied.

"Do you too, my own blood, conspire to torture me?" exclaimed the Count, in accents almost smothered by passion. "Would to Heaven thou hadst effected thy first purpose on her: that thou hadst blasted her fame for ever. Know, that she is the daughter of the accursed Angelo."

Lodovico heard no more: his senses stiffened, and he fell back upon the sofa. The Count perceived, that his manner had been too harsh: he softened his voice, and called upon Julius to attend his master: in a short time, Lodovico returned to his reason. When the Count perceived his eyes again opening, he said, "To bed, to bed, you are weak, and require rest: to bed, and pray that your folly may cease."

Leaving Lodovico for a while to indulge the grief of a despairing mind, we will follow the Count di Ponta, who, with a heart racked by contending feelings, rushed from the house on leaving his son's chamber, as if to draw in air for the sustenance of a bosom smothering under its own rage. The shades of night were beginning to fall, when he entered the garden: he had not proceeded many steps, when Claudio, buried like himself in mournful reflection, met him. It was the first time Claudio had seen him since he had gained the knowledge of his father, and he started back from him, as if the Count had presented a naked dagger to his heart.

"I fear I have interrupted your meditations," said the Count: "the surprise you testified at seeing me, shows your thoughts were abstracted from the scene around you."

Claudio made some evasive answer, and was passing on.

"Stay," rejoined the Count: "we meet happily. I wish for a little conversation with you."

Claudio stopped with a slight inclination of his body, as an affirmative answer to the Count's request. "What can this mean? What can he be going to say?" he silently enquired of his heart.

"Claudio," the Count continued, "I am well assured that you have, especially at this time, more influence over my son than any man living. Will you exert a little of it in the behalf of a request of mine?"

Still Claudio knew not how to reply. The Count again relieved his uncertainty by proceeding thus: "You doubtless have heard, that I have accused to the state, of murder, a man, Angelo di Ponta his name, who has for many years, through my lenity, lived in obscurity, supposed to be dead; but whom his ingratitude has at last obliged me to deliver up to the punishment of offended justice."

Claudio's knees trembled, and almost refused to support his tottering frame: the big drops of agony rolled down his cheeks, and his heart beat against his side with the most painful throbs.— The duskiness of the evening concealed his violent emotions from the Count, who continued to address him in the following words: "The daughter of this man would Lodovico, knowing her to be his child, take for his wife.—You know her well: she is the girl whom you rescued from his entanglements. Would you had not done so; but you could not foresee the consequence."

"You are right," replied Claudio, "*I did not* foresee the consequence: mine was an act of humanity."

"Go to his chamber," the Count rejoined: "first use with him all the arguments of persuasion: if these have no effect in prevailing on him to drive her from his thoughts, tell him it is my resolution, that if he persists in his intention of marrying her, he draws upon himself, not only disinheritance, but a father's curse."

"Consider, Signor," returned Claudio, "that you send me to him as a friend; will such information accord with the character of a friend?"

"I cannot retract a letter of my determination," answered the Count. "Will you go to him?—Remember, that if you refuse to repeat to him what I have said, he may persist in disobeying me; and you may hereafter repent, that you did not use your endeavours to prevent the consequences of his disobedience."

"You have put a spur to my honour," replied Claudio, "which obliges me to go, an unwilling messenger, to my friend."

"You intend to be a just one?" said the Count.

"My honour, I told you, Signor, sends me to him," returned Claudio. These words brought them to the portico: they entered the hall, and parted.

To act with justice to the Count, and honor to his friend, however severe the trial to his own heart, was Claudio's resolve.

Accordingly he ascended to the chamber of Lodovico: at the door, he found Julius. "My master," he said, "has just been visited by the physician, who has strictly commanded, that he must see no more visitors to night: he is, the physician says, already too much overpowered with the exertions he has made in the course of the day.—He has been quite still for some minutes, and I believe is already asleep."

Claudio immediately resolved to defer his visit till the morning: the prison-gates of the Holy Cross were, he knew, closed early in an evening; thus he could see his father no more that night.—

From meeting the Count di Ponta at supper his heart revolted: he accordingly resolved to pass the hours in his chamber. In going towards it, he heard a quick step pursuing him along the gallery: it was the Count. "Have you seen Lodovico?" he asked.—Claudio repeated to him the orders of the physician.—Instead of noticing them, he said, "Are you acquainted, that the reason of my having arrived here yesterday, is in consequence of a letter I received from my son some days ago, requesting my immediate presence here *without* Valeria?"

"I am acquainted, that he wrote a letter to that purpose," answered Claudio.

"Can you also tell me on what account he wished to see me?" rejoined the Count, "for his illness has prevented my making enquiry of him."

Claudio was at that moment wholly inadequate to the explanation, which it had been the intention of himself and Lodovico to lay before the Count, of the mysterious adventures which had befallen him during the course of his life, and their still more strange conclusion: he accordingly said, "I must see your son before I can gratify your excited curiosity: rest satisfied, that it is nothing which can give you uneasiness. Good night."

"You have not supped yet," returned the Count.

"I shall not sup to-night," Claudio answered, and entered his chamber.

In a state of mind which cannot require description, Claudio traversed his solitary chamber, till the light of day was entirely driven from the skies, and the silver moon had usurped her empire over the surrounding scene. Claudio moved to the window of his apartment; and the dusky beams of light which were reflected upon the tall pines, that formed the shadowing wood at the back of the mansion, seemed in unison with his sad heart.—From the scene before him, his busy memory wafted him back to days of mingled bliss and sorrow long gone by; and melancholy was casting her veil of sablest hue across his mind, when a gentle rap at his chamber door, roused him from his trance of thought.

He enquired who was there; and was answered by the voice of Paulo, whom he directly admitted.

"Here is something for you," the old man said, presenting him with a small packet, directed for, "Signor Claudio di Bartelma."

"Whence comes it?" asked Claudio.

"A man brought it just now to the villa," replied Paulo, "and desired that it might be put into your hands without delay."

The hand-writing in which it was directed, Claudio was convinced, upon his first sight of it, was not new to him. A few moments' recollection informed him, that it was similar to that of the note which had been left for him at the pallazo di Ponta, on his return from the festival of the Virgin at Mantua, and which had promised to him the hand of Zelia.

He tore it open. The first paper served as an envelope to the packet: the packet itself was superscribed in these words: *"To be opened by Claudio di Bartelma at the death of the Count Montano di Ponta,* AND NOT TILL THEN."

Strange and incomprehensible was this direction. Was it meant to announce, that the death of the Count was near at hand? or was it simply to be understood as a task for him to perform, when that event had taken place? He asked Paulo to describe the person who brought it to the villa. He replied, that it was a monk.

"Was he tall, and dark?" Claudio enquired.

Paulo believed he was.

"Of what order was he?" Claudio next demanded.

"Of the Benedictine," Paulo returned.

Claudio's heart beat high: he knew not what to hope, what to expect, or, rather, what to fear. The packet had doubtless been brought to him by the very Benedictine friar who had before caused him so much food for conjecture. He dismissed Paulo from his apartment. He read the superscription again and again. He turned the paper on every side: nothing, but what he had already read, was discernible. Sometimes he was on the point of breaking it open; but the emphatic command of NOT TILL THEN dissuaded him from his intention: and he concluded, with resolving, at all events, not to open it that night; but to take it with him, on the following morning, to his father, and be guided respecting it by his advice.

CHAPTER XV.

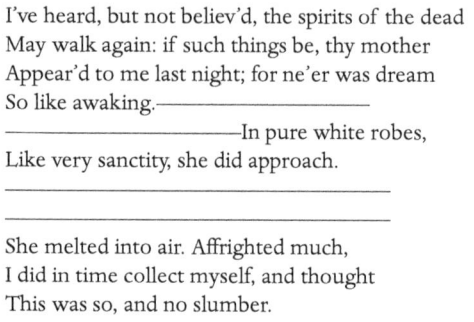

I've heard, but not believ'd, the spirits of the dead
May walk again: if such things be, thy mother
Appear'd to me last night; for ne'er was dream
So like awaking.——————————
——————————In pure white robes,
Like very sanctity, she did approach.

She melted into air. Affrighted much,
I did in time collect myself, and thought
This was so, and no slumber.
THE WINTER'S TALE.

URGED by the earnest solicitations of Angelo and his daughter, or rather induced by the bribe of a ducat offered him by Louis de Saint Pierre, the jailor of the Holy Cross permitted Nina to share the pallet of her father. Angelo was unable to sleep, and Nina declared she would watch with him throughout the night; but her strength was unequal to her will: she sunk to sleep in his arms, and he conveyed her to the miserable bed allotted to them both in the inner recess of the cell.

The unheeded lamp of Angelo burned dim. His thoughts turned not to outward objects: they were centered in his heart. He reclined his wretched frame on the only bench which his cell afforded, and his head fell upon one of his arms, which was rested on the small table that supported his lamp and pitcher of water.

"How uncertain is the fate of man in his short scene of life!" burst insensibly from his over-burthened heart. "How promising was the opening of my life! friends, fortune, a lovely woman: all smiled, and seemed to promise happiness eternal. Now all my fond prospects are blasted. Oh, what a retrospect of agony are the last years of my life! and to look forward—to a scaffold! Oh, God! oh, God! Yet all this could I bear myself, could I cease to think upon my children." The rising tear of parental love choked his utterance, and his exclamations ceased to echo through the unfeeling vaults which enclosed him.

A flash of lightening, which darted violently across the grated window of his dungeon, roused him from his lethargy of reflection: close in succession rolled the bursting thunder. The heavy rain poured down in torrents on the prison roof, and the driven hail ran pattering down its shelving sides. Angelo rose from his posture of reflection: the elemental war above his head, called his thoughts from himself; they returned to his situation in the following exclamation: "How much happier than I am, is the meanest wretch exposed in nakedness and hunger, on some solitary heath, to this storm's fury!" He moved towards the grating. The blue lightening streamed in vivid forkings across the cleaved sky, and the thunder continued to roar with unbated violence; at length, a crash, which seemed the master-effort of nature to dispel the jarring clouds, burst in a tremendous clap over the prison, and the vaults rang with its loud resounding echoes: it was the last, as Angelo had foretold it to be, and the serenity of the elements began gradually to return. He moved to the side of the pallet where lay the affectionate Nina: she was fast asleep: the terrors of the storm had not broken her repose.

"How serenely breathe the lips of innocence!" cried Angelo. "Praised be Heaven that her slumbers are composed!" He returned to his bench, and again placed himself upon it. A stillness, uninterrupted as the silence of the grave, followed the cessation of the tempest: the accidental sighs of Angelo alone broke it, till the loud clock of the prison sounded the hour of midnight.

"Another day is passed," said Angelo, "and all the world but me enjoy oblivion of their cares, and taste the repose merited by them for the labours of the day gone by. My cares will not be lulled in sleep: death now is the only repose to which my wearied brain looks forward. Oh, Horatia! how many pangs of misery hadst thou spared thy husband, thy children, hadst thou been true to me!"

A faint sigh caught the ear of Angelo: he started—in a moment, he recollected the near situation of Nina, and immediate composure returned with the recollection.

He buried his aching head in his hands, and rested them upon the table before him. "Angelo!" was sounded by a faint voice behind him. Again he started, and again he recollected Nina.

A few moments elapsed, and again, "Angelo!" was uttered, in the same faint sounds.

"Ah!" cried Angelo, starting from his seat, "that voice—I know it well—I cannot be deceived in that voice: it is the voice of——"

"Horatia," was immediately added to his sentence.

In wild alarm, he cast his eyes towards the distant side of the cell: his lamp was insufficient to throw more than a dim ray of light upon the white drapery of a figure which stood before him. An icy coldness seized his limbs, and he stood fixed in mute astonishment and dread.

"Have you forgotten me, Angelo?" the figure said.

"Oh, heavenly powers, support me!" he exclaimed: "it is, it is the spirit of my murdered wife which now addresses me."

"Mark me, Angelo," continued the vision: "I was innocent; Montano alone the villain: summon him at break of day to your prison; charge him with his villany. I pardon your error. Heaven will avenge your cause. Farewell!"

The figure retired into the shade, and became lost in the darkness.

"Oh, stay!" exclaimed Angelo: "tell me, I entreat you, tell me——" The figure was no longer visible. "Oh, my injured, my innocent wife!" groaned forth Angelo, and sunk upon the floor of the cell in a trance.

Day had already dawned, when active recollection returned to Angelo: wildly he paced his cell in search of the figure which had that night presented itself to his sight: and in the phrenzy of a disordered brain, he called upon his lost wife—his beloved Horatia. His ravings aroused Nina from her couch: at her approach, he endeavoured to assume an air of greater composure. "My child, a good-morrow, and the blessings of a fair day to thee," he said.

"My father," she replied, "I am blessed in once again beholding you; but you are not well,—your eyes are swollen, and declare that sleep has been a stranger to them."

"Aye, it has indeed been uncharitable," returned Angelo. "Oh, Nina! this has been a night of wonder, of horror, yet of comfort too. I bless Heaven that you slept, and were not moved as I have been."

"By what, or whom?" asked Nina, impatiently.

"By the soul-harrowing, yet consoling voice of death!" replied Angelo. "The spirit of thy deceased mother has this night stood before my eyes: my murdered Horatia has addressed me from the grave."

"You have deceived yourself," returned Nina: "agitated nature has but danced before your eyes a fanciful impression of the form you loved."

"I'll not believe but that it was reality my sight beheld," answered Angelo: "she spoke to me in those thrilling, tender accents of delight, which have so oft before conveyed the faithful epithets of growing love to my fond, listening ear. She told me—mark the words, my child, and think what must have been thy father's feelings at that moment—she told me, that she had never been false to me—that Montano was alone the villain."

"Mysterious Heaven!" exclaimed Nina. "Unfortunate revenge!"

"Drawn from the heart of the innocent mother of my children," added Angelo. "Yet, could'st thou credit it, her sainted shade has pronounced my forgiveness! Oh, powers of mercy!" he exclaimed, and sunk upon the bench.

"Oh, my father!" cried Nina, running to him, and catching his hand in hers.

He rose with a convulsive wildness, and threw her from him. "Stand off!" he exclaimed: "I pray you do not hold me; her forgiveness has left pangs about my heart which I think I had not felt had she cursed me." The orbs of his eyes seemed fixed, and the wildest phrenzy was stamped on his countenance. Gradually his composure returned: he advanced to Nina, caught her in his arms, and, with a fervent embrace, he said, "Sweet child, why dost thou weep? Pardon me, if I distress thee. Uncertainty is a curse, and I wear it rankling in my bosom; but the moment is at hand that dissipates it. I will summon Montano to my prison in such terms, that he cannot refuse his coming. Oh! I will probe his heart; wring from his breast his secret villany; and nail upon his quick of sense those pangs of conscience which, by his juggling, have been vultures to my heart; but which the hand of justice now shall turn to serpents, clinging round his own."

The entrance of the jailor with Angelo's morning repast, put a period to his exclamations: he instantly required pen and paper, which being brought him, he wrote a note to Count Montano di Ponta, which the jailor promised would be conveyed to him without delay.

At an early hour in the morning, Claudio left his restless bed, and proceeded towards the chamber of Lodovico. In the gallery, he was met by Julius: "My master, Signor," he said, "sends me to you, requesting to see you immediately."

"I am now going to him," Claudio replied, and passed on to the chamber. No sooner had he entered it, than Lodovico rushed forward to meet him, and throwing his arms around his neck, he exclaimed, in frantic wildness, "My brother, my brother!"

Easily Claudio perceived the discovery which had been made, to Lodovico. Unconscious how to reply, he lifted the almost fainting Lodovico to the sofa; upon which he placed him, and then said, "My dear Lodovico, what means this emotion?"

With difficulty, Lodovico commanded his utterance. "You are the brother of Nina: consequently, my brother. Behold!" continued Lodovico, pointing to the farthest corner of the chamber.

Claudio turned his eyes to the spot to which Lodovico pointed, and beheld Louis de Saint Pierre.

The old man immediately advanced on meeting Claudio's eye. "Forgive me, forgive me, Signor," he said, "if I have distressed you by a confession from which I hoped to reap benefit for you all. It was I who disclosed to Signor Lodovico, that the unfortunate victim of his father's vengeance is the parent of his friend Claudio, and his beloved Nina. This is the day appointed for the trial of the unhappy Angelo: I learned it but a few hours since; and hastened hither, at break of day, to entreat the intercession of Signor Lodovico with his father, in behalf of one who is so nearly connected with those he most esteems."

"Claudio," exclaimed Lodovico, "you are silent; but you cannot contradict this assertion!"

"I am, indeed," replied Claudio, "the son of the unhappy Angelo di Ponta, and brother of Nina. Is my conduct now explained to you?"

"Oh, my friend!" cried Lodovico, in how bright colours stand your honour and friendship now confessed! and here I swear, if Nina does not frown upon my wishes, I will call thee brother. Let me instantly see my father, that I may dissipate his false arguments by the voice of truth and reason."

Lodovico was moving from the sofa: Claudio caught his arm and detained him. "Hear me, I entreat you, Lodovico: I now come to you, commissioned by Count Montano, to inform you, that disinheritance and his curse are only to be avoided by your forgetting my sister."

"That I will never do," exclaimed Lodovico: "I would have obeyed my father in a point of justice with my last breath; but when his commands are pointed against innocence oppressed, it is my duty to swerve from his example."

"Oh, Signor!" said Louis de Saint Pierre, "how could you, possessing these sentiments, ever attempt a defenceless woman's honor."

"Because," replied Lodovico, "my crimes had then never met punishment to open my eyes to their atrocity. The friendly hand of Claudio gave me the blow that awakened reason from her slumbers, and she shall not again relapse into sleep. I'll see my father instantly, though our eternal separation be the event." In spite of the opposition of Claudio to his purpose, he called aloud for Julius; and when the servant entered the room, he enquired if the Count was risen.

"He has been gone out nearly a quarter of an hour," Julius replied. He desired me to tell you, if you enquired for him, that he was gone to the prison of the Holy Cross, and should return home shortly."

"Get me a gondola instantly," exclaimed Lodovico: "I'll follow him to the prison."

In vain would Claudio have attempted to over-rule this determination of his friend, had not the physician at that moment arrived, and issued his absolute commands, that his patient should not only be prevented from leaving his chamber, but be kept as quiet as possible within it.

On the repeated assurance of Julius, that the Count would in a short time return to the villa, added to the promise of Claudio, that he would not prevent his seeing the Count prior to the commencement of Angelo's trial; Lodovico permitted Claudio and Louis de Saint Pierre to depart.

Claudio returned to his chamber for the packet which he had received on the preceding evening, and then set out for Florence with the old peasant.

The hours at the prison of the Holy Cross, passed in silence, from the time of Angelo's note to the Count Montano being dispatched by the jailor, until the latter announced the Count to be arrived at the prison. Angelo directed his daughter to retire to the inner recess of the cell; and assuming a calm smile of composure, he prepared himself to receive his haughty and imperious tyrant.

With a brow, whereon pride would have sat sole usurper, if the consciousness of guilt had not damped its frown, the Count Montano entered the cell of his victim. A momentary pause succeeded their first meeting, during which the Count, knitting his brow in dreadful sternness, attempted, but in vain, to dispel from the countenance of Angelo, the serenity of innocence, secure in itself. He then spoke. "You sent for me: I do not refuse to visit you, because I consider you as a dying man."

"So do I you," replied Angelo: "we are all approaching to the goal—eternity. Which of us two will meet its messenger, death, with the stoutest heart?"

"Was it to ask me this question, that you sent to see me?" returned the Count.

"It was," answered Angelo, "and I will have it resolved. Look at me, I require not your words to answer me: look at me—my wife was true to me, and you deceived my senses into murder."

An instant pallidness overspread the face of the Count, and he fixed his teeth upon each other to prevent their chattering. After a short pause, in a voice choked by resentment, he said, "Villain, your proof?"

"Your passion, and my calmness," rejoined Angelo, "Heaven

has taught me to inform you, that I was aware my hand had sinned, but not my heart. Which of us two, think you, has the stouter heart?"

A trembling convulsed the Count in every limb, and he exclaimed, "I see thy base, thy pitiful evasion: thou wouldst have me confess, that————"

"Angelo needs not your confession," was the reply. "He only asks you to go and see him die for your crime; then bids you return to hug yourself upon your good, your blessed conscience—to see my orphans weltering in the blood of their basely-murdered father—to see them begging the bread of poverty, while you riot in the viands of luxury, their lawful right, but not to use as you have done."

"Silence, thou wretch," exclaimed Montano, "or my cruelty shall invent—"

"No pang for me it can invent," interrupted Angelo, "so bitter as the sting you feel. I can laugh now. I can smile death in the face. Will you hold out your arms to meet the grim tyrant thus?"

"Will you, insulter?" cried the Count, as with a trembling, but a certain, hand he drew his sword from its scabbard. "Your baseness calls him to your instant wish—this moment is your last!" With these words, he rushed forward to plunge his steel into the breast of Angelo. A convulsive shriek burst from his lips—the weapon of death fell from his enervated arm—Horatia stood between Angelo and his foe, in the same guise in which she had appeared to her husband on the preceding night.

"Well hast thou spoken thine own doom, accursed tyrant," she exclaimed: "this moment is *thy* last!—Angelo, my husband, behold thy revenge!" as she spoke, she drew a dagger from her girdle, and plunged it into the breast of Montano.

"Oh, merciful powers," cried Angelo, "art thou indeed my Horatia? Is this no illusion? Art thou indeed my Horatia, here, and alive?" "I am Horatia," she replied, but no longer *thy* Horatia.— Hear the confession of a penitent heart, and believe it true. With him who lies expiring at my feet, I never was false to thee: never did I disgrace thy marriage bed, whilst thou wert with me as my husband; yet, I have much to repent on thy account. When first I gave to you my hand, you believed me spotless and immaculate:

you took to your bed the mother of a base-born infant. Since I have believed you dead, I have been equally false to your memory. There is but one recompence I can offer you, for the deceit I have practised towards you: may the same action prove the expiation of my guilt.—Farewell for ever!" she exclaimed, and struck to her heart the dagger which she had just drawn from the breast of the Count.—"It's done," she added, "and nothing now remains to me, but the willing task to die.—Powers of mercy, accept my repentance!" she closed her eyes, and sunk into the arms of a friar who attended her.

The voice of death aroused Nina from her retreat, and she advanced to behold her mother in the last agonies of life.

A momentary silence reigned: the approaching voices of Claudio and Louis de Saint Pierre broke it. They entered the cell—Claudio darted forward—his eyes became fixed on the dying countenance of Horatia, and he exclaimed, in frantic wildness, "Oh, powers of mercy! whom do I behold?"

"Thy mother!" returned Angelo, in accents scarcely audible.— "Oh, God! my mother!" exclaimed Claudio, and sunk upon his knees by her side. "Art *thou* my mother?" he added, in the strains of agonized astonishment. "Art *thou* my mother?" he again repeated; for in the dying countenance of his mother, he beheld the once beautiful features of—Viola!

CHAPTER XVI.

————————I beseech you to make it
Natural rebellion, done in the blaze of youth,
When oil and fire, too strong for reason's force,
O'erbear it, and burn on.
ALL'S WELL THAT ENDS WELL.

The blood of youth burns not with such excess,
As gravity's revolt to wantonness.
LOVE'S LABOUR LOST.

In order to account for the enigmatical transactions recorded in the foregoing pages, and the appearance of the Countess Horatia, so long supposed dead by her husband; it will be necessary to return to an early period of her life.

Our readers will remember, that in Viola's account of herself to Claudio, she had deduced her history to that period at which she discovered herself about to become a mother, after the unfortunate death of her Rinaldo; and from this date, it now becomes our task to continue the eventful tale.

Rent by more poignant pangs of anguish than had torn her heart at the death of her father, her loved brother, or even her adored Rinaldo himself, at the conviction of her pregnancy, the first idea which entered the maddening brain of Horatia, was suicide; but the reflection of a few hours, taught her not to accumulate decided vice upon the error of passion; and succeeding days rendered her desirous of beholding the resemblance of him, with whom she had tasted the summit of bliss, and for whom she must now live beneath the bitter scourge of reproach.

The most determined mind is, however, happier under the counsel of a friend; and this slender alleviation of her affliction, Horatia resolved to enjoy. The only woman with whom she had, during her life, been in habits of intimacy—the only woman acquainted with the excess of her love for Rinaldo, was the lady Aurelia, the then newly-married wife of Montano di Ponta.

Aurelia had been a wife rather more than six months, when the forlorn Horatia went to visit her. Aurelia had been wont to be the gayest of the young and beautiful: Horatia now found her melancholy and depressed. A mutual confession of their sorrows soon took place: Horatia's distress arose from her necessity of becoming a mother; that of Aurelia, from her husband's impatience of an heir, and her own inconformity to his wish.

No sooner was the mutual confession of their woes made, than they blessed the Virgin, for the opportunity presented to them of administering to each other's affliction. Aurelia resolved to counterfeit in her own person, the signs of growing pregnancy, and to receive the child of Horatia, at its birth, as her own.

Their plan answered the most sanguine wishes of each: by means of a liberally bribed surgeon and nurse, the exchange was made without the slightest suspicion being entertained by any one of the deceit practising; and she who was really the daughter of

Rinaldo and Horatia, was received with rapture by Montano di Ponta, as the daughter of his wife Aurelia, and named Valeria.

Relieved from the state of dread in which she had been living, Horatia, with returning health and spirits, gained additional lustre to her beauty; and her every charm appeared in its ripest bloom: then it was, that Angelo di Ponta first conceived a passion for her, which, in a few weeks, made her his Countess.

A short time after the entrance of Valeria into the world, Aurelia herself became pregnant; and in giving birth to her son Lodovico, she paid the forfeit of her own life. Horatia received her last breath; and the concern she manifested for the fate of her friend, and the interest she avowed in the welfare of her children, first raised her in the esteem of Montano.

With the care and feelings of a mother, did Horatia continue to watch over Valeria and Lodovico; till the near approach of her second confinement, since her marriage with Angelo, called her back to Placenza. Hither, after the birth of Fulvia, who succeeded her brother Claudio, one year in her entrance into the world, Montano followed. What had at first been merely esteem for the friend of his deceased wife, was now growing into a fierce and uncontroulable passion, which he could not subdue, although he contrived to conceal. Chance soon favored his wishes, by leading him with the appearance of accident, into the dressing room of the Countess, when he knew her to be there alone, and imagined Angelo to be from home. Their great intimacy rendered Horatia unsuspicious of the villanous design which was lurking in his heart under the mask of familiarity; and surprise had rendered her unable to resist his savage embraces, at the moment when Angelo entered the apartment; and, in his attempt to stab the invader of his marriage-bed, sheathed his sword in the bosom of his wife.

The failure of his villanous attack upon the person of Horatia, presented Montano, in its consequence, with an opportunity of triumphing over Angelo, which he had not then awaited, but which the acuteness of his perceptions did not suffer him to let pass unused. He ordered the bleeding body of the Countess to be removed from the apartment; and his order having been obeyed, he closed upon Angelo the door of the Countess' dressing-room, announcing to him at the same time, that it was destined to be his prison, till he should be called upon by the laws of his country, to expiate the murder of his wife by death.

From the death of his great-uncle, Montano had never ceased to envy his cousin Angelo the possession of those domains and that fortune which the death of their near relation had endowed him with; and within the two last years, he had been studiously watching a ready moment to snatch from Angelo his inheritance:—the opportunity, which repeated contrivance had denied him, the hand of chance now placed within his grasp; and he seized upon it with the greediness that a hungry tiger rushes upon his prey. One obstacle alone remained to the full attainment of his proudest wishes: this was, the possibility of the recovery of the Countess. A short struggle between passion and pride took place in his breast; but he decided it, by resolving, that however he disposed of the Countess, her life should not stand in his way to fortune.

On leaving Count Angelo, Montano repaired to the chamber to which had been conveyed the bleeding Horatia. The attending domestics had just staunched the issuing stream of life; but the Countess still lay in a state of languid insensibility.—Montano flattered himself that it was the sleep of death.—The Countess heaved a scarcely audible sigh. "Hark!" said Montano, "she breathes again: her last moments are rapidly approaching. Retire all of you, and send hither father Julio."—Father Julio was a monk of the Benedictine order, a creature in the interest of Montano, who had raised him from the lowest order of society, and who now acted the part of confessor to his house. When father Julio entered the apartment, Montano thus addressed him: "You do not require, my friend, to have repeated to you the object which has occupied my thoughts since the death of my great-uncle: too well do you know my thirst after the aggrandisement of my own person, and the fall of Angelo. There is now but one obstacle in the road to my certain happiness: it must be surmounted.——Julio, has my kindness deserved any recompence at your hands?"

Julio crossed his arms upon his breast; and with the smile of a villain and a sycophant, bowed with the humblest servility before Montano.

"I know thee honest and faithful," replied Montano, with a corresponding smile. "Wait here till I return." And with these words, he withdrew hastily from the apartment.

The occurrences of the last hour had already reached the inquisitive ear of Julio: thus he moved to the couch on which lay extended the fainting Horatia, not to ascertain whose form it was that lay before him; but to indulge, unquestioned, the wanton gaze of passion.

Julio had resided in the family of Montano at the time of Horatia's being a mother, previous to her marriage with Angelo; and to him had fallen the confession of her fault, as the interceder for her crime with Heaven.—This was a secret, which, contrary to his usual custom of unreserved communication of all he knew to his favorer, he had retained sacred within his own breast. From the very first moment of his beholding Horatia, the fire of passion had been lighted by her charms in his heart; and he had resolved not to let Montano participate with him a secret, which might equally serve him with an apology for addressing with freedom her whom it concerned. This privilege he, with a miser's gripe, bound in his own heart, and glutted in private on the happiness of possessing it; but an opportunity had never yet presented itself to him, at which he could hope to derive from it the slightest benefit.

In a very short time, Montano returned to the apartment. Still Horatia lay in a state of insensibility. Montano cast his eyes around in wild and fearful scrutiny; and having convinced himself, that no one but Julio was present with him, he said, as he pointed with one hand to the Countess, and with the other held the friar by the arm, "She must die."

At the first sound of these words, Julio started. A silence ensued, of doubt, fear, and anxiety to Montano; of reflection to Julio. "She is now in my power," whispered to his heart the evil spirit of Julio.

"Do you hesitate this for me?" asked Montano, breaking silence.

"I cannot hesitate when you command," replied the fawning priest.

"Now thou art indeed my friend," exclaimed Montano, pressing the hand of Julio in his as he spoke. "The means of death," he continued, "are easy: in your quality of physician as well as confessor, a draught of eternal sleep may be easily administered to her under the name of a reviving cordial, in the presence of the domestics."

"No time shall be lost," replied Julio. "Summon back the servants."

Montano obeyed; and on their appearance, Julio said, "Animation has not yet returned to the unfortunate Countess; and I fear, that Heaven will not grant her strength to receive the comforts of confession, before she sinks into the awful gulph of eternity: watch over her while I prepare a cordial, which, with the grace of God, may restore her to a short interval of sense."

With a slow and mournful step, he quitted the room; and Montano followed him. "Shall I return with you, and see it administered?" asked the latter, in a low voice, when the door was closed upon them.

"No, no," returned the friar: "rather go you to the Count, and seem to your family to be employed in lending him your aid to bear the misfortunes which are falling upon him." Montano answered by a significant inclination of his head, and they parted.

When the friar had administered to the Countess a dose of a sufficiently powerful nature for his purpose, and perceived that it had taken the desired effect, he summoned Montano to the apartment. "Behold," he said, "your wish is accomplished: now bring hither her husband, and convince him that she no longer lives."

"He has not doubted her death," replied Montano, "from the moment that the blood issued from the wound inflicted by his sword; and he has already refused again to behold her whom he terms an adulteress."

"'Tis well," answered Julio, "and as we could wish. Do you now retire, and come no more to this apartment; lest your visiting it may be construed into a conviction of your love for the Countess' person, which, as the event is, may be doubted, and what is past, deemed only the mad jealousy of her husband."

"I applaud your caution," replied Montano, and departed.

Saying he should himself watch that night over the dead body of the Countess, the friar dismissed the attendants from the apartment. Tediously and anxiously did the hours pass to him between fear and expectation, till he believed the house to be buried in sleep. Had the heart of Horatia ever been laid open to his perusal, half his anxiety had vanished, and the other half been forgotten in the anticipation of certain happiness.

Horatia had, since her marriage with Angelo, conducted herself towards him with the most exemplary constancy; and she had contracted with her own heart, a solemn engagement of continuing to act towards him with the most rigorous duty, while he continued to be the tender husband he had hitherto upon every occasion shown himself to be.

Still a breast like that of Horatia (which had once overstepped the bounds of modesty, and had been deprived of the adored object for whom it had sacrificed duty and honour), could not, however pure its actions, at all times restrain its imagination from wandering to other objects, the contemplation of which seemed to promise an alleviation of her heart's bitterest disappointment. She had espoused Angelo in order to obtain in him a protector, and a situation of eminence in life. She had originally beheld him with a total indifference as to his person; and as she grew into respecting him for his unremitting kindness towards her, and to revere him as the father of her children, still she loved him not as a man; while, on the contrary, her thoughts, though constrained from roaming beyond the limits of her breast, had often wandered to the glow of manly beauty which sat painted on the cheeks of the friar Julio, and dwelt on the intelligent eye which lighted his prepossessing countenance.

Not till the first hour of the morning had sounded, did the friar think himself sufficiently secure from interruptions on the part of the family to awaken Horatia: he then applied to her nostrils an aromatic scent, which, spite of the opiate draught she had swallowed the preceding evening, opened to his wish her languid eyes, and aroused her into sufficient strength to enquire where she was, and who it was that stood before her.

Having explained to her, that it was the well-known Julio who addressed her, he besought her attention to his words; and then explained to her, in a speech which it had cost him some previous trouble to frame, with exquisite art, that Heaven had pointed out to him the means to become her saviour from the mad jealousy of an exasperated husband, and the brutal passion of Montano; that her husband had vowed never to see her more; and that Montano, from the idea alone of her death, had been restrained from renewing his attacks of adulterous love: he added, that he had conceived the plan for her salvation in administering to her the opiate, under whose influence she had for many hours since been supposed to have expired; that he had from his first knowledge of her person been enamoured of it; and that now chance gave him the opportunity of befriending her helpless and persecuted state, it was his pride to rescue her from her tyrants, and would be the summit of his earthly bliss to fly with her from their persecution.

Cast off by her husband, and, but for the offered protection of Julio, abandoned to the brutality of the man whom she above all others detested; the idea of happiness with the long, though silently beloved Julio, was too flattering a temptation to the weak senses of Horatia to be rejected; and to the no less extacy than surprise of Julio, a ready assent to his proposal flowed from her pleasure-breathing lips.

A plan of flight, which will be developed in the course of this narration, was then agreed upon between them; and after the friar had presented to the Countess some refreshments, she, in compliance with his advice, drank a second opiate, which quickly lulled her into the semblance of that eternal sleep, so necessary for her to appear under during the ensuing day.

Towards noon, father Julio went to Montano, in his private apartment, and having represented to him, that the poison which had been given to the Countess required, from the effect it had produced on her person, that her interment should be as speedy as possible, requested that she might be entombed on the evening of the succeeding day.

To this Montano, for his own sake, readily agreed; and the necessary vestments for the Countess' interment being procured, the coffin was ordered to be carried to the apartment where she lay, in the dead of the following night; when the friar promised to attend in person, and to contrive, that the two females who were appointed to place her in it, should be admitted to their office in a duskiness which would preclude the possibility of their observing her change of countenance, and her diversified colour of flesh.

At the hour appointed, the coffin was brought into the apartment in which lay the Countess, extended on the couch on which she was universally believed to have breathed her last.—The men who brought it, having deposited their burden, departed: the friar summoned the females, destined to attire her in the habit of the grave, and from the dimness of the light, permitted to them for the performance of their task, she was placed by them in the coffin, without a suspicion of the deceit that was practising upon them: this done, they threw over her a robe of white silk, as the last covering to her person, and placed upon her face a mask of wax, provided for the purpose. Without suffering them to remove the linen wherein the Countess had lain extended on the couch, the friar dismissed them from the apartment; then cautiously taking the Countess out of the coffin, he bore her back in his arms to the couch, and having carelessly covered her with the linen it contained, he threw across the whole a garment of his own, to increase the appearance of its disorder.

Without loss of time, he placed in the coffin some ancient parchment-records, and other things of more weight than value, which he had conveyed to the apartment for the purpose; and throwing over them the white silk robe, and placing the wax mask in a proper situation, he required to be sent to him the person whose duty it was to infix the closing screws.

Success having thus far attended his plan, nothing now remained to him to perform, but to convey the Countess to one of his private apartments in the pallazo; and having awaited a convenient opportunity for the purpose, he deemed the difficulty of his task performed.

After the funeral obsequies of the Countess were ended, Julio, following Montano into his apartment, thus addressed him: "My Lord, I sincerely congratulate you on the attainment of your heart's most earnest wish: I glory, that it is through me you have arrived at such pre-eminence of happiness, conscious that it is through your friendship alone that I move in the rank of life in which your bounty has placed me, and grateful to fortune for the means which she has put in my power of proving to you the warmth of my recognizance:—but, my Lord, pardon me; we are all subject to weaknesses of the mind: thus actuated upon am I. It will, my Lord, cause me unutterable concern to leave the friend of my life, the fosterer of my good fortunes; but I cannot enjoy life on the very spot where———— You know what I would say—I feel I must quit Placenza."

However the villain for his own ends esteems, or rather pretends to esteem, the perpetrator of those crimes which he has not the resolution to commit in his own person, and is too apt to conceive himself guiltless of, because they are performed by the hand of another, forgetful that the finger which executes is not more culpable than the tongue which dictates; still such a secret villain is always well pleased to have the instrument of his sin removed from his sight. Montano's feelings were of the common nature; and he felt almost delighted, that Julio's presence would not haunt him with the recollection of his murder, especially since it was Julio's own wish to depart from him.

With pretended concern at his leaving Placenza, Montano questioned Julio whither he meant to wander, or whether he had fixed on any spot to which he intended to retire; to which demands the friar only replied, that his sole object being to leave a place which he experienced only misery in viewing, he had formed no plan of future life.

"When do you depart?" asked Montano.

"To-morrow with the dawn," replied Julio, "I can rest no more within these walls."

Montano moved to his desk, and taking from it a purse of gold, he put it into the hand of father Julio. "That purse," he said, "contains notes to a considerable amount, besides the gold you feel in it; let them and this diamond be the slender reward of the services you have rendered me."

Julio pretended to object to the receiving of any recompence for the good he had rendered his patron; but Montano, in the warmth of a man swayed by a mixture of gratitude and fear towards the same object, pressed upon him the offered present; and with the semblance of mutual grief, they bade each other a last farewell.

On leaving Montano, Julio ordered a hired carriage to be procured for him; and desired that it might be in waiting for him at three o'clock in the morning. His next concern was to collect such matters of value as he possessed, and to pack them ready for his journey. He then proceeded to the apartment which contained

Horatia, and whom he found just waking from her long sleep. Having informed her of what had passed during her state of insensibility, he directed her to refresh herself with some wine and biscuits which he had procured for her; and then assisting her to habit herself in one of his ecclesiastical robes, he instructed her to draw the cowl over her face, and to pass thus disguised through the pallazo into the gardens. "In this habit," he said, "if observed by any one of the family, you will doubtless be taken for me: if addressed, hold out your rosary, and answer by signs that you are counting your beads as you walk: it is a common custom with me when I do not choose to be interrupted in my meditations, and it is a whim in which I have never been disturbed. As soon as you have reached the garden, proceed to the statue of Diana, and seat yourself on its base; and when a carriage moving towards the outer road shall pass you, call to the driver to stop. I shall hear you, if he does not, and will question you what you would have: to this demand, reply, that you are a friar journeying to Parma, and would beg for a seat in the carriage, as you are unable from fatigue to proceed any farther on foot. I shall perhaps scruple to admit you immediately, but fear not that I should leave you behind me."

Their plan meeting with no obstruction, Julio and his fair companion travelled to Venice without any longer delays, than such as were absolutely necessary for enabling them to bear the fatigue of their long journey. In the arms of her beloved Julio, Horatia thought no more of that husband whom she believed to have deserted her; and when the report of Angelo's suicide, set on foot by Montano, reached her, and a momentary remorse for the unprotected state of her children stung her breast; again Julio, by his specious arguments and his caresses, lulled to sleep her anxieties.

It has already been said, that Julio, by never hesitating to make himself useful to Montano on any occasion wherein his services were required, had gained his highest favor, and been raised by him from an abject situation in life to that of the confessor of his house; and this being promised, it cannot be necessary to add, that a man of this description had taken care not to be a loser by his acquaintance with his patron's secrets: thus then Julio was enabled to support Horatia with ease for the first ten years after their elopement, in a splendor little inferior to that in which she had been accustomed to live; but at the expiration of this term of years, however reluctantly, he was reduced to the necessity of confessing, that his ability of continuing so to do was upon the wane.

Horatia heard this confession of her paramour's circumstances without surprise; and, with equal calmness, she resolved, that it now became her to exert such means as lay in her power for their future subsistence, in return for the protection she had hitherto been experiencing from Julio.

The ecclesiastical character of Julio having forbidden him to call Horatia his wife, she had lived with him under the title of his sister; and thus believed, she had received from the grand inquisitor, offers of the most liberal nature, in every form but that of marriage.

To this resource, the quick imagination of Horatia pointed in the emergency before her. To Julio, she imparted her design. The idea of becoming dependent was, at first, grating, to the soul of him who had for so long a time been the depended upon; but the necessity of his situation knew no law, and in a few short months, he was compelled to behold Horatia sole mistress of the grand Inquisitor's pallazo at Rome; while the slender consolation alone remained to him, of being protected under the same roof as the brother of the all-favoured fair who governed it.

The woman who has sufficient sense to step forward in the hour of calamity as the saviour of her paramour, is never without sufficient art to reduce, from that moment, the lord of her heart into its slave: thus now stood the fallen Julio. From the gulph of destruction which had threatened him and herself, Horatia had risen to the summit of wealth and power; whilst Julio, still infatuated with those charms which he durst not call his own, was content to live in their contemplation, and to render himself of the most servile utility to their possession, in the fond hope of a smile, like those which had once voluntarily blessed his existence, being made his recompence.

With the sacrifice of her person for wealth, such good principles as had before held a place in the heart of Horatia, began to be weakened by the depravity of the scenes in which she now was living; and the barrier of love, which she had heretofore made the apology of her questionable conduct, being broken down, gusts of freshly imbibed passion were now constantly tossing her heart in the whirlwind of lascivious dissipation. Thus Claudio was not the only youth who had been conducted to the pleasure-breathing chambers of Horatia, nor the first to whom the humbled father Julio had pointed out the ruined arch which, through the intricacies and horrors of the inquisitorial prison, ultimately led to the arms of Horatia.

In the very heat of his passion for Horatia, and in the full possession of her heart, still even then constancy did not rank amongst the virtues of the friar; for not many months after his arrival in Venice, he had contracted an intimacy with a young widow of that place: the consequence of which was his becoming the father of a girl, whose entrance into the world deprived the mother of existence.

The child was named Livia; and, at the death of its mother, was taken under the protection of a maiden aunt, who was entirely ignorant who was the father of her niece.

Without the slightest suspicion of any parental claim falling upon him, Julio cultivated an intimacy with his daughter; for which the unconscious world gave him the applauses due to an ecclesiastic so warmly interested in the fate of an orphan. At his departure from Venice, he exacted from Livia a promise to enter into a frequent correspondence with him, and to consult him, on every important occurrence in her life, with the same freedom that she would disclose her thoughts to a parent.

Livia's aunt was of a morose and resolute temper; and the daughter of Julio found his letters the most consolitary soothers of her life, while living under the influence of this relation. At length, when her aunt proposed to her as a husband that Signor Roderigo di Viratti, with whom the reader is already well acquainted, and would admit of no appeal from her decree; then, with a more than ever ardent pen, did Livia entreat the advice of her friend: in reply to which petition, Julio directed her to fly, on an appointed night, from the house of her aunt, promising to meet her on a spot which he described to her about a league distant from Venice.

This done, he made it his immediate business to petition Horatia to become the protectress of his daughter. For a few moments, Julio's declaration of his being a father startled Horatia; but her composure quickly returned. The friar was now become too indifferent to her for a conviction of his past inconstancy to give her pain; and she knew him to be too useful a minister to her pleasures to be angered by a refusal of his request: accordingly, she, with much good humour, promised to make Livia her companion. Julio accordingly set out on his journey to Venice, when Livia, with much accurateness, adhered to the appointment which released her from the union she had dreaded with the detested Signor Roderigo di Viratti.

In order to render his daughter more secure in herself under his protection, before their arrival in Rome, he confessed to her the affinity by which they stood connected; and she received his confession with the gratitude naturally to be expected from the lips of one who had hitherto believed herself to stand alone in the world. Zelia was the name of Livia's deceased mother; and out of regard to her memory, Julio declared to his daughter his intention of calling her in future by that name: under which title, she was accordingly, with her own ready acquiescence, introduced to Horatia.

When observing the bracelet, the well-known bracelet, on the wrist of Claudio, Horatia doubted not that its timely view had spared her from the commission of incest. Horror-struck by the review of the precipice of enormous guilt on which she had just trembled, she breathed, in the hearing of Julio and his daughter, a solemn vow to reform her life. Her oath was not the gust of a momentary terror, to be calmed by the first succeeding titillation of pleasure: she immediately removed herself from the power of the grand Inquisitor; and, together with Zelia and her father, retired to a sequestered spot, where she resolved to end her days in prayer and repentance.

Zelia had, from her first view of Claudio, been enamoured of his person: this her father had perceived, and imparted to Horatia; whose consent was freely obtained to the exercising of any stratagems on the part of the Benedictine friar, by which he hoped to succeed in bringing about a union between his daughter, and the lawful, though not acknowledged heir, of a noble family. The friar was even more ardent to begin the attempt than was his daughter; for having in his power the secret of Horatia's being alive, he had also the means of restoring Claudio to his possessions: all he first desired to accomplish was, that Zelia should make an impression on his heart; and all that Horatio feared was, that Claudio, from his intimate intercourse in the family of Count Montano di Ponta, might become enamoured of his sister Valeria, knowing her only as the daughter of the Count, and that an incestuous marriage might be the event of his love.

Hence, we think, little farther explanation can be required of the mysterious events which had attended the life of Claudio: it needs only be said, that Julio had constantly been the observer and follower of Claudio through his travels; that it was he who, by means of a phosphoric mixture, introduced the luminous letters into the chamber of Claudio in the inn at Paris; and that the Sieur Fronval was one of his accomplices, who contrived to mix, in the mulled brandy which he invited Claudio to drink, a potion of so strong a soporific nature, as to render him entirely insensible of his being conveyed to the apartment where the promised vision, described in the luminous letters, was shown to him; and that the draught poured between his lips by the Cupid who appeared by his side, was of the same nature with the first potion he had drank, and lulled him into a second sleep, during which he was again removed from the scene of enchantment to his own bed.

At length, convinced by the intelligence of his spies that, were Valeria out of the question, Zelia would be the woman whom Claudio would select for his wife; Julio ventured upon performing the master-stroke of his plan—the marriage of Claudio with his daughter.

This being effected, nothing now remained, but to decide in what manner, and at what time, it would be most prudent and most effective for the supposedly dead Horatia, by her re-appearance in the world, to restore her son to his rights of inheritance; and whilst the means were agitating in the minds of Julio and the Countess, accident opened to them the way to triumph, by bringing to them the intelligence of Angelo's being alive, and at that moment imprisoned by the Count Montano for the murder of his wife.

To right her injured husband, and to free him from the farther persecution of the wretch to whom he owed all his past misery,

Horatia now represented to herself as a step which would ensure her pardon, in a future state, for the ills she had committed in this; and with the enthusiasm with which she had conceived, she executed the plan, which, by giving her again for a moment to the sight of her husband, rescued him from his enemy, and left him no longer reason to regret his union with a woman like herself.

These were the contents of the packet which she had, on the preceding night, sent to her son; to which she had added her hope of forgiveness from him and his father after her death, and a prayer for their future happiness and prosperity.

CHAPTER XVII.

> Let us, who through our innocence survive,
> Still in the paths of honor persevere,
> And not from past or present ills despair;
> For blessings ever wait on virtuous deeds,
> And, though a late, a sure reward succeeds.
>
> CONGREVE.

THE various emotions which filled the breasts of the group collected at the prison of the Holy Cross, may be easily conceived. By the direction of Julio (for he was the friar who had attended the Countess to the prison, and in whose arms she had breathed her expiring sigh), her body was removed to an adjacent convent for interment. Angelo, whose excellent nature prompted him even still to be the friend of his enemy, ordered immediate assistance to be summoned to the bleeding Count Montano, in whom signs of life were yet apparent; but the blow of Horatia's poniard had been certain, and the aid of medicine proved unavailing.

Claudio, in the phrenzy of a mad man, tore open the packet which he had received on the preceding evening, and from which he, with a prophetic divination, expected the clearest developement of the scene before him, which having received, he hastily imparted to his father; and then, regardless of himself, his first concern was to enquire, in what manner the crowd of wonders which had just burst upon them could be best communicated to Lodovico in his present state.

From the tongue of his sister, Claudio determined, that the intelligence (so necessary to be related immediately to Lodovico, lest it should be imparted to him by one uninterested in his welfare) should flow upon his ear in the soothing accents her love would best dictate; and accordingly returned immediately, with her and his father, to the villa di Bartelma.

The means which Claudio had devised answered his expectation in their event: the transport with which Lodovico again beheld Nina, softened the bitter intelligence that she was commissioned to bear to him of the Count Montano's death.

Claudio had passed but a few moments in the apartment of his friend, when he was informed, that some persons in a gondola, at the foot of the lawn, required his immediate presence. Claudio obeyed the summons; and as he advanced towards the margin of the water, he beheld in the vessel, the Benedictine friar, and his wife Zelia. When arrived within a few paces of the river, Julio rose from his seat, and assisting the trembling Zelia to gain the shore, on which the willing arms of Claudio received her, he said, "Claudio, respect my child, and make her happy; for she is good and virtuous. Despise not her, because wayward destiny has compelled her father to wear the mask of deceit. His presence shall never damp your joys: he retires, from this hour, from the world. If you should ever think upon him, be it with a sigh of pity for a repentant sinner. Farewell, for ever!" The gondola was instantly in motion, and Zelia sunk, with a faint shriek, into the arms of Claudio.

The faithful old Paulo was near at hand to lend his assistance towards her restoration; which being effected, Claudio led her into the house with the warmest assurances truth could dictate, that she had not lost the smallest portion of that hold upon his heart which his eyes had confessed her to have obtained upon it, when he, for the first time, beheld her in the apartments of Horatia; and the smile of gratitude and reciprocal affection which Zelia returned to his declaration of love, added to his now; beholding her free from the veil of mystery which had before enveloped her, made her appear, in the eyes of Claudio, more interestingly angelic than he had ever yet thought her, even in his moments of romance.

The *denouement* of a story, like that of a play, being once unfolded, the audience is always glad to be dismissed, as their sympathy goes no farther than the grand event, which puts the whole into a train for happiness: according to this rule, little more remains to be said. Count Angelo, again restored to his possessions, inhabited his pallazo in the neighbourhood of Placenza, where his constant companions were his daughter Fulvia, and her husband Lodovico; and Louis de Saint Pierre took possession of a neat cottage in the vicinity, allotted to him for life by the bounty of Angelo.

Julio, as he had foretold that he should, immediately on delivering his daughter into the hands of Claudio, retired to a monastery, whose laws bound him from ever again appearing in the world.

Valeria, who had, from the first moment of her quitting the convent of the Virgin, rather endured a worldly life than approved it, returned shortly to her mother Abbess at Mantua, in whose seclusion she determined to end her days.

The Signora Clementina, like most ladies of her age and situation who marry, had the misfortune to connect herself with a man who taught her at least one thing: that widowhood upon some terms, is much preferable to a second marriage upon others: and this was all she got by her wedding; except much ill treatment, and large draughts upon her purse, to be lavished on those who really had the charms for her husband of which she in vain wished to convince him she was her self possessed.

Common fame soon informed Signor Roderigo di Viratti what was become of his "dear little Livia;" whether he had the complaisance to wish Claudio joy of his bride, has not been communicated to us; but we can assure our readers, that, according to Lodovico's prediction, their meeting did not produce any more terrible consequence.

From regard to the memory of his deceased benefactor, Claudio resolved, during the life of his father, to inhabit the villa di Bartelma; where, with his Zelia he lived in the exercise of those moral duties which had engraven the Marchese on the hearts of his friends and dependants, and which can alone conciliate the esteem of men and the love of God.

FINIS.

CONTEMPORARY REVIEWS

Critical Review, 2nd ser. 37 (January 1803): 116-117.

Has not Mr. Lathom almost thrown away his time in attempting this work, knowing, as he does, that 'every character in common life has been so twisted, twirled, and strained, into every possible shape and variety, that some of the principal personages in every novel are, at least, cousins, if not more nearly related to some of the most prominent characters in any other you happen to open?' We really give it as our opinion, that this observation of the author is a just one; and we think, that, from amongst the most prominent characters which every novel abounds in, it is a pity some better ones had not been selected to ingraft into the two volumes before us.

Flowers of Literature (1803): 442.

Astonishment is not a misnomer, for there is much mystery and intricacy in the tale. We would wish to see banished from our literature those hobgobliana, which the German school first suggested, and which Mrs. Ratcliffe [sic], by her superior talents, rendered popular. The author, though not destitute of merit, is certainly very far from enchanting the fancy, like the Romance of the Forest.

Lightning Source UK Ltd.
Milton Keynes UK
UKHW012038210921
390974UK00001B/25/J